Staying in Shadow

Staying in Shadow

Georgia Florey-Evans

Published by Georgia Anne Evans
Post Office Box 342
Beecher City, Illinois 62414

Printed in the United States of America
Georgia Florey-Evans
© 2016 Georgia A Evans
All rights reserved
Published by Georgia A Evans
Beecher City, Illinois
First Edition
ISBN-13: 978-0692876459
ISBN-10: 0692876456

Did you know?

www.missingkids.com

I
n 2016, there were 564,676 missing children reported to the NCMEC. In 2015, 460,699 were reported.

This book approaches one kind of kidnapping for one reason. The Proctor group is an organized, polished nationwide organization who have eluded all forms of law enforcement for years.

There will be no sexual component to the kidnapping story nor scenes designed to give you nightmares.

My hope is to share how our Lord is with each and every one of us, no matter our race, gender, or wealth. And, if an innocent child can talk to the Lord like a friend, why can't we?

Please be aware of crimes like the ones in this book, and don't place your children in dangerous situations. Visit the link to see what the NCMEC can do.

Children are God's greatest gifts to us. Let's not take them for granted.

http://www.missingkids.com/Safety

This book is dedicated to all the missing children, those who love them, and the people who get out and do all they can to find them.

When you pass through the waters, I will be with you;
when through the rivers, they won't sweep over you.
When you walk through the fire, you won't be scorched and
flame won't burn you. Isaiah 43:2 CEB

CHAPTER 1

The mean man was going to find her. Gracie Andrews crept back, farther under the brush and tried her best not to cry. If he caught her, he'd take her back to the scary place.

She didn't want to disappoint Bobby. After telling her he was going to fight the big man so she could get out, she cried and begged him to just run away with her. He hugged her and whispered a prayer, asking Jesus to take care of her, and then he whispered something else. "Bobby isn't my real name; be sure to tell your grandma my name is Den— "

At the loud sound of a key, Bobby took a few steps back and and looked like one of the people in the races her brother and his friends watched. As the door creaked open, he turned his gaze to Gracie. "Don't look back or wait for me. You run, Gracie. Run and hide."

It was still very hard to leave when Bobby raced toward the man and jumped high enough to kick his stomach.

"Ow! Oooh!" The man held his belly and bent over. "I'll fix you good this time, Bobby!"

"Go!" Bobby threw a leg over the big man's back and straddled him. Already, the giant was starting to shake him off. "Now, Gracie! Now!"

She made it out the door but was too afraid to go any farther. Until a voice she'd only heard once before came from behind her. "Get back in there, girl, or you'll be hurtin' when I drag you there myself!"

Then, she ran.

Her legs moved faster than any other time during her nine years of life. Just as she stumbled, too tired to keep running, she remembered Bobby's words. "Hide."

She saw the perfect place—this patch of bristly weeds. As she crawled in, Gracie bit her lip to keep from crying. Besides the briars, there were soft plants with little thorns and others with a prickly stem. She hoped even mean men were afraid of being scratched.

"Girl! Come here, you little brat!" She covered her ears. "I know you can hear me! I'll just leave you for the bears and snakes...all kinds of mean animals come out in the dark."

Did he think he was talking to a baby? Animals were her favorite things to read about. And, Billy taught her a long time ago what to do if she saw a snake.

The man's voice changed. "If you don't make me keep hunting you, I won't hurt you at all. I promise. I'll even take you home."

"He's lying. Hold still."

She knew that voice. Jesus had helped her hide when her mom's boyfriend was mad at Gracie for spilling his coffee.

The man didn't listen to Jesus, saying words Miss Tessa had told Gracie's Sunday School class were sinful. She silently peeked through the tall weeds, only to see him coming straight toward her. "Hold still," the soft voice repeated. And, it was no surprise to her when the man said a bunch of evil words and headed the other way.

She waited until she couldn't hear the mean man anymore, and then crawled back out of the briar-filled brush. Grandma was going to be mad at her for tearing so many holes in her clothes, and she wished she had her pretty pink bandages with her. Even so, she just wanted to get away from the man.

Even more brush and branches reached out and scratched her arms and legs as she took off running in the opposite direction of the man. She ran as fast as her little legs would take her.

Chapter 2

Gage Donahue swerved to miss the largest of the potholes scattered on the worn asphalt road and was relieved when he saw the stop sign ahead. Another five miles and he'd be at Ellie's house.

The Shadow Public Library had a sign claiming the community was the perfect place to write the great American novel. He had immediately dropped his cover as a vacationing chiropractor and became a novelist, looking for a place to write.

Unfortunately, the only writing he did was an occasional grocery list, and notes on a case. It had still been a no-brainer when he chose between the two. While his grandmother was under a chiropractor's care, knowledge by osmosis hadn't worked. However, he knew how to hold a pencil and paper. Novelist, it was. Of course, he had promised not to lie to Ellie, and every time she asked about his progress, he felt a knife slice through his heart.

Moving to Shadow wasn't as difficult as he'd expected. The town boasted under ten-thousand citizens, yet surrounding a highly used interstate there were a surprising number of businesses. In fact, at the interstate ramp, there were three convenience stores within spitting distance of each other.

After nearly a year, he'd stopped being shocked to see yet another building going up. City business wasn't why Gage was there. The only real reason was the woman he loved.

Ellie. He'd only been in town a week or so before he met the dark-haired beauty. Telling himself not to rush her was pointless since the first time they met, he couldn't resist asking her out. When she wasn't overly impressed by his efforts, he called a good friend, who told him to man up and be the bull-headed Gage Donahue his team put up with. After nearly two months of painstaking effort, Gage's patience and persistence paid off, and Ellie agreed to accompany him on a date. The first time he took her to church, she began introducing him as her boyfriend.

As he pulled up to the stop sign at the highway intersection, he reached down and opened the glove box. "Ellie," he whispered as he pulled out the priceless photo. In the picture, her dark chocolate

3

hair, which was now cut to frame her lovely face, hung in thick and what he knew to be soft waves over her shoulders. Her eyes, the color of a flawless emerald, glowed. It had always been his favorite picture of her. Of course, if he were to show it to her right now, she would be utterly confused, perhaps even frightened.

The ringing of his cell phone jarred him back to the present, and he realized where he was. Checking to make sure a car wasn't behind him, he answered his phone. He quickly returned the photo to its hiding place as he spoke. "Donahue."

"How is your task coming along?" FSA Section Chief Ross Burnett was his usual straight-to-business self.

"We're growing closer all the time." Gage thought he knew where the big boss was going with this. "I still have nearly eight more months dedicated to this. You signed the papers." He'd gone over his Unit Chief's head because Harold Binkley understood romance about as well as a toddler would the engine of a car. Because Gage and Burnett hit it off, Binkley had the crazy idea that Gage wanted his job.

Burnett's demeanor changed. "I know we agreed to eighteen months, Donahue, and I had every intention of giving it to—"

"What do you mean 'had'?"

"We have a situation, and I'm sorry, but there is nobody else with your talent or record. You are the best of the best, even if you won't acknowledge it." Maybe Gage's voice pattern skills were out of practice, but he was sure the section chief sounded as sorry as a Lotto winner.

"I need time for this, sir." Gage kept his voice firm. "Samantha can take care of whatever situation you have to deal with."

"Oh, Agent Hughes will be right there with you."

Gage's heart went into overdrive. "Is the Proctor case active again?"

"No." At Burnett's answer, Gage deeply exhaled. "We haven't seen any activity from them for over six months now."

"Then, with all due respect, sir, why are you putting both of us on the case?"

As the top officer in a stretch from the north to the south ends of central states, Burnett's orders weren't open for discussion. "Listen, Gage. I'll give you free rein on this new case so you can still

4

work on your other situation as much as possible, but you are going to help me on this." For just a moment, his boss sounded sympathetic.

"What is it?"

"A child has gone missing from Pattinton—only ten miles from you."

Gage couldn't keep the incredulity from his voice. "Samantha can handle that without me."

"The boy is a Senator's only grandson, Donahue. I'm going to need you and Agent Hughes both on it." The brisk tone of voice was back.

So, they would do whatever it took because of the senator. While Gage hoped the child would be found, this was in no way fair. He wasn't the one pulling strings, though. Besides, now that he knew about the kidnapping, if something happened to the boy and Gage hadn't done all he could to help, he wouldn't be able to live with himself.

"Senator Wilder would be an easy target," Burnett wasn't insulting the politician. Throughout three terms, Wilder had infuriated constituents by making unpopular and unexpected choices. The man thought himself invincible.

"And our missing boy? What's his name?"

"Dennis Wilder."

Chapter 3

Ellie Walker looked at the phone in her hand as though it might roll over and perform a trick. She was unsure of her feelings with emotions fluctuating between surprise and unhappiness. Gage Donahue had just canceled their date.

For the first time, she realized what an ardent suitor he'd been, practically from the moment they met. What if he was losing interest in her? While it hurt deeper than it should, there was nothing she could do about it

Never one to sit and feel sorry for herself, she placed her phone on the end table and stood. She'd just change into comfortable clothes and fix a frozen pizza.

Thirty minutes later, she found herself sitting on the sofa, staring at the television screen and trying to eat while batting a fat cat away from her food. A re-run of an *"I Love Lucy"* episode was airing, and Ellie found her mind drifting.

Her life during the past fifteen months had been unusual, to say the least. She miraculously survived a crash that probably should have killed her. Although she suffered some significant physical injuries, none of them impacted her like the loss of her memory. Doctors determined her loss was around five years prior to the accident. With no physical reason for the condition, her neurologist and psychiatrist agreed that relaxation should help, and a change of scenery might prove beneficial. She'd moved out of the apartment over her father's garage in Atlanta to Shadow.

This community was a logical choice. She would start over, but not alone. Her paternal aunt and uncle lived there, and her cousin Luke, who had always been more like her brother, owned the old family farm. His wife hadn't sold her house in town yet, so, Ellie was pleased to rent it.

Ellie was a psychologist, but didn't remember her recent employment. Given how she loved and excelled at working with children in Gibson Clinic, she couldn't believe she was fired or quit. There seemed to be no other answer, though.

She wasn't proud of herself after being dismissed from the hospital. The directions for others to tell her nothing was sound. It was just that nothing seemed right and having to remember with no help overwhelmed her.

After catching her sister crying, Ellie realized she was only thinking of herself. This was not her family's nor her friends' idea of a lovely time. They were hurt both by their desire to help and her behavior. At least, her love and compassion seemed familiar.

After she had moved to Shadow, the situation grew ridiculous. Since she couldn't ethically practice psychology, she relied on her office skills to obtain employment. The problem with that was her office skills were laughable. Her cousin and his wife put in a word, and suddenly, Ellie was Clay Richmond's assistant at Richmond Insurance Agency. It wasn't the job of her dreams, but it took care of expenses.

All in all, she had a good life in Shadow. She even had friends. In fact, a group of them were scheduled to have a girls' day tomorrow. Shopping, manicures, good fun. Then, she was supposed to have a date with Gage. Unless he canceled that one, too.

She addressed the cat. "Well, Fat Ollie, it's not as if Gage is the only man in Shadow who pays attention to me." In fact, her boss asked her out at least once a week. "It's a shame his blond hair, blue eyes, and perpetual tan just doesn't do it for me." Of course, that could partially come from her knowledge of his regular dye jobs, bright blue contact lenses, and the tanning bed he invited her to use. The man had a stricter beauty regimen than most of the women Ellie knew.

No. Gage's coal-black hair and dark blue eyes, coupled with his larger, muscular frame, did funny things to her heart. She must like her men tall, dark, and handsome.

Since no knight in shining armor showed up to claim her after the accident, Ellie could only assume she hadn't been involved with anybody. In fact, only her father, Ryan, and younger sister, Annie, had come to see her in the hospital.

When her dad took Ellie home to her apartment, everything seemed wrong. The clothes hanging in the closet were much more expensive and dressy than her usual wardrobe, and the shoes! What had ever possessed her to buy that many pairs of shoes? Her dad just shrugged, and Annie reminded Ellie they couldn't answer questions like that.

As soon as she was dismissed from the hospital, the first place she visited was the beauty salon. She had always worn her hair in a face-framing style, yet the tresses left after the surgeon was finished were long, clear over her shoulders. To top it off, she still didn't look right after the carefully cut style covered her freshly growing hair.

Then, Annie had taken her clothes shopping. Again, she knew the jeans and T-shirts were more her style, but they somehow felt wrong. It had taken weeks for her to feel like the old Ellie again.

In fact, it wasn't until she was settled in Shadow that she began to rejuvenate. It was a fresh start. She would never tell her family, but sometimes she hoped those years were permanently gone. This new life was about as good as she could imagine.

Chapter 4

Crystal Stanley was working late again, all because her boss was at a convention in Reno, Nevada. She couldn't imagine what an expo attended by sporting goods store owners would be like, but she carefully avoided any situation which would result in an invitation. Keeping books at the store was enough.

She knew next to nothing about sporting goods, and some records confused her. With a deep yawn, the smell of leather, metal, and sweat filled her mouth. She reached into her desk drawer and pulled out the small can of air freshener. The rose-scented spray put up a losing battle, a few hours at best, but at least there was a break from the gross smells. "This should have never been my job!" Steam was liable to ooze from her pores if she didn't calm down.

Remembering her job as the county sheriff's dispatcher brought her temper right back on top. Mitch had fired her, and the man was smiling. Of course, her peers thought it was hilarious, too.

She could still see Mitch with a piece of notarized paper. "I'll let you read these formal reasons, but basically, you have been selling information to a reporter and left a teenage boy in the all-purpose room where there were weapons on hand."

She'd been forced to sit while he gave her a list of not only rules she'd broken, but laws, too.

Yes, she occasionally made a little money on the side, but nobody ever got hurt because of her. In fact, she was devastated.

First, Karl King, the reporter for the Shadow Sundown, washed his hands of her the moment he found out she lost her job. All he'd ever cared about was the information she leaked to him.

Then, when she applied for the administrative assistant at Richmond Insurance, she was certain the job was hers. The way Clay Richmond looked at her; she thought he was interested right from the start. To show she had good taste, she went right out and bought an expensive tie she couldn't afford.

She could still remember walking in and seeing Ellie Walker sitting at the desk—Crystal's desk.

"Are you a temp?" She had been sure he only had one of the perfect Walker family filling in until he reached Crystal.

Ellie smiled, all roses and sunshine, and knocked Crystal's world out of orbit. "I'm Mr. Richmond's new assistant. May I help you?"

Of course, Crystal asked to see Clay. There had to be a mistake. Only, after Ellie buzzed his office with the news of Crystal's presence, the former homecoming queen had covered the mouthpiece and addressed Crystal. "What is your visit concerning?"

Determined not to be humiliated, Crystal insisted everything would be clear as soon as she spoke with Clay. He finally consented. When she walked in, it was with confidence. She proudly presented him with the tie.

"When I saw this, I immediately thought of you. It'll perfectly match your gray suit."

He reluctantly accepted the tie and looked at her with confusion. "Please accept my apology. I may have seen you around town a time or two, but have we actually met before?"

Her smile froze on her face. "You interviewed me for the job and all but promised it to me. Surely you remember."

The businessman took over for the man, right in front of Crystal's eyes.

"I interviewed several people and am positive I didn't promise the job to any of them."

Then, he compounded Crystal's embarrassment. "Please, take the tie. I don't feel right accepting it under these circumstances."

Always a fighter, Crystal had rallied one more time. Deciding a wealthy boyfriend was even better than working for one, she produced a big smile.

"Would you care to join me for a home-cooked dinner?"

Her final humiliation came when he apologized and told her he hadn't meant to give her a false impression.

Clay had seemed sympathetic. "You are a lovely lady, but I'm not interested in pursuing a relationship with you. In fact, my life is so busy, I have no time for dating."

Knowing perfectly well his reputation as a womanizer, she stiffened her spine and told him to keep the tie. She wasted no time in getting out of there.

At least, now she had Bryan. She'd been working for Bryan Cosart for six months and dating him nearly as long. A little over a year ago, he leased the building and moved Cosart's Sporting Goods in. Shortly after opening for business, he hired Crystal—even though her only qualifications were a couple of on-line courses taken some years ago.

Bryan was handsome—not like Clay, of course. More in a rugged, outdoorsy way with dark blond hair and hazel eyes. Unsurprising, since he owned a sporting goods store, he liked to camp, fish, and hunt. It was too bad he hadn't found the time to partake in any of those activities in Shadow.

He wasn't a romantic man, but he took her out regularly. She assumed a past broken heart was why he took things slowly. That had to be why he rarely talked, too.

The shrill ringing of the phone interrupted her thoughts. Who would be calling the store after ten o'clock on a Friday night?

"It's me, Crystal." The handsome, but lower class, head salesman was on the line. "I know the big guy is out of town, but I need to speak with him. It's urgent."

"I'm sorry. Clay left me with strict instructions not to bother him at the expo."

The voice erupted from the phone. "Just give me the number! Or the hotel. I need to inform him of something immediately."

The second apology was more difficult, what with him yelling at her. "I'm really sorry, but I'm not allowed to give Mr. Cosart's number to anybody." The little buzz down her spine reminded her that she didn't even have it. And, if the man on the other end of the phone knew that, he'd be sure to make a laughingstock out of her. "Is there anything I can do for you?"

He was angry, but at least he lowered his voice.

"I'll just talk to him later. He's not gonna be happy with you when he finds out you didn't let me get this to him sooner."

She was certain her position as Bryan's girlfriend would trump a salesman. "You go on ahead and do that."

A loud snort was the only thing she heard before the phone went dead.

She looked back at the computer. She was never going to understand how inventory worked. It seemed to her like they had much less merchandise coming in and being sold than the paperwork showed. Of course, she'd never counted items and compared them to the computer statement. If the inventory sheet said there were forty-four tents on the premises, she was sure they were there somewhere. Probably in the places left empty by the seventy-eight reported sold and shipped out.

No. This stuff would never make sense.

Chapter 5

Gracie ran past a group of trees and came to an abrupt halt at the sight of a cabin. Maybe somebody in it would help her.

Her knuckles hurt when she knocked too hard. There weren't any sounds like she thought there should be. She turned the doorknob, but it wouldn't open. Somebody had to be in there!

A table and chairs were on the porch, so she crawled up on the table and peered through the window. At first, she wasn't sure what it was, but with her face pressed to the window, she recognized sheets covering furniture. Her best friend, Laura, went with her whole family to California for the summer. Gracie had helped cover their furniture the day they left.

A tear ran down her cheek. Nobody was home. Then a flash of black caught her eye. She'd seen pictures of old telephones, and there sat one! Right there, on a table. She couldn't remember her number, but she could call 9-1-1 to get help. She was already going to be in trouble for tearing up her clothes, so she didn't care if going into somebody else's home made Grandma madder.

Only, after trying to open the front door and few reachable windows, she realized there wasn't a way to get inside. She was hungry and very thirsty. More tears began pouring down her cheeks, and she buried her face on her knees and wept.

Chapter 6

"Talk about five-star lodging." Gage whistled as he looked around the elegant sitting room. The subtle blue carpet was thicker than some mattresses, and the pleasant smell of roses filled the room. He softly whistled again as he knocked on the table in front of Samantha. "This probably cost over three thousand."

She frowned. "Dollars? Three thousand dollars?" Gage almost laughed when she leaned over and carefully examined the table. She looked up at him, still standing to her side. "It's just a wooden table like they sell down at the Queen-mart. Maybe Illinois has more expensive furniture than Atlanta."

"You'd have to visit a top-notch furniture store to buy one of those. It's solid cherry." Then the nearest painting caught his eye. "That is an excellent reproduction of daVinci's *Madonna of the Carnation.*" The depiction of a chubby Baby Jesus reaching up to Mary wasn't Gage's favorite, but still an incredible piece.

His gaze traveled through the doorway leading to Samantha's bedroom. "This hotel's decorator has a thing for fat babies." He nodded toward the next artistic creation. "That painting is another da Vinci, named *Benois Madonna*, also called *Madonna of the Flower.*" Now, this was one he liked. "Look how young Mary appears." While the painting first seemed joyful, the little "trinket" in the baby's hand was a kind of cross. Even when Jesus was a baby, he had the cross in his future. "We all forget she was so young and had the faith to raise her son to die, don't we?"

Samantha was studying her hands as though they contained some magical power. As she looked up, she rolled her eyes. "You know how I am about that mumbo jumbo. It makes no sense, and if it doesn't make sense, it's not true."

If only she knew how fervently her co-workers prayed for her.

While Gage disliked many of Samantha's methods, she was God's child, just like everyone. Even when unnecessary, she often lied to witnesses, and the men...it saddened those who worked with her when she disavowed their Lord. Maybe, one day.

"So, these are knockoffs of famous paintings?" She changed the subject.

"Not exactly knock-offs." He was finished with the art lesson. "You must be on Binkley's good side."

"Harold Binkley doesn't have a good side. I was afraid I'd pull back a nub when he handed me the credit card." Freckles formed a straight line when she wrinkled her nose. "They just gave me these hoity-toity digs because we're looking for a senator's grandson. I'm not sure how I feel about it."

"I know what you mean." Only, he could easily describe his feelings—unhappy and frustrated. Before she could bring up their bosses again, he changed the subject.

"What do we know about the case so far?"

Samantha indicated he should sit as she opened the folder in front of her. "And before you ask, yes, these are handwritten. My tablet isn't working."

He usually liked to tease Sam about how his handwritten notes were much more thorough than the notes she typed into that contraption. Not today. "The child, Samantha?"

She quickly put her glasses on and looked at the paper in her hands. "Dennis Wilder; age thirteen, red hair, green eyes, approximately five-ten, and around one-twenty in weight. He's physically active and in good shape. It says here that he's a wrestler in the middle school league, Kickboxing, Ju-Jitsu, and Karate..." Sam looked up at Gage. "I've seen some of this on television; isn't it teaching children to fight?"

"Not if they're correctly instructed ." Gage was impressed that a thirteen-year-old kept a high GPA and was so active. He'd seen all the basketball and baseball trophies. "The main idea with each of those, at least as far as I can remember, is defense."

Samantha stood. "So, he might be able to take on his kidnappers and get away?"

"I hope not."

His statement floored Samantha. "But—"

"If the kidnappers are short-tempered and have guns, even the boy's best defense won't stop them. In fact, I think it might make

15

them so angry they'll hurt him." Gage drew a deep breath. "So, for now, at least, I'm praying for Dennis to be calm until an opportunity presents itself."

That wasn't all he was praying. If only the people who had the Wilder boy wanted money from the Senator or his family, Dennis might have a chance. Gage's gut told him something was wrong here. He said a silent prayer.

Samantha shook her head as though shaking the fighting talk away. "The boy was last seen yesterday afternoon, at approximately three-thirty." She slid another page from the folder and read from it. "He left a ball diamond in Pattinton to walk twelve blocks, His friends were with him the first eight blocks, but he was on his own for the final four. He disappeared somewhere within those four blocks. No witnesses have been found or come forward. No contact or ransom demand has been made."

And, there was another bad sign. The felons were either geniuses with a grand plan or more likely, not sure what to do with the child. Maybe they'd ask for money, soon.

"What do you think we should look at?"

As unpleasant as Gage found it, the first suspects were always the same. "Did his family check out?" They had to investigate the heartbreaking possibility a parent would try to cover up a tragedy with a "kidnapping."

"Father—Rod Wilder—is vice president of the local bank. Dozens of witnesses verify he was in his office all afternoon." Samantha read further down the paper. "Vicky Wilder was at the library, where she volunteers until three o'clock, and then she stopped at Miller's Market for groceries. The store's security tape shows her checking out at three forty-seven." She flipped through the pages in the file. "There is no extended family in the area, other than the senator. He resides primarily in Washington, but maintains a second home in Pattinton."

What did the Senator have planned? "Where was he when the boy went missing?"

Sam looked up with a big smile "In an office packed with other old fuddy-duddies. If Proctor joined them, we'd have it made. They each have a problem, and they want to tell you all about it." She shoved an errant curl behind her ear. "You know what? You would have fit right in with those guys."

Was his unhappiness over being called back to duty so obvious? Uncomfortable about sharing details of his marriage with a coworker, he pushed the subject aside. "I assume the local department has decided to be involved." Gage had learned long ago to never underestimate local law enforcement.

"They've gone door-to-door along the entire route." Sam slid a sheet of paper across the table. "There were no sightings of anything unusual or out of place," she continued. "They're in the process of checking all known sex offenders in the area."

Gage considered the information they had and tried to come up with a plan of action. "I'll start by walking the boy's route." Things always looked different from a child's perspective.

"It's good to be working with you again." Samantha's fair complexion reddened at the admission. "Atlanta just isn't the same."

"How's the unit?" While he would rather focus solely on Ellie, he missed his team.

Sam's South Alabama accent only appeared when she was emotional, and it was there in spades. "It doesn't feel like we're a unit anymore. The boss sends us off, one at a time, on odd jobs. Troy is loaned out to just about anybody who asks, and so are Elijah and Bridgett. Jess claims she has now been in every FSA office in the country, and Kurt has been gone nearly as long as you have, on some hush-hush mission who knows where. The only one besides me to stay in Atlanta is Eric. It's awful. We haven't worked together for over six months." She hesitated before her next words. "We need you there, Gage."

Although technically he was in charge, Samantha worked every bit as hard as any of the other members. There was no purpose in lying "I'm not ready. I wouldn't even be on this case if there was any other choice."

Her expression became somber. "How are things going with Ellie?"

"Great." Thank the good Lord.

"How will it affect her when she remembers everything?" Sam crossed one hand over the other. "How will she react?"

"I need her to remember." Growing uncomfortable discussing Ellie with Samantha, he stood. "It's why I'm here."

Samantha rose to her feet. "Just be careful, or you both might be hurt."

Gage's jaw clenched. "This isn't any of your concern." He turned toward the door. "I'll see you tomorrow.

"I'm sorry if I overstepped my bounds." Samantha sounded near tears, and Gage shouldn't have been so rough. He turned back around. "I'm sorry, Sam. I am about to go out of my mind, wanting to be with her so badly and having to work cases. I have to fight to keep from looking like a stalker."

Samantha's face strongly resembled a speckled strawberry. "Can we just forget it happened?"

"Sure."

"And, what about if Ellie sees me around? We've never come up with a plan." Samantha crossed her arms. "I won't intentionally capture her attention, but you know I have to be out and around. And what about if she sees me with you?"

The truth was whenever that question came to his mind, Gage put off thinking about the possibilities. If Ellie remembered, she wouldn't have a problem with Samantha, but right now,"I guess I'll deal with that when it comes up."

Samantha's voice was a murmur. "I understand."

At least one of them did.

As he walked out into the sunny afternoon, a prayer sprang to his heart. *Please, Lord, I need some help here.*

Sam was right about one thing. There was a huge chance this would wind up hurting Ellie and destroying anything they may have had. And, Gage would be the one to hurt her.

God was in control His chest felt lighter as he unlocked his car. Sometimes, it was hard to remember life wasn't a leaderless journey.

Chapter 7

"Do I look like a strawberry in this dress?" Haley Davis twisted side to side.

Ellie looked at the other woman's relatively tall, perfectly put-together body. How even for one minute could she not realize how beautiful she was?

"Why must you always compare yourself to a piece of fruit?" Melissa Willis pulled her thick, auburn braid out of the way to straighten her necklace. "You've been a lemon, an orange, and overripe banana. Exactly what color is left, to stop you looking edible?"

The small group of women who were gathered at the dressing rooms laughed. Missy was right, though. Haley had been a veritable smorgasbord throughout their shopping excursion.

"You look great in that shade of blue." Mavis Shepard cocked her head. "But I think this shade of red would look fantastic with your hair and eyes."

A wave of melancholy came over Ellie when she looked at a reflection of the dress Mavis held. Unable to look away from the lovely frock, she instantly saw herself wearing it, snug in Gage's arms as they danced. Only they had never been dancing before. Then she realized something.

"I like to dance." She looked at her friends in wonder. "I remember. I like to dance."

Tessa Landon stepped over and gave her a hug. "That's great, Ellie. Maybe your memory is all starting to come back."

Holly, her cousin-in-law, smiled brightly. "Do you think so?"

Then Ellie's heart sank as she realized the error in her thinking. "No. I just remembered something I haven't done in a long time. It's not something unique to the years I lost."

Consolatory murmurs from her friends nearly brought Ellie to tears, but she took a deep breath and stood straight. "I'm going to ask Gage to take me dancing."

19

"That sounds like a good idea," Mavis agreed. "And you can wear this dress." She held the garment out. "Just try it on and see for yourself."

A few minutes later, Ellie did see for herself. Again, she flashed to an image of being wrapped in Gage's arms, wearing that dress. "Wishful thinking," she murmured.

"How's your job with Clay working out?" Holly asked several minutes later as they sat at a large table in the food court.

Since Clay had once flirted shamelessly with her cousin's wife, Ellie knew she had a kindred spirit in Holly. "He takes no for an answer enough, but he seems to think if he keeps asking, I'll change my mind."

"Are you and Gage getting serious?" Haley asked.

Ellie was surprised. "We haven't known each other for even a year. I have feelings for him, but it's too soon for there to be anything serious going on."

Haley's loud laughter attracted attention from other diners. "Beau and I hadn't known each other for more than a month when we realized we were meant to be together. When God gives you the knowledge that you've found your intended, time doesn't matter."

As the other women weighed in with their opinions, Ellie let her mind wander. How did she feel about Gage? She was startled to realize her feelings were growing deeper every day. Maybe Haley was right, and they had a future. Of course, that would take two, and Gage hadn't spoken of it. She decided to push tomorrow out of her mind and focus on today.

"Who is that?" Tessa's shocked voice brought Ellie out of her reverie.

She joined the other women in looking at the petite woman Tessa spoke of, and nearly fell out of her chair. Gage was sitting with her! And, not across the table. No. They had their chairs scooted together. Gage's date had red curls brushing her shoulders, and freckles that made her look like a cute, farm girl. That wasn't the worst of it, though. Ellie watched in disbelief as the woman and Gage put their heads together and huddled over some papers in front of them. Then, her astonishment grew as the other woman said something that made Gage laugh. Ellie didn't have to be a psychologist to see the familiarity and comfort in their body language.

"Now, Ellie, don't let your imagination run away." Mavis knew Ellie better than the other women did, and was probably the only one of them to have witnessed Ellie's temper.

"It's not my imagination," Ellie spoke through her teeth. "I'm pretty sure I'm looking at the reason for our canceled date." Exactly what kind of a game had Gage been playing with her?

Before any of them could stop her, Ellie nearly knocked her chair over as she stood. She left her stunned friends and stomped straight to Gage's table.

"Want to introduce me to your date?" She had trouble acting civil as she spoke.

Gage looked up, surprise evident on his face for a moment before being replaced by guilt. "This is Samantha Hughes."

Surely, steam was coming out of Ellie's ears. "Well, I guess I know why you canceled last night."

"It's not what you think." Gage seemed to be regaining his equilibrium.

"Then, what is it? Because I'm pretty sure you were with her instead of me last night." Somehow, Ellie still managed to keep her voice down. "Am I wrong?"

"No, but it's not—"

"what I think." She glared at him. "You can do what it is I think you're doing to your heart's content. Tonight's date is off, and I'll go to church with Mavis tomorrow."

Guilt clouded his blue eyes.

"You were going to cancel our date again tonight, anyway, weren't you?" If that lovely little imp said so much as one word, Ellie was mopping the floor with those perfect curls.

"Ellie, please." Gage stood up. "I'm sorry. Please understand."

"I understand perfectly." And, suddenly, she did. "You've been playing some sort of game for the past several months, pursuing me, and now that you've caught me, you're done. Well, bucko, so am I."

21

She turned and started to walk away, but his hand on her arm stopped her.

"Please wait." Gage stepped close to her and softened his voice. "I haven't been playing a game. I have feelings, deep feelings, for you. It's just that something has happened that's out of my control."

"Well, so am I." Ellie pulled her arm out of his grasp and walked away. She hoped Mavis would drive her home because she didn't think she could see through her tears well enough to operate a car herself.

Chapter 8

Gage carefully examined his surroundings as he followed Dennis Wilder's route. His home was in one of the more upscale neighborhoods, and the nearer Gage came to it, the less traffic he saw.

The houses, even those with larger front lawns, were close enough together, that at any given time, the boy was visible to at least four of them—two on each side of the road. The odds of somebody snatching the teen without garnering any attention were slim to none.

"Oh, no." As he approached the Wilder home, the bushes, each planted at an angle to the sidewalk, created a border of sorts. Rod and Vicky Wilder had undoubtedly intended to beautify their lawn with the landscaping, but instead unintentionally provided a criminal with a good thirty feet of cover to grab their child.

This told Gage two things. Dennis was only visible to the single house across the road, and the kidnapper was a pro. Grabbing the kid so close to home would be another feather in his cap. "We'll get you," he promised the unknown subject. A Senator's grandson or not, Gage wanted to find Dennis Wilder.

Samantha wouldn't appreciate a phone call in the middle of a meeting with the chief and FSA behavior analyst. This was something important, though. He pulled his phone out and dialed his co-worker.

"Hughes." Sam sounded angry.

"It's me." They had been partners too long not to recognize each other's voice.

"Found anything?"

"I'm pretty sure I know where he was snatched, and there's only one house with a view. I'm going to talk to the residents and see if there's anything they might have forgotten to tell the police."

"Okay." He could hear her speak to somebody in the background, but then she was there. "What do you need from me?"

"I want to speak to those boys Dennis was with. Can you set that up for me?"

"Of course," Samantha spoke to someone off the phone again. She sounded troubled when she came back on the line. "There's something you need to know."

He could hear her twang; this wasn't going to be good. "What?"

"It's the Senator," She huffed. "He is determined to hold a press conference." Anger filled her voice. "In my entire career, I have never seen such a stubborn man. He wouldn't listen when I explained why it's not a good idea. He's even going to offer a reward bigger than my annual salary for the safe return of his grandson."

Gage considered the idea. "Every nut and his granny will be calling in, but he has enough clout to have a team of law enforcement answering. Other than that, it shouldn't hurt anything."

"What if all they're after is the ransom? Do we know for sure money isn't the reason?"

"Since he's been gone for nearly four days now, and there hasn't been a ransom demand, I doubt money is the motivation for this kidnapping." Before Samantha could start another argument, Gage decided he needed to stop procrastinating and talk to the residents of this house.

Either a gigantic yawn or a deep breath came across the line. It didn't matter to Gage which it was. Before she could get back to her griping session, he hit the power button on his cell and stuffed it into a hidden pocket his seamstress-stepmother had placed in all his suits.

Please, Lord, give me the words I need. He stepped onto the huge porch.

The woman must have been watching out the window because the doorbell had barely begun to ring when the door opened. An elderly woman stood there.

Gage pulled out his badge and held it so she could see it. "I'm Special Agent Gage Donahue with the Federal Safety Agency, ma'am. Would you mind answering a few questions?"

"Is this about that poor little boy?" The short, heavy-set woman with snow-white hair and wire-rim glasses appeared near tears.

"Yes, ma'am."

"Well, I guess you can come in." She opened the door and stepped aside.

As he stepped past her, the scent of his mom's favorite perfume filled his nose. When was the last time he'd visited her grave?

The lady's voice pulled him back to the present. "You'll have to overlook the mess. I haven't had time to clean today."

What mess? Gage wanted to ask. He was certain the agency's best fingerprint expert would be hard-pressed to find anything in this house. He pulled his small notepad out of his shirt pocket. "Is it okay if I take notes while we talk, Mrs. —?"

"Kennard. Marion Kennard." She indicated he should sit on the sofa before taking a seat on an uncomfortable looking chair. "Why don't you have one of those fancy tape recorders or telephones police use?"

Something about this woman assured him she would help if she could.

"It's easier to find something in my written notes than to locate it somewhere on a tape."

"You were a good student, weren't you?" the elderly woman asked. "I used to teach English, you know. Nowadays, they let students do reports on videotape. Soon, nobody will remember how to write."

Gage quickly realized that once Marion Kennard began talking, she wasn't inclined to stop. Within a few minutes, he knew she was a retired teacher whose husband had been taken by heart disease more than ten years ago. She had four children, six grandchildren, and eight great-grandchildren. And would he like to see their pictures?

After viewing numerous photographs and snapshots, he was finally able to steer their conversation back to the missing child.

"Can you tell me what you remember about the afternoon Dennis Wilder went missing?"

Her smile was immediately replaced by a sad look. "I'm sorry. I was watching Dr. Phil. I never miss him. I told the nice officer that, you know. Why do you want me to say it to you, too?"

"Sometimes, we see something and don't even realize it at the time." Gage needed to handle this carefully. "Is your television in another room?"

"I keep it in the parlor." Her chin rose. "It's rude to sit and stare at a picture show while you have guests, so I don't even tempt myself. Avoid bad habits, young man."

"Yes, ma'am." He could see the teacher she used to be. "Did you sit there during the entire program, or might you have gotten up for something? Maybe a glass of water?" He wasn't the best one of his team at interviews; it was too bad his champion questioner agent wasn't there.

Mrs. Kennard's frown deepened for a moment before her cheeks turned bright pink. "I had to use the restroom. I rushed during a commercial so I wouldn't miss part of the show."

"When you walked to the bathroom, did you pass any windows that look out onto the street?" At least she was trying to help.

"The picture window of the parlor and the bathroom window both do."

"Okay, Mrs. Kennard," Gage spoke encouragingly. "Did you happen to glance out?"

"I don't remember" Her gaze went down, and Gage thought she was going to cry.

"Ma'am, you haven't done anything wrong."

"That's what Maybelline Tinker told me during Bible Study this morning, but surely you're familiar with the difficulty in pushing guilt away."

He felt guilty, alright, with too many images of parents, begging him to find their child and becoming angry when he explained their team worked on assigned cases. Even his efforts to make sure they had local help couldn't stop the sick feeling of not helping a broken-hearted parent.

"I can see from your eyes—such deep blue eyes...now there's a beautiful color." She quickly became businesslike. "I can see from your expression that you're familiar with guilt."

"I am." He remembered what his pastor had told him. "But, I try not to be. The feeling of failure pulls us away from the Lord. Don't

26

you think the Scripture that tells us worrying won't add a day to our lives would apply to this?"

"I believe it would, but if only I had been able to help that boy." She tilted her head as lines creased her forehead. He needed to get to this before she became so sad she couldn't focus on the kidnapping.

With a smile that felt like it might reach his ears, he shifted his happy demeanor into place. Mrs. Kennard smiled back, so he knew she was all right. He softened his voice. "Just relax and think back. If there was something strange out there, you'll remember it."

Her eyes half-closed as she thought. Then, her brows shot up, and she put her hands over her heart. Wide eyes met Gage's gaze.

"There was a truck parked on the side of the road. It was a TV Repair truck. I remember it because nobody gets their televisions fixed anymore. They just buy new ones. My son, Kevin, made me buy a new one not six months ago, so I know what I'm talking about."

Gage was encouraged. "Do you remember the name of the TV repair company?"

"No." She frowned in concentration again. "I only remember seeing a large picture of a television with a bandage and cold compress. Like an injured television."

There surely couldn't be many of those around. "What color was the truck?"

"I'm pretty sure it was white, and the television was black. The bandage and compress were colored...the bandage was red because it looked bloody! And the compress was that ugly mustard yellow."

Gage wrote everything down.

"Have I helped?" Her nearly translucent fingers intertwined on her chest, and a tear slid from pale blue eyes to her chin.

"Very much," he quickly assured her. "Would it be okay if a sketch artist visits you?" He was afraid the station would disconcert her too much. "If you describe the truck, he'll be able to draw it. That will help us identify the company."

27

"I'll be happy to do that." A dimple appeared on her face as she clasped her hands tightly. "I like young Dennis. He's a polite, thoughtful boy who respects his elders."

After several more minutes of a discourse on the manners of today's youth, Gage finally found himself back on the sidewalk. A television repair truck was more than he had before speaking with the retired teacher.

He retrieved his phone and dialed his boss's number. "I need a favor."

Binkley didn't even try to hide his dislike for Gage. "What do you need?"

"Troy Martin."

"Is that all?" Sarcasm oozed through the phone. "Your team hasn't been activated, and you want me to ask Burnett to send our very best sketch artist to a small town in Illinois? Aren't there any local artists?"

"Three things, sir." He'd been ready when he called. "First, you want this senator's grandson found. Second, Burnett said there hasn't been any Proctor activity, so Martin isn't needed there. And third, our boss gave me free rein on this case. I'm telling you, I need him here."

He was met with dead silence for a moment. "I'll have him on a plane first thing tomorrow." His voice sharpened. "It must be nice to be the boss's favorite and get your way all the time."

Gage knew better than to participate in this conversation."Thank you." The line went dead before Gage could say anything else. Both of his bosses would choke him to death if they found out Troy Martin was coming to sketch a repair truck. But the reason Burnett wanted Gage on the job was his history and instincts. Right now, they were telling him something big was coming. For once, he hoped it was wrong. He wanted this case over so he could focus entirely on Ellie again.

Ellie. Had he blown it with her? Neither he nor Samantha knew the local law enforcement well enough to hand off data and were, therefore, buried under paperwork. He hadn't even made it to church yesterday. Ellie would undoubtedly have reached the conclusion he was with Samantha again.

He couldn't tell Ellie everything, but maybe he could tell her part of it. Would it hurt for her to know he was an FSA agent, and that he was working on a case? Then, he could tell her that Samantha was his partner, not his girlfriend.

He'd led her to believe he was a writer, renting a country house and working on a book. Would his not telling her the truth right off the bat damage the progress of their relationship? He needed their relationship to be solid, for more than one reason. What should he do?

There was only one option--to call Dr. Becker. Ellie's doctor would advise Gage of what was best for her.

Just as he reached his car, his phone rang.

"I may scream," Samantha warned him, and unless Gage wanted a two-hour griping session with her, he knew better than to ask why Samantha was upset. After a brief silence, when she was most likely expecting to be questioned, the pleasant tone of voice jetted away. "I have your boys ready to come in tomorrow and be interviewed. And, this man—the Senator—isn't only stubborn; he is absolutely the grumpiest human being on this earth. I've tried everything, but I can't change his mind."

Now wasn't the time to admit he, too, was concerned about the press conference. There were too many things going on and not adding up. It was out of Gage's hands. They'd all better pray that Senator Wilder was right.

Chapter 9

Gracie had slept in the gross doghouse, afraid the mean man would show up and grab her while she was asleep. Then he'd take her back to the scary room, where Bobby and the strange man were. She knew that the man was different because Grandma had gotten furious when a teenage boy said something about a man being tired. "He's special," Grandma had knelt to whisper, "and you just forget what that boy said. He used words we don't like. Okay?"

Of course, Gracie wouldn't call anybody names, anyway. Her Sunday school teacher would be disappointed. But, even now it confused her. "A-tired" was a silly thing to call anybody.

It wouldn't matter what she called anybody now. She would be grounded for the rest of the summer, maybe clear until Christmas, because she was going to break the window. She wanted her grandma, and that phone in there was the only way to get her.

She remembered Billy hitting a baseball through Mr. Jennings' window. It only made a little hole, but Grandma had to pay money for it. She hadn't been mad at Billy, though, and just told him to be sure to bat in the other direction from now on.

It wasn't going to be like that this time, though. Gracie was going to make a big hole. She had scoured the yard and finally found something that should work. She could barely lift the chunk of concrete to her waist, but that was high enough.

Her arms shook as she hefted the heavy mass to the windowsill. She swung her arms in as close to her tummy as she could and then pushed the concrete into the window with all her might. Closing her eyes, she jumped backward while glass fell out.

Thinking she would be with Grandma before she knew it, Gracie opened her eyes. "No." Her eyes burned, and tears streamed down her cheeks. This couldn't be. The jagged glass was everywhere. Glass that might cut her so bad a Band-Aid wouldn't work.

Now, what would she do? The phone was right there where she could see it, and she still couldn't get inside.

She had to get to the phone. She needed to be a big girl and stop crying, but she was scared. That mean man might find her, and he was even angrier since she got away. Would he hurt her?

She sniffled and looked around. Maybe if she thought real hard, an idea would come to her.

Chapter 10

Bryan Cosart looked at the scenery fly by the window. Soon—too soon—the train would stop in Pattinton. Then, after a short drive, he would be back in the latest hick town his boss consigned him to. Circumstances dictated he set up stores in unobtrusive locations, but the big guy had found a dandy one this time. A population of not even ten-thousand; how was he supposed to convince people his sports store was a legitimate business and selling like crazy?

At least he managed to hire a blue-ribbon ditz as his "assistant" at this store. All it had taken was a cheap, knock-off diamond tennis bracelet for Crystal to forget about the inventory discrepancies she'd asked about. While it was quite a chore to appear attracted to her, such tactics, coupled with the small amount of legitimate business he participated in, ensured she was no danger.

Hopefully, he wouldn't be in this Nowheresville much longer. He'd meet the regular quota of deals and then close the store—just so he could head to his boss's next chosen destination. It was a vicious cycle, but necessary if he expected to become even wealthier. With money his boss knew nothing about, he'd bought land in Washington state. After his house was built, he'd kiss this gig goodbye.

By the time he reached Shadow, one deal should have been taken care of. Maybe they'd make enough money the boss would require less stock before relocating them. Yeah, right. Cosart's boss was a money-hungry, ruthless person unable to care about any other human being. Bryan had just spent the past three days hearing how wonderful his boss's plans were. He'd like to tell the person who paid him that he didn't care about wonderful; he just wanted to be rich.

Of course, leaving this business was difficult. A couple of drivers had gone missing after they tried to quit. But, Bryan had insurance—papers exposing everybody in the gang, including the person in charge. Then, another poor sap could take his place. Cosart would even pass on the computer system he took from site to site. Now, there was a plan.

With that daydream in mind, he sat back to enjoy the remainder of the ride.

Chapter 11

Ellie stapled the last set of papers together and placed them on the tray to be filed.

"You're doing an outstanding job." Clay Richmond's voice jolted her. "I'm sorry. I didn't realize you didn't hear me."

"That's okay. My mind was elsewhere, I guess." Like in a farmhouse seven or eight miles outside of town, where a certain author should be writing.

"I've been meaning to tell you I really appreciate you being here." It seemed that her boss wasn't bothered by her daydreaming. "I hope you're happy here. Let's keep it our secret, but business has more than doubled since I took over for my grandfather."

She had to be honest. "I appreciate having steady employment." Her smile wavered. "I just miss the work I used to do. It was a very challenging and rewarding career."

Clay stepped near her and leaned against the wall. "What did you do in Atlanta? You've never actually said."

He hadn't asked. He hired Ellie as a favor to Luke and Holly. "I'm...I was a child psychologist."

His brows shot up. "I don't mean to be nosy, but surely you had a good job. Why did you leave?"

Ellie sighed. "The last day I remember before the car accident, I left the office to drive home. When I woke up, my father told me I hadn't worked there in over four years. I don't know why I quit, or what I'd been doing since."

"It must be difficult to have a chunk of your life you can't remember."

She was surprised by his empathy. This was a new side of him. "It's not so bad since I moved to Shadow. I've made friends and found a church."

"And you have a family," he added.

"I don't know what I'd do without them." She remembered the first few weeks after being released from the hospital. "Dad and my sister, Annie, tried, but they didn't know how to help me. It wasn't anybody's fault, but I felt like I had to live up to expectations of a person I couldn't remember being. Right away, people here accepted the person I am now, with no questions asked."

He sat on the corner of her desk. "Don't think I'm trying to start trouble here, but I have to ask. How did you get hooked up with Donahue?"

Ellie did not want to talk about Gage Donahue, but it was a reasonable question. "We met each other, and I guess we clicked."

For the first time since she'd met the man, Clay produced what appeared to be a sincere smile. "It's a shame Donahue got your attention first. I'd like a chance to show you I'm not all that bad."

Maybe he wasn't the kind of man people thought he was. "I just might give you that chance."

She nearly laughed as his eyebrows jumped up to visit his hairline. He recovered quickly, though. "Then, would you like to have dinner with me this evening? It's Monday, so I won't try to make it into a late night with dancing or a movie. I know what a tyrant your boss can be."

The image of sparkling dark eyes gave her second thoughts. What was she doing? She and Gage had been dating steadily and exclusively for nearly a year. The image of him with that cute pixie made her stomach hit her knees. Maybe she'd better move on.

"I'd be happy to join you for dinner."

"I'll pick you up at six." Clay produced a boyish smile; his smugness seemed to have disappeared. "I'd better let you get back to work before we both get behind."

Her feelings were mixed as she turned to the computer a few minutes later. She realized it wasn't so much anger at Gage as hurt feelings. Gage should have told Ellie about the absentee girlfriend. Now, what a joke. Evidently, their relationship had never been as exclusive as Ellie assumed.

Oh, well, it didn't matter now. Ellie had a date with Clay Richmond. Gage Donahue wasn't the only one of them who could play the field.

Chapter 12

Rod Wilder apparently hadn't inherited his father's desire to live in the public eye. Within the fifteen minutes Gage had been there, the senator's son resembled a child playing hide-and-seek, ducking and dodging as if reporters could see through heavy drapes. If somebody didn't calm him down soon, Gage was afraid Vicky Wilder would become too upset to speak.

At the moment, it was evident that the poor woman was trying to listen to Behavior Analysis Specialist Rex Towers while keeping an eye on her overwhelmed husband.

Gage stopped one of the officers walking through the room. "Can you do us all a big favor?"

The young man, G. Hennings, according to his name tag, nodded.

"Will you take the boy's father into the kitchen and have him do something that keeps him busy? Have him fix a glass of tea, or make a whole pitcher or whatever busy work that might help him gain control. The man is going to have a nervous breakdown, or cause one if he doesn't get it under control soon."

"Yes, sir." The officer seemed pleased to receive specific instructions and lost no time in approaching Wilder.

Gage turned around and heard Towers going over what Mrs. Wilder needed to say and how to act while the entire country watched. A well-known Senator's grandson was missing.

A soft ping notified Gage of a text message. Turning with his back to the people, he pulled out his phone.

There are already three national networks out here. What is going on?

Now, of all times, Gage realized Samantha had never helped orchestrate a press conference of this size. He typed in his reply. Senator Wilder has a very public profile. Networks like him because they never know what he'll say. Samantha hated asking for help, so Gage finished his message. We won't handle this one any differently than we do other conferences. It's fine.

Thank you popped up on his screen.

"Just remember to use Dennis's name as frequently as you can," Rex Towers' voice pulled Gage out of his musings. "We want his kidnappers to see him as a person, not an object. Talk about the fishing party he's supposed to go to this Saturday, and how his friends in the youth group miss him. Even mention that his puppy needs Dennis to be here to take care of him."

Officer Hennings was still with Rod, maybe baking cookies by now. Rex would speak in depth to both Dennis's mother and grandfather about handling all kinds of questions and comments. Gage decided it was a good time to visit the boy's bedroom.

His first impression of the room was that a typical thirteen-year-old boy lived here. The bed was made as neatly as any child his age would do, with a blue denim bedspread pulled haphazardly across it. The computer, minus the CPU, which was being examined, took up half the desktop in front of the window, with posters hung on each side. One was a photo of the Fighting Illini football team, and the other was the Chicago Cubs. The trophies scattered around the room indicated the boy was a decent batter and second baseman for the Pattinton Pirates. A bulletin board was covered with photos alongside certificates celebrating his martial arts skills. This boy was a fighter. Please, Lord, tell him to remember a gun can stop him.

The bookshelf held well-read biographies of famous sports figures and age-appropriate mysteries. When Gage opened the closet door, he wasn't surprised to discover jeans and shirts hanging randomly. Dennis's shoes were placed in no apparent order on the floor. A rather large black box with the boy's name written in white was the only thing on his closet shelf. Knowing the bomb squad and their dog had swept the house and found nothing of interest, Gage pulled it down and readjusted his grasp. It was heavy.

He smiled as he saw the paper with Property of Dennis Wilder. All snatchers will be prosecuted. As silly as the child's warning may be, it told Gage that whatever was in here was dear to him. Lifting the lid, the first thing Gage saw was a photo of Senator Wilder and Dennis fly fishing. As he leafed through, there were pictures of his parents and an older woman who, from the resemblance, was likely Vicky Wilder's mother. Most of the photos were either of Dennis

37

with his grandfather or the senator on stage. Then, Gage saw a thick folder. Grandpa's Dreams–This should have been taken in to examine. He lifted the ragged cover and saw newspaper articles, some about Dennis winning a game for the team and academic honors, but again, Senator Wilder took center stage.

The last paper Gage slid out was a letter from the senator to his grandson. After only reading a few sentences, Gage refolded it and put it back. This boy had a very close relationship with his grandfather, and the deep love was returned. The letter detailed their plans for a church father-and-son camping trip. Rod hadn't been able to get off work for the event, which Gage imagined was a frequent occurrence.

All in all, there was nothing in the bedroom to raise any red flags.

"Yeah, you just try it!" A voice came from very near the bedroom's window.

Gage pulled the mini-blind aside and looked outside. Cameras flashed as a heavy-set man shoved a skinny man sporting a reporter tag.

"Walk away," one of the security guards spoke to the larger man. Instead, the angry man drew back a fist. Just as Gage decided to go help, out of nowhere, Samantha stepped up to the man. Too close—if he hit her, it would cause damage.

Gage nearly ran as he hurried to help his partner. Just as he made the corner, Samantha and the angry man walked around, and miracle of miracles, he was laughing.

"Lou, this is my partner, Gage Donahue." Sam smiled like Lou was her best friend.

"Howdy,"

Gage nodded. "Howdy."

"We were just going around the house to sneak in on the other side of the group," Samantha explained. "Lou lost his temper because a reporter spoke out of turn."

So, she was finding him a place as far from the reporter as possible.

"Good idea." Gage turned and headed for the news conference. Samantha had handled that like a pro.

The reporters were moving into a somewhat organized group, so Gage decided to stand in the semi-darkness of the open garage. He didn't plan to be on camera, but he needed to be out there watching while staying in the background. Maybe he'd get lucky and spot somebody who just didn't fit.

He had to rethink that idea a few minutes later as he surveyed the people gathered in the Wilders' front yard. There wasn't simply one who appeared strange; there were several. Apparently, some of Richard Wilder's opposition, as well as his fans, had decided to take advantage of his appearance in a relatively small town.

If Gage were going to arrest people based on their weirdness factor, he'd have to start with the woman in the tie-dyed T-shirt and denim shorts. She was waving a sign around, proclaiming Wide than Wider and Wild than Wilder! And then he'd move on to the man in bib overalls with the poster reading I didn't vote for no Wilder animal. He'd have to give the senator his due, though, because the man was focused solely on his daughter-in-law at the moment.

Just as Gage started to make his way to Sam, his phone rang. It took him a minute to reach the garage, where it was quiet enough to hear his caller.

"Gage, this is Simon Fisher."

He'd wondered when this call would come. "Listen, Simon, I don't want to be stomping around in your backyard any more than you want me to. You'll have to talk to Burnett or Binkley if you don't like it." If he were stationed as the head agent in a territory, he wouldn't appreciate other officers being brought in under his nose either.

"I'm calling because another missing child has just been reported."

All kinds of bells and whistles sounded in Gage's mind. Two missing children in a relatively small area...this may only be the beginning of a nightmare for the entire community.

"A nine-year-old girl named Gracie Andrews, from Shadow was last seen on Friday, the day after Dennis Wilder disappeared."

39

Gage couldn't believe it. "Friday?" He forgot all his manners, as well as the presence of reporters. "Why in the blue blazes is she just now being reported?"

"It's a mixed-up mess. Burnett told me to turn it over to you, though." Fisher sounded relieved to be passing it on to Gage. "You're supposed to get to 3986 South Mackinville Street as soon as possible to speak to the girl's family. Sheriff Mitch Landon is expecting you. You'll be talking to Gracie's grandmother and brother."

Gage didn't understand. "Burnett already has me on the Wilder case."

"This is coming straight from him. After looking over whatever Binkley sent, they've both decided that there's reason to believe Proctor is involved in this little girl's disappearance."

Nothing more needed said. "I'll be there as soon as possible."

Gage stuck his phone back in his pocket and headed back to the crowd. It took him a minute to get Samantha's attention, but the two of them soon stood at the garage door.

To say that his coworker was shocked to hear the news was putting it mildly. "Senator Wilder won't be happy to find out you're on a different case, Gage."

"Both Burnett and Binkley think Proctor is involved." Gage waited a moment for his words to sink in. "Besides, Sam, there are a lot of people looking for Dennis Wilder. The Andrews girl is every bit as important."

"I know." Samantha threw a worried glance over her shoulder. "Do you still want to talk to the boys? They're supposed to meet you at the police station in the morning. I guess I can talk to them if you can't make it."

"I'll be there." Why was this all happening at once? "Let's just hope that for once, my gut is wrong."

"You really think Proctor's here, don't you?"

Gage didn't want to say it aloud, but he needed to. "I've had a bad feeling ever since Ross called me. Dennis Wilder is too old for Proctor's purposes, but Gracie Andrews is a different story." He pulled the picture from his shirt pocket and handed it to Sam.

"The little moppet could pass for four years old." The color drained from his partner's face.

That would be within the range. There was another sign of how serious this was. "We both know that Burnett wouldn't be pulling me off this case if he didn't think Proctor was involved."

Samantha slowly nodded. "You're right. I guess I was hoping Proctor had closed up shop and rode off into the sunset."

"He won't quit--they won't quit. What did Elijah figure the last time we looked at money?"

"Close to a billion dollars." Her lips turned down. "And we can't reach it because it will come out that Elijah hacked what? Five banks?"

Before Sam could start

Gage nodded. "Proctors love money. That's all they care about."

She seemed to come to a decision. "I'll smooth things over with the senator. Let me know if there's anything I can do to help in Shadow." Samantha turned and headed back to the now quiet group.

What neither of them had said was if it was determined that Proctor had anything to do with either kidnapping, it was going to take more than just the two of them to work the case. Gage hoped it wasn't Proctor. Maybe...no, he knew selfishness controlled him right now.

Father, help me focus on these children for their sake. Please help me make the right decisions for their benefit. You know how badly I want to work things out with Ellie. You've put such a strong love for her in my heart...but please, be with the children and families. Dennis Wilder may be in mortal danger.

Gage realized what his first choice would be if it came down to Ellie's love and the children's lives. Ellie—his Ellie—would kick him in the seat of his pants for even considering her over a child's life.

Please let me do Thy will and not my own. You are a sovereign God, full of love.

Gage saw a small boy sitting on the side of a hospital bed, listening to his mother's last words to him. Her faltering voice still sounded in his ears. But he'd remembered.

"Jesus loves you, Gage. You're God's child, so be sure to act like it."

Chapter 13

Gracie looked at her stinging knee. Not only wasn't she in the house, but slivers of glass had also fallen and cut her as she tried to kick the glass. Now it was bleeding. Just like Billy's nose when Mommy's boyfriend hit him once.

Thinking of Billy made her start crying again. He was the best brother in the world. When Mommy drank the stinky stuff and acted wrong, Billy took care of her. He loved and helped her just like Daddy would if he wasn't in the war. And since Daddy lived in heaven, Billy did what he thought their dad would want.

Grandma loved and took care of her, too, but Billy made her feel safe. He'd never have let either of those guys get close to her. Even though Billy wasn't as big as that guy, her brother would've beat up the mean man.

Mrs. Landon read a story once in Sunday school, about a very brave man staying in a cave full of lions. The man's name was Daniel, but she knew Billy would have gone in there with those lions. She wanted her brother now. He'd know what to do.

She curled into a ball and let the silent sobs come.

Chapter 14

Ellie fastened her earring and looked at her reflection with disgust. "What was I thinking?" Fat Ollie licked his paw in response to her question. "I'm not attracted to Clay. Gage has been my boyfriend, and I feel the same as I always did." She needed to stop kidding herself; she was using Clay to get even with Gage, which was very wrong.

The doorbell startled her. She should have known her boss would be early.

Only it was Mavis on the other side of the door.

"I brought the soda." Mavis held up a six-pack. "Did you remember to buy a pizza?"

Ellie hadn't remembered their plans to share a pizza and movie. "I'm sorry, but I completely forgot our arrangements, and now I have a date."

Mavis reached out and patted Ellie's shoulder. "That's okay. I'm just glad you and Gage worked things out."

Her guilt increased. "We didn't. I'm going out with Clay."

The other woman's mouth hung open for a moment before she sputtered, "After nearly a year with no interest in the man, are you trying to tell me you suddenly find him irresistible?" She reached over and touched Ellie's cheek. "The Ellie I know would never do this. You're in love with Gage, so what are you doing? Using Clay to hurt Gage?"

Hearing her thoughts spoken aloud resulted in more misery than ever. "That's exactly what I'm doing. What now? I don't want to lead Clay on."

"Be honest with him." It sounded simple coming from her friend's lips. "Just tell him you were reacting to being hurt by Gage and not thinking straight."

Mavis was right. "I'll do that. The minute he gets here, before we go anywhere, I'll be perfectly honest with him."

"It'll be all right," her friend assured her. "Call me later if you need to talk."

Mavis opened the door to step out, only to find Clay with his finger poised over the doorbell. The two of them exchanged greetings before he walked into the house.

His eyes took in Ellie's caramel-colored skirt and shimmery top. "You look lovely."

"Thank you." She needed to confess. "Please come in and have a seat. I need to tell you something."

His smile disappeared, only to be replaced by a puzzled expression. "Okay." He sat on the edge of the sofa as if he might jump up and bound away at any moment.

Ellie took a deep breath. "I'm afraid I've given you the impression I'm romantically interested in you." She could do this. "The truth is, I have deep feelings for Gage, and he let me down. I honestly didn't mean to, but I realized tonight that I'm only going out with you to try to hurt him. I'm very sorry, but I just won't lead you on like that."

His laughter took her completely by surprise. "I don't mind being used by a beautiful woman. We can eat and have a lovely evening without there being any romance involved. Donahue might see us together and assume it's something else. That would probably open his eyes."

"You've surprised me again," she had to admit. "You're not like I thought you were at all. Why haven't you found the right woman yet?"

Clay's smile disappeared. "I did find the right one, but it didn't work out as I hoped."

Ellie couldn't help but wonder if any relationship ever did.

Chapter 15

The furniture in Rita Andrews' kitchen wasn't designed for men Gage's size. He held his breath as he felt the legs on his chair wobble. Once he was situated, he looked around the table at the faces of Rita and her grandson.

Sheriff Mitch Landon, who evidently did this often, had parked his large frame on the most marked up chair. He nodded at Gage and settled in. He'd have to ask Mitch later if there was a trick to sitting on rickety furniture.

Mitch cleared his throat, bringing Gage's attention to the sheriff.

"Rita has full custody of her grandchildren," Mitch explained. "She hasn't seen Gracie since Friday night."

Gage schooled his features so as not to seem judgmental. "This is Tuesday, Mrs. Andrews. Can you tell me why it's taken so long for you to report this?"

Tears welled in the woman's blue eyes and the boy's fists clenched. Before she could reply, her grandson spoke.

"Don't you look at my grandma that way. We thought Mom took her."

"Billy." His grandmother placed her hand on the young man's arm. Then she turned back to Gage and Mitch. "Gina has been threatening to try to regain custody of the children."

"Not because she loves us or anything," Billy reached over and touched his grandmother's hand. "She wants money the air force sends us. It's because of my dad dying in the war." The defiance left his face for just a moment before returning in full force. "The judge said Grandma gets that money because she's the one who takes care of Gracie and me. Mom only wants it so she can buy more booze."

"It took us this long to find her." Rita seemed ashamed to make the admission. "She was at one of her...friend's...houses, and she didn't have any idea where Gracie was."

Gage no longer needed to ask why they hadn't gone straight to the sheriff. For all the harsh talk and bluster, that boy loved his mother. And, while he should consider the soft-spoken Rita a suspect, an astonishingly profound and pure love seemed to emanate from her. Gage didn't need his gut instinct or luck...This woman would give her life for her grandchildren; she would never harm them. Procedure or not, Rita Andrews would not be considered a suspect.

"I know how much these children mean to you, Rita. The important thing is finding Gracie." Apparently, Mitch was thinking along the same lines.

"Where did you last see her?" Gage included both of them in his question.

Gage had never seen so much shame on a woman's face. "Friday night. I listened to Gracie's prayers and tucked her in around nine o'clock."

"When I went to get her up for breakfast on Saturday, she was gone." Billy finished. "Mom has a key. That's why we thought she took her."

"Does your mother have a friend she might have left your sister with?" Gage wasn't ready to rule the woman out just yet.

"The only friends my mom has are drinking buddies. Gracie would never go willingly to any of their places. She's little, but she saw our mom do some pretty bad things." For the first time, the teenager's voice wavered.

Although it didn't seem to bother either of the Adams,' Gage planned to see that new, solid doors with deadbolts went up on this house as soon as possible. Even though he didn't believe Gina Andrews had anything to do with it, they were going to take a closer look at her. If she were desperate for money, a child offered unthinkable options. He could only pray she didn't choose any of them.

"Here's the picture Rita gave us." Mitch held out a five-by-seven photograph. "It's her fourth-grade school picture."

The first impression Gage had was that the blond pigtailed moppet appeared much younger than nine years. If he had to guess, he'd say he was looking at a five or six-year-old. His stomach turned; that age was on the high end of Proctor's spectrum.

"Can you find my sister?" Gone was the angry, defiant young man. In his place was a frightened brother.

"I'm sure going to try." It was the best Gage could offer.

"Thank you." Rita appeared relieved. "I know you must hear this all the time, but Billy and Gracie are my life. They came to me at a time I was feeling lonely and unloved. All of a sudden I have two children who I love unconditionally and who love me back."

"I understand." Gage often heard this from heartbroken parents. Some might have lied, but not this woman.

"You..." She looked at Gage. "You're an FSA agent. Why does your agency care about my granddaughter?"

With no hesitation, Mitch answered. "He was here to work on another case, so when Gracie went missing, he came to help us."

As Mitch spoke to Rita, Gage excused himself and walked to the little girl's bedroom. A plain white twin bed with a pink quilt covering it stood against one wall of the small room. He discovered neatly folded clothes in the child-size chest of drawers and a closet rod that was lowered to the child's height. Gage pulled out a dress and was unsurprised to see that the articles of clothing were a size five.

There was no blind on the window a pink gingham curtain adorned. There was no lock, but it was an old storm window. An intruder would have had to use a screwdriver to gain entry. He couldn't see a kidnapper risking the time to replace the storm window, let alone keeping a little girl under his power while doing so. No. Gracie didn't leave the house by this window.

Just as he lowered to his knees to look under the bed, a black ball of fur streaked past his legs. Either the Andrews family had a black cat, or there was an enormous rodent roaming their house.

Gage stood and pulled out his phone. The receptionist at the local field office put him right through to Simon Fisher.

"Are we looking at Proctor?" Fisher didn't beat around the bush.

"It's too soon to make that call." Even though his gut was screaming Proctor's name. "I need some help, though."

"Name it."

47

"We need a full check on Gina Andrews." Sheriff Landon had already told Gage his small department wasn't equipped for a crime of this magnitude, and he would appreciate the AMAR team taking control of the investigation. "Also, I'd like a tap and trace placed on the grandmother's phone as soon as possible. I'll call Elijah and have him send a state of the art device, but will you try to dig something up until it gets here?"

"I'll get on it as soon as we hang up."

Gage felt movement and looked down to see the cat rubbing against his legs. It gave him an idea. "Simon, do people let cats out like they do dogs?" Gage couldn't judge another cat according to Ellie's pet. Fat Ollie was a slowpoke of the highest degree.

Confusion was in Fisher's voice. "I suppose some people might. I think they use litter boxes, too, though. Why?"

"Just a hunch." But maybe a good one.

After promising to let Gage know if he ran into any snags, Fisher disconnected the call.

Gage walked back into the kitchen, where the family still sat.

"Who does the cat belong to?"

Rita looked at him strangely. "He's a family pet, but I guess Gracie pays the most attention to him. Why?"

His hunch was heading to the stars. "Would Gracie have opened the door to let the cat out on Friday night?"

The woman shook her head. "I've told her not to let him out after I'm in bed."

Billy spoke up. "If Elmo wanted out, Gracie would do it anyway. I've caught her letting him out before."

"Why didn't you tell me?" Surprise and disappointment warred in Rita's eyes.

The teenager shrugged. "I handled it."

For the first time in his life, Gage watched a woman scold her grandson without harshness or anger. "I know you had to be a parent when you were with your mother, but you're with me now. You can be the teenager you're supposed to be."

"So, you're thinking somebody snatched her when she let the cat out?" Mitch interrupted the familial dialogue.

"It makes sense." Gage couldn't think of any other way to consider. "One of the local FSA members will be here this afternoon to hook up a wiretap."

"Will that trace calls too?" Billy asked.

"If you can get them to stay on the phone long enough." Gage made a mental note to tell Fisher to reassure them and try to focus on Billy. His rudeness and anger would rile the kidnapper, and an angry criminal usually made mistakes.

Mitch promised the Andrews' that his wife and a large group of volunteers would be ready with posters and banners first thing in the morning. Finally, he and Gage said their good-byes and left.

As they walked to their, Gage decided either they were about to be attacked by a giant bear or Mitch was a hungry man. The sheriff shrugged. "Tessa's at the church organizing the search, so I haven't eaten all day. Do you want to stop at Wilkins Diner and have dinner with me?"

Gage realized that with this case consuming all his time, a quick breakfast was all he'd eaten. "That sounds good. I'll meet you there."

>>>>><<<<<

A few minutes later, Gage pulled into a parking spot just in time to see Mitch close the door of his squad car. "This place has food about as good as Tessa's."

They had just given their orders to the waitress a short while later when Mitch looked up and let out a low whistle. "Well, look at Shadow's Romeo with his date. Clay has a beauty with him this time."

Gage glanced over, but then he did a double take. Even from the back, he could tell he was looking at Ellie.

He stood up and walked over, leaving a curious Mitch.

"What do you think you're doing with my—" Gage caught himself. He looked at Ellie, only to see her face covered in guilt. "Why are you with him?"

Defiance replaced guilt. "You lied to me so you could be with your cute little red-head. Where is your girlfriend, anyway?"

Gage took a deep breath. "I thought I was looking at her."

49

"Well, then, where's your other one? You know, the one who's so important you can cancel dates to spend most of your time with her?"

Only the smug smile on Clay's face kept Gage from confessing. "You don't understand, Ellie." At least, Gage had her listening. "Look, I want to explain everything, but not here, not like this. Will you come to my house for dinner tomorrow?"

Clay smirked. "It's kind of tacky to try and make a date with a woman when she's out with another man, don't you think? Besides, Ellie and I have plans for tomorrow night."

Anger made a sudden appearance as Gage turned once more to Ellie. "Are you really going to throw away y— months of a real relationship without even giving me the chance to explain my side?"

Finally, uncertainty appeared in her eyes, but then her gaze sharpened and focused on something behind him. "I think your side just sat down at your table."

Gage turned to see Samantha take the chair across from Mitch. Fantastic timing.

"Excuse me." Ellie stood and brushed past him. "Clay, are you coming?"

If Clay pushed his chest out any farther, he would tip over. Gage turned, so he didn't have to watch the happy couple leave.

No, he'd rather hit something—anything—as he sat back at his table.

Samantha must have seen Ellie and realized what happened. "I messed up again, didn't I?"

Gage fought back his frustration. "It's not your fault, but the timing...why are you here?" As a mottled reddish color rose in her cheeks, he realized the answer before she gave it. She was lonely and stressed. "I'm sorry, Sam. This is driving me insane."

Samantha's eyes were glued to the napkin in her hands.

Well, this was great; he'd chased off the woman he loved and hurt his partner's feelings within the same five minutes. Maybe, to top it off, there was a puppy to kick or baby to scare nearby. He may as well earn the title he would receive in this small town.

And, the look on the happily married sheriff's face reminded Gage of how quickly small-town rumors started. If—no, when Ellie remembered everything, he didn't want her new friends wondering what the excuse was for him not acting committed to her. He couldn't bear the thought of doing anything that would embarrass or disrespect her.

With a groan, he leaned back in his chair. If this Proctor case was leading him to the edge of a cliff, trying to romance a woman who didn't remember their actual relationship might just shove him right over the edge.

Chapter 16

"Come out, come out, wherever you are!" The mean man hadn't seen her yet. She backed further into the doghouse. "I know you're here. I know you're hurt, too. What were you trying to do? Get to that phone in there?" Gracie suddenly felt warm arms around her, and her head rested on a solid chest. It might have frightened her, but she knew who held her. She silently asked, "Jesus, please make that man go away."

Somehow, she knew the Lord had come to comfort her, not be an angry Jesus and bop the mean man over the head.

"Thought you'd want a new mommy and daddy who will buy you anything."

She almost answered him. She was happy with Grandma and Billy. Why would she want a new mommy and daddy? She leaned over and took a quick look. He bent over and looked at the biggest bloodstain.

At least she hadn't dripped blood between the porch where he now stood and the doghouse. The tattered, old towel she'd found had made the bleeding stop.

"You are in my hands. Believe, Gracie." The comforting arms slowly disappeared. He probably told her that to remind her even if he didn't talk or hold her; he was still with Gracie. Always.

"Well, it won't do you any good to get to the phone now!" The man reached in through the hole Gracie had created and unlatched the window. He then calmly raised it before sliding through, into the house.

Why hadn't she thought of that? She could be home by now.

A sob burst forth before she could stop it. She slapped her hands over her mouth and held her breath, too terrified to cry.

The mean man hadn't heard her from inside the house because he opened the door and walked out like he owned the place.

She pressed back into the dark corner, squeezing her eyes tightly shut. She was too big to think doing that made her invisible, but she wished it did.

Please, Jesus, don't let him find me. I want my grandma, and I need to help Bobby.

The mean man laughed. "I don't care where you're at. You can stay there. If you don't bleed to death, you'll still die without food and water. And I made sure the phone won't work. I don't care. Little girls are easy to come by."

She held her breath as she heard him finally get in the ugly van and leave. He might have been trying to trick her like Billy sometimes did, so she was going to stay right where she was for a while.

Chapter 17

Gage's eyes glowed with love as he led her around the dance floor. The ruby-red dress she was wearing sparkled in the candlelit room. Even though there were people all around them, all she could see was Gage. He smiled before lowering his mouth to hers—

Ellie sat straight up in bed, her heart hammering. Where had that dream come from? It seemed so real, she expected to feel Gage's kiss when she awoke. And the dancing. . . their dream counterparts had danced with an assurance only gained by familiarity and time. It was as if they were two halves of one person, moving in perfect synchronization.

She looked at the clock and was surprised to see it was nearly six o'clock. There wasn't any sense in trying to go back to sleep since she'd have to get up in an hour.

An enormous ball of bright yellow fur seemed to appear from nowhere and launched himself onto her lap.

"Ollie!" She gave up and petted him. "What am I going to do? Gage is interested in another woman enough that he'd rather spend time with her than me. And now, I've somehow ended up dating my boss, only I guess it isn't actually dating since he knows how I really feel. And how do I feel? Well, that's the really fantastic news, Fat Ollie. I'm pretty sure I've gone and fallen in love with Gage Donahue. Isn't that just peachy?"

The cat's purring grew louder as he arched his back.

"You don't fool me," she told him. "You love Gage, too." She hadn't forgotten when her cat climbed up on the back of the couch and stuck his head between their faces right as she and Gage kissed. "He had quite a coating of cat hair on his lips," Ellie told Ollie as she rubbed his neck. "Talk about a mood-breaker." It was a good thing Gage's kisses weren't too passionate, or he might have coughed up a fur ball.

Not that she thought Gage didn't want to be passionate. As a fellow believer, he never showed anything but high respect for her. Sometimes, though, under the surface of a kiss, she could feel something strong waiting to break free.

"I guess I shouldn't have taken our relationship for granted." Purring like a long-haired tractor, Fat Ollie's eyes closed in ecstasy as she continued petting him. "Gage was just so interested and determined to romance me, the thought of him walking away never crossed my mind."

Ellie pushed Fat Ollie to the floor as she stood and stretched. Knowing where she was headed, the cat beat her to the kitchen. After fixing his dish of cat food, she prepared a bowl of cereal for herself.

Since the television was in plain sight of the dining room table, she had gotten into the habit of watching as she ate. "I know it's rude, Ollie, but you can't talk." A few weeks ago, the mayor's assistant, Pearl French, showed up with postcards Ellie had promised to mail. As Mrs. French walked into the dining room, she suddenly sat on a chair–hard. Ellie feared the other woman was suffering a cardiac arrest until she followed Mrs. French's gaze. Ollie was on a dining room chair, bathing anything and everything. "Oh, my" were the only two words she spoke before leaving.

Just as she shoved that embarrassing memory out of her mind, the local news came on. Ellie dumped half a box of cereal on the table. Two area children had been reported missing. Kidnappings in Shadow were too much to comprehend.

There were still no leads in the Dennis Wilder case. A clip of his mother pleading for Dennis's safe return and another one of his grandfather offering a reward that was so large, surely someone would have the right information to share.

The spoon clattered to the table as Ellie's heart stopped.

"Gracie." She was one of the little girls in Tessa Landon's and Ellie's Sunday school class. With an exceptionally large number of students, she and Tessa co-taught. A video clip showed Gracie's grandma, Rita, in a plain housedress. She had tears in her eyes, and her lips were shaking as she told whoever had her granddaughter that she and Gracie's brother loved her very, very much and begged them to please give her back. They could just take her to a hospital or fire station, and let her out. Rita didn't care who they were; she just wanted her Gracie back.

55

"No." Ellie rubbed her burning eyes. Crying wouldn't help.

Billy stepped over and replaced his grandmother at the mics. "Okay, kidnappers." Ellie felt sick to her stomach as she realized what whoever was in charge had this boy doing. Depending on the ages of the kidnappers, a teenage sibling talking could have an adverse effect. They'd show the runt on television.

Whoever allowed it must have been happy with Billy to let him talk. And, boy, was Billy talking. "Does it make you feel good to steal a little girl? Big, strong men all rough and tough with a nine-year-old girl?" He was battling tears and apparently won. A man was looking from Billy's eyes. "Come and try it with me--I guarantee you it will be the last time you try to kidnap a child."

Ellie's heart broke for Rita and Billy. Tall and muscular for his age, she didn't doubt for one minute the police would have to pull the teenager off their suspects. Luke had told Ellie about how Billy saved Holly, and that was before his growth spurt.

Since he worked on her cousin's farm during summer vacation, Ellie had met him, and he'd been nothing but polite while speaking to her. It was common knowledge that while he tried to act all tough and macho when it came to his sister, he was a marshmallow. She suddenly felt a strong need to visit them.

"I'll just go over my lunch hour," she told Fat Ollie. It seemed like the right thing to do.

Chapter 18

The over-sized closet Mitch Landon called his multi-purpose room was giving Gage claustrophobia. Samantha had set up his appointments with the boys here, though, so he was going to have to tough it out.

"Will you be my wingman?" he asked.

She looked up from the pad of paper in front of her and smiled. "Sure. I won't say a word unless you give me a nod."

The door opened, and Haley Davis stuck her head in. "Here's your first interview."

A boy walked hesitantly into the room.

Gage smiled welcomingly. "Have a seat." He indicated the chair at the end of the table, between him and Samantha. "You must be David, right?"

"I'm David Connors." For just a moment, dimples appeared as the boy smiled shyly.

It didn't take long to determine the fourteen-year-old hadn't seen anything or anybody out of the ordinary.

David's younger brother Trace provided them with some interesting information, though.

"I thought the van was an ice cream truck for a minute. I remember. I was mad 'cause I didn't have my allowance with me."

It was encouraging, even though the boy couldn't positively identify the sketch of the television repair van.

It was the youngest of the boys, eight-year-old Jason Connors, who gave them the most information. That didn't really surprise Gage since the youngster would have been more easily distracted by a silly sign on the side of a vehicle.

Gage nodded at Samantha, and she held the sketch out for Jason to see.

"I saw a van with that stupid picture on it." And apparently, it hadn't impressed him.

"Where did you see it?" Gage hoped this would take them somewhere.

Jason frowned. "When me and my brothers were walking home from the park last week. Maybe Wednesday." He shook his head, "No, because we have youth group on Wednesdays."

Samantha sat straighter.

Gage had to fight the rising hopes this boy's story was giving him; younger children were rarely considered reliable witnesses. In Gage's past, he'd seen too many testimonies be tossed, simply because it was difficult for young victims and witnesses to tell only the accurate facts. They were used to seeing such events on television or in those games that no child should play. He had to push his thoughts back to the little boy patiently waiting.

Samantha must have thought Gage was finished. "Was the van heading to the park or away from it, Jason?"

"The first time I saw it, it was a couple of houses away, going to the park. Then, I saw it again headed away from the park. Who would think their TV needed a Band-Aid?" The boy snorted.

Samantha's head tilted to the side with raised brows. She was undoubtedly wondering if Gage had gotten back from the trip his mind took or if she needed to take over. He nodded before speaking. "Think carefully, Jason. Do you remember if you saw the person driving the van?"

Jason's brow furrowed as he thought. "No. I only remember that stupid picture."

Gage thanked him and let him leave.

"Looks like our repair truck is a substantial lead," Samantha observed.

"It's the only thing we have right now, so we'll work on it."

Samantha turned and smiled at the boy walking into the room.

Fourteen-year-old Carter Rayne not only remembered the van, he remembered that its driver was wearing a red baseball cap, like his dad's Cardinals hat.

"Have you ever seen that man anywhere else?" Gage sent up a prayer for a "yes."

Carter frowned before his brows lifted. "I think I saw a man with a hat like his in the park once. I don't remember when, though."

"Not that day?" Gage's hopes were circling the drain.

"It was a day when we rode our bikes to the diamond." The teenager seemed confident. "I remember 'cause the chain came off Jason's bike, and we had to stop and fix it."

Gage had to ask the next question, even though he already knew the answer. "Would you recognize that man if you saw him again?"

"Maybe, if he had his hat on."

Just as Gage expected. The baseball cap was tied in too closely to the identification of the man.

"Thank you, Carter. You've been a big help."

The boy was almost out the door when he stopped and turned back to face them.

"It's my fault."

"Why do you say that?" Gage made a mental note to send someone to these boys' parents. He was positive that Carter wasn't the only one who felt guilty.

Carter's cheeks took on the hue of a tomato. "I borrowed Dennis's bat. If he had his bat, he could have gotten away. He wouldn't be kidnapped."

Gage couldn't let this boy blame himself. "Don't think like that. There's no way to know whether a bat would have helped. It could have been taken away from Dennis and used on him."

Carter emphatically shook his head. "You don't know Dennis. He's not afraid of anything. He fought. Even without his bat, I know he fought. I just hope my friend comes home soon."

"We're doing everything we can to make that happen."

Samantha waited until the door closed behind the youth before she spoke. "You know, Gage, if Dennis put up too much of a struggle, he may be hurt—or worse."

"Let's not go there." That wouldn't do anybody any good, and if he spent very much longer breathing in this damp air, he would be sick.

"I haven't had the chance to ask about the other case yet." Samantha slid her glasses up her nose. "Do you think it's Proctor?"

"It's too soon to tell, but the girl sure fits his target group."

"She's nine, though. The oldest child, as far as we know, is five." It was apparent that Samantha hoped they weren't going to have to deal with Proctor again.

"See for yourself." Gage pulled a photo of Gracie Andrews out of his shirt pocket and slid it across the table.

She's a baby." Dismay filled Sam's voice. "They could have easily thought she was younger."

Just as Gage was about to reply, Mitch Landon rushed through the door.

"Another child's gone missing."

Chapter 19

It was too dark. Gracie had waited and waited to make sure the mean man was gone before she crawled out of the doghouse.

When she first came out, she couldn't believe it when she found the front door still unlocked. Certain it was a trap, she ran back and hid for a while longer—until it grew dark.

Now she was in the house and couldn't see anything.

"Ouch!" The sharp corner of what felt a coffee table scraped her knee and elbow.

Once, at Sunday School, they had covered their eyes and walked around the room. Miss Ellie had wanted them to know how frightening it would be to not be able to see. Then, when they removed their masks, she told them a story about Jesus healing a blind man.

"Quit feeling sorry for yourself," she said, trying to sound like her PE teacher. He scared her.

She closed her eyes and tried to remember where everything was, and then began a slower journey.

Just when she thought she was most likely going the wrong way, she felt the hard plastic phone. When she put it to her ear, it didn't make a sound. Something hit her leg, and she realized it was the curly cord that should be stuck in the other part of the phone. The man had torn it out.

She was a growing girl and knew it wouldn't do any good, but she shoved the end of the coiled wire into what felt like the right place. *I am with you.* Those words gave her the courage to touch the buttons on the phone and carefully counted them so she could press nine-one-one. Praying for it to work, she told the broken phone her name was Gracie Marie Andrews, and she wanted to go home.

Chapter 20

When Ellie told Clay she was going to visit the Andrews home and offer support during her lunch hour, he told her to take as long as she needed.

"I know Gracie is in the class you help teach, and I like Billy. The kid has had it rough, with his mom the way she is and then losing his dad."

He had once more surprised Ellie. "What's changing you? You're like a different man."

Clay shrugged. "The way I've been isn't the way to get a lady to jump up and yell they want to be my one true love. I decided I'd better change into a likable man. Then, my next step will be to make new friends, and hopefully find the woman I need."

"That's not me," she gently reminded him.

"I know," he readily agreed. "But she's out there, somewhere."

"I hope you find her." Ellie realized she honestly did wish good things for her boss.

"Thank you." Clay smiled. "Tell Rita and Billy I'm praying for them and Gracie."

Ellie thought of the changes her boss was going through as she drove across town a short while later. She was shocked to see a familiar car in the driveway. It couldn't be Gage's though because he barely knew the Andrews family.

Hank Stone, the friendliest deputy sheriff on Shadow County's force, answered the door, "Hello, Miss Walker."

"Hi, Hank."

"You looking for Gage?" Hank started to turn, which confused Ellie. Was her ex-boyfriend here after all?

"I'd just like to speak with Rita and Billy."

Hank leaned closer. "Nobody's been here to offer support. They're such nice people."

"Well, then, I'd say I'm the gal you need because that's pretty much what I plan to do."

For a moment, Ellie thought the deputy was going to hug her. He stepped back, though. "You head on back to the dining room, and I'll fetch 'em for you."

He had just left the room when a familiar voice came from the hall.

"And I'm telling you they're connected. We need to get started right away." Gage was using a tone of voice Ellie would never have imagined. "Fine. Since you're breaking your promise and are not giving me what I need, then let me get back to my life."

Then Ellie heard a woman's voice. "Calm down, Gage."

"Good." Satisfaction filled Gage's voice now. "I'll have the sheriff set us up somewhere. We'll have a base of operations ready by the time the team gets here."

"I didn't think even you could pull the team back together this fast." The woman was speaking again. "Good w—"

Ellie looked at the doorway, where Gage and the redhead he'd been seeing stood. Flames of rage filled Ellie's chest when she saw the other woman's territorial pose--her hand on Gage's arm.

"Ellie, what are you doing here?" Gage took a few steps toward her. Then the things she'd overheard started spinning through her head, and for only a second or third time during her life, Ellie was speechless.

"Ellie, sweetheart, are you okay? You're so pale. He seemed upset by what he said. Maybe it was calling his old girlfriend the name he should only be calling his new love. Or old love? Who knew what he'd been doing before they met. His voice was deeper than ever. "Are you okay? Why are you here?"

After the stuff she heard, this had something to do with his new girlfriend. The wheels in her head turned, driving down a very bumpy road.

"Ellie, can you tell me why you're here?" Gage repeated as he stepped closer. She backed away.

Too much input was going to be the death of Ellie. There was too much confusion to allow her to bicker with him. So she was too confused not to answer. "I came to see Rita and Billy." Ellie looked at the other woman. "Gage, what's going on? What did she mean by team?" This wasn't right. "Who is she?"

Gage closed his eyes for a moment, and when he opened them, they were liquid silver. "Samantha is my partner. I'll explain, Ellie, but not here." He looked at the other woman. "Can you handle things for a while?"

"Don't worry about this. Go take care of your w–relationship." Samantha waved them away.

"Thank you," he told the woman. Then he turned to Ellie. "Come," Gage whispered. "Please, come with me, Ellie."

Ellie finally nodded, but if he just wanted her alone to tell her they were over, he could do it right here. She turned to him.

"Gage, let's not make this so difficult. You're with the woman you love and are ending this with me."

"Ellie." The woman—Samantha—seemed to carefully choose her words. "Don't worry about me. Gage and I work together—that's all."

Gage silently placed a hand on Ellie's shoulder. She wasn't ready for a hug, so she brushed his hand away.

"The–this is too much. I don't know what's true, or who to trust."

Gage reached over, grasped her arm and gently tugged her to the door. "Me, sweetheart. Hurting you is killing me."

Ellie's mind was flipping quicker than her father's pitiful card tricks.

With Gage urging her forward, she finally fell into step beside him, in such a stupor she couldn't ask any more questions or argue. Neither of them said a word as he drove to the park, or as they walked the short distance down a secluded path to their favorite park bench.

They had just sat down when Ellie found her voice. "What do you mean, she's your partner? You're a writer. Writers don't have partners. Is she your agent?"

Gage's gaze didn't waver. "I take notes most people could never understand. I'm sorry I lied about the author thing. I studied law enforcement at college, and right after graduation, the FSA offered me a job. Guess they'd been watching me for a while."

"Federal agent? Right out of college?"

"Yes. With this job, I could make a difference, help people, Ellie. When the FSA decided to put together a team focused on kidnapping, I was offered the job of supervisor. When we chose the members, I was tasked with finding the best.

"I've never even heard of the kidnapping group you named." His non-writer status didn't surprise or anger her. Somehow, in the back of her mind, she'd always known the novel was a lie. "This makes the tiniest smidgen of me want to slap you."

"If a slap will help you forgive me, go ahead and slap away."

Ellie realized one thing. She may not best him in a scuffle, but he'd have a fight before she gave in. She realized how absurd that thought was; he had several inches on her and was unbelievably muscular.

"Ellie, please just listen for once." He stood and knelt before her.

"What is that supposed to mean?" His face was close enough to smack. "Are you calling me bossy? Or just a motor-mouth? I can see why you'd go to your so-called partner. What game have you been playing? You should have just lef--"

A soft kiss shut her up. Before she knew it, his hands gently framed her face as he let it get more...more everything. When he pulled a few inches away, a small smile rested on his face, "Tell you what. Listen to what I have to say." He caressed her hair in a way that had sanity jumping out the window. "And if you want me to, I'll leave you alone,"

Confusion waved goodbye and joined sanity.

His gaze didn't move one centimeter. "I needed a break, so I took a sabbatical. I'd still be doing nothing, except these kidnapping cases came up." His handsome features were troubled while he pleaded with her to understand. "It's what I was hired to do. My boss didn't give me much choice."

He rose far enough to slide on the bench beside her. Ellie was stunned. "You're really an FSA agent."

Gage swiveled and took her hand in his. "Listen, honey. I'm still the same person who's spent the last f— several months with

65

you. I'm a to-the-death Braves' fan, even when they hit a slump. I'm still not fond of Fat Ollie's kisses. I'm still the same man who has spent time talking, laughing, living with you. I'm still the same man who is in love with you."

She was genuinely trying to process everything, but his last words captured her attention. "You're in love with me?"

Her heart jumped around like an acrobat when he smiled at her.

"More than I ever thought possible."

Ellie smiled tremulously. "I'm in love with you, too. Why do you think I became so angry? If she hadn't quit touching you, she'd look like a scarecrow."

"She's my partner," Gage spoke firmly. "Samantha and I have worked together for six years. We're coworkers. We've never been anything more." He slid his arm around Ellie and pulled her closer.

After dealing with confusion and frustration, Ellie had to admit her imagination had turned a simple touch into something more.

"You with me?" Gage asked.

Shoving away the disturbing thoughts of Gage's relationship with Samantha, Ellie remembered more of his words. "Your sabbatical is over?"

"Interrupted." His free hand was on her neck, slowly massaging. "During the past six years, Sam and I have been working the same case."

Hearing Gage refer to "Sam and I" working together for six years sent her heart to her feet.

He pulled her around to see his face, and as though he'd read her mind, he said, "Partner, Ellie. Partner."

She managed to nod. "I know." Maybe she had no reason to feel threatened, but she did. She forced herself to calm down. "And this case is active again?"

"It had gone cold, but I believe these recent kidnappings are connected. My boss needs me to work it. We need to catch these people."

Ellie thought of Gracie's sweet smile. "What kind of case? How does it involve children?"

The smell of honeysuckle wafted in on a breeze as Gage pulled both of his hands back to his lap. "A child abduction ring."

"I don't understand. Kidnappers working together—here? In Shadow?"

Just when she thought he wasn't going to explain, he spoke. "A person with money wants a child—a blond-haired boy with dimples. An order is placed for that child. This organization, we call it Proctor, has people in places all over the country. A child is found to match the requested one, he's taken, and sold to the individual who put in the initial 'order.'"

Ellie was horrified. "So, Gracie might already be in another home. Being abused?"

"No, sweetheart." Gage gave her a quick hug. "That's one thing we've found to be thankful for. It seems our kidnapping ring has morals. The children we've managed to recover were all given to decent people who wanted a child so badly, they were willing to pay unbelievable prices. In one of the cases we solved, the so-called new parents paid right at a million to get their little red-haired girl."

There had to be some kind of explanation. "The parents a child is taken from are what? Abusive, neglectful?"

"No. They're loving parents and usually middle to lower class. We've speculated that Proctor probably considered wealthy parents better than the ones they were taken from."

"But, that's not right!" Ellie thought of how much Rita and Billy Andrews loved Gracie. "Just because people have more money or a nicer house doesn't mean they'll provide a better home for a child."

"You just jumped onto my soap box with me." Gage's lips turned down, and his forehead creased. "What they're doing is wrong on every level. The FSA formed the AMAR team, and we've been trying to break them up for years. Their widespread teams make it more difficult. A child snatched in California might end up in New York within days."

Something wasn't making sense to her. "Won't Gracie tell people who she really is? I know she's learned about 'stranger danger' at school."

67

Gage appeared troubled. "I have to admit, I'm a little concerned about Gracie Andrews. A just-turned five-year-old is the oldest we've ever seen them take before. I'm afraid they didn't do their homework well enough, and she looks younger than she is. They may not have realized her age."

"This is awful." Ellie leaned over and buried her face against his neck.

His arms wrapped around her and held her tightly. "This is what I do, Ellie. I'm sorry I didn't tell you before. I just didn't want to complicate things."

She straightened to look into his eyes as another thought occurred to her. "What would you have done if these kidnappings hadn't occurred? At the end of your sabbatical, would you have just told me 'so long, it's been nice knowing you'?"

Gage held her gaze. "I intend for us to be together. I plan to stay at the Pattinton office."

"But, when were you going to tell me about the FSA?"

His eyes clouded for an instant. "I promise I wasn't going back to work before you knew about my job."

What more could she ask?

His eyes appeared bottomless. "So, are we okay? Can you live with me doing this job?"

Ellie sighed. "Since I'm crazy in love with you, I don't really have a choice."

A smile lit his eyes before he tenderly kissed her.

The moment their lips met, a detailed image appeared in her mind. Gage, in a black vest with FSA emblazoned with white letters, was rushing toward her. The moment he reached her, he pulled her into his arms and his lips found hers. It seemed so real it took a moment for her to come back to her senses.

"Hey, are you okay?" Gage pulled her around again. "You're terribly flushed."

Ellie shook it off. "I'm fine. I just imagined our future." What else could it have been?

His eyes searched hers. "Are you starting to regain your memory?"

"No." Ellie gave him a hug. "But, don't be worrying. If I had a boyfriend bigger than you, he would have shown up by now."

She felt more content than she could remember feeling as he held her in his arms. Everything was going to be okay.

Chapter 21

Gage looked with satisfaction around the renovated health clinic. The FSA Advanced Multiple Abduction Recovery team had arrived from the home office in Atlanta and were currently settling in their newest center of operations.

When Binkley gave Gage free rein to choose people for this team, all the hours of research paid off. That information, coupled with all the interviews, landed him a talented team with the highest number of rescues.

Each one of these agents was an expert in their field. During his first year of college, Elijah, "Don't call me Eli" Pryce had managed to hack not one, but two heavily protected government systems. After the FSA supervisors met Elijah and realized his potential, they paid for all his education. More likely they hired him because they didn't want him out there trying to get into the FSA computers.

Jessica Bannon's blond hair was streaked with blue today and in no fewer than five pigtails. She was hands down the best at bringing in a suspect. She could pass for a small, bubbly teenager, when in reality she was twenty-eight and at last count, held five degrees.

In one instance, Jess rapidly and adamantly told a reporter from a major magazine "no." The overconfident young man started to write something, then stopped. "Wait. You won't do an interview?"

Her response should have been chronicled as a masterpiece. "I'm going to be polite since you probably think FSA stands for Fun and Sunny Grade A nincompoops. The truth--a promise if you write one single word about me, or for that matter, about this Federal Investigation Unit, I will sue you. And, I have the law degree to be successful."

In reality, all she had to do was quote the mandated response from her contract with the FSA, and the consequence of being on the wrong side of one of the country's strongest teams. Unless the reporter had pea gravel for brains, that usually shut them up.

At the moment, she was already hovering over the small computer Elijah left on the table.

The computer expert had immediately claimed the biggest office and was currently hooking six monitors up to what Gage thought might be a Central Processing Unit, and at least five other pieces of hardware. The FSA had funded the endeavor and given Elijah free rein to buy the most reliable system, even he had to design and build one. Knowing his soft heart when it came to Jessica, he had probably left his iMac Book so Jess could use it. She was currently arguing with the automated voice search engine. "Shut up, Syrie. What kind of a name is that, anyway? Her interest was taken off Elijah while he put together his systems. Jess launched into a heated, one-sided argument with the search engine. And, she was the most intelligent person on the team. Oookay.

Elijah probably had the most power with the government agencies. Not knowing if they might need him later, the head honchos tended to look the other way when he surfed the net. He also wore his hair longer than FSA regulations, but again, nobody approached him.

Except for Jessica, who once went on a month-long campaign to make him look patriotic with red, white, and blue hair. He finally stood his ground and told her he'd let her color his hair when the Dodgers went to yellow floral team uniforms. He was very calm; the best candidate for his job.

The opposite of Jessica, Bridgett Monroe, a former Kansan was the other woman on the team. She was usually silent, so when Bridgett voiced her opinion, E.F. Hutton couldn't compete with the silence as she spoke. Shy with others outside the team, Jess thought she came across as standoffish. Instead, her office back at the Atlanta base had at least two dozen trophies for her success in mixed martial arts, and Gage gave up trying to keep track of her certificates and awards for her work as a forensic scientist.

Once, when Eric asked her why she wasn't on a job that paid more money, she looked near tears. According to the intel, of which there was little on her, Bridgett's past was unknown to Eric. When orders came down from so high they specified that Bridgett would be considered completely an agent with no distinctions, Eric didn't have to be told his job would blow away like a dandelion's tufts.

In a different way, she fit in on the AMAR team. She didn't talk much or share, so the team didn't know who she really was. A psychiatrist once theorized that she stayed with AMAR because she felt safe.

Her forensic skills were remarkable, and she had to have someone who truly cared about her high in the system, because most of her reports were redacted.

And as for Dr. Eric Grant, as far as Gage knew, the man didn't own any apparel other than suits. In his late sixties, he was the oldest agent on the team. With salt and pepper hair, the psychologist could pass for a distinguished professor. At the moment, he was busy with his antique laptop, which Elijah had repeatedly hypothesized might still be set for dial-up internet. As talk of Eric's retirement or teaching grew, Gage had come to realize that a fresh start might be what Eric needed. The enthusiasm he showed when he first joined AMAR had lasted less than a year, and ever since, he had slowly sunk to the same level of enthusiasm and pleasantness as the Grinch.

Troy Martin, who had been in town for a couple of days, seemed content to be back with the team. His computer gear was mixed in with a sloppy pile of sketch pads and pencils. At the moment, it appeared he was drawing a caricature of Eric—something to irritate the other man, no doubt.

Gage wondered what assignment Burnett had pulled Kurtis Wright from. The tall, muscular African-American looked bored at the moment. Of course, he didn't have much to prepare since, as an ex-special forces operative, his expertise was in the fields of stealth, weaponry, and physical combat. He didn't have any bombs to dismantle or guns to play with, and his favorite pastime--tormenting Jess—would have to wait, since she was focused on Elijah's computer.

Of course, Sam, being her usual OCD self, had prepared and left color-coded packets on the table before leaving. "Let's get started." Gage waited until each of them had taken a seat before he moved around to stand in front of the situation board.

"I have to say I don't like the circumstances, but it's nice to see all of you again." He looked around the room, making eye contact with each of them. "We now have three abductions in the area, and I believe two of them are connected." Gage stepped aside, so the pictures of the girls were visible. He indicated the blond-pigtailed girl with bright, blue eyes. "This is Gracie Marie Andrews, nine years old, taken from her home sometime between last Friday night and Saturday morning."

"She's nine?" Bridgett voiced the question on all their faces.

Gage nodded. "We think she was mistaken for a younger child."

"The other girl is four-year-old Destiny Jones." Gage waited until his team's attention was on the toddler's picture. "She was at home with a babysitter, fifteen-year-old Amy Brock. Brock tucked the toddler into bed at eight-thirty, and then went back downstairs to watch television. When the Jones' got home shortly after ten, the father ran the sitter home. While he was gone, his wife went in to check on their daughter, only to find her missing. She called the local PD immediately."

"Poor baby," Bridgett murmured.

At least he had more information than they did for the Andrews kidnapping. "The girl's bedroom window was found open, and a ladder was left propped against the house."

Jessica jumped to her feet. "Don't tell me the girl's dad left a ladder lying around in plain sight. Why didn't they just lay out a path to her room and mark it with neon signs?" Jess had little patience for parents who, in her opinion, as good as assisted the abductors through mere carelessness. "Why didn't they leave the ladder with a big red circle on their daughter's window? Why—"

"It was locked in the garage." Had he not interrupted Jess, she would be stringing Destiny's parents on light poles and using Kurt's gun to shoot their toes off. As Jessica silently sat down, Gage indicated a photo of the property he'd tacked to the situation board. "You can see the side door was forced open."

Kurt looked up from the paper he'd been studying. "Have the parents and babysitter all been cleared?"

73

"The parents have a solid alibi. Their waiter remembers them being at the restaurant because they were celebrating a promotion on a Tuesday night. He said they didn't leave until around six-forty-five, and since it's a fifteen-minute drive, they're clear."

Gage checked the board before he finished his response. "Fifteen-year-old babysitter, well known and trusted, no boyfriend. She keeps busy as one of the most sought-after babysitters in town. There's a note here stating this was only the second time she sat for the Jones family. They're not financially able to spend many evenings out."

"Any other possibilities?" Elijah looked up from his tablet to ask.

"Every person in Destiny's life is being checked out, but it sounds like a stranger abduction."

"Since we're here, you must believe Proctor is involved." Leave it to Eric to state the obvious. "Why don't you explain your logic?"

Gage remembered Samantha asking the very same question. They had "discussed" his theory quite vigorously before she finally conceded defeat and agreed he should call. It was time to see if the team agreed with him. "He's shopping." The words made his blood run cold. "Proctor wanted a white girl with blond hair and blue eyes. He had Gracie Andrews. I think he realized she was older, so he needed Destiny Jones to replace her." He didn't need to tell them what most likely happened to Gracie after she was replaced.

Eric gestured toward Dennis Wilder's picture. "He has to be what, fourteen? How does he tie in?"

"He doesn't." At least, not as far as Gage could see. "Since he's a senator's grandson, and comes from an affluent family, his kidnappers may be biding their time until they make their demands. Burnett is sending agents from Chicago to assist Sam on the case." He leveled a gaze at his team. "You all know me. I've always relied on my instinct, and it's never led me wrong. It's telling me these two girls were taken by the same person. Yes, it's too soon to state unequivocally that Proctor is involved, but he's been out of action for a while now. This just feels like his doing."

Elijah's eyes sparkled, but not with happiness as he turned to Eric. "I'm not a shrink, but I trust Gage's gut. I think we should at least be on the lookout for signs of Proctor's involvement."

Gage couldn't help but sigh with relief as he heard the murmured assents. Eric was the only one of them who appeared unhappy about the situation, but Gage thought he knew the real reason for that. As the others began talking about the cases, Gage headed over to update Eric on his progress. He'd only taken a few steps when his phone rang.

Mitch Landon was on the line, and he didn't take time for niceties.

"My dispatcher is on the emergency line right now, listening to a little girl claiming to be Gracie Andrews."

Gage motioned for the others to be quiet. "Has she told your dispatcher where she's at?"

"We can hear her, but she can't hear us. She's just saying her name, and she wants to come home."

The room was silent as Gage spoke. "Where is the call originating from?"

Mitch's voice was troubled. "It's coming up as unknown. Shadow County doesn't have the technology to trace it at the drop of a hat. It has to be in the county, though, since the nine-one-one call came to our office instead of the state's."

Gage met Elijah's eyes. "Just a minute, Sheriff." He held his phone against his shirt. "Elijah, a child is on the phone with the caller's origin coming up unknown. They don't have the technology for an immediate trace, and we need to know where she's at. What can you do?"

Elijah stood and picked up a tablet computer. "I'm not linked into the phone system yet, so I'll have to be on site. Let me grab a couple of cables, and we'll go."

"We'll be there in a few minutes," Gage told the sheriff. "Whatever you do, don't let the call get disconnected." He stuck his phone in his pocket and addressed his crew. "Kurt, Bridgett, we'll go to the station with Elijah. It'll be easier to follow the sheriff to the

75

location once we know it." He turned to Eric. "We'll need you with us."

Eric was even more unhappy. "I'm not trained to work with children. We need an agent who is."

"I'm working on it," Gage assured him. "Until then, you're just going to have to do your best."

After what seemed like hours, but had to have been only minutes, he found himself approaching a group of people gathered around the dispatch table. Silent tears flowed down Haley Davis' face as the sobs of a little girl came from the phone's speaker.

"Sheriff Mitch Landon, this is Special Agent Elijah Pryce. He'll trace the call." Gage stepped aside to let Elijah move closer.

Mitch didn't waste time. "What do you need?"

Elijah set his tablet on the desk next to Haley and pulled a cord out of his pocket. "I just need to get to the phone."

Without being told, everyone backed away as he worked on the device. For just an instant, it seemed as though the line went dead, but the child's soft crying resumed.

"I wish she could hear me." Haley seemed about to lose it. "She is so frightened."

Gage assumed like most police stations, they recorded their calls. "Can you play back the recording of the call without disrupting Elijah?"

Haley gestured toward the computer. "I can't access a live line on it, but I can pull up what's already been recorded."

"Please play it."

Haley scooted her chair from the dispatch table to the computer. A few moments later, a voice came from the speakers.

"My name is Gracie Marie Andrews. My name is Gracie Marie Andrews. I want to go home. I want my grandma and Billy. My name is Gracie Marie Andrews." It sounded as though the little girl was speaking more to herself than the phone.

"I've got the address, but we have a problem." Elijah's voice caught everybody's attention. "She has company."

The room went dead silent as they listened. The child's sounds had stopped, but it was apparent somebody was searching.

"I know you're here somewhere." Although he wasn't very close to the phone, the man's voice was audible enough to hear pure cruelty.

Elijah handed a piece of paper to Gage. It was the address.

"Know where this is, Mitch?"

The sheriff looked at the paper. "We need a map, please, Haley. One of the county and enlarge the east side."

"Something wrong with the GPS in your squad car?" Gage asked.

"This address won't be on any GPS."

"Hide, Gracie." Bridgett murmured.

Mitch accepted the map Haley had printed out. "Let's go."

"I'll meet you at the hospital," Eric looked like a banty rooster as he posed by the doorway to the sheriff's office.

Gage bit back a frustrated retort. Eric knew he might be needed on site, but it was apparent he was using the urgency of the situation to get his way. Kurt threw a disgusted look the older man's way and stepped toward him, leaving Gage in no doubt if he said the word, Eric would be accompanying them. Gage caught Kurt's eye and subtly shook his head. They didn't have time to waste.

A few minutes later Gage sat in the front seat of a squad car. The image of Eric's smug expression finally faded when the sheriff, behind the wheel, captured his attention.

"The place is a good twenty miles out of town." Mitch was yelling to be heard over the siren. "North Forty-first turns into nothing more than a glorified cow path past Wichita Road. I can't even remember a house out there."

"That's the kind of place kidnappers like." And patent Proctor.

Mitch gave Gage a sidelong glance. "I may just be a county sheriff, but I'm not stupid. The FSA is here, and now you have a team working out of the old clinic. What exactly is going on in my county?"

Gage had planned on telling the sheriff everything after they knew for certain it was Proctor, but now was as good a time as any. "We're the FSA Advanced Multiple Abduction Recovery team. Our job is to locate and stop child and adult abductors, and we have reason to believe the area kidnappings are the work of a group we call the Proctor Organization. Gage felt the familiar flame growing in his chest. "They set it up to be a store-like business."

"They sell kids to perverts?" Mitch asked sharply.

"They're facilitating illegal adoptions. So far, the children we've recovered have been found in upscale homes. The new parents had various reasons for using Proctor. In one case, conventional adoption was difficult because of the wife's health issues. Another extremely wealthy couple simply didn't want to wade through the legal process."

"If they were wealthy, couldn't they find a surrogate and have their baby?"

Gage hid his scowl. "These people don't care anything about genetics. The couples I've met were irritated, not guilty. After all, they buy everything else they want; why not a baby who looks like their family." Just remembering the movie star and his wife had Gage's stomach rolling. Their three-year-old wouldn't stop telling the world she wanted her real mommy and daddy. They had placed a three-year-old child into their tanning bed, and her thin skin blistered before they got her out. Neither would take responsibility for helping her.

Mitch slammed the gas pedal a little too hard, and lumps of dirt flew past the fences on either side. "What did they do to her?"

"I'm sorry." Gage took in the officer's ruddy cheeks and realized the man was about three minutes from losing his breakfast.

"I'm okay." Mitch's appearance said the opposite, but if he wanted to know, Gage would tell him.

"It seems brutal to us, but I think the parents call Proctor and complain, and in four cases we discovered parents who could see no difference from trading in a car for a much nicer vehicle. They're trading in one model of a baby for one they like better."

Anger seemed to have rid Mitch from the sickness. "How does something like that work?"

It had taken years of hard work and the capture of a sole perpetrator to learn what they knew. "It's all done on computers. A screen will appear with the offer to fill their order. They complete a form and pay half the fees online, and when the dropoff occurs, they pay the rest in cash. Then, the child is delivered, and that's it.

"And this Proctor kidnaps the children himself?"

"Proctor has teams all over the country. We believe there are four people on each one. Two or three who snatch the kids and take care of them, and one who receives the orders from Proctor and ships the kidnapped children out."

Mitch looked at him incredulously. "If you know all this and the guy's name, why don't you arrest him and bust it up?"

"First of all, Proctor isn't his or her name." Gage was a little embarrassed to admit this. "We found a bunch of high-end cleaning supplies, with a case of Proctor and Gamble, at a farmhouse after they abandoned it. When one of my team members remarked about it being the perfect product, we began calling the organization Proctor. You can imagine how it evolved into the Proctor ring, and it stuck. Now we use it for the boss's name and the organization" The ring itself or its creator–Proctor was a handy name for both.

"But you know what they're doing."

"We have no idea how many teams are out there. We've only been able to catch a member of one of them." Gage remembered how God surely had his hand in things that day. "As usual, we got too close, and they ran. Only this time one of the people taking care of the children was left behind." Kristen Baker had fought like a hundred-pound ball of fury. "Her partners left her, not realizing she was out of gas. We caught her because she forgot to fill up her tank."

Gage felt like his teeth were going to rattle out of his head as the squad car careened over what was supposed to be a road. The bumpy ride made further talking impossible. After what seemed like forever, they rounded a corn field and there it was—a small house in the middle of nowhere. Both squad cars pulled up and parked.

"No other vehicles in sight," Kurt observed as he and Bridgett joined the sheriff and Gage. "Could be he parked down the road and walked, though."

They glanced at one another before all six of them silently pulled their guns.

"Donahue and I will take the front door." Mitch indicated the house. "You two come in through the back." Gage watched his agents wordlessly nod. Mitch turned to his deputies. "Hardy, you and Jeff look around out here."

Gage kept repeating the same prayer as he and Mitch approached the door. *Please let her have found a good hiding place.*

The door was standing open, so the team walked in, guns raised. In response to Mitch's signal, Gage checked the living room while the sheriff checked the kitchen. Bridgett and Kurt were in the bedrooms. "Clear," he called when he heard the others do the same.

They met in the living room. Mitch's brow was furrowed. "If the person we heard was her kidnapper, he may have her again."

Gage knew that. "If anybody else found her, they would have brought her to the station." Coming so close, yet failing to rescue the child turned his stomach.

"Want us to check around out back?" Bridgett respectfully addressed the sheriff, who nodded. Kurt followed her down the hall.

Gage noticed the telephone. The receiver's cord was poking out of the base at an odd angle, so he walked over for a closer look. "Sheriff, you need to see this." Mitch joined him as Gage carefully straightened the coils nearest the phone. The wire had been torn from the phone and appeared to be stuffed into the slot. "Somehow, it connected."

"It's a miracle." The sheriff's voice was full of amazement.

But not enough of one to save her. Gage looked out the window. He was just about to suggest searching the cornfield when a movement caught his eye. The sheet covering the couch had shifted just a little, as though a breeze had brushed by. Only it was a hot, windless day. There weren't any breezes. "Sheriff." He waited until Mitch looked at him before pointing to the couch. The sheriff looked at the sheet and nodded.

"Gracie, if you can hear me, my name is Gage Donahue. I'm with the FSA. Sheriff Landon is with me, and we've been looking for you. Your grandma and Billy miss you."

This time the sheet moved farther.

"You probably don't remember me, but I go to your church. I sit with Miss Ellie. I've seen you there with Billy lots of times. I'd sure like to take you back to him."

A tiny dirt-covered face popped out from under the sheet. From what Gage could see, her hair was matted.

"Is the mean man gone?" Her voice quivered.

Gage hadn't noticed Harding Davis walk into the room until the deputy spoke. "There isn't anybody here except the people who came to take you to Grandma and Billy. You called nine-one-one and told Miss Haley you wanted to go home, didn't you?"

The child slowly crawled out from behind the sheet, where she'd been hidden in an incredibly small space under the couch. Gage noticed a dirty towel encrusted with what appeared to be dried blood wrapped around her leg.

"Will you really take me home?" Big, blue eyes were fastened on Gage.

He knelt in front of her. "You need to go to the hospital first and have a real bandage put on your leg, but I'll make sure Grandma and Billy are there. Okay?"

Mitch stepped closer to the child. "I'll even turn on my siren so we can get you to Grandma and Billy faster. How's that?"

She looked from Mitch to Gage. "I'm a big girl, but just this once can you carry me? My leg really hurts."

Gage stood and scooped the little waif into his arms. *Thank you, Lord.* Gracie Andrews was safe.

Chapter 22

The smiley face balloon blew down and bumped the top of Ellie's head as she got out of her car. The hospital parking lot was full for a Thursday morning.

She exchanged smiles with the man sitting in the truck next to her.

"Wife took sixteen hours to get our baby here." Once Ellie looked at him, she saw exhaustion. "Had to get out of there for some fresh air."

"You're feeling guilty?" The man didn't have to be a child for Ellie to realize what was wrong.

"Yep. If Monica could struggle for that long, I'd at least ought to be in there with her and our baby."

"Know what?" Ellie's heart ached for the man with such mixed feelings that he had no idea how to handle. "I don't know for sure, but I'm almost positive that long in labor wore your wife out. She's probably in there sound asleep."

His shoulders seem to drop as he produced a giant sigh of what Ellie believed to be relief.

She didn't want to leave him like that, though, because he would return to his guilt, and their poor baby would have two parents with postnatal depression.

So, normal talking it was. "Boy or girl?"

A real grin appeared on his rugged features. "A—" An ambulance, with sirens roaring, pulled in across the parking lot and headed to the emergency bay. "A boy," he finally managed to speak loudly enough.

"Congratulations." She produced what she prayed was a cheerful smile and lifted the cat. "I have to get this to a little girl. I hope you and your wife enjoy your son."

"We will." He appeared much calmer since their talk.

She turned and headed quickly toward the visitors' door. Their conversation had been pleasant, yet something niggled at her mind. Why did the subject of a baby make her feel sick? There was no way she could have been pregnant since she hadn't done anything to get that way. Once more, her imagination seemed to be in charge.

Ellie looked at the cat. "You know Clay was very understanding when I told him my plans." The stuffed toy was about as conversable as the fat feline she had at home.

The doctor admitted Gracie after being rescued and treated for severe dehydration and an infected gash on her leg. Ellie tried to tell herself it was because she hadn't been able to see Rita and Billy the day before, but the truth was, she felt deeply drawn to visit the little girl.

When Gage called the day before to give her the news and tell her he might be busy for a while, she asked if it would be possible to visit the little girl. He was silent for just long enough to make Ellie wonder if he'd hung up. But, when Gage finally spoke, there was something close to eagerness in his voice. He even asked why and seemed disappointed when she reminded him that the child was her student.

Ellie felt guilty because she hadn't been entirely honest. It was just she didn't understand her compulsion to see the child, let alone try to explain it to Gage.

Ellie glanced at the non-talking, yellow, stuffed cat that resembled Fat Ollie. She'd picked it up on a whim; she didn't even know whether Gracie liked cats.

A few minutes later, she had to shuffle the cat and balloon's string in her hand to dig out her wallet and show her driver's license to the receptionist. "I'm sure you're a nice person, but I have to see a photo ID before I can tell you where that patient is. And I still need to make sure you're on the visitor list."

"I understand." Ellie wondered why she felt almost normal going through this routine. She just about jumped out of her shoes as a loud alarm howled through the hospital.

The gray-haired lady frowned as she looked at a computer screen in front of her. "All the muscle on that boy must be draining his brain cells."

Ellie waited, wondering if she should be taking cover.

"Been trained for a month now!" The alarm stopped, so the receptionist sighed. "My nephew needed a job, and they gave him a good one. He keeps setting off the wrong alarms, though. My maternity ward light is red, so that means it's something to do with that department."

"I hope it's nothing bad." It would be too much of a coincidence for this to involve the man from the parking lot and his new family, so Ellie pushed it out of her mind.

"I can't say." The gray-haired lady looked up from a paper. "You're on the list. She leaned toward Ellie and lowered her voice. "You shouldn't be misled by her room's location." The receptionist looked around them and whispered, "She's in the ICU for security reasons, rather than health."

As Ellie stepped into the elevator and pressed the button for the third floor, a sense of Deja vu struck her. She saw herself with a stuffed cat and balloon in a different elevator, on her way to see another little girl.

The memory had to have been from her work in the clinic, but how strange that she couldn't remember a particular event. She was still puzzling over it as she once more showed a nurse her driver's license. The doors buzzed, allowing Ellie into the intensive care unit.

Hank Stone and Billy Andrews sat at a small table in the hall.

"Rummy." Billy placed his cards on the table and grinned.

Hank's brows went up. "Are you sure you're not cheating?"

Billy started to reply, but then saw Ellie. "Hi, Miss Walker."

Hank turned and smiled. "Gage told me you were coming."

Ellie took note of the look in Hank's eyes and the pistol in its unsnapped holster and realized Hank wasn't as laid back and relaxed as he seemed. Gracie was safe.

Billy stood up. "Isn't it great, Miss Walker?"

"It sure is, Billy. Is Grandma in there with her?"

The teenager's smile wavered. "Grandma only leaves the room to use the bathroom. She even orders hospital food and eats in there."

Ellie smiled gently. "I can understand her not wanting to let Gracie out of her sight. How is your sister?"

"I'm really glad she's okay." Billy appeared troubled. "But it's very hard to be in the room with her right now."

Ellie exchanged glances with Hank, silently thanking him for providing Billy with a distraction. "Why is it hard?"

It took a moment for Billy to answer, but when he did, it gushed forth. "Because I'm so mad. Not at Gracie. Never at Gracie. It's just she has an awful cut on her leg and so many bruises. And she was filthy when they brought her in. The doctor said it's why her leg is infected."

"It's natural for you to be angry," Ellie assured him. "You should be furious at the people who took your sister. But, you should be very proud of her, too. She's only nine years old and somehow managed to get away from them."

The teenager's eyes glistened. "Agent Donahue told us Gracie had to hide from the kidnapper after she got away. He said she hid so well, he and the sheriff almost didn't find her." He produced a nervous smile. "She's good at hide-and-seek. I play it with her a lot."

"Think about that when you're with Gracie." Ellie thought the young man had every right to his feelings. "It's okay for you to be angry, but it's probably not a good idea to be angry around Gracie right now. She just needs to feel safe and loved. I know you're a strong, young man. If you set your mind to making your sister feel better, you can do it."

She put her hand on his shoulder. "It's okay if you need help, too. I'm certain the doctor can find somebody to listen to you—somebody it's okay to be angry around."

Billy's smile grew. "I like talking to you. Could you maybe spend some time with me?"

Ellie made up her mind in an instant. "I'll visit your sister, and then if your grandma says it's okay, I'll see if Agent Donahue is free anytime soon, and we'll talk him into treating both of us to a pizza?"

The boy's response was beet red cheeks.

"Hey." Hank winked at Ellie. "If you're not going to take her up on her offer, I will. A man should never turn down a chance to spend time with a pretty woman."

Billy looked shyly at Ellie. "Pizza sounds good."

"Why don't we try another hand of Rummy while she visits your sister?" Hank shuffled the cards. "I'm bound to win sooner or later. Ellie left the two of them resuming their card game when she opened the door and walked into the room.

Rita was sitting in an uncomfortable-looking chair pushed as near to the bed as physically possible. Her hand was over Gracie's, and the little girl was asleep. She was pale and bruised, just as Billy described, but her hair looked freshly washed and brushed out. An IV was pumping badly needed fluid and nutrients into the child's body.

It appeared as though Rita was asleep, too, until she began to speak. "I thought I'd lost her. That it was going to be like all those kidnappings you see on TV, where the child never turns up."

"Of course, you were afraid." Ellie set the balloon weight and cat on a small table and walked closer to the pair. "But Gracie beat the odds. She's safe and sound, back with people who love her."

Rita looked up at her, and Ellie found herself looking into bloodshot eyes. "I didn't care when Billy's friends talked him into joining the church's youth group. I didn't care when he started taking Gracie and going every Sunday. But, the truth is, I thought it was a waste of time. Until yesterday, at ten-forty-seven in the morning." Her gaze didn't waver. "Billy bowed his head and asked God for his sister back. He no more than said 'amen,' when the phone rang. It was Haley Davis, telling me they'd found her."

Goosebumps covered Ellie's arms. "Sometimes, miracles seem even more astonishing than we can imagine. It looks like God made sure Billy knew he was listening."

"Well, so will I from now on," the older woman declared. "I'll never doubt God's power again."

Ellie silently thanked the Lord. "More than one miracle was brought about by that phone call."

Finally, Rita smiled. "I guess that's true. I grew up in the church, you know. But, when Virgil drank himself to death, and then I watched my only child marry a woman who gave her life to the bottle, I just lost faith."

"You're finding it now, though, and if the Lord is part of your family, your grandchildren will be even better off."

Rita's gaze lowered to her granddaughter's face. "The psychologist from the FSA and doctors have tried, but she hasn't been able to tell them what happened yet. The doctor says she wasn't...assaulted. And it looks like the bruises and scrapes are from her escape."

"Does Gracie remember anything?" If not, Gage would be disappointed.

"She heard the cat outside her window. We never leave him out at night, so she went to let him in. She doesn't remember anything past opening the door." Rita shook her head sadly. "She thought I'd be mad at her. I told her repeatedly not to open the door after I was in bed, so I'm afraid she thinks the kidnapping is all her fault."

"It might help Gracie to talk to somebody who can help her understand," Ellie gently suggested. "Your doctor can recommend a therapist."

"Grandma?" Gracie's eyes were open. Ellie's heart broke to see how sunken they looked.

"I'm right here," her grandmother assured her.

"We have to go get Bobby." The little girl was agitated. "I forgot, I was supposed to tell you he's there." She started to cry. "He knocked the special man down and told me to run. But Bobby didn't get away. We have to go get him, Grandma. We have to."

With no conscious thought, Ellie stepped closer and spoke calmly. "We'll go get Bobby if we can find him. Can you tell me where he's at?"

Gracie shook her head. "Bobby said we were in an underground house. It looked like the place they keep dogs—a kennel. Only I was in one of the cages, and Bobby was in another."

Ellie fought back her revulsion. "How did you get out of the cage?"

The child's tears slowed. "Bobby broke a little piece of wire off. Then, he messed with the lock on his cage. After he got out, he got the keys off the nail and unlocked my gate. But the door that would let us outside was locked on the other side, and Bobby wasn't strong enough to kick it open."

"What do you remember, after you were outside?" Ellie gently prompted.

"I was too scared. I just ran."

"That was a smart thing to do." Ellie didn't know where the questions were coming from, but she had to ask. "Do you remember if it was morning or not?"

Gracie frowned. "The special man brought bowls of oatmeal for breakfast. Then, we had peanut butter sandwiches right before Bobby got the locks opened. I remember, because the sandwich was too sticky without jelly, and the water tasted funny. Bobby said the special man wouldn't be back until it was time to eat again. That's when he got us out."

Ellie realized they must have waited until their captor was bringing their evening meal before Bobby put his plan into action. "Do you remember if the sun was in your eyes, Gracie?"

The little girl scrunched her face. "I don't remember the sun." She suddenly looked worried. "Am I in trouble?"

Rita spoke up. "You're not in trouble for anything, precious. You were brave, and I'm very proud of you."

What had Ellie done? She had just interrogated a child as if she were an FSA agent. What had possessed her to do something so inane? "I need to call-Agent Donahue so that he can find Bobby. One of his friends might need to talk to you again, but it'll just be so they can find Bobby. Okay?"

"Okay." Gracie looked past Ellie. "Where's Billy?"

"I'll send him in." Ellie needed to leave and clear her head. "You shouldn't worry about anything."

But should Ellie?

Chapter 23

Bryan Cosart fought the urge to knock every blasted object off his desk. This job should be easy. They had it made. With somebody out there grabbing a senator's grandson, nobody would have time to worry about finding a regular kid. But the girl was all over the news, and his people had messed up. He didn't understand what was going on with them; they had worked in much riskier environments.

Maybe he should have insisted on somebody besides that crazy family. Of the mother and her two sons, the younger man was the only one whose spark plugs didn't seem to misfire. If instead of his brother, he'd have overseen the brat, the kid would have never gotten away.

At least the girl was replaced in time for the shipment. He wondered what new parents would be awaiting her arrival. He didn't envy those people. They still had to go through the reconditioning process with her. It amazed him the technique had as great of a success rate as it did. Out of the hundreds of children they "adopted" out, only a small number failed to succumb to it. Bryan didn't know what happened to those children, nor did he want to.

He glared at the phone he'd just placed on the desk. For some reason, his boss had suddenly decided Bryan couldn't do anything right. After all, he already failed part of his assignment. But it wasn't his fault. It wasn't supposed to be his job to eliminate problems, but that was exactly what he'd been instructed to do. Set up shop in this Podunk town and take care of Ellie Walker. Since the problem with Miss Walker was due to Bryan's mishap, he had no choice. He would do it.

But, she had a guardian angel or something. Every single time Bryan had a perfect plan, something would ruin it. And, then Gage Donahue showed up. His boss finally agreed, with the agent so close, it was too high of a risk to rid the world of the woman.

So, why had he received the call? His boss couldn't possibly know of the Andrews girl's escape. Maybe it was just to keep him in line.

He satisfied himself with the knowledge he was an irreplaceable component of the operation.

Crystal's cackling announced her impending arrival. He took a deep breath and plastered on a smile. Romancing her was becoming quite a chore. One he'd gladly quit any time. If only he could.

Chapter 24

"If she ran through the woods the entire time, she had to either come from the north or east, Gage." Bridgett made the observation. "Cornfields are on the other two sides."

Gage looked around the lawn of the small house where Gracie hid out. "Who owns these woods, Sheriff?"

Mitch, standing between two of his deputies, turned and looked at him. "All of the acreage covered by trees and brush is owned by Mel Carmichael."

"What do we know about him?" If the man was new to the area, they might have a suspect.

"You'll be wasting your time if you go after Mel." The sheriff gestured around the area. "This land goes all the way back to his great-grandfather. There's a thick forest on the property, but Mel can't help us out much there since losing his leg. He just farms now."

"He told me there's nothing man-made in there, other than a small family cemetery," Deputy Jeff Fielding offered. "He doesn't think there's even a clearing large enough for a structure."

"Exactly what type of structure are we looking for?" a female state police officer asked.

The others in the large group of officers waited for Gage's answer. "The girl was in what she called an underground house." His heart leaped when he remembered Ellie had instinctively led Gracie to recall what happened. "Since she ran out the door, instead of climbing, it must be built into a hillside."

"Let's spread out and walk the woods." Mitch gave the order. Soon, the agents, officers, and deputies were trudging through trees and forest fauna.

As he shoved his way through thick underbrush, Gage recalled his conversation with Eric that morning. It seemed the psychologist thought Gage should pass this case off to Samantha and the Chicago crew. The AMAR team should be working the Wilder case. The way Eric saw it, Gage was jumping the gun on deciding this was a Proctor case, and frankly, the team could benefit from earning points with a senator.

91

Gage had barely restrained his anger as he informed the older man it did not matter whether Proctor was involved; these children were every bit as valuable as Dennis Wilder. And since they were set up to deal with multiple abductions, it made more sense for AMAR to take this case. Eric left Gage's office in a snit and was nowhere to be found when the team gathered to join the search. Gage wondered what Eric's problem was lately. Maybe it was time for him to leave the team. They could make it without him if—

The thought of Ellie's phone call dragged his mind a different direction, and at that moment, he couldn't have stopped his smile with a bulldozer. She reported her session with Gracie Andrews like a pro. He tried to caution himself. She was a child psychologist for years before they met, and she may be falling back on those skills. No. He had spent a lot of time with her during the past year, and this was different. She was different. He'd first gotten a glimpse of his Ellie when she yelled at him for his supposed cheating. He had real hope of her memory returning.

Exactly what would it mean? There were many questions about the accident only Ellie could answer. His entire world might collapse when she did, but it was a risk he had to take. He needed her to remember.

"Ouch," he muttered as a thorn of some kind scratched the back of his neck. He'd thought a long sleeve T-shirt would be adequate, but even as he shoved his way through the brambles, the sleeves were beginning to look like Swiss cheese. And to think, the little girl, scared senseless ran through this. Gage was amazed that she wasn't even more injured.

"She only had on shorts and a T-shirt, no shoes." Sheriff Landon's voice and the crackle from his radio came from Gage's right.

He thought Hardy Davis was to the left of him, but the seasoned deputy would be silent.

Gage stumbled on a root and stopped to look around. How could there be an underground house out here? He could see what Mel Carmichael meant about no clearings. The longest distance he walked at one time without a mass of brush or dense forest was six or seven feet. One good thing—if the structure were out here, it would be hard to miss. He wondered if the helicopter crew was having any luck. Jess was most likely driving the pilot crazy. Before they landed, she'd know how every gadget in the chopper worked.

Gage heard crackling brush right before Hardy Davis stepped into sight. "Good thing I'm a country boy at heart."

During all the televised uproar, Gage had admired the man beside him. "I remember seeing you on television. You took down the drug-running syndicate in Chicago." It had been all over the news. "Pardon my asking, but with success like that, why are you a small-town deputy? I mean, what a past."

"One I don't like to remember." Hardy fell into step beside Gage. "Going undercover and becoming a part of the criminal world for five years almost cost me everything."

Gage remembered something else. "Elliott Lawrence is your brother-in-law, isn't he?"

Hardy grinned. "If he'll claim me."

"He'll claim you." Gage knew first-hand how Lawrence felt about Hardy. "I was partnered with him on the Brast federal prison escape. Inspecting cells was about as dull a job as they come, so we talked a lot. He's very proud to call you family."

The two of them shared a companionable silence for a few minutes.

"Do you have anybody undercover in the kidnapping ring?" Hardy seemed hesitant to ask.

"We've never gotten close enough," Gage admitted. "We've only been able to access their website a few times. I don't understand the technicalities, but the trail from a post ends up in the deep web, and even with Elijah Pryce's crazy mad computer skills, we can't find it."

Hardy let out a low whistle. "I wondered if he was the genius. Didn't the FSA bust him for hacking into their system in Texas?"

Gage chuckled. "Not the FSA computer system. We caught him after he'd finished taking over two other agencies I'm not allowed to share."

"So the FSA ended up with a man known around the country for hacking the government."

Hardy didn't know that those government agencies were only half of Elijah's crime-filled portfolio. One case had received so much publicity; Gage could talk about it. "Want to know the kind of man Elijah Pryce really is?"

"I have to admit, coming from crimes that dangerous, how he could be in the FSA, let alone an elite unit like AMAR, puzzles me."

"One of his first hacks was in a small-town hospital. A childhood friend was dying from cancer, and with research, Elijah discovered his friend wasn't receiving all of the meds on his list."

"Let me guess—they didn't believe him because of what they had on the computers."

"Exactly. Elijah spoke to everyone he thought might have the clout to get things straightened out, but when his friend passed away, he was finished with the hospital staff. You can imagine why he hacked their system."

"I saw it on the news, but they didn't include the reason he did it."

"No, because the hospital insisted it be kept quiet. Several patients were being incorrectly treated and had the complete story came out, the hospital would have been in big trouble."

"So, the criminal known for hacking important agencies, did so out of anger?"

"Not at all." Gage had liked Elijah from the beginning, and after a year of watching every move he made, Gage received an all-clear to hire him and put him on the then brand new AMAR team. "He had reasons for all of his crimes. Even I don't know what they were; nor do I want to. Elijah's a good man."

"Sounds like it." Hardy glanced at his wrist. "I've enjoyed talking with you, but I'd better get back over. I can't imagine how, but I'd hate to miss anything out here."

As Gage watched the deputy walk away, he considered Davis' suggestion. Undercover agents could pose as wealthy would-be parents and try to connect with Proctor. Only, the single most important missing link was how Proctor knew which couple would be willing to buy a child. After making it to the Proctor site once, only to see it disappear, Elijah picked up a brass statue and beat on his tablet until it was in tiny pieces.

Anyway, the agency couldn't afford to create and maintain a wealthy couple for an extended length of time, and the cover would have to be deep to fool Proctor.

Sometimes he wondered if they were wasting their time, trying to stop the organization, but then he would look at pictures of missing children they thought Proctor had taken, and his resolve was strengthened. It might only make a dent in the crime of child abduction, but he was going to take Proctor down. If it was the last thing he did.

Chapter 25

Crystal looked at her reflection and admired the diamond necklace. Bryan told her when he saw it in Reno, he imagined it "right around your neck."

It didn't matter if he didn't talk with fancy love words. It seemed difficult for him to show his feelings: lots of people had trouble doing so. He obviously cared for her, if he thought about her while they were apart. Maybe he'd even told people she was his girlfriend.

He would be there to pick her up any minute. They were going to O'Leary's. She was a little disappointed because it was a Wednesday night, and the people she most wanted to impress would all be at Bible study.

Maybe Bryan would take her to the Diner Friday night. The necklace was a little flashy for such a place, but it would be worth it to see Haley Davis or Ellie Walker's envious expressions.

Crystal Stanley was just as good as those women. On the arm of a wealthy man like Bryan Cosart, she was better.

The doorbell interrupted her thoughts.

Holding a bouquet of roses, Bryan stood on the doorstep.

"Are you ready?"

Why hadn't he complimented her appearance? "Do I look okay?"

"You look fine." He shoved the flowers at her. "Are you ready?"

She was disconcerted. "It'll take me a minute to put these in water, but then I'm ready."

As she found the vase in her kitchen cabinet, she once more reminded herself Bryan simply wasn't the kind of man to use words. He was showing his feelings with gifts and flowers. As a couple, they were fine.

Chapter 26

"Richmond Insurance." Ellie placed the phone on her shoulder and shoved a ridiculously detailed policy aside.

"Ellie?"

A warmth filled her heart, and the truth popped out. "I've really missed you, Gage."

"Not more than I missed you." A chuckle came across the line. "I guess we're about as cheesy as they come, huh?"

"Maybe, but I don't care." Ellie probably looked like a grinning fool.

"I'm sorry about Bible study last night." Gage's deep sigh wiped away any light-heartedness she felt.

"You haven't found the place, have you?"

"No, we haven't."

"So, the boy is still..."

"They still have him."

"Is there anything I can do for you?"

His silence made her wonder if he was unable to speak out of sadness. She was just about to say something when his voice stopped her.

"Pray for the boy, please, and all of us looking for him."

She'd already been begging the Lord to take care of the child and help the searchers. "I will." Good thing God didn't set limits as to how many times she could pray for the same thing.

"I have more bad news. At least I hope you wouldn't call it good."

Ellie started to come back with a lighter retort when she realized there was nothing light-hearted about this situation. "You're expanding the search area, aren't you?" Why that popped into her head, she didn't know.

"Yes, and I'm sorry, but I won't be able to see you today."

Ellie forced her disappointment to the outfield; the man she loved needed her support. "You have too many obligations to worry about me. I'm not going anywhere."

"I wish I could see you, but we're looking farther in case

Gracie was confused about the distance."

"I understand, and trust me--I'll still be right here."

After they had exchanged goodbyes, Ellie sat back and tried to figure out why there was such a sense of deja vu about their conversation. In fact, she felt like they had similar conversations—more than once.

The door opened, and Ellie looked up to greet the customer. Instead, she hopped to her feet and rushed around the desk.

The older women enclosed Ellie with her arms. "I miss you, my darling."

Ellie smelled Aunt Vi's scent and wanted to cry.

The women released their grasps and stood a few feet apart.

Ellie couldn't believe her eyes. "What are you doing in Shadow?"

The tall, slender, silver-haired lady smiled lovingly. "I'm meeting with my partner in Chicago. I had the driver make a bit of a detour."

"You still won't fly." Ellie shook her head. "You're probably the only person in the country who would travel from Atlanta to Chicago by car. Do you know how strange that is?"

Vivian Wolfe raised her chin. "What I believe strange, is putting a monstrously huge chunk of metal in the air and expecting it to stay there."

Ellie knew her godmother was wealthy, but to leave her office closed had to cost money. Unless... "Who's manning the helm while you're gone? Don't tell me you finally hired somebody."

"For your information, Miss Smarty Pants, a young and ambitious attorney named Adam Spencer began working for me nearly nine months ago." The twinkle in Aunt Viv's eyes belied the sternness of her voice.

"Wow." Ellie was impressed. "How long–?"

"Excuse me."

Ellie turned to see a very curious Clay Richmond.

"Clay Richmond, this is my godmother, Vivian Wolfe. Aunt Viv, Clay is the man kind enough to hire an embarrassingly inexperienced person as his assistant."

He didn't even bother to hide his enthusiasm to meet such a

sophisticated lady. He about knocked Ellie onto her desk as he stepped over and shook Vivian's hand.

"Vivian smiled warmly at Ellie before she spoke to Clay. "I know better than to believe the only reason you hired my goddaughter is that you're nice. She's probably the most gifted woman on the face of the earth."

"Are you in psychology, then? Like Ellie?" Clay politely asked.

As always, Viv's smile was beautiful. "Some people would undoubtedly say I'd benefit from psychiatric assistance, but I'm an attorney."

Ellie wouldn't be at all surprised if he were silly enough to drop to his knees. He'd probably get Viv's purse upside his head.

"What kind of law do you practice?" Had Clay swooned?

Ellie decided to shift the man's attention away from her godmother by answering him. "Aunt Viv takes just about any case she believes in." Ellie was proud of the woman. "Lots of times, she represents clients who can't afford a lawyer." Ellie remembered her father's words. "She helps Daveys take on Goliaths."

"So, you're from Atlanta."

Vivian didn't like to field personal questions, but she was too dignified and polite to ignore Clay "Yes. I'm passing through on my way to Chicago and thought I'd stop in and see if I can spirit Ellie away for brunch." She placed her hand on Ellie's shoulder. "I miss her since she moved."

"Of course." Clay was quick to be accommodating. He turned to Ellie. "Take all the time you need. It's not every day you have an important visitor."

"I love her, Clay, and she would be important to me even if she lived in a box."

Viv didn't say anything; the stately woman placed her hand on her goddaughter's shoulder and steered them toward the door.

A few minutes later, Ellie found herself wondering why she'd chosen the Diner, of all places, to bring her distinguished visitor to. With her swanky hairstyle and designer suit, Aunt Viv looked about as out of place in the restaurant as a chrysanthemum in a patch of onions.

"I'm sorry, Aunt Viv." Ellie looked around. "Maybe you'd rather go to O'Leary's. It's more to your taste."

"Nonsense." Vivian pulled the laminated menu from between the napkin holder and condiments. "Diners like this always have the best food."

Sandra, a waitress who might just be Betty Crocker, herself, seemed taken aback when she brought ice water and got her first look at Vivian.

"Hi, Sandra." Ellie greeted the older lady. "How's Joshy?"

The question brought the woman out of her stupor. "He's starting to walk. Tasha thinks handling a baby is bad; wait until she's taking care of a mobile one."

"I'm Ellie's godmother, Vivian Wolfe." Vivian smiled warmly and held her hand out to shake Sandra's. "Are you talking about your grandson?"

"Great-grandson." And just like that, Aunt Viv had put the other woman at ease. Ellie sat back and waited as the two women discussed children. Sandra sympathized with Vivian's woes over having no grandchildren of her own to look forward to.

It had always puzzled Ellie that even though Vivian was such a nurturing person, she never married and had a family. Someday, when the time was right, she'd ask her.

"How's life in Atlanta?" Ellie asked after Sandra left with their order.

"Pretty much the same." Vivian leaned forward as though sharing a confidence. "I had dinner with your father. He's suffering from empty nest syndrome since Annie moved out."

"I feel sorry for Dad." He had raised his daughters alone since their mother died shortly after Annie's birth. "But Annie is twenty-six now, Aunt Viv. She needs to have her own life. Dad will just have to understand."

"I am proud your sister chose to teach at an inner city school, but I'm still frightened for her." Poor Annie had probably faced quite a battle when she announced her plans.

"If Dad would do like most men his age and retire, he could come visit me in his hometown whenever he felt like it."

Brows raised, Vivian leaned toward Ellie. "Ryan Walker will be performing heart surgery until he's too old to stand up. Even then, he'll probably just try to scoot his wheelchair closer." Vivian's gaze narrowed. "Speaking of retiring, though, you might be interested to know Zane Gibson is retiring at the end of the year. Lou keeps asking me if you'd come back."

Ellie had worked with Lou Reese for Zane at the clinic in Atlanta from the time she was certified until her memory stopped. "I just can't go back. I don't know why, Aunt Viv, but it's just not me anymore."

"I understand." The older woman reached over and patted Ellie's hand. "I'm sorry I brought it up. How is your life in Shadow, then? Anything exciting going on?"

"I have good news." Ellie knew she was smiling from ear to ear and didn't care. "I've fallen in love with the man I've been seeing."

Aunt Viv's forehead wrinkled. "What is this boyfriend's name?"

"Gage Donahue."

Her godmother's sigh was followed by a smile. Had Viv been expecting someone else? Ellie wanted Viv's blessing.

"I feel blessed, Aunt Viv, because he loves me very much."

"That's wonderful."

Why had her godmother seemed so relieved about Gage's name? Why would she worry at all unless—Oh?

Ellie's heart sank with the possibility she was cheating. She couldn't remember or imagine loving anybody other than Gage. She still needed to ask and be sure she was doing the right thing.

"I know Dr. Marx said I have to remember everything on my own, but you'd tell me if I wasn't free to commit to Gage, wouldn't you? If I was already in a relationship with somebody else?"

Amusement lit the older woman's eyes. "I promise, my darling, you are not involved in any relationship that would be affected by your committing to Gage Donahue."

A pent-up breath of apprehension left Ellie.

The women waited while Sandra set their plates on the table. "Is that pumpkin pies I smell, or merely wishful thinking?" Vivian always had a sweet tooth.

Sandra beamed as she answered Viv. "We have a new cook who says pumpkin pie is her specialty. We don't typically serve it this time of year."

"Well, put me down for a piece," Elllie's godmother looked like someone had handed her a pile of diamonds.

"You, Miss Ellie?" Sandra's pen hovered over her notepad.

"Apple for me."

"I'll bring them out after your meal." Sandra appeared even more pleasant than she usually did as she headed toward the kitchen.

Vivian's gaze followed Sandra and then turned to look at Ellie. "Mr. Richmond seems gentlemanly enough, but surely you don't plan on making insurance your career."

"I don't." Ellie speared a broccoli floret. "I just haven't decided what I want to do yet." The image of Gracie Andrews' face flashed into her mind. "I helped a young kidnapping victim remember some things that might help, and it felt good. Maybe I should consider doing some kind of therapy for the police department."

"No." Viv spoke quickly. "I mean it would be too stressful. If you want to practice psychology again, I'll set you up in a private office."

Ellie knew Viv's offer came from the heart. "I'll keep it in mind when I make my decision." She sighed. "There probably isn't any need for a child psychologist in law enforcement, anyway."

"I wouldn't know." Vivian was battling with a cherry tomato. "Sometimes, I wonder why we don't, as an entire population, throw our eating utensils away. Then it would be appropriate to pick up food and eat it." Her lips trembled as she looked at Ellie. "Why, we could lick our fingers! And, won't babies be better off learning to dip fingers in a jar of liquefied beets and smear them anywhere within reach?" With a wink, she picked up the tomato and popped it into her mouth.

"Aunt Viv." Ellie giggled. "You lose your appetite when a baby burps loudly."

"Oh. Well, is burping any more pleasant than recycled baby food adorning everything?" She waggled her brows, and Ellie knew

Aunt Viv was finished with the joke.

Five years of memories with this amazing woman were gone. To keep herself from crying, she feigned a keen interest in her chicken salad sandwich. "I don't remember it, but I've read about your remarkable accomplishments—the formation of the United Legal Assistance Network."

"I'm pleased to be a part of such a beneficial organization."

"So, you have how many attorneys in the network now?"

Ellie had come across a box of newspaper clippings while visiting her godmother. During the past four years, Aunt Viv had developed a network of attorneys across the country, all committed to helping the less fortunate. Her original partner Lyle Crawford was based in Chicago. He had often flown to Atlanta and joined the Walkers and Vivian for dinner. Ellie could only remember seeing him once—when he came to dinner with Vivian. Ellie had wondered if there might have been a little romance brewing, but nothing seemed to come from it.

Viv regaled her with trial stories as they ate. Ellie wasn't surprised Aunt Viv had taken the case of a down-on-his-luck man. She not only helped him keep the visitation rights his ex-wife was trying to take away; Viv helped him gain more hours with his children. And, of course, she'd taken the case pro bono.

"It always amazes me when God uses you as he does," Ellie said in admiration.

The other woman appeared uncomfortable. "I have watched you grow into a woman with values and faith in Jesus."She shrugged. "I've just seen too much hatred and anger to believe in a loving deity."

"Aunt Viv, don't you see how God uses you to remove those negative feelings from others?" Ellie felt nearly desperate to get through to Vivian. "Every time you help someone, you're helping one of God's children. You're making a big difference."

Vivian reached across the table and touched Ellie's cheek. "I wish I had your kind of faith. I really do."

"I'll pray for you." Ellie wasn't ready to give up. "I intend to spend eternity in Heaven, and I want you right there with me."

"You are truly a precious child." Was that a tear sliding down the older woman's cheek. Before Ellie could ask, Viv seemed regenerated and back into her normal mode. "Now, let's eat. I want that piece of pie before I get back on the road."

Chapter 27

Gage was dirty, sweaty, and exhausted after spending an entire day in the woods. A state tracking dog smelled the shirt Gracie had on when she was found and gave all of them a shot of optimism when the dog found the scent and took off like a Greyhound. The entire group of searchers abandoned their designated areas and fanned out behind the dog and his handler.

They made it a good two miles into the woods, and the dog lost the scent and went gallivanting through a high wheat field. Even as disappointed and tired as they all were, the dog hopping through the field like a rabbit gave everyone a chuckle.

After Mitch had assured the dog handler nobody blamed him, they focused on the spot where he seemed to lose the scent. Every person who was there practically tore the area apart, going out in a hundred-yard radius, hoping to locate a hidden door. After over five hours of intense searching, they had to give up.

After a quick shower, Gage fixed himself a sandwich, even though he was too tired to be hungry. Dennis Wilder had been missing for a week. Sam and the crew of agents from Chicago continued working the case, leaving the AMAR team to focus on the Jones girl and the boy they knew only as Bobby.

Even though Elijah had worked his magic, none of the missing children were Bobby. He found a Robert out of state, but he had been missing long enough to be in his twenties by now.

Troy Martin was going to the hospital in the morning to see if he could get a sketch of Bobby from Gracie. Under protest, Eric was going with him. This was the type of situation where their specialist was needed. She would coax a description of Bobby out of the little girl with no muss or fuss. The thought made him realize he hadn't spoken to Ellie since early that morning.

A glance at the clock told him it was late, but he decided to call her anyway. Her sleepy voice immediately flooded him with memories.

"Did I wake you?"

105

He heard her yawn before she answered. "I must have dozed off while I was watching the news. Did you just get home?"

"Yes."

Her voice was full of empathy. "I can tell by the tone of your voice it wasn't successful."

Gage fought back his frustration. "If there's any kind of building in those woods, I don't know where it is. The dog couldn't even find it."

"So, what's your next move?"

His heart twisted as he realized how much he missed this. Late night conversations about their days. Soon. "As quick as Burnett can persuade the powers that be, we're trying to get the National Guard. Their nearest base is in Pattinton, but they and all the others we contacted are out on assignments." Gage knew as well as anybody that bombings, shootings, and controversy about the police would be more important than a few kidnapped children. It had to be, or agencies and military would be hopping all over the country while the people who wanted them destroyed became even closer. Still, the state and county police were helping the FSA.

"Do you think your boss will get through to them?"

"Truthfully, no. The country's shootings are keeping our guard busy. And, as bad as I feel saying this, a kidnapped child out of over two thousand a day won't garner much attention."

"Really?"

"Yes, and almost half of them are taken by a parent, but sweetie, can we talk about something else?"

"Of course." Her words didn't surprise him at all. Ellie had never wanted to talk about work after going to bed. She wanted alone time. And she sounded sleepy.

"You're tired. We should get off here so you can get to bed."

"Unless you don't want to, I need to talk to you. It makes my day complete." She had the strange tone of voice he was getting used to. A memory was tugging on her mind.

"Just one more thing, Ellie. Don't worry about Proctor being in Shadow. My instincts say it's one of his teams, but to my knowledge, they've never let a child escape."

106

"You have good instincts." Ellie's reply was instantaneous. "I've always trusted them, from the first time we met."

They had "met" when he stole her chair in Wilkins Diner and gave her a corny line about a country song. "What do you mean?"

Once again, her response was immediate. "You knew that family needed help, even though you didn't understand a word they said."

Gage fought to remain calm. "I don't remember. Where were we?"

The line went silent. Finally, she spoke. "We met in the diner when I came from the restroom to find you sitting on my chair."

His heart fell. "You said something about a family being there." He couldn't see how a little prompting would hurt.

Determination filled Ellie's voice. "I'm just more tired than I thought. I must have been dreaming again."

It looked like she still wasn't ready. Gage forced a teasing note into his voice. "Have you been dreaming about me?"

"Maybe a time or two."

He chuckled. "I hope I behave like a perfect gentleman in them."

Ellie's voice softened. "You do. I have on a beautiful dress, and you take me dancing in a romantic, candlelit room."

An image filled Gage's mind, and he spoke without thinking. "You looked exquisite in that red dress."

He was met with dead silence, and then she spoke so softly he could barely hear her. "How did you know the dress I dream about is red?"

Gage thought fast. "Aren't all beautiful dresses red?"

"I guess." Her uncertainty was apparent.

Maybe it was because he was so tired, but he made an instant decision and spoke before he could change his mind. "A sketch artist is visiting Gracie in the morning, to try to identify Bobby. Since you've already established a rapport with her, would you like to be there to help?"

"Yes." Then, concern crept into her voice. "I'll have to ask Clay if I can come in late. I don't think he'll mind, though; he was so accommodating when Aunt Viv showed up."

"Vivian is here?" Fabulous. He tried to cover for his blunder. "You've never mentioned an aunt before."

Ellie didn't seem to notice his slip. "Vivian Wolfe and my mother grew up next door to each other. They were inseparable, more like sisters than friends."

"You don't have to talk about it if it hurts too much." Plus he wouldn't have to hear his tired brain saying the wrong thing.

"Do you mind if I share? You must be exhausted."

Ellie D–Walker, your voice is the most pleasant thing I've heard all day. Go ahead, but don't feel like you have to finish."

During the silence, he was certain she was carefully considering his offer.

Then, a much firmer voice came through the receiver. "Aunt Viv took the role of godmother seriously when Mom died. I don't know what Annie and I would have done without her."

"She sounds nice. How long is she staying?" He hadn't seen Vivian since moving to Shadow, and he missed her.

"She only stopped in for a short visit on her way to Chicago." He heard Ellie's deep sigh. "Aunt Viv absolutely refuses to fly. She travels everywhere by car."

"Does she want you to move back to Atlanta?" Of course, she did.

"She did mention my former employer is retiring, and the psychologist I worked with wants me to come back."

Gage choked back words of anger–words Ellie wouldn't understand. If Lou Reese had his way, Ellie would never remember who she was—at least not before the rat could persuade her she should be Ellie Reese. "Are you considering moving back to Atlanta, then?"

"No." Ellie sounded confused. "Somehow, it doesn't seem like I belong there anymore."

Mixed feelings flooded Gage. He visualized a house in a suburb of Atlanta, sitting just as it had been left over fifteen months ago. But he loved a person, not a place. "Shadow seems to suit you."

"It does." Then she asked worriedly. "Will you have to relocate because of your job?"

Gage remembered Burnett's promise of more time. "If a move is necessary, the team will go on without me. I have something here that is too precious to leave, even for a job."

Silence came from the phone until the most angelic voice Gage had ever heard spoke. "That is so sweet, Gage." The sound of a muffled yawn came across the line. "Excuse me."

"I'm keeping you awake." He glanced at the clock. "I'll pick you up at eight."

She sounded pleased. "Even though it's late, I'm going to call Clay tonight. I'm looking forward to helping Gracie."

"I love you, Ellie."

"I love you, too."

After saying goodnight and hanging up, guilt showed up and knocked on the door. Was he doing the right thing by asking her to work with Troy? Would he be helping, or making things worse?

He decided he didn't care how late it was. He was putting both of Dr. Marx's daughters through college with what he paid him. They may have managed to make it appear to Ellie her insurance was adequate, but, thanks to excellent investments, Gage could handle the rest.

Several minutes later, he concluded that the call was worth it. Although the doctor didn't appreciate being phoned at a late hour, he was extremely encouraging. It seemed to him Ellie remembered bits and pieces. And, since she had taken the initial step of speaking to the child, he believed encouraging her would be beneficial. After Gage had hung up, he was even more hopeful that the real Ellie would soon be back.

Chapter 28

"Come on in, and we'll see if we can find Troy."
Ellie walked past Gage as he held the door open. She found herself in a large room, with a group of people gathered around a table, eating.
A tall, buff, African-American man was arguing with an incredibly petite woman who, with purple and orange pigtails, couldn't be more than twenty.
The man didn't seem willing to give up. "You said you wanted an omelet. Those banana pancakes are mine, sister."
The tiny woman didn't seem phased. "You need a hearing aid. They're mine."
Jess always did like banana pancakes. The thought came from nowhere. Of course, Ellie imagined it.
Just then, a tall, black-haired beauty looked up and saw Ellie with Gage. "Ellie." The woman's smile widened.
The table grew quiet as they all turned and looked at Ellie. Then it seemed as if they all greeted her at once, each happy to see her. She was befuddled by their demeanors.
Gage's throat clearing quieted the room and got everyone's attention. "They all feel like they know you because I've told them about you." Ellie didn't miss the strange look he directed toward them. "Right?"
Before Ellie had time to ponder their actions, Gage took her arm and led her to the table. He gestured toward the woman who had managed to claim the pancakes. "This is the Queen of Brains, Jessica Bannon. She looks like a teenager, but she's actually a few years younger than you. She is also our top talent for convincing a suspect to come in for questioning."
Jessica? And Ellie had imagined her name was Jess. How odd.
The energetic woman started to stand, but after exchanging a look with Gage, she sat back down. "It's nice to meet you, Ellie."
Ellie had to ask. "Do we know each other? You seem familiar."
Jessica's eyes widened as she focused on Gage.
"Jess has that effect on everybody." He spoke smoothly. "The man

sitting next to her is Kurtis Wright. If it's a weapon, he knows it."

The handsome man looked pointedly at Jessica's breakfast. "I also know I picked those pancakes up for myself." As he turned to face Ellie, an intense moment of déjà vu made her light-headed. Evidently not noticing or sharing her trip to the stars, he gestured toward the Styrofoam container. "Would you like to share the omelet I'm stuck with?"

Feeling semi-normal, Ellie wondered why she felt so connected to this man? Kurtis seemed to be a paradox, with muscles on muscles, yet calm-tempered with a friendly smile. "I already ate breakfast, but thank you just the same."

Gage continued introductions. "The other woman on the team is Bridgett Monroe. She's an expert in forensic science, and she fools around with mixed martial arts."

"She has a lot of trophies and belts for someone who just fools around," the man who could have just stepped out of a GQ magazine, winked at Ellie.

"Be quiet, Elijah," Jessica ordered.

The tall, svelte woman with long, black hair smiled in a friendly way. "Don't mind them. Jess argues with everyone." She reached across the table to shake Ellie's hand. "It's wonderful to see you."

Ellie returned her smile. "I'm glad to meet you, too."

The tall, brown-haired, GQ man stood and offered his hand as Gage introduced him. "This is Elijah Pryce, our technology expert."

As she shook his hand, yet another strong feeling hit her chest; she knew this man. Even her hand in his felt disturbingly comfortable. She must be more tired than she realized.

"Gage saved the best for last." A man appeared to be in his mid-sixties with short, gray hair and the surliest face Ellie had ever seen. His smile seemed to cause him pain. "I'm Dr. Eric Grant, the team's criminologist, and psychologist."

"Hello." It was all Ellie could say. The whole experience had taken on a surreal quality.

"Gage saved the best for last all right."

Ellie turned to see the man who had entered the room. He had cropped blond hair, and the widest smile Ellie had ever seen. And

111

somehow, he looked extremely familiar.

Gage spoke up again. "And here is the man we came for. Meet Troy Martin. He is considered the best sketch artist in the country."

As Ellie started to speak, Troy swept her into a hug. Before she could decide what to do, he released her.

"Ellie?" Gage's disembodied voice came from beside her. "What's wrong? Tell me so I can help."

"I think I need to sit down."

Eric, who was closest to her, stood so Gage could get Ellie off her feet.

Ellie closed her eyes and took deep, calming breaths.

Gage knelt beside her. "I'm sorry. I shouldn't have heaped so much information on you like this."

She managed a shaky smile. "It's not your fault. I've just been feeling a little off-kilter." She had to shake this off. She sat up straight, full of resolve. "We need to get to the hospital."

Gage's fingers gently traced her cheek. "Are you sure you're feeling good enough to go?"

Ellie stood up. "I'm sure."

A few minutes later, without thinking, she climbed into the back seat of Gage's car and let Troy sit in front.

"Has Sam checked in this morning?" Gage asked Troy.

Troy turned to his boss. "I think you need to make an appearance at the senator's house. He has been giving Samantha a hard time about his grandson playing second fiddle to the other missing kids in the area."

"I'll get over there as soon as I can." Gage's eyes met Ellie's in the rearview mirror. "I'll make myself scarce while you're working with Gracie. She won't need an audience, will she?"

Ellie had been thinking about that. "Would you mind getting Rita out of the room? Maybe you could take her and Billy to the cafeteria." She felt strange, requesting assistance,, yet it seemed natural. "They wouldn't mean to, but they would distract Gracie."

"I can do that."

A few minutes later, Ellie wasn't surprised to see Hank hovering outside Gracie's hospital room.

"Where's your Rummy buddy?" she asked the deputy.

Hank's seemingly perpetual smile grew bigger. "Your cousin came and picked him up to spend the day on his farm." The deputy's phone rang. "Guess I better answer this."

Ellie gave the young deputy a little wave before turning to the men behind her. "Let's go see Gracie," she instructed. As Ellie walked into the room, with Troy and Gage behind her. Rita looked with trepidation at the men, but relief instantly appeared on her face when she sighted Ellie.

"Hi, Miss Ellie." Gracie sounded much perkier.

"Hi, Gracie." Ellie stepped next to the bed. "You look lovely today."

A missing top tooth showed when the little girl smiled. "Miss Tessa brought me some new hair ribbons last night, and Grandma fixed my braids and put the pink polka-dotted ones in this morning. Isn't it pretty?"

"It sure is." Ellie heard Gage and Rita murmuring. Troy stepped up beside her.

"This is my friend Mr. Troy. He likes to draw."

Gracie looked questioningly at Troy. "Do you draw cartoons? Mickey Mouse is my favorite."

He reached up and rubbed his chin. "Hmmm. I might be able to do that. Just a minute." Troy pulled a packet of pencils out of his shirt pocket and flipped his sketch pad open.

Rita approached the other side of the bed. "I'm going with Mr. Donahue for a little while. Will you be okay with Miss Ellie while I'm gone?"

Just when Ellie was certain Gracie was going to tell her grandmother not to go, Troy held out his sketch pad. "Here you go."

They looked at his drawing. Mickey Mouse was sporting a long braid, complete with a polka-dotted hair ribbon.

Gracie giggled. "Mickey Mouse is a boy, silly."

Troy looked at the picture. "Oh." He shrugged. "I guess he's a boy with a braid."

Gracie's giggles were like music. "What else can you draw?"

"I'll be back." Gracie barely looked at her grandma. Troy had enchanted her.

Ellie pulled a chair up beside the bed. "Mr. Troy would like to draw a new picture, but he needs your help."

"How can I help? My crayons are in the drawer, but I only know how to color with them." Her gaze went to Troy. "Do you want me to do that?"

Ellie accepted the sketch of Mickey Mouse from Troy. "That isn't the best way you can help, but you can use crayons on the picture of Mickey while we talk."

Troy situated the drawing on the tray in front of the little girl, while Ellie went to the drawer and found her crayons.

"As Ellie handed her the crayons, she asked the Savior to *please let her do this without frightening or hurting this precious child*. "You remember Bobby, don't you?"

Gracie looked up from seeking a crayon, her eyes desolate as they met Ellie's. "I still don't know where he is."

"It's okay." Ellie rushed to reassure the child. "But, do you think you can help Mr. Troy draw a picture of Bobby?"

The little girl frowned. "I guess."

Troy walked around the bed and pulled a chair next to it.

Ellie wasn't sure how, but she knew what to ask. "Is his face round like a circle, or does it look more like an egg?"

Gracie's crayon started moving again. "It's not like Mickey's. It's more like Billy's."

"Then it's oval, like an egg. Does Bobby look a little bit like Billy?"

Gracie nodded. "Bobby's hair was a different color, but it was cut like Billy's."

Ellie thought of the teenager's appearance. "So, it kind of lies straight around his ears and onto his forehead a little. What about his nose? Does it look like Billy's?"

"No." Gracie's lips turned down. "Bobby's nose is little, like my friend Emmy's. Grandma calls it a button nose, but I don't know why since it wouldn't do any good to stick it in a buttonhole. It would just come right back out."

Troy glanced up from his sketch to share a smile with Ellie. Ellie turned to look at their witness. "What about Bobby's mouth? Does he have plump lips like Billy's or thinner ones like Grandma's?"

"He looks a lot like Billy when he smiles." The little girl's lips trembled. "He wasn't happy, but he smiled anyway. He wanted me to feel better and not be so afraid."

This boy was brave, whoever he was. "What about his cheeks? Do his cheeks have circles when he smiles?"

"He has dents in his cheeks when he smiles, like Miss Haley."

She knew what Gracie meant by that. "He has dimples."

Gracie stopped coloring and frowned at Ellie. "No. He doesn't have those things Billy tries to scrub off his face. He has dents in his cheeks."

"Okay. I'm sorry." This wasn't the time to explain dimples.

"He has polka dots on his face." Gracie smiled at Troy. "Not big ones like Mickey's ribbon. They're little, like some of the kids in my class have."

After adding some lines, Troy flipped the sketchpad around. "Does this look like Bobby? Are his eyebrows like this, or are they bushier?"

Gracie's brows went up. "It looks like Bobby, but he's not old enough. Bobby is bigger."

Before Ellie could say anything, a light of recognition came to Troy's eyes, and he began to sketch. He soon turned it to show to Gracie again.

Gracie put her crayon down. "That's Bobby! Can I have that picture?"

Ellie placed her hand on the child's shoulder. "I'm sorry, sweetheart, but the police need the picture to help find him. I'll make a copy of it for you later, though, and bring it."

Pacified, Gracie picked up her crayon and resumed coloring.

"I need to find Gage," Troy murmured.

"Why?" Ellie walked around the bed. "He'll be back shortly."

He turned the sketch around, and this time, she realized what he was talking about. "I just drew a picture of Dennis Wilder."

"Dennis!" Gracie yelled. Her face was as white as the hospital sheets. "Bobby's name...he told me to remember his name is Dennis."

Troy stopped in his tracks and turned around. Ellie was sure her expression mirrored the stunned one on Troy's face.

The little girl's lips shook. "Am I in trouble?"

"Of course not," Ellie assured her. "Mr. Troy and I are just proud of you for remembering his real name."

Troy's head barely nodded before he turned and headed for the door.

Gracie was coloring, so Ellie allowed herself to consider the new information. Gage was all but certain the Proctor gang was responsible for the girls' abduction, but he said they didn't take children over five years old. Wasn't the Senator's grandson fifteen? Did this mean Proctor wasn't involved after all? Her head spun with the possibilities as she sent up a prayer for Gage to find the answers.

Chapter 29

Bryan picked up his phone and carefully placed it in a desk drawer. He didn't want to destroy another phone; replacing it would leave a paper trail. His eyes searched the room and landed on a perfect object. A few seconds later, the keyboard hit the ground with enough force to break it to pieces. Bryan had never been this angry in his life. Through absolutely no fault of his, they had a massive problem, and now it was up to him to solve it.

Every single employee knew how the system worked. At last count, there were twelve teams scattered across the country. Each had a supervisor, like Bryan. He was contacted by his boss's second-in-command, given the specifications and a deadline.

He let his top man know what child to look for. Then, that man located and abducted the product. In this instance, Brother with a Brain was the hunter, and the only one of the three Bryan wanted to deal with.

The younger brother took care of the children, and with his size, he should terrify children. But, this guy was a giant teddy bear who wished he could stay when he brought their food. They could play Old Maid or some other silly game.

To top it off, their mother was shy two wheels of a bicycle. Bryan had spoken to her one time and immediately called his boss afterward.

The big guy's assistant was as far as Bryan got, and that man was somebody Bryan didn't want to mess with. So, when the sound of a gun being cocked came across the phone, Bryan didn't argue one bit when he was told, "Boss isn't getting rid of that family. I'm telling you right now—you even mention losing them, and you'll be driving off a bridge."

So, even with their...problems, they should have been able to pull this off without a hitch. But, just an hour ago, the member of the team who Bryan would least expect to do something this stupid waltzed into his office and calmly told Bryan they had a boy in the kennels. It seems his mother decided she was lonely and wanted a child to keep for herself. She sent his slow-witted brother out with instructions to find her a "Bobby like the Brady Bunch has."

The fools had a boy all right; they had Senator Richard Wilder's grandson. It was thanks to the Wilder boy that the girl managed to get away, and the kid almost got away too many times to count. His man told him this kid was a fighter and had left bruises, scratches, and even a bite mark or two on the big man.

And what had prompted the confession?

"After I saw the kid and recognized him, I figured there might be some way to make some money. And I planned to share with you."

Bryan stood. "Stop lying. Don't be telling me your brother didn't have help when he took the kid. The reporters talk all the time about how he fights, and you've admitted he's left marks on your brother. You picked him up."

He hadn't denied it, but instead began whining because he couldn't set up a "rescue." Not with two teams of the FSA present, the boy's face adorning billboards and television appearances, and a substantial reward offered by the Senator.

Now Mr. Brainless was asking Bryan for help. After all, Bryan had orchestrated a few side deals before. Bryan unkindly pointed out he'd never been foolish enough to go after a kid so old, and certainly not a legislator's grandson.

One option Bryan would absolutely not consider was killing the teenager. He had no control over what others did, but he would never go so far. So, how was he supposed to take care of it? The girl was confused enough she was leading the FSA on a merry goose chase. A fifteen-year-old boy; however, would lead the police right back to them.

As if thinking of the boy conjured it, Dennis Wilder's parents appeared on the television screen. His lovely mother begged for her son's release. The father seemed to be in a trance. After her boohooing and the kid's dad seeming fascinated by the sky, the senator appeared. The amount of the reward had nearly doubled.

An idea formed, and the wheels began to turn. Bryan had found his way out of this mess.

Chapter 30

"So, you finally decided to grace us with your presence." Senator Wilder's eyes were cold as he spoke to Gage. "And here, I'd just gotten used to second string—only now I don't even qualify for them."

Had nobody explained the situation? "Sir, I'm s --"

"To top it off, they left that bossy wit—"

"Okay, that's enough." At Gage's stern words, the older man looked at him as though Gage had a second head and six-foot-tail.

Gage didn't deny Sam could be stubborn and had a temper, but the team was a family of sorts, and Gage stood up for each of them.

"I've worked with Agent Hughes for nearly seven years, and I guarantee she'll put forth every effort." Wilder wouldn't be thrilled had he known that the Chicago crew were regular FSA agents and unfamiliar with AMAR methodology. Their lack of training hadn't stopped them from working around the clock.

In fact, the Chicago crew was exhausted enough that when Burnett told them AMAR had it covered, they didn't argue or ask questions. One agent almost as large as Kurt—Craig, Gage thought, confided that with all the drug, theft, kidnapping, and even murder in Chicago, nothing had ever affected him as much as the filthy place they kept innocent children. How could Gage do this all the time?

"I've experienced every emotion working this case," Gage had confessed. "After we finished with an aspect of the case, I learned to let it go. Sometimes, it's mighty hard, but being able to focus on a recovered child—that's a gift from God."

"ARE YOU EVEN LISTENING TO ME??" jolted him out of his musings. But, before Gage could apologize, the domineering man's voice rose even more. "And, what is it I'm hearing about the Proctor organization being involved in my grandson's kidnapping? I was under the impression the monsters only abduct much younger children. What makes you think they took Dennis?"

Gage had no problem with legislators being informed of the FSA data. But, he did not like the ease and quickness with which they could collect or read it. In Gage's opinion, it did more bad than good. "We are operating in the same manner as we would with any multiple abduction case, regardless of whether Proctor is involved. And I would think you'd be relieved to know the country's top abduction recovery team is on your grandson's case."

Suddenly, the older man's shoulders drooped and his shining eyes lifted. "I'm sorry. This is taking a lot out of me. I'm used to making things happen and accomplishing seemingly impossible tasks." He closed his eyes for a long moment. "Now, when my only grandchild is involved, I'm forced to wait. The only action I've been able to take was to offer the reward, and I'm sure you know how that turned out."

"The response you've received is typical." Gage found himself feeling sorry for the senator. "The nuts fall out of every tree when money is involved. We have to hope one of the calls will be the real deal."

Senator Wilder appeared bewildered. "One woman managed to get my personal number. She informed me she saw Dennis in cake frosting. He was in a circus, surrounded by clowns. How are people with that level of mentality allowed to roam the streets?"

Gage immediately thought of the people who, because of budget cuts, no longer received adequate care. The man in front of him was broken, so Gage kept his response short and sweet. "There are many people like that out there."

An uproar of voices coming from the living room kept the senator from responding. After exchanging curious glances, they walked into the room to investigate.

Once there, Gage and the senator were met with a confusing sight. It seemed like everybody in the house was huddled around something.

The senator's deep voice boomed out. "What's going on?"

There was immediate silence.

"Grandpa?" The boy's voice came from the midst of the crowd.

"Dennis?" The crowd parted as the child appeared. The grandfather froze for just an instant before rushing to the child. "My boy." Tears poured shamelessly down the senator's face as he gathered his grandson into his arms.

State police officer Delroy Potter appeared with a red-haired woman Gage remembered seeing before.

"This is Crystal Stanley." Potter introduced her. "She's who found the boy."

Gage met the woman's eyes. "I'll need to speak with you in a few minutes. Officer Potter will take you to the study and make sure you're comfortable."

"Am I in some kind of trouble?" Her voice was shrill.

"Why?" Gage gave her a measuring look. "Should you be?"

"Of course not." She blustered. "I brought him straight to his grandfather the minute I found him." To the man who offered the reward, not the parents or authorities.

Gage nodded anyway. "Good. I'll be with you shortly."

He left Potter to escort Miss Stanley to the study as he walked to the senator and his grandson. The older man had his hands on the sides of Dennis' face, examining the dirt, scrapes, and bruises on the boy's cheeks and forehead."

"I'm sorry to interrupt," Gage understood their need to be with each other, but he had a case to solve. "I need to ask Dennis some questions before the ambulance gets here."

The senator turned disbelieving eyes on Gage. "Hasn't my grandson been through enough? Look at these cuts and bruises." He indicated the young man's face. "He has a black eye." His arm was wrapped firmly around his grandson's shoulders.

"Are you a policeman?" Dennis had the attitude of a grown man, even with a shaking voice.

"I'm FSA Special Agent Gage Donahue." Gage returned the handshake Dennis offered him. Bravery and good manners—this teenager didn't stop amazing Gage. "I'm in charge of the team that has been trying to find you."

The too-thin, pale boy pulled away from his grandfather and focused entirely on Gage. "Did Gracie make it? Is she safe?"

"She's safe and sound at the hospital in Shadow. She'll be relieved to know you're okay."

121

"He is not okay!" The senator was irate. "I insist that you have to wait."

"No, Grandpa." The young man's voice was stronger. "I have to tell him everything I know, so he can stop those people."

Something resembling pride showed in the senator's eyes as he reluctantly nodded his acquiescence.

As the young man drew himself to his height, Gage dug his notebook out. "What can you tell me about the people who held you, or where you were kept?"

Dennis frowned. "I only saw it a couple of times, but I'm good at remembering. We were in some kind of room dug into the side of a hill, close to the woods. There was a wheat field next to the trees."

Gage picked up on his words. "It wasn't in the woods?"

"It was in a place with trees hiding it, but not really a forest. And," the boy looked apologetic, "I'm sorry I can't tell you more. I tried to keep track of turns, but the guy who brought me to town must have driven all over the place to mix me up."

"It's okay." Gage hadn't expected a fifteen-year-old would even think of keeping track of directions. "What about the men? What can you tell me about them?"

Dennis's eyes narrowed in thought. "There were two of them, and they wore wigs and fake mustaches." One side of his mouth lifted. "The biggest guy–at least six-two and stronger than he looked– was the one who grabbed me. He leaned over and gave me some story about dropping a hundred dollar bill." Dennis drew in a deep breath. "I just kept walking because I know a con. I figured he was someone who thought I'd help him get to Grandpa." For the first time, fear flashed across the teen's face. "He shoved me so hard I lost my balance, and then..."

"Are you okay, Dennis?" The senator asked.

The teen nodded. "Yeah, but when I tried to stand back up, he grabbed me and stuffed cloth in my mouth." His grandfather placed a hand on the boy's shoulder, and Gage knew if Dennis became very much more upset, their interview would end. "He taped my mouth closed," Dennis's voice wavered. "I kept thinking what if I choked."

His eyes met his grandfather's. "All those fighting moves--I'm sorry to disappoint you, Grandpa."

The senator cleared his throat. "I put you in all those classes to protect yourself, but you learned that even your best moves won't help in some situations. With the man so large, you couldn't have done better. Don't you ever think I'm not proud of you. Got it?"

"Yes." While Dennis appeared relieved, he also was visibly tired.

Gage hurried. "Did they both take care of you?" If they were a Proctor team, each would have had specific duties.

"I saw the guy who grabbed me every day, but I was glad I only saw the really mean--evil--man two times, when he brought the girls in and threw them into the cages. But, then, last night, he came in and said he was taking care of me."

Gage saw the boy shiver. "Did he hurt you?"

"I fought and tried to get away, but..." Dennis's gaze drifted to a painting on the wall. "I got in a couple of punches and kicks that'll leave him with bruises, but he won."

"Did he give you that black eye?" The senator seemed ready to send the army after this man.

Although Gage, himself, wanted nothing more than five minutes alone with the man who beat up a child, he needed to stay on track. *Please steer me away from this anger to help this boy.*

"Let's talk about how the men looked." Gage wanted to change the subject as much to calm himself as to ease the tension building in Dennis.

The boy's voice wavered. "The guy who took me had something wrong, like some of the kids at school who need extra special help." His eyes glistened. "He's bigger than the other one, but he's not too smart."

"You said girls. Do they have another girl? One named Destiny?"

His lips shook as a tear traveled to his chin. "Yes. I tried to talk to her, to tell her it would be okay. I wanted to come up with a plan to get her out, but she just cried and said she wanted her

123

mommy and daddy." His chest sunk. "I couldn't get her out like I did Gracie."

"You were brave." Gage knew the young man was most likely in shock. He'd been kept too long and obviously knocked around. Gage bent down until his face was lined up with the boy's. "You did more than most people would. You managed to save a terrified little girl, and now you're giving me information to help catch those men." He had to stop himself from making a promise. Too often, they were not kept. "And when we do, we'll do everything we can to get Destiny back."

"I don't think it's just those two men." Dennis's voice cracked. "The one who took care of us said something about a woman one day. That she'd be mad if I didn't eat the food she fixed for me, and they would put me in the dog cage thing."

Gage hated that there was no easy way to do this. "Dog cage thing? You mean the pens they put you and the girls in?"

"No." He raised his eyes to Gage. "It was a small one like people keep in their houses for a dog. I almost got away when he first tried to punish me, and then he hit my stomach so hard, I couldn't breathe for a minute." He stared through Gage, probably seeing the horrors he went through. "But, I was too big, and after he cussed at me, he threw me back into my cage."

The senator spoke softly, but hatred practically glowed. "Did either of them...did they--"

"No, Grandpa. They weren't like that."

Gage would have told him that, but the AMAR team had discovered long ago, parents didn't believe it until a doctor confirmed the child's answer.

But, teams. Shipping a child off. He didn't know why this teenager had been abducted, but Gage was sure they were dealing with Proctor.

"The ambulance is here." Sam had silently walked up to stand by Gage.

"Thank you, Dennis." Gage reached out and shook the boy's hand. "Agent Hughes is following you to the hospital, so if you think of anything else, you can tell her."

124

"Dennis!" A woman's voice announced Rod and Vicky Wilder's arrival just seconds before they grabbed their son.

Gage murmured to Sam, "Please let me know if Dennis remembers anything more. I'm going to speak to Miss Stanley."

As he opened the study door, a nauseating scent seemed to burst from it. After he was certain his gag reflex was gone, he walked in to find the woman in her lemon-yellow dress pacing back and forth.

"Please have a seat, Miss Stanley." Gage kept his voice pleasant. "I just need you to tell me what happened."

He noticed that her too-red lipstick was on her teeth, something Jessica told him happened when a woman tried to drive and apply the cosmetic. "I'd prefer standing, thank you."

"Whatever makes you comfortable." She could tap dance on the coffee table and yodel the national anthem--as long as she talked. "Just start at the beginning."

Crystal's perfume once more threatened to overpower him as she stepped closer. "I was at work. I'm Bryan Cosart's office manager, you know."

"He owns the sporting goods store." Gage had seen the man a handful of times.

"And manages it." Gage unobtrusively stepped back as she drew nearer. "Anyway, he and I were working in our offices when I heard a noise. Bryan likes to wedge the back door open just enough to let fresh air circulate. You wouldn't believe how awful sports equipment smells." She wrinkled her nose. "And that's before people use it and cover it with sweat."

"You heard a noise..."

He waited as she redirected her thoughts. "Oh, yes. So, I got up to make sure a stray cat hadn't come into the store. It happened once, and a salesman ended up having to shoo it out the front door. Who knows what kind of damage—"

"The noise, Miss Stanley." Why hadn't he let Samantha take care of Crystal Stanley?

She appeared affronted at being interrupted again. "I could tell the noise was coming from the alley, so I opened the door to see what it was." Her cheeks reddened. "A van was sitting there. Right

125

when I opened the door, a man yanked the poor boy out of it. Then he slammed the door shut and drove away. Just like that. It all happened very quickly."

Gage knew he was hoping for too much, but he had to ask anyway. "Did you get a good look at the man?"

"Not for very long." The pretentious necklace she wore looked tight enough to choke her without the woman nervously tugging it.

"I remember, though, he had long, greasy-looking hair and a mustache badly in need of a trim."

Most likely the wig and fake facial hair Dennis Wilder had described. "What about his build?"

Her gaze traveled from the top of Gage's head to his toes, and her eyes lit with interest. "I'm not sure, but I think he was a little taller than you." Gage was six-two, so they weren't looking for a short man. "Of course, he wasn't nearly as well built." Gage bit back a smile as he thought about Ellie's likely response to the ogling woman in front of him.

He decided the best thing to do was continue the questioning. "What was he wearing?" A uniform of some sort would help identify him.

"Faded jeans and a T-shirt. I think it was a baseball shirt, but I don't know which team. I don't follow sports." Her fake giggles grated on his nerves. "And here I am, working in a sporting goods store."

"What about a hat? His shoes?"

Crystal squinted her eyes. "He wasn't wearing a hat. I think he had work shoes on."

Gage bit back a sigh. "What kind of work shoes?"

She gave him a puzzled look. "Like those the farmers or factory workers wear. Those brown ones with tan soles."

"I'm going to arrange for you to sit down with a sketch artist, and see what we come up with." Troy may never forgive him. "We'll also get some baseball emblems and see if you recognize one. Would you be willing to meet with him back in Shadow?"

Crystal appeared uncertain. "I'm a single woman, living on a tight budget. I already used gasoline I couldn't afford to burn, driving the boy from Shadow to Pattinton. Wasn't there something about a reward?"

Why wasn't he surprised? "I'm sure Senator Wilder will keep his word, but right now he's caught up in the joy of having his grandson returned." He pulled his wallet out and slid a few twenties from it. "Here. This should help buy your gas in the meantime."

She eagerly accepted the money. "Do you think the press will already be looking for me? I'd like to get my hair done before they start snapping pictures."

If Gage didn't get away from this woman soon, it would be his patience snapping. "The press will probably focus on Senator Wilder and Dennis first."

"Oh." Crystal's disappointment was obvious, but then she smiled with false cheer. "Well, that's good. I'll have time to look my best. I don't want to shame Bryan. He's not just my boss, you know. We'll be married soon.""

Gage most certainly did not want to hear about this woman's social life. Especially since there were so many tells that a first year FSA trainee would know she was lying. "Thank you for your time. There will be somebody waiting for you at our headquarters in Shadow. We're in the former health clinic building. Are you familiar with the location?"

"That's Dr. Ryman's old office building." She went straight from answering questions to gossiping. "It was a shame when he moved to Tennessee. Who moves to Tennessee if you don't have to?"

"An agent will be expecting you," Gage managed to say.

He was downright ecstatic to see the woman leave. It took him a few minutes to call Troy Martin and give him the bad news, and then he spoke to Jessica. "Please tell Elijah we need a thorough investigation of Crystal Stanley, and he may as well check Bryan Cosart out while he's at it. Something about her story doesn't feel right. And I'm sure the local police are already on the scene, but I want you and Bridgett to scope out the sporting goods store."

"Finally, I get to use my brain," There was a lilt in Jessica's voice. "And my brain likes you, so it will be friendly."

127

After a few more calls, Gage stuck the phone in his pocket and took a deep breath. Everything that could be done was taken care of. So far, even with a call from the senator, the Guard was unable to come. So, half the women and men from all the churches from town formed their own search party and were currently on an expanded search for the basement home. State and County police joined forces to look for Destiny Jones—men were working their regular nine-hour shifts, plus another nine hours determined to find a little girl.

He needed a break. He needed some time with Ellie. It was time to steal an evening.

Chapter 31

Ellie thought she must be seeing things when she opened the door. Gage stood there, the ends of his hair damp enough to curl them. He looked like a country-and-western singer in his faded jeans and T-shirt. And the flowers in his hand were a perfect shade of blue.

Wait a minute. "You've never brought me flowers before. How did you know blue daisies are my favorite?"

He shrugged as he handed them to her. "Lucky guess."

She didn't remember any conversations regarding flowers, but she decided it didn't matter. She led Gage into the living room and left him to get comfortable while she put the flowers in a vase.

"How did you find the time to see me?" She asked as she sat next to him on the sofa.

He looked steadily into her eyes. "I'll always make time for you."

Her heartbeat picked up speed, but she tamped it down. "Have you had dinner?"

"No." Gage slid closer to her. "But if you don't mind, I'd like nothing more than a delivery pizza. Then we could curl up on the sofa and watch an old movie."

She had to tease him. "Curling up on the sofa? Are you trying to put the moves on me? Because I'm not that kind of woman."

He shook his head and chuckled. "You can sit at the opposite end if you want. I'll even give you a foot rub. That's always been your favorite way to ease stress."

"What do you mean?" Ellie was once more confused. "You've never massaged my feet. In fact, I'm pretty sure I've never had a foot rub before."

"I'm more tired than I thought." He smiled ruefully. "Is my name still Gage Thomas Donahue, or do I have that confused, too?"

"I'm pretty sure it's still your name." She reached over and picked up the phone book. "I'll order a pizza."

She heard him messing with the television while she called the order in. She ordered a large supreme with no black olives on only one-fourth of it, and no mushrooms on the other three-fourths.

129

"Sounds like you've placed this order lots of times." The man on the phone joked.

"No." Strangely enough, she and Gage had never shared a pizza before. "This is the first time."

After she had given him her address, she walked over and dropped to sit at the opposite end of the couch, silently ordering her confusion to go elsewhere. Then, she decided to ask Gage.

"Do you like supreme pizzas?"

He gave her a lazy smile. "Is there any other kind?"

She had to ask. "Is there any topping you don't like?"

"I'm not fond of mushrooms." Gage looked puzzled. "Why? Did you order a supreme with mushrooms?"

The room started spinning, and her mind felt like it was full of electricity. She leaned back against the sofa as thoughts snapped into place.

Gage leaned toward her. "Ellie, are you okay? I can just pick the mushrooms off. It's not a big deal."

She looked at him in disbelief. "How?"

He frowned. "How what? What's wrong, sweetheart?"

Ellie was at the edge of a precipice, and she wasn't backing down this time. "How did you know the dress was red? How do you know about the daisies? How do you always seem to know what mood I'm in?"

She barely noticed when he moved over and knelt in front of her. She stared at the floor as she asked her questions. "How do I know so many things about you?" Her mind was suddenly flooded with facts. "Your favorite color is blue, but you like it best when I wear red. You hate seafood. Your first car was a Mustang, and you drove it until it fell apart. You sleep on your side because you snore like a buzz saw if you lie on your back."

Tears were pouring down her face as she lifted her gaze to look into those blue eyes. "Please. You have to tell me how I know those things."

Gage reached up and gently wiped the tears from her face. When he spoke, his voice was barely above a whisper. "Don't cry, my love. I want to tell you everything, but Dr. Marx says you need to remember on your own."

Only one thing made sense. "We knew each other before you came to Shadow, didn't we?" Like a movie screen, images flashed through her mind. Gage standing at the door; Gage dressed in a tuxedo waiting at the front of a church, both laughing as he carried her into a hotel room; wearing the red dress and dancing in his arms; his head on the pillow next to hers. "We knew each other very well."

He smiled gently. "As well as a man and woman can know each other."

The impact of his words took her breath away, but she suddenly knew one truth. "We were married."

His gaze didn't waver. "We are married."

A plethora of emotions ran through her, with joy and confusion battling over first place.

"You're my husband."

If she hadn't already been light-headed, the intensity of his gaze would have made her so. "You're my wife, and I love you more than I can find the words to say."

Ellie nearly knocked him over as she threw herself into his arms. He managed to keep them both upright, as he stood and held her tightly.

She wrapped her arms around his shoulders and buried her face against his neck. How could she have ever forgotten this? This was where she was safe and loved and cherished. When she felt his chest shake, she pulled her head back far enough to see his face. Gage was crying. Her strong, tough husband was crying.

"I love you so much." Her lips found his, and the last piece snapped into place. She was Ellie Donahue and had been for nearly six years. She wrapped her arms around him even tighter, and his arms pulled her closer.

It was a long time later when Gage rolled over and turned on the bedside lamp. "Are you okay?"

Ellie snuggled against his side. "I'm better than okay. I know who I am."

A loud noise from the vicinity of his stomach made them both laugh. "Maybe we should get up and eat the pizza." He made the suggestion but didn't seem in too much of a hurry to move.

"I wonder what the delivery man thought when you answered the door barefooted and your shirt on inside out." Ellie giggled.

"I couldn't help it. I had to dress fast."

After a few kisses, they finally made it out of bed, and into the dining room. Ellie was completely relaxed and comfortable as they worked together to heat the pizza and fix their plates. It didn't even bother her that she was in his shirt, and he wore only jeans. They had done this many, many times before.

As they sat at the table eating, she noticed the cat sitting on the back of a chair, glaring at them. "Fat Ollie is pouting, you know. Because I shut him out of the bedroom." The giant, yellow fur ball huffed and turned around, so his back was to them.

"I hope you're not planning on letting that cat sleep in our bed." Gage raised one eyebrow as he looked at Fat Ollie.

"I don't know," she teased. "He likes the left side."

Gage reached over and stole a green pepper from her pizza. "Well, Fat Ollie better understand that a husband comes first." He looked back toward the cat. "Fat Ollie, I'm glad you've helped Ellie, but I'm her husband. Husbands trump cats, so you need to make new sleeping arrangements."

Ellie looked at the cat just in time to see him straighten his hind legs and raise his tail.

"Did he just moon us?" Gage chuckled.

"Probably." Her smile faded. "What are we going to do now? We can't live apart any longer."

"How would you feel living out in the country?" The house Gage had leased was just remodeled, so it was very nice. And the closest neighbor was a couple of miles away. It was peaceful and relaxing, a good place to recoup.

Ellie thought of his supposed writing and suddenly realized something. "You left your job and followed me, didn't you?"

Gage shrugged. "Dr. Marx said you had to remember on your own, but I wasn't about to take a chance on your not remembering me. I hoped since I won your heart once, I could do it again."

"And you did." So many things made sense. "No wonder I fell so deeply in love with you so quickly. I already was." Tears of joy escaped her. "God brought you to me once, and now he has again."

A chuckle was his response as he leaned past the table corner and kissed her. "Maybe God was tired of listening to me beg for you to come back—to be my Ellie."

"He probably decided we should be together because we were both asking for the same thing. Back in the day, we both liked—"

She had realized something else. "I still don't remember the accident."

"Maybe it's too traumatic." Sadness shone in his eyes but was gone so quickly she thought she must have imagined it. "You'll remember when it's time."

It made sense, but— "I don't remember why I left the clinic, either. What did I do for a living after we were married?"

He frowned. "I probably told you too much helping you remember us. Please don't ask for more." He reached over and touched her chin. "Those are the doctor's orders, and we have to trust he knows what he's talking about."

Ellie started to argue, but then she realized he was right. Besides, she was beginning to feel a little overwhelmed by the memories flooding her mind like a river.

A strange look crossed his face. "Maybe I should go and let you rest." He appeared to search for words. "I shouldn't be pressing you to move so fast. We can back up and take things slowly."

She set her milk glass down. "Please don't leave. Stay the night. I'll pack up and move in with you as quickly as I can." If there was one thing she knew, it was that she wanted to be with her husband. "Luke and Holly won't care. They'll just put this place back on the market."

His eyes searched hers. "You're sure that's what you want?"

"Absolutely." She didn't understand his sudden concern.

Gage seemed to hesitate again, but then all traces of doubt disappeared from his face. "I'll have to be up early. I need to run home to shower and change before I go to the hospital."

"Why are you going to the hospital?" Ellie's heart plummeted. "Didn't Gracie get to go home this afternoon?"

"I'm sorry I haven't already told you." Gage smiled wryly. "I just wanted to forget everything but us for a while. Dennis Wilder is in the Pattinton hospital."

She was surprised. "You found him? Is he all right?"

"Dennis has fractured ribs, a black eye, and a lot of nasty looking bruises and scrapes, but otherwise he is amazing."

"He fought to get Gracie away from the kidnappers."

Sadness reigned supreme on Gage's face. "We don't know the half of it. Bridgett watched his examination and said it would be easier to touch a bruise or injury than find an uninjured spot."

"Where did you find him?"

"Supposedly, he was dropped off at a sporting goods store." Skepticism was evident on his face. "He was dumped in the alley behind Cosart's. Cosart's assistant claims a man shoved Dennis out of a van the exact instant she went to the back door to check a noise."

"You don't believe her, do you?"

"It's not necessarily that I think she's lying." Gage frowned. "It's just the timing bothers me. It took Crystal Stanley a while to get to the back door. By all rights, the vehicle should have at least been pulling away. It's like the abductor waited for Crystal, and presented her with the boy."

"It does sound strange. I assume since you're here, Dennis wasn't able to tell you where he was kept."

"Not exactly, but he did say it was in a part of the field where a group of trees hid them. We've been looking in the woods, instead of around them."

"What about Destiny Jones? Is she okay?"

Gage sadly shook his head. "She's been taken away. If I'm right, and this is Proctor, she's already being delivered to her new parents."

Tears welled in her eyes. "Dale and Erica Jones are good parents. They're not well off, but they always make sure Destiny doesn't lack for anything." Then she realized something. "Why did they let Dennis go, anyway?"

"I'd like to know the answer to that, myself, but I haven't yet figured out why Dennis was taken in the first place." Gage's frustration began to show. "Proctor has never ventured past four years before."

Ellie was suddenly struck by a powerful urge. "If you think it will do any good, I'll talk to Dennis. Maybe I can help him remember something he doesn't realize he knows."

Worry lines covered his forehead. "Are you sure?"

She nodded. "I don't have to be in the insurance agency on Saturdays. I can't explain it, but talking to Dennis seems like something I should do."

"Then I'd like it very much."

Ellie looked at her husband and felt extremely content. "Since you can't do anything about the Proctor case tonight, and we both have an early start tomorrow, don't you think we'd better get to bed?"

A light glowed deep in his eyes. "That's exactly where we should be."

Chapter 32

"I told you. I arrived at the store at seven-thirty yesterday morning, and I didn't leave my office until Crystal screamed for help. I ran out into the alley and saw her with the boy." This was at least the sixth time Bryan had given the same answer. The auburn-haired beauty scrutinized him over the glasses that kept slipping down her nose. He wasn't stupid; he knew perfectly well she was trying to trip him up. Well, FSA agent or not, Samantha Hughes was no match for him.

"Why did you say you were there so early, again?" She finally pushed her glasses up. After she straightened her hair and began typing on her pink tablet computer, he wanted to grab that hideous orange eyeglass chain and choke her.

Digging deep for strength, he kept his face as emotionless as possible. "I was at an Expo a few weeks ago, and the paperwork piled up while I was gone. Remember, I'm owner and manager. I have double duty."

He didn't like the calculating look that appeared in her eyes. "That's right. You've owned and managed a sporting goods store in several states. None of them lasted very long. Why is that?"

Because they were each a cover for his boss to work behind. "I've had bad luck choosing sites. Business wasn't good."

"You didn't move much product, then?"

As she leaned closer, Bryan seriously considered telling the agent she needed to back off on the sore-muscle cream.

"Mr. Cosart?"

He gripped his denim-clad legs to keep from smacking her.

"That's what I meant by saying business wasn't good."

"Yet, according to your records, you had an awful lot of merchandise coming and going at each location. Exactly how do you ship merchandise?"

This was one path Bryan did not want the agent to go down. Since leverage was his boss's chosen way to maintain control, Bryan was worried about the so-called computer clean off. "I use several companies. I can get a list for you."

"You do that." Agent Hughes abruptly shifted gears again. "Did you notice a van anywhere around the store when you arrived yesterday morning?"

"No. I would remember one like the sketch you showed me." It was a good thing he'd thought to tell those fools to get rid of the television repair logo.

A buzzing sound came from the agent's phone. She picked it up and looked at the screen before returning her attention to him. "You'll have to excuse me for a minute. I'll be right back."

Bryan exhaled deeply as he watched the door close behind her. Maybe he should have arranged for the boy to be "found" by somebody else, like a person clear across town, or even out in the country. If his plan failed, he might as well decorate the police station with his posters and directions to his house.

On the other hand, if his plan worked, he would take care of two problems at once. He was growing increasingly weary of the romantic charade with Crystal. Thanks to the senator's reward, she would soon come into a sizable amount of money. A large enough sum the excitement should outweigh any disappointment their breakup would cause. He hoped she would be upset to the point of quitting her job. If she didn't, he'd have to wait a couple of weeks and fire her. It wouldn't be an exaggeration to say she was inept.

At least Tweedle Dee had called to tell him the loony trio managed to close the premises. As always, Bryan had purchased a second base right after he moved to town. Or, according to the paperwork, Hubert Balden was the proud, new owner. If the FSA made it past good old Hubert and all the other so-called owners, they'd track it to a nonexistent company in Colorado

Fortunately, the woman and her sons were experienced enough not to have left anything behind. Because, thanks to the boy, the site would be discovered any time now. In fact, it was probably what the agent's call was about.

His suspicions were reinforced when the door opened, and the deputy who was nearly as tall as the sheriff walked in. "You're free to go." The man, Hardy, he finally remembered, waited until Bryan stood. "Agent Hughes said not to forget the list you promised.

He stepped forward so only the table stood between them. "This town is friendly and trusting. Don't break that trust." The deputy placed his hands on the table and leaned forward, so close to Bryan, he could smell the coffee on his breath. "You hear me?"

Bryan didn't like to take directions, but he wasn't stupid. "I'll have it at the station by noon." That would give him just enough time to make sure it passed muster. His boss would be beyond furious if anything else went wrong with this operation. And with all that was going on, Bryan didn't think an angry person so powerful was a good idea.

Chapter 33

Just a minute." Before Ellie headed out his front door, Gage stopped her with a gentle touch. "Before we leave and our duties pull us apart, I need to do something."

Ellie's cheeks turned a rosy shade of pink. "If you keep kissing me, I'll never make it to the hospital, and you won't get out to the abduction site."

His smile grew as he leaned down to kiss her forehead. "That can wait until I do this." He captured her left hand and slid her diamond ring and wedding band on before sealing it with a kiss. He was already wearing his.

She looked at her hand and smiled beautifully. "I can't believe I forgot what it felt like to wear your rings."

He winked. "Now I'm going to kiss you." And he proceeded to do so, quite thoroughly.

After he finally forced himself to release his wife, he stepped back. "Let's pray you're able to come up with a better sketch than Crystal Stanley's." The man in Crystal's completed picture was a dead ringer for Abraham Lincoln on a horribly bad hair day.

During the drive, Gage listened to her chatter about a project the Sunday school class was doing. Finally, he could take it no more."

Gage hoped he hadn't misunderstood his wife the night before. "So, about us living together, do you want to move in with me right away? If you —"

"Let's pack my stuff and move this evening if we have time." Her hand was soft and warm against his cheek. "I love you, Gage, and I remember everything about us."

Gage returned her smile, but he couldn't quite push away his fear the other shoe might drop at any time. So far, she seemed content and completely in love with him.

"You know what?" Her hand slid down to his shoulder. "Working with Troy to help Gracie was very satisfying. And I'm looking forward to repeating the experience. It's disappointing that you don't need a child psychologist on your team." She pulled her hand down and playfully punched his shoulder. "I'd be tempted to dust off my

139

credentials and apply."

"Oh, you would, would you?" Gage couldn't quite believe the words came from her mouth.

His heart leaped at the genuine joy in her laughter. "I don't know if I'd be able to give up my job at Richmond. It gets pretty exciting in there, entering all the data and answering the phone."

"You can quit if you want to." Wasn't he an Albert Einstein clone? "We can live comfortably on my salary. Our house is paid for."

Ellie's mouth dropped open. "Our house! You didn't sell it? I remember, we talked about selling it and moving out of town."

"I'd never do anything so significant without your input." Besides, it was full of their life together.

She studied her rings. "Do you like Shadow?"

"Yes." He had been expecting the question. "It's a friendly place with folks who treat you like family. Why?"

"It feels like home." She rushed on. "Of course, my home is wherever you are, but there's just something about Shadow."

He had lain awake with her sleeping peacefully in his arms, thinking about this. "I'll see about working out of the Pattinton office."

"But, what about your team? They can't all locate to this area."

"There are plenty of qualified agents, like Samantha or a local agent named Simon Fisher. When it's time for the team to move on, I'm staying here."

Ellie smiled uncertainly. "Are you sure?"

Gage reached over and took her hand. "After dealing with Proctor and so many kidnappings, I'm finished." As it was, some of the children were emblazoned on Gage's brain."Why don't you start looking for a place to buy?" They wouldn't have any trouble selling their house in Atlanta.

They discussed what they wanted in a new home for the remainder of the drive.

Gage opened the door and waited for Ellie to walk into the building before following her.

Jess was walking across the floor with a coffee pot in her hand. Today, her entire head of hair was a bright grape-toned shade of purple and reminded him of the little girl on the Flintstones shows.

She froze, staring at him. "What is on your finger?"

Before he could answer, Jess jumped up and down, sloshing coffee all over the place. "She remembers!" She looked around and evidently didn't want to take the time to walk the short distance to the table. She just leaned over and set the coffee pot on the floor. Then, before Gage could stop her, Jess yanked Ellie to her and hugged her like a champion calf roper. "You remember!" Jess finally released Ellie and stepped back. "You're wearing your rings. You know who you are."

Gage didn't like the confused look on his wife's face. "She remembers we're married, but she doesn't remember everything yet." His eyes met Jessica's, and he sent her a silent message. She must have understood because disappointment replaced her enthusiasm.

"I'm sorry." Ellie smiled shakily. "Of course I must have known you before. You work with Gage, after all."

Jess put her hands on Ellie's shoulders. "You'll remember us. I believe that."

Troy walked into the room, carrying his art satchel. "What's all the commotion about?"

Gage winked at Ellie. "Jess was just excited to see my wife." He watched Troy's face as it sank in.

Always a calm person, Troy nodded. "That's good." Then, he raised his satchel toward Ellie. "Well, Mrs. Donahue, are you ready to get back to work?"

"She doesn't remember everything yet." Jessica cautioned him. "She doesn't remember us yet."

Troy frowned for a moment before his smile returned. "She will."

Lord, please grant the miracle of her memory returning." No matter the outcome, Gage hoped his wife remembered.

Troy walked over to Ellie. "I hate to rush, but we need to leave now if we're going to get to the hospital on time."

Ellie turned to Gage, confusion on her face. He placed his mouth near her ear. "What's wrong?"

She smiled uncertainly. "Do you usually kiss me goodbye in front of your co-workers?"

Laughter bubbled up from inside him. He looked at Troy and Jess. "Turn around." He barely waited until they followed his directions before he had Ellie in his arms, putting all the love he could summon into this kiss.

He liked seeing the smile on her face as she walked out the door with Troy a few minutes later.

Jessica waited until the door closed before she turned to face him. Her eyes narrowed. "I'm guessing from the look in your eyes, Ellie regained her memory last night."

"Wow." Gage felt happier than he had in months. Years, even. "You are a genius." He sobered. The team had been on the site for at least an hour. "Has anyone called to keep us up to date on the hideout?"

Her smile disappeared as she tightened the rubber band in her hair. "Bridgett called and says it's hidden in plain sight. The lane goes along a tree line and then turns a ninety-degree angle north for a short way before another ninety-degree turn, this one west."

Elijah was holed up in his self-proclaimed office, determined to discover Proctor's deep-web activities, and undoubtedly working on at least four computers at once. Samantha was in Pattinton, trying to appease the senator, who was now demanding his grandson's abductors be brought to justice immediately, if not sooner. She'd met him at the crack of dawn since he had a major press conference scheduled later. "Where's Eric?" He hadn't seen or heard from him.

Jess rolled her eyes. "He's pouting. After all his whining about being forced to work with children, he bulled up and said with Ellie back, there was no need for him to go."

He had to sit down with the older man soon. "We need to get to the site. Are you ready?" He headed to the door, somehow reassured by the woman behind him. Jessica Bannon was one of the most honest, brutally sometimes, compassionate women he knew.

Once they were inside the car, Gage turned the GPS on.

Jessica's small hand landed on his. "Huh uh, Mr. Donahue, sir." She held out what he could already see was a map. One with a bright red arrow.

"No GPS?" While Gage wasn't into all the technology, he relied on the earnest man's voice telling him where to turn.

She spread the map across her legs. "I'm as frustrated as you, Gage. I've never heard of this, but the place has no address; it doesn't even exist if you try to look it up. Elijah broke up with his monitor before I left his office."

They followed the map and drove on roads which cows would have to walk single-file to fit. And when they finally reached the lane, they drove right past it and had to back up.

"If there had been a good rain, they'd have been stuck," Gage observed.

Jess grasped the panic strap as they bounced along the dirt lane. Her voice shook with the SUV's vibrations. "After the first turn, you're no longer visible from the road, even though it's still pretty far to the woods."

"Hold on." Gage downshifted to drive up a steep hill. "How come nobody warned us about this?"

"I don't know." Jess's tiny body was bouncing off the seat as far as the seatbelt would allow. "But I might just take Kurt's precious pistol away from him and clunk him over the head for good measure." She always used Kurt's gun in her threats, claiming her little Glock wouldn't do enough damage.

"What will you do to Bridgett?" Jess's revenge plots were always amusing. "She's who called, isn't she?"

Jessica's brows lowered. "I'll pour some of my neon green hair dye in her shampoo bottle. She'll glow in the dark for a week."

Gage steered around a giant rut. "It really would be easy to get stuck back here. They must have had at least one four-wheel-drive vehicle."

"What about escape?" Jessica looked out her window. "If they'd been discovered, there's nowhere to go."

"They were evidently confident they wouldn't be found." He finally pulled in between the sheriff's squad car and Kurt's truck. Kurt was the only one in sight.

"Hey, Boss." He greeted Gage.

"Why didn't you warn us about that lane?" Jess marched over

143

and took up a defiant stance in front of him, which looked comical since the top of her head barely hit his chest level. "Give me your gun. I'm going to shoot you."

Kurt grinned and tugged Jessica's hair. "You won't shoot me. You love me."

Gage knew better than to let those two get started. "Before you begin your love-fest, can you tell me what you found, Kurt? Where are the others?"

"They're in the structure." Kurt sobered immediately. "Come over here for a minute, though." He led the way to a flat and bare patch of land. "You can see where they've had maybe a sixteen-foot trailer parked."

Jess wrinkled her nose. "I don't see any water or electric hookups."

"They probably had a generator." Kurt frowned. "But I can't imagine it being a very sanitary way to live."

"What about tire tracks?" Gage hoped the make and model could be identified.

Kurt indicated the indentations in front of them. "Bridge said the ground's too hard and dry for getting a good tread." His gaze swept the length of the area. "Boss, didn't the boy say there were two men and maybe a woman?"

"Yes."

"Then, we're most likely looking at a family." Kurt turned back to the empty camper spot as he spoke. "No fully grown men and a woman are going to share a camper this size unless they're related."

Unless it was an unmarried couple living together with someone else.

It was no surprise when Jess voiced that very sentiment. "We can't think about the unsubs as a family when there are so many people who live together."

Kurt shocked her speechless when he agreed. "I'm wrong. Buttercup is right. We have no idea of the orientation of anybody living here." Not that Kurt was ever rude or too silent, but Gage knew he only said what he meant. The weapons expert turned his gaze to Jessica. "Sorry to upset you."

Gage was about to speak in support of his weapons expert

when a noise coming from their left drew his attention. The sheriff and Hardy Davis had hold of Bridgett from each side, and were headed toward him. Gage had never seen her so pale or weak enough to need help standing.

"Sheriff. Davis." Concerned about his agent, Gage took a couple of steps toward her. "You okay, Bridgett?"

Troubled brown eyes met his. "I have my sample collection kits inside, ready to collect specimens, but I had to get out of there for a minute."

"She had fruit for breakfast," Hardy supplied. "I may never be able to eat a slice of cantaloupe again."

"TMI, TMI," Jess called out to the deputy. Gage was glad she beat him to it.

Bridgett held up one of the pills she'd been prescribed and took it dry. Gage could tell she was worse than usual, and as much as he would have liked to let Bridgett leave, they would need forensics for proof.

The stoic sheriff held on to her arm until she was steady. It was then that Gage realized Mitch was almost as shaken as Bridgett.

"I don't know what the other places these Proctor people kept kids in were like, but this is unspeakable." The big man's voice shook.

Gage would never forget some of them. "They've all been pretty unpleasant."

Bridgett shuddered. "Not like this one."

Hardy appeared to be holding up better. "I'll go back in with you if you need me to."

"Thank you." Gage liked the deputy. He would make an excellent agent. "We have a better chance of not missing anything with three sets of eyes."

Jessica twisted an escaped lock of hair. "Maybe I should wait out here. I'm the brains, not the brawn."

Gage hated to do this to her. "I'm sorry, Jess, but I need your brain." He thought of something that might help. "Think of the kids."

"I'll go with you, Princess." Kurt tugged on Jessica's hand and fell into step beside her, matching his long stride to her short one.

Just as Dennis described, the structure appeared to be nothing more than a large hole dug into the side of a hill and outfitted with a door.

It's an old cellar," Hardy said. "You can see the rotted wood, even on the ceiling, and I have to say, those children had angels because it could have come down at any time."

"Thank you, Deputy. Everybody, watch for any sign of it falling in and get out if it so much as creaks." Gage made it about two steps inside the door before he had to act unmanly and cover his mouth. Never before had he smelled something this nauseating.

"Yuck! Gross!" Jess wasn't shy about expressing her opinion. "How about if I drive to a store for some air freshener? I'll be back in an hour or two."

As usual, the candid agent was dealing with stress by relying on humor. "Jess, please check the lock and hinges on the doors. See if you can find a manufacturer."

Then he saw what had Bridgett so upset as he looked on with a mixture of disbelief and disgust. His stomach rolled as he lifted his gaze. Three large cages made of a double thickness of chicken wire with steel rod posts holding them in place took up most of the room. This was low, even for Proctor.

"I'll give you three guesses which one they kept Dennis in." Hardy's voice came from behind Gage.

Gage saw what the other man meant. He walked to the farthest one. There were so many dents and bulges in it, it was more egg-shaped than cubic. The filthy blanket meant for sleeping was torn into strips still tied to the wire. There were what looked like busted plastic plates and silverware on the ground. Dennis Wilder had tried everything to break out.

Kurt spoke. "Maybe this is why they gave him back."

"Oh, this is...this is..." Jess didn't run out of words. Ever. "I wouldn't keep an animal in one of these." She turned to the man next to her. "Give me your gun, Kurt. I'm g—going—"

Gage couldn't recall Jessica crying except while waiting for news of Ellie. Before he could decide what to do, Kurt placed his arm around her and pulled her against him.

"It's okay, Jess. It's okay."

With the man she loved like a brother holding her, she soon stopped crying. "I'm okay. These people are evil."

Kurt slid his arm down and grasped her hand. "Come on, Princess. Let's see if we can figure out where they bought this stuff. Maybe it'll lead us to them."

"You need to see one more thing." Hardy indicated Gage should follow him as he walked past Dennis' cage. He shone his flashlight in the dark corner, illuminating a second dog crate. Dennis had told him about this horror, but to see it... Disgust was rapidly changing into anger, so Gage prayed. *Please, Lord, help me stay calm and focused. I want to help these kids.*

Then he turned to see what Hardy was showing him, and with no need of checking, Gage realized he was looking at the source of the odor.

The deputy's voice was full of anger. "They put them in this filthy place and took away their dignity."

This was classic Proctor. "The people at this stage of the organization think of the children as nothing more than a product. They're paid to snatch kids and keep them until they're shipped, not to care."

Hardy's voice was calmer. "Times like this are when I almost wish God hadn't given us free will."

"I know what you mean." Gage had entertained the thought himself—many times.

Just as Hardy's flashlight went off, Gage saw a fleck of white. "Shine that back over there," he instructed Davis. "There." Gage covered his mouth and rapidly walked over and picked up the object. When he held the paper closer to the flashlight he saw it was a receipt from a department store in Pattinton, time stamped and dated for four-seventeen a.m. on what would have been two days before Dennis was released.

"What did they buy?" Hardy asked.

"I'm not sure." He read it aloud. "S-T-F, T-Y, seven-ninety-nine." He walked back past two cages to the first one. "Hey, Jess, see if you can figure out what they bought."

Kurt helped Jess stand up from the sad excuse for a floor,

and Jessica accepted the receipt. She squinted. "The light's too dim."

Hardy stepped closer and shone his flashlight on the paper.

"Oh." Jess looked at Gage. "They bought a stuffed toy."

Gage felt a flash of hope. "Maybe the store will have our kidnapper on film."

Finally, for the first time, they might have a real chance of catching an entire Proctor team. Of getting to the head and taking the organization down.

Chapter 34

Ellie checked her watch again.

"It's thirty seconds later than the last time you looked." Troy's amused voice came from beside her.

They had now spent nearly ninety minutes sitting in the hospital's fourth-floor waiting room and doing exactly that—waiting.

"I understand the senator wants to celebrate, but something about this just doesn't sit right."

Troy leaned toward her and whispered. "I know what you mean. It's almost like he's using the boy for publicity."

At his words, she realized that was exactly what the politician was doing. "He could have called a press conference and formally presented the reward money to Crystal Stanley anywhere. Why would he want to have it in the hospital lobby? Why would he subject Dennis to the press?"

Troy shrugged. "Politics, I guess. It's an election year, and his term will be up."

"I just can't believe the man who seemed so elated to have his grandson returned would turn around and use the situation to his own advantage." She cried nearly every time the frequently aired clip played. "Didn't you see them showing the senator get out of the ambulance with him? He acted happier to see Dennis than the boy's parents did."

"You've always been good at reading situations."

She was confused for a moment. "You seem to know me pretty well. We must have been friends."

A smile lit Troy's face. "We were exceptionally close friends."

Gall rose in her throat. "You don't mean..."

His eyes were circles, and the rest of his face was strawberry red. "No." He produced a nervous smile. "You're the closest thing I've ever had to a sister. That's it, Ellie. In fact, Gage is glad we get along so well."

She closed her eyes. "I wish I could remember. I don't understand why I can't."

"Your mind must not be ready yet." His lips were pursed as

he stared at the ceiling. "It seems like you remembered an awful lot last night. Your brain is just keeping itself from overloading."

Whether true or not, she appreciated his empathy. "Thank you, Troy. I can see why we're friends."

"Don't get your hopes up, but it sounds to me like Dennis is coming back."

Ellie could hear a group being way too noisy for a hospital. She stood and walked to the door to check. Sure enough, surrounded by no less than six security men, Richard Wilder was pushing his grandson's wheelchair back to his room. "I hope Dennis isn't too tired to do this."

"Kids are resilient." Troy stood up and joined her, his canvas satchel in hand. "Let's get this show on the road."

And a show is what it looked like. A very dramatic display of security with two guards remaining outside the room ala Buckingham Palace and the other four accompanying the senator and his grandson through the door.

Ellie had to fight back giggles, and she heard Troy snicker as each of the second duo seemed determined to be the first through the door. She wondered if they'd be so eager in a dangerous situation. "Me! Let me get shot!" "No! I want to get shot first!"

Troy put his mouth close to her ear. "I've seen that look before, Ellie. You're up to your eyeballs in mischief."

Even though she knew they had been close friends, she was surprised that he knew her well enough to read her facial expressions. Their relationship was platonic; she knew that. But it must be strong. "You're not actually my brother or something, are you? My dad didn't sow any wild oats?"

"No, but I wouldn't mind being a member of your family." He seemed unperturbed by the idea. "My parents live in Montana, and your father is like a dad to me. Does that help?"

A half-formed thought entered Ellie's mind, but before she could grasp it, the senator and his four guards left the room, headed toward them.

Senator Wilder was curt when he spoke to Ellie. "I hope you don't tire my grandson. He's had quite a bit of excitement today."

"And whose fault—"

150

Troy quickly stepped in front of her. Unless she wanted to dance around behind the sketch artist, Ellie had to listen to Troy.

"We'll take our cue from your grandson. You have my word we won't wear him out."

Ellie nudged the back of Troy's left calf, causing him to wobble long enough so that she could speak to the senator. What was wrong with Troy, anyway? She was merely going to ask the senator which had the higher priority there—a press conference, or identifying the man who took Dennis?

Sometimes political correctness irked her. "Your grandson will be all right, Senator. We won't push him."

The politician looked down his nose at her. "Well, see that you don't, Miss Walker."

Ellie couldn't help herself. "It's Mrs. Donahue. Mrs. Gage Donahue."

Surprise showed on the senator's face before he masked it. He frowned as he spoke. "I suppose you and your husband fancy yourselves some sort of heroic crime-fighting duo, but I assure you, you will not rise to fame at the expense of my grandson."

Well, if that wasn't the rooster calling the donkey noisy. "Excuse me, but—"

"We'll be sure not to overdo it, Sir." Troy ushered Ellie past the senator. "Man. You really are back. Temper and all."

In fact, Ellie was still miffed. She might just put her thumbs in her ears, waggle her fingers, and blow raspberries at the rude man.

"Come on, Ellie." Troy tugged her away. "Don't even think about doing whatever it is you're planning."

They had taken only a few steps when the nearest security officer stopped them and asked for identification.

Ellie gestured behind them. "Didn't you just see us speaking to the senator?"

"Yes, ma'am, but I still have to do my job." The man's face would surely crack if he smiled. "Identification, please."

Ellie watched as Troy flipped open his FSA badge and identification, and immediately pictured herself doing the same thing. She pushed the silly image aside and managed to dig out her driver's license. Seeing the name on it, Ellie realized it should be changed back to Donahue right away.

By the time they made it into Dennis's room, she had managed to regain her composure and focus on the task at hand.

The freckles stood out on the boy's face as he looked curiously at them. "Who are you?"

Ellie smiled at his adolescent bluntness. "I'm Ellie Donahue. You can call me Ellie." She indicated Troy. "This is FSA Special Agent Troy Martin. We're here to help you identify your abductor."

Dennis appeared interested in her now. "Are you related to Agent Donahue?"

Her heart flip-flopped at the mere mention of her husband. "I'm his wife." She pulled a chair toward the bed. "Can I sit down?"

"Is it like those guys on TV who pick out eyes for the picture, and then keep finding the features?

Troy pulled a chair around and sat beside Ellie. "Not exactly." He pulled his sketch pad out and set his bag on the floor. "Ellie will talk to you, to help you remember things you may not even realize you know. I'll just draw while I listen."

Dennis looked skeptical. "Are you sure this will work?"

"Agent Martin and I have done this many times. It always works." Ellie wondered what Troy's strange expression was about, but she forced her attention back to the boy. "You saw two different men, right?"

"Yeah, but I only saw the mean one a few times. Just when he dropped off the g—girls, and after Gracie was gone. He knocked me down and kicked...that's how my ribs are fractured."

Ellie glanced over at Troy to see, like her, he was unsure whether to remain calm or go find the guy and kick his ribs a few times. Only, that wasn't the way God wanted his children to speak. She turned her attention back to the boy.

After a ragged sigh, the teen spoke. "He brought me to the alley and shoved me out." I guess the other kidnapper was supposed to be taking care of us." His lower lip quivered, telling Ellie not to say anything about his situation. He would share when he was ready.

Ellie kept her voice as soothing as she could. "Let's talk about him, then." She considered the boy's words. "You say the other man is average, so that must mean this one isn't. Can you explain?"

It was evident Dennis was uncomfortable with the question, but he drew a deep breath. "I go to church. I know I'm not supposed to make fun of people, and honest, I'm not. But the man is different, like the kids at school who go to special classes."

"Could you tell by the way he looked or did you have to wait until he spoke?"

Dennis answered immediately. "The way he looks."

"Okay." Ellie glanced at Troy. "Will you answer some questions?"

"Yes," Dennis answered.

"Good. Did he have a round face or more of a thin one?" Ellie noticed Troy begin to sketch.

"Kind of like a thick rectangle with curved edges." The young man was more comfortable with this question.

"And his forehead—could you see a lot of it, or was it small?"

The boy didn't seem to find it difficult to picture his abductor. "I know he had a big forehead because the wig he wore didn't cover his head like it was supposed to. I think his head was too big."

"So, he was a big man?"

"Yes." Dennis appeared insulted. "If he wasn't so big, I'd have gotten away when I got Gracie out of there. I know how to fight."

"I'm sure you would have," Ellie spoke quickly to assuage his feelings. "Was he big like a football player, or big like somebody who's overweight?"

Dennis frowned. "Like a football player, I guess, except I don't think he worked out or anything. He's just strong."

"And was he tall?"

"Not really." The boy looked at Troy. "Not as tall as you are. I think he's a couple of inches shorter than you."

Ellie didn't stop to ask herself how she knew Troy was five-eleven. She now knew the kidnapper was roughly five-nine.

"Let's talk about his face again." She smiled encouragingly at Dennis. "Was his nose long or short?"

"His nose was big—like too big—great big holes like he probably picks it a lot."

He sounded like a teenager now.

"Were his eyes close to his nose or farther away from it?"

"Close to it, and when he looked at me, one eye moved, and the other one didn't."

"Could it have been a fake eye?" She tried to stick with terminology he would understand.

Dennis shook his head. "I don't think so. It moved a little, just not like the other one."

"Were his eyes round or oval?"

"Ovals."

Ellie saw he was growing paler. "You're doing a great job, Dennis. Are you okay, or do you need to rest?"

Determination covered the boy's features. "I'm tired, but I want to catch this guy."

"Okay, then, think about his mouth. Was it large or small?"

He was silent so long, Ellie was close to asking if he had forgotten. But, then in his weakening voice told Ellie, "Kind of small, I guess, but it was hard to tell under the fake mustache."

"Could you see if his lips were thin, or full?"

"I could only see the bottom one, and I don't know what you'd call it, but it didn't look fat or anything."

"And what about his ears? Were they visible?" She doubted they were if he wore a wig.

For the first time, Dennis smiled. "Those things stuck out so far, the long-haired wig didn't cover them. One time, when he brought me food, I got hold of one of his ears and gave it a good yank."

Amazed by the courage the boy in front of her possessed, yet unable to tell him he did the right thing, Ellie managed to return his smile. "What did the hair look like?"

"It's brown, like the mustache." Dennis shrugged. "Like I said, I don't think it fit the guy right because you could see some kind of rubber stuff around the front of it."

"You said it was long. Did it come down to his chin? Or maybe his shirt collar?"

"I think it was supposed to come down to his shoulders, but it didn't reach." A crooked grin appeared on the boy's face for just a moment. "The guy's head was gigantic."

154

"One more thing, and then we're finished. Think of his neck." Ellie gave him a moment. "Was it thick or thin, and long or short?"

Once more, the boy paused to consider his answer. "It was short because I could hardly see it, and it was thick."

"You've done a fantastic job, Dennis." Why hadn't she found out what he liked to read and brought him a book as a reward? She used to always stay on top of things like that. Where are these ridiculous statements coming from? *Father, please don't let me go crazy.*

Troy turned his pad around. "Does this look like the man who took you?"

Wide-eyed, Dennis' mouth hung open for a moment. "How did you do it? It's him. It looks just like him."

Ellie spoke up. "You did it, Dennis. Agent Martin wouldn't have known what to draw if you hadn't told him."

"Wow." He had yet to take his eyes off the sketch. "Do you think you'll catch him now?"

"We'll take this straight to the police, and it will be on the news. If anybody sees the man, we'll catch him."

Troy closed his pad and slid it back into his bag. "And he won't be so quick to try to grab another child. He'll be worried someone will recognize him."

Ellie and Troy both stood. "We'll leave and let you rest." Ellie hoped his family knew what a remarkable boy he was. "Thank you, Dennis."

"You're welcome." Suddenly, as if of its own volition, his lower lip quivered. "I hope you find Destiny. She wasn't there very long, but she was more scared than Gracie. Gracie talked to God a lot."

I promise we'll do everything we can to get her back." Ellie just hoped it was enough.

Chapter 35

"No." Crystal Stanley couldn't believe her eyes. She stood and walked closer to her television.

"These are the two men suspected of kidnapping three area children, one of whom is Senator Wilder's grandson."

Crystal hit the TV's pause button when the men, whose identities she was already certain of, suddenly filled the screen. Close, the images were even blurrier, but the photograph taken with a store's security camera showed an undisguised Mike Campbell buying a fuzzy rabbit. What he would need with a stuffed animal, she couldn't imagine, but the fact remained—it was Mike.

The sketch was just as easy to identify. The long hair and mustache appeared almost as authentic as those black plastic glasses with attached noses. The drawing faded away, to be replaced by an excellent representation of a disguise-free Mike.

And they both worked at Cosarts. Todd was the head salesman, and popular with the customers because of his friendly, easygoing attitude. With his height and build, he was a favorite of the female clientele.

Mike Campbell worked odd hours, doing maintenance at the store. There was something wrong with his mentality, but that wasn't what gave her the creeps. No. It was his eyes. The slowness of one eye made it appear he was actively looking in two directions. She tried never to be alone with him when the store was closed and didn't fully understand why Bryan would...Bryan! What would he do? He'd still be at work and most likely didn't know about this. He'd be horrified to discover two of his employees were child abductors. Whether he knew or if she had to tell him, Crystal would be there to comfort him.

Since she'd received the reward money, she felt more on equal footing with Bryan. Not that she had even a fraction of his wealth, but at least his girlfriend wasn't as poor as a church mouse. Right now, she had to get to him.

She rushed around and pulled her car into the dark parking lot right before twelve o'clock. The store closed at nine-thirty, but

Bryan worked until midnight most nights. Crystal used her key to let herself in the back door.

"Bryan?" She didn't want to startle him.

"I'm in here." From the irritation in his voice, she knew he was having trouble with the books.

She walked into his office to see him sitting at his desk. "I'm so sorry. I came to tell you before you saw it on the news. It's just terrible."

He wasn't any happier. "What are you talking about?"

"It was on the news. Pictures of the men who kidnapped the Wilder boy."

Bryan stood up, a frown firmly in place. "What does that have to do with me?"

"They work here." Crystal hated to give him the news, but she would comfort him. "It's Todd and Mike Campbell. I know it's hard to believe, Bryan, but I'm certain of it."

An unreadable expression replaced his dour one as he reached down and slid a desk drawer open. "Have you called the police yet?"

Joy filled Crystal when she realized Bryan was worried about her. She smiled at him. "I haven't called anybody. I wanted to tell you first. I'll do it now, though." She stepped to the desk and reached for the phone.

His arm rose. The blood rushed to her head when she saw a pistol aimed directly at her. "I can't let you do that." His voice was void of emotion. "Those fools are liable to lead the police right back to me."

Bryan loved her; she knew that. Crystal laughed nervously. "What do you mean? This isn't funny." His expression didn't change. "Put that gun away."

"You just don't get it, do you?" The gun didn't waver as he walked around the desk. "Starting with, you are the last woman this side of Mars I would build a real relationship with."

"What?" She couldn't have heard him correctly. "You bought me—"

"Upper-end costume jewelry. I'd have stuck with the kind out of those kiddy machines, but even a simpleton, man chaser like you would recognize plastic."

"You...we..." Crystal felt the world shift. Was she having a nightmare?

He motioned toward the door with the weapon. "I guess we'll just go for a little ride, and I'll explain everything. And then, maybe you'll understand."

Was he going to explain, and then it would be all right? A gun...he was going to shoot her. Cold dread conquered her confusion. She had to get away. Before she took one step, he grabbed her hair and yanked her back. Then, she felt a cold hand against her neck.

"Walk out that door, or I'll shoot you right here and now."

As clear as a bell, Crystal heard her mother speaking through sobs. "Steal. Lie. All to trick a man into marrying you. But unless you change, you'll never be the kind of lady men fall in love with." Her mom had been right.

Chapter 36

"Do you want to ride with me?" Mitch was already halfway into his car.

"Samantha and I'll be right behind you." Gage slid in and had barely closed the passenger door before being jerked back and hearing the tires squeal.

"Maybe I should have driven." He quickly fastened the seat belt. "I forgot what a crazy driver you can be."

"I'll show you crazy." She took a corner on what felt to Gage like two wheels, staying close behind the sheriff's car. At this rate, Gage would end up in Mitch's car yet.

At least a dozen calls had come in during the first twenty minutes of the newscast, and they all said the same thing. The men were brothers who had lived in the area for a couple of years. It had taken some "creative" web searches, but Elijah located two properties linked to their names. Tim Cambel had a maxed-out credit card, using the address of a rental house on the east edge of Shadow. The funny thing was, Tim had the same social security number as Todd Campbell.

As for the others, Elijah found a farm five miles west of town, and when he pulled it up on satellite, there was a camper they assumed was the one near the cave. Then, it was discovered that Dixie Campbell belonged to a mail order movie club and ordered an average of ten a month. The addresses matched up. These people were not ace criminals, which confirmed Gage's contention that the kidnappers had a boss.

Simon Fisher had the area FSA agents and a passel of state police with him. Gage glanced at his watch and saw they should already be at the townhouse by now. The sheriff's caravan was on their way to the farm.

"Do you think we'll get there before they leave?" Sam scared Gage by taking her eyes off the road to glance at him.

"Depends. Hopefully, the lane out here will be in as bad shape as the one we already found." With her at the wheel, he may not make it with all his appendages in place, anyway.

Samantha smiled. "I heard about that. And heard about it some more. Jess was shooting nearly every limb on their bodies before she finished."

Gage felt he needed to warn his partner. "Just don't lose Davis back there. Kurt is with him, and we may need his shooting skills." He hoped he was wrong, but he had a feeling these people weren't going to gracefully surrender.

His phone rang, and he was surprised to hear Simon Fisher on the other end.

"We were fired upon when we approached the house. It's been confirmed there's at least one man inside. We have the place surrounded, so nobody's getting away this time, Gage."

"Do what you have to," Gage instructed the other agent, "but try to take him alive. You have Eric with you. Set up communication between them and use him. This is the best chance we've ever had of moving up the food chain in this organization."

"I understand. I'll do all I can."

Gage summarized the call to Sam as soon as he put his phone away.

Samantha responded without hesitation. "So, it's most likely Todd Campbell, the younger son, in the house. From what people have said, and especially what Dennis Wilder told Ellie, I doubt if Mike Campbell would be capable of holding off the FSA."

"If you're right, there's a good chance Mike and his mother are at the farm." Gage thought of what they knew. "Mike may be manageable, but Dixie Campbell is a wild card."

Samantha glanced at him again. "Elijah could only find the basics on her. She's never been in trouble. Maybe she just goes along with her sons."

"Maybe." He hoped that was the case.

The car skidded sideways as Sam followed the sheriff onto a poorly graveled drive. The lights of a house appeared to be a quarter of a mile away.

Samantha's vibrating voice reminded Gage of Jess. "These people like long, bumpy lanes."

"Apparently."

The sheriff stopped behind a white panel van, and miraculously, Sam pulled in behind him.

Just as Gage opened his door, "Achoo!" No little ladylike sneezes for Samantha.

He took advantage of the time it took her to work up another. "Are you okay?"

She answered with three consecutive sneezes. Finally, she pulled an inhaler from her coat pocket and after another squeal, puffed relief into her mouth. "These weeds stir up my allergies, but this medication is nearly immediate."

Within moments, they joined the group gathered around the sheriff.

Mitch's jaw twitched. After leaning into his car and adjusting the radio, he held his wireless mic to his mouth. His voice rang out.

"Mike Campbell. Todd Campbell. This is Shadow County, Sheriff Mitch Landon. Come out with your hands up."

The only response was a light in an upstairs window shutting off.

Mitch turned to the others. "Get low and scatter. He may plan on sitting up there and picking us off. We need the place surrounded." He turned to Hardy, Hank, and a group of state police officers standing behind his deputies. "You guys split up and circle around. Look for a back way in."

Gage turned to his agent. "Kurt, use your night scope. Find a place with clear vision, and lock in on anybody with a gun." Kurt started to walk away. "No kill shot, Kurt. We need him to talk."

"Understood." Gage watched as Kurt, with his rifle over his back, effortlessly climbed a tall tree several yards away.

Mitch's voice came over the loudspeaker again. "You are surrounded. Come out with your hands up."

Gage's hand-held radio crackled. "Okay, Kurt."

"I can only see two subjects in the house, but both appear to be armed. The male subject has a handgun, and it's too dark even with the lenses, to tell whether she's using a rifle or shotgun.

"Where are they?" He'd bank money one was in the upstairs room.

Kurt's deep voice came from the radio. "Male is on the lower floor, the third window from the west; the female is in the middle window upstairs."

So, they could be certain it was the woman in the darkened room. "Do you have a clear shot?"

"Easily." Kurt wasn't bragging, just stating a fact.

"Stay on the alert. Let me know of any movement." Hopefully, the Campbell's would surrender without a fight.

The sheriff looked at Gage. "We know where they're at. Maybe we can get to the house without being seen." A low-volume beep came from his radio. He pulled the hand-held from his shirt pocket. "Landon here."

Hardy's voice came from the speaker. "We have a problem. The entire north and east sides of the property are enclosed by a stone fence that looks like it was built over a hundred years ago."

Mitch was obviously perplexed. "Climb over it."

"Hank did."

"Well, then?" Mitch was as close as Gage had seen him to losing his temper.

"Besides it being eight-foot tall, barbed wire is on the top. I gave Hank a lift, but I can't climb this."

"Grab one of the officers around you and have him get you over the fence. I need you in there. Got it?"

"Those guys are in the camper. One of them smelled what he thinks is meth, and they're all over that."

"Mitch, these people aren't drug users. They'd never be able to pull off something like this." Gage didn't need a complete profile on any of them to know this was the truth.

"Jerry?" The sheriff's eyes didn't move from Gage.

"Yes, sir."

"Be careful, but go ahead and look inside the camper."

A couple of minutes later, the deputy was back on the radio. "No meth, Sheriff, but there's a significant smell from an unemptied septic system."

"Let me guess; Robert smelled the meth."

Another voice came on the radio. "I'm sorry, sir. I ain't never smelled sewer gas." Before Mitch could speak, a ragged sigh came from his radio. "I reckon I ain't smelled meth, either."

Mitch looked at Gage. "We will deal with this later, Rob."

"Uh oh" Hank's uncharacteristically angry voice followed Rob. "Sheriff, you won't believe the setup they have. It's some kind of racetrack; I'm not sure what breed their dogs are."

The sound of barking was audible, first on the radio and then in the night air.

"Get out!" Hardy yelled loudly enough that he could be heard without the radio. "Those are Pit Bulls, and they aren't friendly! We gotta get over the fence!"

The sheriff shook his head. "Hardy's off his game. He's the best officer I know. He'll have this job soon."

"We're out, Sheriff," Hard breathing came from the radio.

"What did you do to make them mad?" The sheriff seemed a bit aggravated with his most experienced deputy.

"They're Pit Bulls, and nothing but skin and bones," was Hardy's response. "Hank counted four of them before one managed to bite him."

The Campbells would not have the capabilities to care for a pet, especially after finishing a job caring for kids. Gage would have liked to share this information with Mitch the moment the dogs were spotted. The sheriff had made it pretty clear what he thought of Gage's observation about drugs, and they didn't have time to test another theory.

Mitch leaned forward, his brow furrowed in concern. "Is he injured?"

Hardy's voice was dry as he answered. "No, but he'll be needing the seat of his pants patched."

The ring of a shot being fired and a barn window to their right shattering kept Mitch from replying. Everyone ducked.

Gage didn't need Kurt to tell him the woman was shooting slugs with a shotgun. The gunfire was too loud for a rifle, and from what he could see of the area around the window, the shots were spread.

Samantha spoke from close beside Gage. "Bad aim?"

"Or a warning." He keyed the radio. "Make it dark out here, Kurt."

"Got it, Boss."

Five shots rang out in quick succession, and with each one, an exterior light crackled and disappeared.

There was awe in the sheriff's voice. "Does that man ever miss?"

Gage answered honestly. "Not unless he means to."

Kurt's voice came from Gage's radio. "We've got movement. The male subject is sitting in the living room." Even on the static-filled radio, Gage could hear the bewilderment in his agent's voice. "I think he has his thumb in his mouth."

"You know who we need." Frustration was on his partner's face. "It's not right to risk lives when she would have this over within minutes."

"She hasn't remembered this part of her life; she will when it's God's time."

Apparently, Samantha was going to argue. "She remembers enough. Look at how she worked with those two kids."

The vibration indicating his phone was ringing gave Gage an excuse to ignore Sam. He turned and answered it.

Simon Fisher did not have good news. "Todd Campbell is en route to the hospital with a self-inflicted gunshot wound to the head. I'm sorry, but I don't think he'll make it, Gage."

"Not your fault." Gage shoved the phone back into his pocket. Now, the only hope they had of catching Proctor was getting these people, or at least one of them, to talk. He stepped closer to Mitch. "Sheriff?"

Mitch's eyes glowed in the moonlight as he looked at Gage.

Gage said a quick prayer he was making the right decision. "Do you have a deputy who can drive my wife out here?"

Eyes wide open, Mitch swiveled to face Gage. "Donahue, you're a great agent, but to have your wife here? "

"Please let me explain."

"I know you just reunited, but do you think this is the time or place for canoodling?"

"That's not what I need her for." Not that he'd mind being alone with Ellie instead of dealing with this situation.

"She doesn't remember it, yet," Gage explained to the sheriff exactly why he wanted Ellie there.

A wild shot rang out and hit the barn, followed by another that put a pattern on the hood of a junked car. So far, the hits were all east of them. "Okay," Mitch spoke into his radio again and instructed his dispatcher to get Jeff Fielding out of bed and thrill him.

In Gage's experience, there was always one grump in a police department. Fielding had earned the title in Shadow.

"I know he's exhausted, Ray. We all are, but I need him to fetch Ellie from Donahue's house, and bring her here." A groan came from Mitch's chest before he spoke again. "Not that it's our place to judge, but they are very much married. Now, get Fielding and fast."

A cacophony of shots surrounded them as glass shattered and aluminum siding pinged.

"That woman's going to mess around and hit one of us." Samantha made the dry prediction from a crouched position behind the sheriff's squad car.

Gage called Kurt on the radio. "Is it just the woman firing?"

Kurt still seemed disbelieving of what he was seeing. "She's on her knees with the shotgun braced on the windowsill. The man is now rocking back and forth, with his thumb in his mouth, and he's holding the pistol right up against the side of his head with his other hand."

Please, not like his brother had. "Does it look like he's going to shoot himself?"

"Not yet." Kurt paused. "It's more like he's holding his head, and the gun just happens to be there."

Gage still didn't allow himself to feel relieved. Things could change at any moment. "Sit tight, Kurt. Ellie's coming."

"Good."

Now, Gage could only pray this wouldn't harm his wife.

Chapter 37

Ellie still couldn't believe she was doing this. After a long telephone conversation with her dad, she'd been curled up on the couch, reading an exciting mystery. She had just about decided to give up on staying awake until Gage came home when the doorbell rang.

Then, when she answered the persistent pounding on the door and saw Jeff Fielding, her first thought was something had happened to Gage.

But, no. Jeff told her the sheriff sent him to fetch her. All he knew was he was taking her to a farm. There was evidently some danger because they were going in dark.

Now, in the car, she looked at the deputy's profile. "Exactly what am I supposed to do at a dangerous crime scene?"

Jeff shrugged. "I don't know. I'm just following orders."

"Is Gage there?"

"As far as I know, everybody is out somewhere." His frown was visible in the dashboard lights. "The dispatcher called and got me out of bed."

No wonder he was a bear. "I'm sorry."

"No." Jeff sighed. "I'm the one who's sorry. I've just been working too many hours, with these abduction cases. I shouldn't be taking it out on you."

"I understand."

They rode in silence, but Ellie had to constantly calm her frazzled nerves. She still hadn't come up with a logical reason for her unexpected summons, when Jeff slowly came to a stop.

"Here we are." He shut the car lights off and turned onto a dirt lane. "Give me a minute to get my night vision."

As they sat, the images of gravel sparsely spread on what appeared to be tire tracks with grass growing between them became visible. Jeff began to drive ahead. Just as they rounded a bend, and pulled up behind a squad car, three shots rang out in rapid succession.

Panic struck Ellie. "Is somebody shooting at us?"

Seemingly unaffected, Jeff shut off the car and opened his door. "Sounded more like they were aimed east of us, but it's probably the reason for the lights-off order."

Ellie opened her door and very reluctantly slid out of the car. Without interior lights, it felt wrong—dangerous, even. As she took a step, her mind was screaming at her to stop, and her feet said they were going as slow as they could; they might even decide to shift into reverse.

What could they want with a child psychologist or an insurance receptionist? Maybe the sheriff needed new targets. He was tired of being shot at, so he thought he'd let her have a turn. Suddenly, she didn't care how irrational she was being. "Huh uh. No way." She turned back around and headed to the car.

"Ellie?" Gage's voice, from directly behind, startled her. "Where are you going?" He took her arm and stepped in front of her.

She turned and waved in the general direction of the shooting. "You just get yourself a spotlight and make shadow puppets for whoever that is to shoot at. I'm not going to be a target."

There was laughter in his voice. "You're really back, aren't you? My Ellie is really back."

Well, duh. "Yes, I am, and unless you're planning on becoming a widower, you'll move and let me back in the car."

He placed his hands on her shoulders and turned her to face him. Even in the dark, his expression was so loving, she almost asked why they both couldn't get in the car and go home. "I know you still don't remember everything, but I believe there's a part of you that does. The part who worked with Troy and helped those kids—you don't remember why you can, but you did it anyway."

"Okay." She looked past him at the car. "But what does that have to do with being shot at?"

"Ellie." She was startled by the solemnity in his expression. "I'm going to ask you for something I know you can do. Something you can do very well. And, even though you may not know why you can, please trust me when I tell you it's true."

Hold on. "Am I an expert marksman or something?"

"You barely passed your qualifications."

This wasn't making any sense. "Qualifications for what?"

Gage shook his head. "Never mind. You're just not a good shot."

He didn't want her to serve as a living target or a sharpshooter, so... "Just what is it I'm supposed to do?"

"There's a woman we know nothing about in the house, shooting at us. Her son, the man Dennis told you about, is currently sitting and rocking back and forth. Kurt says he has his thumb in his mouth and a pistol flat against the side of his head."

Ellie thought of the description Dennis had given them. "But he's liable to unintentionally shoot himself!! You have to get the gun away from him."

Gage's fingers felt warm on her cheek. "That's why you're here. You need to persuade him to surrender peacefully. Then, you can start working on the woman."

Her mind was racing. "How do you expect me to do this? Talking to a disturbed adult is much different than working with a child. I'm not trained for this."

"Just try, Ellie." His eyes were twin lasers. "Please trust me, and try."

"The sheriff says to tell you they found a body on the other side of the house." Jeff had appeared out of the darkness. "Hardy has identified her as Crystal Stanley. Mitch says we need this to stop now."

Gage hadn't taken his eyes off her. "Ellie?"

She stiffened her spine but immediately ducked when bullets struck metal again. "I must be crazy." She straightened to as near of a standing position as she dared. "Take me to the megaphone or whatever you call it."

"Ellie's on her way," Gage spoke into his radio.

Right. Ellie was most likely on her way to creating an even larger mess than they already had.

"Thank you for coming." Mitch greeted her when they reached his squad car.

She had to voice one more protest. "You know I'm not really qualified for this. Maybe you'd be better off—"

"Trust me, Ellie," Gage spoke firmly as he handed her a

microphone.

As she felt the weight of the device in her hands, she wondered exactly how she should begin. "What are their names?"

"Dixie and Mike Campbell, a mother and son," Gage answered. "There's another son Todd, but he's being taken to the hospital."

Please, God, help me out here. Ellie took a deep breath. "Mike? Hi, Mike. My name is Ellie."

A round of shots was the immediate response. She ducked, even though they all hit the building to their far right.

Kurt's voice came from the radio Gage was wearing. "He's standing and looking around. I don't think he knows where Ellie's voice is coming from."

Ellie keyed the microphone. "I'm right outside, Mike. Why don't you come out here so we can see each other?"

"Leave my son alone!" A woman's loud voice echoed through the yard.

"I want to help Mike, Mrs. Campbell. I'd like to help both of you."

Kurt spoke again. "He's looking out the window."

"What can I do to help you? Do you need anything?" Ellie was running on pure instinct.

"I need Bobby!" The woman's voice was strained. "He's always happy."

They now knew "Bobby" was Dennis Wilder, so exactly who did the woman want? "If you come out, I'll see about getting Bobby for you."

"I want Cindy, and Peter and Jan, too." Her voice had taken on a plaintive note. "Marcia and Greg are too old."

"Oh, for crying out loud," Samantha spoke from her hiding place behind the car. "She wants the kids from the Brady Bunch."

"Cool it, Sam. She's sick, not someone to gripe about." Gage's voice was nearly a whisper.

Samantha smiled ruefully. "I'm sorry, Gage. I'm exhausted and put my mouth in drive while I still had my brain in park."

Gage's whisper continued. "I'll remind you."

169

Mitch half-smiled. "Maybe her son stole a Bobby for her, and Proctor found out."

Ellie tuned out the others' voices and focused on the people inside the house. "Why don't you and Mike both come out, and we'll see if we can find Bobby and Cindy? I'll help you look."

"He's becoming agitated," Kurt's voice advised.

Of course. "He may not want his mom to have other children." Now, what was she going to do? "If I make one of them happy, I'll upset the other."

Gage spoke quietly. "We need one of them alive, Ellie."

She looked at him. "You'd better not be asking me to sacrifice one life for another." She closed her eyes and prayed for the right words. Then she knew. She lifted the microphone again.

"Todd needs you. He's at the hospital, and he's asking for his mom and brother."

"What's the matter with Todd?" There was more curiosity than concern in Dixie Campbell's voice, but she seemed interested.

Gage's radio crackled. "The male subject is headed for the front door, gun in hand."

Ellie spoke quickly. "They don't allow guns at the hospital. If you want to go see Todd, you'll have to leave your gun at home."

"What's the matter with Todd?" Dixie was becoming more belligerent.

"He has a broken arm." Ellie sent up a prayer she was doing the right thing. "He fell down when he was playing with Bobby."

"Male subject has put gun on table and is moving toward door. He's going to come out," Kurt notified them.

Mitch spoke into his portable radio. "Unarmed male subject is coming out. Do not shoot. I repeat, do not shoot."

"That Bobby played hard." The woman cackled. "Mike got lots of bruises from playing with him."

"Here he comes." At Gage's soft words, Ellie looked up and saw the man Dennis described—minus the long hair and mustache—walk out of the house. He still had his thumb in his mouth.

"He's stopping." Sam's concern was evident.

Sure enough, Mike had made it about fifteen feet from the house and stopped. Suddenly, Ellie Lynette Donahue knew. It was all

170

right there, as if waiting behind a closed door for her to open. She moved quickly before Gage could stop her. She dropped the microphone and headed toward the man.

"Ellie! No!" Gage was right behind her.

She turned to face him. "I remember everything." She looked into his eyes, willing him to see the truth. "Now, you need to trust me."

Emotions warred in her husband's eyes. "At least wear this." He handed her a Kevlar vest with FSA across it in big white letters. Somehow, she knew it would fit her perfectly.

Wordlessly, he helped her put it on.

"I'll be right back."

He smiled grimly. "You'd better be."

Ellie raised her voice as she walked toward Mike. "Mrs. Campbell, it's Ellie. Mike wants to go see his brother, so I'm just going to help him. Okay?"

"You'll have to watch them." The woman could have been discussing the weather. "They can be sneaky."

"I know." Ellie chuckled loudly and kept moving. "Boys are like that, aren't they? I don't have any children yet, so I hope I can handle yours."

Dixie sounded friendly now. "Well, if they don't mind you, just give their seat ends a swat."

Mike quickly moved his hands protectively over his derriere, so Ellie spoke to him. "I'd never spank anybody. I'd rather just help you do the right thing."

"Will you take me to see Todd?" Mike slowly lowered his hands. "I don't like Bobby anymore. He don't play nice. He even bit me."

Ellie spoke loudly enough for his mother to hear. "I'm taking Mike to see Todd. I sure wish you'd join us. I know Todd wants his mom there." She was within arms' reach of Mike. It was only as she held her hand out and watched him take it, she realized how big he was. She fought back her fear and smiled at him.

"Are you coming, Mrs. Campbell?"

Behind Mike, a woman appeared in the open doorway. Ellie

told herself not to panic; Gage wouldn't have allowed Dixie Campbell to so much as head in the direction of the door if the woman were still armed. Ellie smiled encouragingly and waited.

Even though she knew these two people had been involved in taking children, her heart went out to them. The woman walking toward her was every bit as disturbed as her son, just in a different way. Her life was probably so miserable, she lost herself in television programs.

"I'd better take Mike's other hand," Dixie said as she reached them. "He gets excited, and he might run out into the road."

Ellie saw Gage and the others headed their way. Her steady voice halted them.

"Thank you, Dixie." She glanced at the officers and felt a smile tug on her lips when she saw nearly identical, confused expressions.

Gage motioned for everyone to step back.

Ignoring them, Ellie turned to look at Mike. "I'll just walk you over to the sheriff's car. He can get you to the hospital faster than I can. Okay?"

Mike's childish voice came from beside her. "Can I turn on the siren?"

"I don't know." Ellie raised her voice. "Sheriff Landon?"

Mitch stepped forward, disbelief in his eyes.

"Mike wants to run your siren. Could he do that before you take them to the hospital?"

The sheriff, apparently still dumbfounded, replied. "That'll be okay."

After a tense group of people had observed the fugitives cheerfully follow Ellie's instructions, Hardy pulled away with a content Mike in the back seat of his car. Dixie was loudly lecturing Hank Stone about being a careful driver as he pulled away with her in his vehicle.

As Gage and the others took care of Crystal Stanley's body, Ellie sank onto a nearby tree stump.

She was an FSA agent. She'd joined the AMAR team as a child psychologist, not six months after she and Gage were married. Then, at the group's urging, she earned her credentials as an agent.

She remembered all of them. She and Troy had developed a method of identification that proved so successful they received requests from all over the country.

Jess was a walking database with an incredible sense of humor and was usually threatening to take Kurt's gun away from him and shoot somebody.

And Kurt. He taught Ellie how to fight when he realized she wasn't a sharpshooter. The memory of taking him down one day still made her smile. As for shooting, Kurt had done his best to teach Ellie, but she still barely made it into the unit. Kurt told the rest of them if she ever started shooting, they should just stand where she was aiming. She'd miss them for sure. He was one of her favorite people.

Bridgett was a contrast in character. She would be sickened by disgusting sights one minute, and up to her elbows collecting samples of muck in the next. Her other skill, which she rarely used, was as a fighter trained in nearly every form. Another detail popped into Ellie's head. Bridgett never shared her past. When Gage had admitted he knew next to nothing about her, just that she came with virtually no background information. That would take help from someone with clout. Ellie often found herself wondering if Bridgett was covering a tragedy.

Elijah—put a computer in his hands, and he was unstoppable. He could handle a room full of computers all going at once. Extremely handsome, he was teased by the other men on the team. She had been in their office in Atlanta when an agent practically begged him to pose for photos. He could be the next Fabio. The other guys teased him sometimes, but Elijah laughed as hard as his buddies.

At sixty-four, Eric Grant was the oldest member of the team, and Ellie's counterpart in that he treated adults. Her hope to be working with him ended when he made it very clear he strongly disliked children.

What had the AMAR team done during the last fifteen months? Did Eric step up to the plate and fill in for her? If so, she'd wager it was under protest. He would be the first to say children were on his "avoid" list.

"You okay?" Samantha's voice pulled her from her thoughts. "If you're not, I can borrow a squad car and run you home." She knelt in front of Ellie. "You've remembered so much, but I have to tell you how glad I am to see you back.:

Ellie saw honesty in the other woman's face. "I owe you an apology." There. Ellie had just blurted it.

Samantha's brows formed a perfect v on her forehead. "What for?"

"I as good as accused you of having an affair with Gage when it couldn't be further from the truth." Ellie looked up at the face of her husband's partner. "God is front and center in our marriage. That's what keeps it unbreakable and why I'm never worried."

"Maybe it isn't you who should—"

"Are you okay?" Gage's deep voice startled both women.

Ellie produced a weak smile. "I'm more tired than I realized."

He knelt in front of her as Sam headed toward the cars. "Do you really remember everything?"

She considered the question. "Almost. I remember going to bed one night, and the next thing I knew, I was in the hospital. I can't remember the time right around the accident." It troubled her.

Ellie was in worse shape than she thought because to her tired eyes, Gage appeared relieved. "Give it time. Look how quickly everything else has come back to you. This won't be any different."

A yawn exploded from her before she could stop it. "Can we go home now?"

He leaned in and kissed her forehead. "I need to wait until we've done all we can with the crime scene. We'll get you a ride home, though." He stood and pulled her to her feet. "I'm really proud of you."

"Thank you." She yawned again. "Samantha offered to borrow a squad car and run me home."

He pulled her into his arms and turned to face the cars. "Take the SUV, Samantha."

She nodded. "Whenever she's ready."

Ellie decided she didn't care who might be watching. She pulled Gage's face to hers and received her good night kiss.

How could she have ever forgotten this? She prayed she

never would again.

Chapter 38

Bryan paced the floor, from the dining room table where he'd dropped the newspaper's special edition to the kitchen door. He had to get control of himself and think. He could still walk away from this unscathed. Somehow.

Todd Campbell had been DOA due to a self-inflicted gunshot wound. He couldn't talk. But Dixie and Mike...Neither of them had a line on their fishing poles, but could one of them manage to point the authorities toward Bryan?

He had to think about this logically. If the Campbells told police the brothers worked for Bryan, he'd just have to convince his interrogators that they were confused. They were his employees at the store. And, how could they think a respectable businessman would want to take part in kidnappings? Okay. That seemed feasible.

But Crystal. She begged, pleaded, and promised anything if he'd let her live. Especially after he confessed, she would be his first homicide. He honestly regretted giving in to his emotions and acting in haste. The article on the front page of the morning newspaper stated that while the pictures were still on the screen, over twenty callers had identified the men who allegedly kidnapped the senator's grandson.

Panic and frustration had paired with his dislike of her, and for once, he let his emotions rule his head. Had he been thinking clearly, he would have found a way to let her live. He could have snowed Crystal. Now, he'd have to be the distraught boss and grieving boyfriend who couldn't believe what his employees had done.

At least he had enough sense to come up with a story. Crystal had to have seen the pictures and recognized the men. Then, most likely out of love for Bryan, she had gone to try to talk Mike into turning himself in. Only, huge, unstable Mike killed her with a length of rope he stole from the store.

Yes. Bryan simply needed to remain calm and stick to the story.

After the debacle this mission turned out to be, the Shadow ring was finished. As soon as everything died down, Bryan would be on to the next location—with a new team. Bryan was indispensable so his boss would have to overlook this mess. His boss had proven how valued Bryan was by helping him out of the last disaster he'd been dragged into. He felt better just thinking about it.

Bryan Cosart was going to come out on top. He always did.

Chapter 39

It was a good thing Clay Richmond wasn't Gage's insurance agent. If he were, Gage's premiums would have undoubtedly skyrocketed today.

To say the man was unhappy when Gage came into the office to retrieve his wife was an understatement. Richmond didn't appear to be over the initial shock of discovering his assistant was a happily married woman before her husband showed up to claim her.

But Gage needed Ellie. The Campbells were being picked up from the state police station any time now and relocated to a federal mental institution. After they were there, it would be difficult to see them.

He had to find out about Mike's boss before they were picked up. Eric was questioning Dixie, and Ellie was now in an interrogation room with Mike. Nobody else could get him to utter a word. The giant had refused to look at the men who tried, and both Samantha and a female police officer had the same results when they tried.

Gage looked through the two-way mirror where Eric and Jess sat with Dixie. The woman lived in a world of her own creation, which was comprised partially of her limited surroundings and largely of television shows. She had spoken about so many fictional characters; Gage gave up trying to keep track of the programs she was referencing. Jess was there to help the conversation move along when Dixie's Television-World befuddled Eric.

Sam leaned her shoulder against the glass. "Well, so far she's camped out in her living room with the Partridge Family, shared bananas with Gilligan, and sewed buttons on Laura Ingalls' dress."

"And about a dozen other shows." Gage had to add.

"I'm glad I'm not in Jess's shoes right now." She nodded toward the end of the room. "How's Ellie doing?"

Gage walked over to the second window. He wasn't surprised to see Ellie with a deck of cards. Mike's voice came through the speaker as Gage turned the volume up.

"You got a turtle?"

"You peeked." Ellie handed him a card. "Do you have a duck?"

The big man stomped his foot in glee. "Go fish!"

Ellie drew a card from the stack on the table. "I didn't get a duck. It's your turn."

"I think I'll go make nice with the state boys," Samantha murmured from beside Gage. "There haven't been any jurisdictional issues yet, and I'd like to keep it that way."

Gage glanced over as she left the room. The door hadn't closed all the way when it reopened, and Mitch Landon, in jeans and a T-shirt, walked in.

"What are you doing out of your jurisdiction?" Gage made sure to keep a teasing note in his voice. Like Sam had just said, they were all working well together.

Mitch seemed embarrassed. "I still can't believe what Ellie did last night. Hardy had to deal with a similarly inclined man last year, and nothing got through to him."

Pride welled in Gage's chest. "Ellie has a God-given gift to bond with children, especially ones with mental problems." Gage shrugged. "Guess we'll have to start having her talk to adults, too."

"Well, I was in Pattinton, and just couldn't resist seeing her in action again." The sheriff glanced at the glass through which Ellie and Mike were visible. "Do you mind?"

"Not at all." Gage was confused, though. "How did you know Ellie was doing this?"

A big grin split the giant's face. "Are you kidding? Clay Richmond is crazy-mad. It's not enough he hired an unqualified woman as a favor to his friends. Now, her big-shot FSA husband thinks he can just waltz in and take her with him whenever he wants."

"What's the man going to do when he finds out Ellie's real profession?"

Mitch chuckled. "I don't know, but I sure hope I'm there to see it." He rubbed the bridge of his nose. "Are you still smelling that place?"

Unfortunately, Gage would have to answer yes. "When something smells that bad, it gets up into the nose and settles in the nerve endings or something. It'll go away eventually."

"Good, because Tessa is blaming her cooking or her perfume, everything to do with smell. I tried to tell her what I could, and she ordered me to shut up."

Gage knew what that was like. "Before Ellie joined AMAR, she went so far as ear buds topped with ear muffs. And just to make triple sure she wouldn't hear me, she'd belt out some of the worst rock songs in history."

"That's too—"

Ellie's laughter caught their attention.

As she shuffled cards, she casually spoke. "Do you play cards with Todd very often?"

Mike picked up his cards. "Todd don't play with me."

"What do you and Todd do together, then?"

The big man frowned. "We just work. That's all Todd ever wants me to do.

Ellie was leading him in the right direction.

"Do you have a rabbit?" She was sticking with their card game.

That perked Mike up. "Go fish."

Ellie asked another question as she picked up her card. "What work does Todd make you do?"

Mike sighed unhappily. "I always have to clean. I sweep and mop and wipe things off. Toilets are nasty, and the ones in our keeper house wouldn't flush. I told Todd they were buckets, but he wouldn't listen to me." His brows wrinkled as his face turned red. "Bobby was so mean, he tried to throw one at me."

"He's escalating," Mitch observed.

Gage patted the sheriff's shoulder. "Don't worry. My wife is aware of everything the man is feeling."

And, sure enough, Ellie pulled through. "Mike, did you see the duck's feet? She picked a card up and held it out for him. "Look at his feet."

The big man began giggling like a child. "Ducks don't wear boots, do they?"

As their duck-shoe discussion continued, Ellie gradually pulled him back into the game. As they played, Ellie gleaned information from Mike in bits and pieces.

Mike worked in the "keeper rooms, " and they never smelled good. He had to give food and water to the kids, and the kids didn't even say thank you or please like they were supposed to.

It was only when Mike mentioned Bobby that he grew agitated again. "Bobby is the meanest boy in the world. I should have showed him how to behave."

Ellie smiled sympathetically. "I think maybe all little brothers are mean, sometimes."

They resumed their game and discussion with no more mention of Bobby.

Gage's ears perked up when he heard a new name mentioned.

"Bryan tells me what to do." Mike then went on a tangent about the many chores he did for Bryan.

That piqued his interest. He turned to Mitch.

"Both Campbell brothers worked for Bryan Cosart, and so did Crystal Stanley, right?"

Mitch nodded. "I hadn't thought about it, but yeah, they did."

"Dennis Wilder was dropped off at Cosart's store, and now the woman who found him is dead." Even Burnett would figure this out. "There are three of Cosart's employees somehow connected to this case. It seems like more than a coincidence."

"I'm sorry to tell you, for too long, I haven't been able to put much energy into any part of my job except this Proctor thing. Frankly, I'm out of my league, and the deputies need to focus on our community. I should have told you before now, but I'm embarrassed to admit I've been a coward."

"There is no reason to be embarrassed; you are about the furthest from a coward as it gets. It's hard for any of us to know which to take when more than one case needs work." Gage had done that when Burnett called with the Wilder case.

181

"Thanks."

Gage observed Ellie long enough to make sure she and Mike were peacefully playing their card game before he returned to the subject of the store owner. "What do you know about Bryan Cosart?"

"Just the basics, I guess." Mitch seemed to think for a moment. "He moved to town, maybe a year-and-a-half or two years ago. Then, not too long after he arrived, he bought the empty bicycle shop and opened his store."

That was right. Elijah had discovered Cosart's history of several failed businesses and declared that children's lemonade stands were more professional than the mess Cosart seemed enraptured with. Suddenly, the taste of lemonade mixed with body odor and cleaning supplies, and Gage couldn't keep from shuddering. Since he didn't want to be sick, he focused back on Bryan Cosart. "What about his personal life? I don't remember seeing him around town."

Mitch frowned. "He's not exactly sociable, but I guess he really liked Crystal."

"Why do you say that?"

A battle seemed to be going on in the sheriff's head. Mitch drew a deep breath."She dispatched at the station and sold information to a reporter."

"Please, don't tell me he used it."

"I wish I could, but he described a crime scene at our veterinarian's office, and his front-page spread wasn't only filled with information he shouldn't know; it was graphic."

Gage was trying to find the words to console Mitch, but he couldn't imagine any member of his team, even Grouchy Eric, trading AMAR business for money.

Mitch glanced at the first window and froze. A slow smile filled his face.

When Gabe turned to look, why was he not surprised that Jess was doing a dance from the sixties or seventies? Eric didn't exactly look like he wanted to stand up and join her, but Daisy Campbell did. As usual of late, Jess was forming a better bond with a female prisoner than the FSA's psychiatrist. What was going on with

Eric? He told himself for the hundredth time to remember his strange-acting agent.

"Crystal didn't have any other training I know of, so I don't see how she could have been qualified to work as a secretary or whatever Cosart called her."

Gage pulled his thoughts back to the case, but his response was halted when he saw the door behind Mike open. A police officer with two large men in scrubs stood there.

"Ellie's not going to like this," he murmured.

The officer stepped in, with the men behind him. "It's time to go, Campbell. These men are here to pick you up."

Mike glanced over his shoulder. "I don't know you. I want to play cards with Ellie."

The men took a couple of steps toward Mike, their intention clear. Gage wasn't the least bit surprised to see his wife stand up and insert herself between them and Mike.

"What is she doing?" Mitch seemed unsure of what he was seeing.

"Treating Mike Campbell with respect."

Ellie's voice, calm and clear, carried through the speaker. "Gentlemen, Mike and I are playing cards. You'll have to wait until this hand is over."

It was plain they all three wanted to argue with Ellie, but she stood her ground and stared them down. Then, without another word, she walked around the table and sat down.

They all watched with varying degrees of disbelief as an attractive woman played a rousing game of Go Fish with their patient. Only after she'd exclaimed to Mike over his winning yet again, did she pay attention to the others in the room.

She stood and looked at the attendants. "Mike, this is David and Chad." She'd read their name tags. "They probably don't play cards any better than I do. Will you go with them and show them how to play?"

Mike turned in his chair and frowned at them. "Where are we going? I don't want to go to the keeper rooms."

Ellie sounded cheerful. "You're going to a better place. People will be friendly and want to help you." She looked pointedly at the attendant nearest her. "Isn't that right, David?"

The man, visibly perplexed, answered. "Yes."

"So, Mike, what do you say we go with them? I want to see the van you're riding in."

Mike still seemed unsure. "Are you going with me?"

"You'll have so many new friends, you'll be too busy for me. I'll try to visit sometime soon, though." She held her hand out for him to take. "Come on, let's go."

Mike stood but immediately froze, an uncertain look on his face.

Ellie smiled encouragingly. "You can turn the siren on for a minute—like Sheriff Landon let you."

That roused the shell-shocked David. "We can't really—"

"You can do it because you're being so good." Ellie once again ignored the other men.

"Wow." There was awe in Mitch's voice. "She's not going to back down, is she?

"No." Gage watched as his wife held the gentle giant's hand and led him through the door. "When it comes to her patients, my wife won't give in."

David had turned to Chad before they followed Ellie and Mike out of the room. "Where did she come from?"

Chad leaned close to his coworker. "I don't know, but I'll take one."

Mitch chuckled, and Gage smiled. But then he sobered. "I have to go. My wife needs me right now." Gage quickly left the room, not giving Mitch time to voice the question on his face.

He walked through the jail house, past busy officers, and out the door. He found her right where he'd expected, standing where the institution's vehicle had been parked.

"Come here." Gage pulled a softly crying Ellie into his arms. "You did a fantastic job with Mike. He'll be taken care of now."

"He's a child," Ellie said through her tears. "I don't think he's ever intentionally hurt a living soul. He was used. One of the people who should love him more than anything used him." She sniffled and pulled back to look at him. "Did you hear how upset Mike was about the keeper rooms? He only became worked up about having to take care of those rooms and the kids."

Gage framed her face and with his thumbs, wiped away her tears. "I heard."

"I'm sorry I couldn't get a name out of him." She lay her head on his chest. "He just talked about his job at the store."

He wrapped his arms tightly around her. "I'm not too sure about that. We'll worry about it later, though."

"I'm going to call Aunt Viv." She sounded determined. "She'll contact Charles Crawford, and they'll find a lawyer who'll do what's best for Mike."

"I hope your interview went better than ours." Jess had walked up beside them, with Eric and Samantha behind her.

Gage wasn't quite ready to let go of his wife, so he turned and spoke over her head. "Did you get anywhere with Dixie?"

Jess's blue-streaked thing—a waterfall, she called it, shook with her declaration. "We've been to an island, a school, a farm, and even Mayberry, North Carolina."

"Don't forget the American Bandstand." Eric seemed sociable. Of course, the man didn't do happy.

Gage hated to spoil the doctor's very strange mood, but he took a deep breath and asked, "So what are your diagnoses of Dixie?"

And, there went Eric's good mood. He glanced at Jess and spoke in a more sedate manner. "She lives entirely in a world of her own making. Her sons and the inside of whatever house she's living in are the tangible components of her existence. But then she has a complete fantasy world in which she places herself into television shows."

Ellie slowly backed out of Gage's embrace to stand beside him but intertwined her fingers with his to keep his arm around her. "Mike only did what he was told. How involved was Dixie?"

"I think she only knows they 'get' children because she's the one who fixes food for them. There was nothing to suggest she's even aware they work for somebody else." Gage didn't miss the irritation Jess directed toward Eric as he spoke. Was the agent getting on everybody's wrong side?

Samantha's phone belted out the theme for Hawaii Five-O "Sorry." She glanced at the screen and rejected the call. "What's our next plan of action?"

"I don't think he's Proctor, but Bryan Cosart is now a person of interest." Gage went on to explain the basis of his conjecture.

"Are you reaching?" Save the headlines on a national newspaper, Eric was once more a naysayer.

"Maybe," Gage conceded, "but I'm still going to get the ball rolling." He would have Elijah dig deeper into Cosart's life. They needed to know as much as possible about the store owner.

"Are we questioning him?" Jess seemed eager.

"Not yet." Gage ignored Eric's glare. "If he's connected, he'll be expecting us at any moment. If we let him wonder when we'll be there, we might throw him off his game."

Samantha rocked back on her dress shoes. "And, if he's innocent, we're no worse off."

"Sounds feasible," Jess said, and the other two women lost no time voicing their agreement. Eric was back to normal, maintaining a stony stare for all of them.

"I'm sorry, but I need to get back to Shadow." Ellie stepped away from Gage. "Clay is on his own, and he has three appointments this afternoon." Her cheeks reddened. "I was planning to give him notice this morning, but my husband showed up and whisked me away before I had a chance."

That wasn't going to wash. "You can't tell me you'd rather sit at a desk than do this."

Ellie's smile was beautiful. "You do know me, don't you?" Her gaze went past Gage and froze. "That dress."

Gage spun to see what she was talking about, and gall rose up and burned his throat. Two women were walking on the sidewalk, and one of them was wearing a blue and white dress exactly like the one forever frozen in his mind.

"What about a dress?" Eric wouldn't remember; he'd been too busy complaining about having to cover for Ellie.

"I wore that dress." Ellie was in a near trance-like state. "I wanted to look extra nice for lunch, to show Dad and Viv–" She turned wide eyes to Gage. "My dad and Aunt Viv are engaged."

"Yes." But that was hardly the key point here. "Ellie, you're talking about the day of the crash."

"What should we do?" Jess stepped around Gage and placed her hand on Ellie's arm.

Eric cleared his throat. "We need to calm down. She may only be remembering bits and pieces."

"You drove the car." Ellie was focused solely on her husband. "The Explorer was low on gas, and you didn't have time to stop. So, we switched vehicles."

Gage's heart sped up. "That's right."

"We're not in the right place for this." Eric stood as tall as a five-ten body could. "You need to take her somewhere else, Gage."

"Do you want me to call her doctor?" Jessica offered. "To see if there's something we should do."

"I hardly think that's necessary." Eric appeared affronted. "In fact, I think I can help—"

"I want to remember." Ellie turned pleading eyes to Gage. "Please, help me remember."

Chapter 40

Ellie looked at the people sitting around the table. Each of them—well, nearly each of them appeared eager to help her. Gage had taken Jess's advice and called Dr. Marx. He was pleased Ellie was remembering the day of the accident on her own and didn't think prompting from her friends would hurt. However, he still did not recommend volunteering information she had no memory of whatsoever.

Before Ellie quite knew what was happening, she and Gage were at the AMAR headquarters, where the entire team waited.

Jess pulled out the chair next to her. "Come sit next to me."

Since Gage didn't suggest otherwise, Ellie walked around the table and sat by the blue-haired woman. "We're good friends, aren't we, Jess?"

Jessica grinned. "The best."

"We're all your friends." Troy spoke from the other side of the table. "In fact, during the years we've worked together, it seems almost like we're a family."

Ellie realized that was how she felt—like she was sitting with a family to which she belonged and was welcome. Drawing a deep breath and silently asking the Lord for strength, she spoke. "Let's start."

Gage's expression was unreadable as he sat between Troy and Eric. "What do you remember?"

"I remember hurrying out of bed to beat you to the shower." She bit her lip to keep from smiling. "I used too much hot water, and you ran out."

A reluctant smile appeared on her husband's face. "That could be just about any morning, Ellie."

"Oh." Of course, he was right. But she continued. "You had meetings at the regional office all day. You weren't going to be home for dinner." She waited while he nodded. "I planned lunch with Dad, Annie, and Aunt Viv." She had to be wrong about the reason. "Dad and Aunt Viv aren't actually engaged, though, are they?"

"They told us at dinner, the night before the crash." Gage waited expectantly.

Images slowly crept into her mind. Her dad's joy, Aunt Viv's uncertainty of Ellie's response...She disappointed both of them when she couldn't muster the enthusiasm they hoped for. Later that night, guilt and an open mind kicked in. "I set up the lunch to apologize and celebrate their engagement."

"Yes."

"So, do you remember getting to the offices?" It seemed Troy could wait no longer. "I beat you for once."

Ellie focused on him and tried to picture the scene. Rushing to get there on time because she'd stopped and filled the tank on the SUV. "You practically ran me over when I walked in." It was coming back. "We had an appointment at someone's house...Peter Durmont. His wife was a Federal Judge."

"An attempted abduction was made on his five-year-old daughter, Carrie," Troy prompted. "Durmont's son—"

"His name was Morgan. He was eighteen, and he refused to speak to us."

"Yeah, and you weren't any happier about it then than you are now." At Troy's statement, a chuckle came from Kurt's side of the table. "We interviewed the girl, though. You sat on the floor and played Barbie dolls with her while she gave us a description of Gargamel from the Smurfs."

Frustration pounced on her. "I still say it doesn't matter if Morgan was so focused on his sister he didn't look at the man. We could have gotten a sketch out of him."

"Calm down, Ellie." Gage's gentle voice brought her back to the present.

Jess leaned forward. "It's my turn, isn't it?"

Elijah arched an eyebrow. "What about me?"

"Quiet, Computer Man." Jess raised her hand and shooed him away. "Elijah and I had been working on a map of the Proctor sites when you walked back in. We were in his office. You heard us arguing and stopped by to see what we were doing."

Just like that, Ellie saw the tiny woman with her finger bouncing around the computer's monitor, claiming it made sense, and she had to laugh. "You figured out there was a McDonald's within twenty-five miles of several known Proctor sites."

Kurt snorted. "A nationwide kidnapping ring run by a clown."

Jess smacked his arm. "You just be quiet, or I'll edit your face onto a clown photo and place an ad to rent you out for birthday parties."

"Hey, what about me?" Elijah's affront might have looked authentic if he wasn't smiling. "You joined us in my office."

Ellie remembered. "McDonald's gave us an idea. We looked for a business with a franchise near each Proctor site." They had come up dry. "We worked on it until I left for lunch."

"We can't help you remember lunch," Bridgett said.

"It's okay." Ellie didn't mind. "I'll focus on it later. Let's keep going with this."

"I can tell you what you did right after lunch," Kurt volunteered before producing a large smile. "You scared the blue outta my jeans."

"What do you mean?" She drew a blank.

"You were supposed to take your qualifications the day after the accident. If you didn't pass the shooting portion, you would lose your pistol, so, I—"

"You drove me to the indoor range to practice." She remembered longing for jeans and a T-shirt. A dress and heels weren't exactly conducive to shooting a pistol. "I hit the target, didn't I?"

Kurt winked at Gage before turning back to face Ellie. "You hit three targets—the edges of yours and all over the ones on both sides of you."

Laughter erupted around the table. Ellie reached across the table and patted Kurt's hand. Remembering stress wasn't good for Ellie, he'd lightened the atmosphere in the room; teasing had turned tension into erupting laughter around the table.

"If you go bowling." Elijah gasped. "You better throw your ball down the lane next to yours."

Gage, who now wore a huge grin, shrugged. "I told you, you're not a marksman." Suddenly, he sobered. "Do you remember what happened next?"

The laughter stopped almost immediately.

Ellie focused. She saw herself walking into the building, with Kurt behind her. Then she'd gone into her office to work on.... Nothing. "Who was with me?" Maybe she just needed another prompt.

It made no sense to her why Bridgett looked at Gage and waited for his nod before she spoke. "You returned alone, and then received a phone call."

"That's all you should say." For the first time, Eric voiced his opinion.

Bridgett frowned. "I wasn't going to say anything else. You know, Eric, why are you acting so authoritatively lately? Last I heard, you were the same–"

Gage spoke up. "Later, you two." Then he looked at Ellie, who suddenly felt ill. "Do you remember who called you?" If Ellie didn't know better, she would think Gage didn't want her to. It had to be her imagination.

She closed her eyes and thought back to that day. Still nothing. After she her return to the office, it was as though the day ceased to exist.

"I can't remember anything past returning to my cluttered desk." The hill she'd been climbing turned to sand. Ellie didn't think she would get through this without screaming.

Ever observant, Jess spoke gently. "Maybe you need a break. You've remembered an awful lot."

"Yeah." Ellie stood and allowed Jessica to guide her from the room. Neither of them spoke as they entered the restroom. Jessica pulled a handful of paper towels from the dispenser and soaked them with cold water.

"Here." Jess handed them to her.

Ellie looked at her reflection as she pressed the paper to her face. Suddenly, the mirror became the windshield of a vehicle. The rails of a bridge were growing close. Too close. She was going to die.

191

"Ellie." Jessica's name came from far away. "Ellie! Snap out of it! Please." Ellie finally managed to process her friend's pleas.

Then she remembered the mirror--window.

"I need to remember the accident."

Jessica immediately took her hand. "You're so pale, please sit down before you fall."

"No." The implications of her memory were too much. "I want to know everything about it." She dropped the paper towels into a trash can. "I need to talk to Gage. Now."

They were just outside the conference room when Eric's angry voice became audible.

"I told you to let it go. Now, Ellie's bound to remember she wasn't alone, Gage. I know you don't want to know about their tryst in that cabin, but facts are facts. And when Ellie remembers, you're going to have to live with the entire truth."

Ellie couldn't fathom what she was hearing. She wasn't alone? A tryst? This was too much. She stepped into the room.

"I don't care what Dr. Marx says. You are going to tell me everything."

Chapter 41

Gage couldn't remember ever in his life being so confused. He had taken Ellie home three days ago and given her the facts. The SUV plummeted over fifty feet off a bridge, flipped completely over, and landed on the rock-covered bank of the river.

The male was found approximately fifteen feet from the vehicle. There wasn't enough skin intact to fingerprint, and his teeth were broken off. The coroner claimed even if they miraculously found the other teeth, they would be impossible to reassemble.

Days later, when Kurt brought the paperwork to the hospital, Gage had even more to be thankful for. While neither she nor the passenger was wearing seatbelts, the airbag held Ellie firm.

The part Gage could barely stand to hear was the words of a middle-aged agent who should have known better. Though a nearby coworker told the man to be quiet, the braggart proudly reported that the road they were on was seldom used, and he quickly determined Ellie and her passenger had been headed back to town from a nearby cabin. Signs indicated the couple had been there and most likely enjoyed a romantic interlude.

The smart agent tried to grab the folder as the arrogant man handed it to Gage, but the photos fell out. Even now, gall rose as he remembered rumpled sheets, and Ellie's necklace—the one Gage watched her put on that morning—was at the base of a pillow. The delicate chain had snapped.

He had been as honest with Ellie as possible, but there were things he would never tell her. Like, when an officer made a crude remark about Ellie, Kurt had to pull Gage off the man. How he tried so hard to cling to the hope that when she regained her memory, she'd explain everything. It hadn't been enough, though. He'd spent the past fifteen months with the knowledge there might be another man in his wife's life.

He wasn't going to burden her with the pain he'd gone through. He would never forget the sight when he rushed into the emergency room. EMTs and nurses were working feverishly over the nearly unrecognizable body of his wife. The polka dots on her dress, once white, were now stained with blood. As soon as the doctor examined her, she'd been rushed straight into surgery. He had no recollection of doing so, but Ryan said Gage called him. Ryan and Annie arrived and joined him in the waiting room. Vivian Wolfe had shown up shortly afterward.

The four of them sat in silence, each with their own thoughts and prayers, for nearly five hours. Just as Gage decided to go check at the nurses' station and demand to hear something—anything—about his wife, the doctor walked in.

Annie cried when the doctor told them that they had lost Mrs. Donahue twice on the operating table, but Ellie was a fighter. She suffered significant damage to her internal organs. Removing her appendix and spleen without re-starting bleeding had been difficult, but the Holy Spirit was with Ellie. After explaining those events, the surgeon turned to Gage and spoke with sincere regret in his voice. He and his staff did their best, but there was damage to her reproductive system, and a partial hysterectomy had been necessary. She would most likely never be able to conceive.

Even now, that seemed insignificant. Ellie would live, and that's what mattered most. For over thirty-six hours, he sat at her bedside, unwilling to leave before she opened her eyes.

Hazy green replaced her sparkling emerald eyes. Then he kissed her and told her he loved her—right before his world shattered. Right before she looked at him and asked who he was. He told himself it had to be the medication, but after three more days she smiled politely and asked if he was one of the doctors on staff. He'd managed to say something noncommittal as he left.

Somehow, he found his way to the hospital chapel, where he dropped to his knees and finally gave in to the pain.

How long he begged God for his wife to come back, or he cried, Gage couldn't say. When Ellie's dad found him, Gage slowly regained control. The doctor wanted to speak to them. Then, Ryan hugged Gage and reassured him no matter what, Ellie loved him. She would realize it soon.

Only the neurologist, who came in with the doctor, told them it most likely wouldn't be soon, if at all. One injury she sustained to

194

her head had damaged an inoperable section of her brain. Whether it would mend or not was in God's hands. In the meantime, they shouldn't tell Ellie what to remember. They should act as though the lost time hadn't occurred. The past four to five years hadn't occurred. They hadn't occurred.

Gage cried again when Annie slipped the rings off Ellie's finger as she slept and handed them to him. When he'd placed those rings on her finger, they were supposed to stay there for a lifetime.

He planned to use the vacation time he and Ellie had been saving for a trip to Hawaii. Since Gage knew Binkley would have denied his request on the spot, he contacted Burnett. The man shocked Gage when he immediately approved the time and told Gage to let him know if he needed more. They would be taking his salary out of a support fund for family emergencies. They may be stuck with a local vacation, but if he had his wife back, he didn't care if they camped in the backyard.

He'd been able to focus on this new Ellie as he romanced her and clung to the hope he would win his wife back. He had to be with her. The thought that she might mourn this other man and settle for Gage made him sick, so he forced it from his mind.

His favorite Bible verses, Matthew 6:26-27, had comforted him for most of his life. Look at the birds in the sky. They don't sow seed or harvest grain or gather crops into barns. Yet your heavenly Father feeds them. Aren't you worth much more than they are? Who among you by worrying can add a single moment to your life?

And all this time, he'd waited for her to explain what had happened in the cabin. Instead, after he gave her the pictures, she distanced herself from Gage.

"Do you have a plan for questioning Cosart?" Sam's voice, coming from the driver's seat, pulled him from his thoughts. "What has you worried so much you didn't speak during this long ride?"

While it was rude to ignore the driver as they made their way from upstate, collecting items from the accident, he would not apologize. As for answering her question, even if it were appropriate, he would never talk about his marriage with Samantha.

"Sorry." He knew she was upset when her lips formed an

upside-down smile. Well, she'd have to get past that, too. The situation between him and his wife was more important than any case.

He vowed not to worry as he focused on Cosart. "We're going to catch him off balance. He had to have been expecting the police to show up any minute." The sheriff and state police had agreed to sit tight and let the FSA handle it. Gage appreciated how the jurisdictions in this area worked together. "Two FSA agents showing up at his place of business on a Friday afternoon should be a surprise."

Samantha glanced over at him. "So, what is our plan of attack?"

"We'll see if he slips up and tells us anything we don't already know." Plain and simple, but hopefully productive.

"I like this guy for a Proctor goon." Sam didn't seem to realize they were accelerating. "I stopped in the store, and he waited on me, himself. He gave me the heebie-jeebies." She suddenly brought them to a near stop. "Do we park in back, or right out here in front for the world to see?"

"Throw him off balance, remember? Let's go in through the front."

Samantha pulled in between two spaces. With only one other car there, Gage decided not to order her to move. "Looks like it's the middle of rush hour." Her voice was pure sarcasm.

The first thing Gage noticed when they entered the building was a large amount of merchandise fit into a relatively small space. There appeared to be merchandise haphazardly stacked or hung on every available surface.

A tall, teenage boy immediately approached them. "I'm Ronnie. What can I do for you today?"

Gage pulled out his badge. "I'm Gage Donahue, Special Investigator for the FSA, and this is my partner, Samantha Hughes. We're here to see Bryan Cosart."

Ronnie seemed impressed; Gage guessed federal officers didn't often show up in the store. "He's back here in his office. I'll show you."

Gage fell into step behind Sam as she followed the young man through the store. They stopped right outside the office.

"We're okay from here," Gage used an "in charge" tone of voice that usually worked.

"I don't know. Maybe I should—"

"Thank you, Ronnie." As Samantha smiled at him, his face reddened, and then he turned away.

"That was cruel, Samantha. One of these days, that game will explode in your face." Gage kept his voice to a murmur.

"It worked, didn't it?"

He let it drop. Sam's actions weren't dangerous, and her lifestyle was between her and the Lord.

Gage followed Sam through an empty office—Crystal Stanley's perhaps—right into the room occupied by Bryan Cosart. The man was bent over his keyboard, and he didn't seem aware of their presence.

Gage cleared his throat.

Bryan's head bobbed up, but he hadn't actually seen them since his gaze flew back to the monitor. "I'm sorry, but this room is restricted to employees only."

This time, Gage stood quietly while Sam spoke. "I think you'll want to talk to us."

As soon as Bryan recognized Sam, an instantaneous look of panic briefly appeared before a mask of despair covered it.

"I'm so glad you're finally investigating this." Bryan stood. "I can't believe this happened to me."

"Exactly what happened to you?" Gage stepped closer to the desk. "I don't know of any crimes being committed against you."

Bryan flushed. "I didn't mean actually to me, but my girlfriend was murdered. And the man responsible worked for me. I'd never thought Mike capable of strangling somebody."

They had purposely held back the cause of death, only calling it a homicide. Yet, this man knew.

"Just to be safe, we need to Mirandize you." Samantha's smile didn't seem to have the calming effect she too often relied on. Instead, Bryan stood and began pacing from one end of his desk to the other.

Not to be dissuaded, Samantha calmly recited the rights. As she finished, she asked if he understood.

"Yes! Are you trying to tell me that I'm a suspect?" Bryan demanded.

"Why would you think that?" Sam calmly responded. "You can ask anybody in this situation, and they'll tell you we do that just to stop any future problems from occurring."

Gage could easily see the other man knew very well he was under suspicion. If he was a member of Proctor, he should have several lawyers at his disposal, so why wasn't he calling them?

"So, how long have the Campbells worked for you?" Samantha seemed unaware of Cosart's disbelief.

"Ever since I opened," he readily replied. "Nine months ago now."

Samantha spoke up. "What did they do for you?"

A flash of fear disappeared as quickly as it had come. "Todd was my head salesperson. He strictly worked the floor."

"And Mike?" Gage asked.

Turning to Gage, Bryan began what looked like washing his hands with no water. "He was maintenance." What Gage assumed was supposed to be embarrassment appeared on his face. "You know, he's kind of slow. It was better for him to work where customers wouldn't encounter him. I couldn't have him scaring them."

Gage spoke again. "In my experience with the man, he's timid and shy."

The corner of Bryan's mouth lifted. "He can't be too timid. He put a rope around my girlfriend's neck and strangled her to death."

Samantha immediately caught the gaffe. "What rope are you talking about, Mr. Cosart? I don't recall any mention of one in the media."

"Well, I just assumed." Bryan grimaced. "Some came up missing right before she was found, so I figured Mike took it to use on her."

"It sounds like a little too much preparation for Mike Campbell," Samantha observed. "I doubt that he's capable of planning ahead like that."

"Then, maybe Todd took it. He had just as many opportunities. He could have even been the one who—" Bryan's voice faltered, and he covered his eyes.

Sam looked at Gage and rolled hers.

As far as Gage was concerned, he was finished watching Cosart's performance. "Speaking of Crystal Stanley, how long had she worked for you?"

Bryan made quite a production out of wiping his eyes, which looked bone dry to Gage. "You'll have to excuse me for being so emotional. You see, I was on the verge of proposing to Crystal."

"I'm sorry." Sam sounded sympathetic, but Gage knew better. "Of course, this is difficult. But you want justice for her murder, don't you?"

"Of course I do." The man sniffled.

Samantha continued. "Well, that's what we want, too. Now, how long did she work for you?"

"I guess about seven months." He produced a weak smile. "I tried to take care of the office work on my own, but as you can see, my business is too brisk for a one-man operation."

Gage decided since Sam was getting Cosart to talk, he would just observe.

"So, exactly what was her job?" Samantha sounded so pleasant, it wouldn't have surprised Gage if flowers and rainbows sprouted from her mouth.

"She was my assistant—my office manager. Crystal was supposed to keep track of sales and inventory, as well as payroll." Bryan smiled sadly, which appeared as genuine as a Michelangelo painting of a clown. "She just made a mess of things most of the time, though."

Sam leaned toward him. "What do you mean?"

"She wasn't qualified for the job. But the moment I saw her, I was captivated." His lips twisted into a ghoulish version of a smile. "I knew it wasn't good business to hire someone simply because I was attracted to her, but surely Agent Donahue can understand." The man's gaze pivoted to Gage. "Doesn't your wife, Ellie, work with you?"

199

News traveled fast in a small town, but how did this reclusive man know about Gage and Ellie? Regardless, merely hearing his wife's name come from Cosart's mouth sickened Gage. "That's an entirely different situation."

"It's just strange." Samantha had also apparently reached her limit because her friendly voice became ice-cold. "Two of your employees were involved in a child abduction case, and a third is dead after finding one of the kidnapped children. You're the only common factor unless perhaps Miss Stanley and the Campbells were somehow working together."

Cosart nearly tripped on his tongue to jump on Sam's suggestion. "I just can't believe it of the woman I love, but—" He was going for a heartbroken appearance again. "Todd was pretty popular with the ladies, and he and Crystal worked together a lot. Since I'm often out of town on business..."

Gage thought of the information Elijah had managed to dig up. It was time to switch gears. "Can you explain how a man with no fewer than thirteen failed businesses is able to accrue an account the size of Alaska in an offshore bank?"

Bryan instantly lost all traces of sadness. He stood straighter. "I don't know where you obtained your information, but it can't be legal. I want you to leave immediately, or I will charge you with harassment."

"We'll go," Samantha said.

It seemed the businessman was determined to have the last word. "I don't want to see you again unless you have a warrant."

Samantha turned to leave, but Gage stood his ground. "Don't worry. We'll also have computer forensics here, going through every gigabyte of your data." Gage didn't even have to try this time: he smiled. "And, in case you didn't know...you can delete to your heart's content, but it's never actually gone."

Bryan finally appeared scared, but he had to bluster one more time. "You want to find data in the store, you come right ahead; I don't have anything to hide."

Once again, Bryan Cosart was lying. Just because Gage rarely used his profiling skills didn't mean they were gone.

Gage followed Samantha as they took their slow, sweet time walking back through the store. He couldn't help but notice the blatantly curious stares from Ronnie and two customers who were in sight. Gossip about their visit to Bryan would be all over town by sundown.

"What are we going to do?" Sam had waited until they were on the way to their building. "Unless pathetic acting is a crime in Illinois, we don't have anything on him."

"I think we have enough to put him under surveillance, though." Gage's instincts were on high alert. "I'd like to hear who he's calling and what's said. Maybe we'll even get some names. Let's talk to Binkley and get this set up."

"Sounds like a plan." Samantha hesitated. "Something's bothering you. It's Ellie, isn't it?"

He ran his hand down his face. "Maybe I shouldn't have told her about the crash. Maybe it would have gone better if she remembered it on her own."

"You had to tell her." Tires hit the wake-up bumps along the highway before Samantha steered back onto the lane. "It would have come back to her anyway—soon. And then, how would she have felt about you keeping it from her?"

"But the man—" He couldn't finish the thought.

"You know what I think. I've told you before, and I'll tell you again." Samantha's eyes left the road and met his for a moment. "No matter what it looks like, your wife would never be with another man. Keep the so-called faith, and when she remembers, everything will be clear.

"Thank you, Sam." Unshed tears caused his voice to be gruff. Gage was quiet as his memories stirred.

He'd never forget the day over four years ago when he met Ellie. Not while he lived.

Gage needed to question a five-year-old boy about his abductor. The child was the first one they recovered from the Proctor organization, and his information was crucial. Spanish was the parents' primary language. Gage's translator was unavailable, and the boy spoke English just fine, so he decided to wing it. The problem

201

was he hadn't been around kids too much, and after a couple of questions, the child became extremely upset. Consequently, so did his parents. It turned into total bedlam.

Gage could still see the dark-haired beauty storm into the room. She spoke to the parents and calmed the boy, just like that. Then she asked if she could have a word with Gage—privately.

He took her to his office and had no more than closed the door when she let him have it. She yelled like a basketball coach. "What are you trying to do? Traumatize the child further?" She smacked her hand on the desk. "Where is your degree in psychology, because you shouldn't have been speaking to that child without one."

"I—"

"How would you like to be a parent in a room, listening to your son being questioned in Latin?" She drew a deep breath. "You, sir, do not have the sense of a drunken grasshopper."

He fell in love with her on the spot.

Unfortunately, she had been a little slower to commit to him. In fact, he asked her out every day for two straight weeks, until she decided she either had to say yes or file a harassment suit. Those had been her exact words when she finally agreed to have dinner with him.

Miraculously, Ellie fell in love with Gage. He proposed to her, and they were married before God and every member of their families six months after they met. Their marriage was strong. Or it had been. No. He wasn't going to think about the mystery man anymore. Ellie would remember, and she would explain. He was going to cling to that with everything he had.

Chapter 42

"There is nothing I can do." Bryan had never been the recipient of his boss's fury, but desperation was at the door.

"I'm telling you, this whole thing is going to blow up in my face. You took care of the last...situation. If you don't figure out how to get me out of this, Donahue and his precious AMAR team will have me. And I won't go down alone." He let the threat linger.

"They'll never link us, and you'll be a fool if you try." The voice on the phone would cut diamonds. "You'd better think of exactly who you're speaking to, and what I can do. Do you really think I'd be so foolish as to not have a plan for this?"

Bryan fought to keep the fear from his voice. "Are you threatening me? Because you would do well to remember I don't take kindly to threats."

Laughter came from the phone. "What are you going to do? Hire some more mentally ill people to do your dirty work? Or allow another uneducated trucker to make a fool of you?" His caller paused. "From what I understand, you're not well known in that town. I doubt if anybody would mourn your demise."

"I have insurance." Panic knocked desperation out cold and walked right in. "If something happens to me, crucial computer data will find its way to the authorities. I kept backup copies of everything you thought was destroyed." He played his top card. "And there's enough there to bury you."

"We both know you're bluffing." There was no doubt Bryan's boss believed it. "As of now, our association is terminated. If I were you, I'd make sure all my doors and windows are locked. I hear life can be dangerous in a small town."

The line went dead.

Bryan dropped the phone onto his desk and buried his face in his hands. What was he going to do? The backup flash drives would take his boss's organization down. But what good would it do him if he were already dead? And he wasn't going to kid himself. He was living on borrowed time.

No. Bryan's boss—former boss—needed to believe Bryan

would follow through. And he'd have to act fast before a "visitor" showed up on his doorstep to finish him off. How could he prove his capabilities without losing his proof?

He thought of what he had, and what he knew. Slowly, an excellent plan began to form. It would work. It had to. "There is nothing I can do." Bryan had never been the recipient of his boss's fury, but desperation was at the door.

"I'm telling you, this whole thing is going to blow up in my face. You took care of the last...situation. If you don't figure out how to get me out of this, Donahue and his precious AMAR team will have me. And I won't go down alone." He let the threat linger.

"They'll never link us, and you'll be a fool if you try." The voice on the phone would cut diamonds. "You'd better think of exactly who you're speaking to, and what I can do. Do you really think I'd be so foolish as to not have a plan for this?"

Bryan fought to keep the fear from his voice. "Are you threatening me? Because you would do well to remember I don't take kindly to threats."

Laughter came from the phone. "What are you going to do? Hire some more mentally ill people to do your dirty work? Or allow another uneducated trucker to make a fool of you?" His caller paused. "From what I understand, you're not well known in that town. I doubt if anybody would mourn your demise."

"I have insurance." Panic knocked desperation out cold and walked right in. "If something happens to me, crucial computer data will find its way to the authorities. I kept backup copies of everything you thought was destroyed." He played his top card. "And there's enough there to bury you."

"We both know you're bluffing." There was no doubt Bryan's boss believed it. "As of now, our association is terminated. If I were you, I'd make sure all my doors and windows are locked. I hear life can be dangerous in a small town."

The line went dead.

Bryan dropped the phone onto his desk and buried his face in his hands. What was he going to do? The backup flash drives would take his boss's organization down. But what good would it do him if he were already dead? And he wasn't going to kid himself. He was living on borrowed time.

No. Bryan's boss—former boss—needed to believe Bryan would follow through. And he'd have to act fast before a "visitor" showed up on his doorstep to finish him off. How could he prove his capabilities without losing his proof?

He thought of what he had, and what he knew. Slowly, an excellent plan began to form. It would work. It had to.

Chapter 43

"And just when you think you can't take even one more step, our Lord shows up and takes it with you." Pastor Rollins' sermon was winding down. Ellie felt her shoulder brush against Gage's. Her eyes filled with tears when she realized it was the first time they had touched each other in nearly a week. She should be listening to the sermon, but her mind was full of pain, thinking about losing her husband.

After an awkward night with her nearly falling out of bed, so he didn't have to touch his cheating wife, she silently started fixing sheets and a pillow on the couch and sleeping there with Fat Ollie. It had been excruciating when Gage didn't even voice an objection.

She automatically looked at the screen behind the altar and began to sing the hymn.

"I go to the garden alone, while the dew is still on the roses—"

With a stifled sob, she got up and blindly rushed out of the church. She barely made it to the car before the pain became unbearable. She doubled over and let the tears come.

"Ellie, don't." Gage's voice broke through her sobs at the same time she felt his hands on her shoulders.

"Don't touch me," she managed to say as she stepped away from him. She was crying harder than ever. "I'm not good. I cheated. You think I cheated."

"Ellie, please listen to me." Gage was once more beside her.

She couldn't answer him; she was crying too hard. Her heart was bound to fall onto the ground at any moment and shatter into little pieces. He didn't even try to deny that's what he believed of her.

"You'd better let me." She heard her cousin's calming voice.

"Luke." Ellie managed to turn and found herself in Luke's arms, held safe and warm. "Luke, take me home with you. Please."

"Ellie, you have to listen to me."

"I think she'd better come with me." Luke's voice rumbled through his chest as he spoke firmly to Gage. "I don't know what's going on, but it's plain to see you're upsetting her."

"I just need to talk to her. We can—"

"You can talk to her when she says she's ready." Luke interrupted him. "Holly, will you drive? I'm going to sit in back with my cousin."

Ellie vaguely noticed a growing crowd of onlookers as Luke effortlessly swept her into his arms. She glimpsed Gage's pale face as her cousin carried her to his car.

"I'm sorry, Holly." She finally managed to speak once they were on their way.

"You have nothing to be sorry for." Holly's compassionate voice sent Ellie back into deeper sobs.

"Ellie, you're going to make yourself sick if you don't stop. Try to get hold of yourself, honey." Luke spoke from beside her. "Holly, do we still have some of those wet wipes they gave us at the fried chicken place?"

"There should be some in the center console." Holly's calm voice came from the driver's seat. "Can you reach it, or do I need to stop and get them?"

"I can reach it."

After some movement and the sound of paper tearing, Ellie felt Luke place a damp paper in her hand.

"Wipe your face off, Ellie," he gently suggested. "It'll calm you down."

She inhaled deeply several times, her chest hitching with each breath. Then she placed the cloth on her forehead.

"Don't get that thing too close to your eyes," Holly warned. "I used one to take off mascara once, and it burned like crazy."

"She made me stop and let her wash her eyes out," Luke supplied. "Then she complained all the way home because of the 'stinky stuff and dirt everywhere' in the restroom."

"Well, you took me to the filthiest place in the state," Holly scolded. "I was too blind to see where we were until I got my eyes rinsed out. By then it was too late."

Ellie felt her lips twitch as a small smile came to them. She loved these two people.

"Yeah, and you should have seen her, Ellie. She almost ran a little old lady over; she was in such a hurry to get out of there. I

207

couldn't even keep up with her." It was apparent Luke enjoyed teasing his wife.

"Believe me, I would have been doing her a favor if I kept her out of that bathroom."

"Maybe you'd better tell me where it is, so I can avoid it." Ellie's voice shook, but the tears were under control.

"It's a little convenience store on the other side of Pattinton. I can't ever remember the name of it." Holly's eyes met Ellie's in the mirror, and she winked. "Only gossipy, old men and your cousin are regulars."

This time, Ellie's smile came easier. By the time they pulled up at the white, two-story farmhouse that used to belong to her grandparents, Ellie felt almost like herself.

She even laughed a little when Clarence the wonder dog—as in she often wondered if he was only a dog—galloped out to greet her.

She looked at his multi-directional hair. "Have you ever thought of getting a shampoo and perm, Clarence?"

Clarence immediately sat down. "Harooo! How, how harooo!"

All three of them burst into laughter.

"Is that a no?" Ellie asked Luke

"Probably." Her cousin reached around her shoulders for a brief hug.

"She's not threatening to give you a bath," Holly told the dog. She looked at Ellie. "I believe he understands every word we say."

Clarence nodded his head in agreement.

"Maybe you and Clarence would enjoy a walk while Luke and I finish fixing lunch. He's trying out some prime rib and garlic potato concoction."

Luke had developed the habit of gourmet cooking while recovering from a gunshot wound. Since he once more worked the farm, he contented himself with preparing their Sunday meals.

Ellie looked at her dress and sandals. "I'm not really dressed for a walk in the woods."

"Come inside, and we'll fix that." Holly and Ellie were about the same size, so a few minutes later Ellie was comfortable in a pair of shorts and a tank top. Holly's sneakers were a little snug, but Ellie wouldn't be walking far enough to get blisters.

"Where are we going?" she asked Clarence as they started down a path.

Clarence answered by crawling under a fence and starting down a trail.

Deciding she would not fit under the wire, Ellie opted for going over it. She soon found herself walking a path she remembered well. It had been her comfort when she needed to get rid of the muck in her mind.

Her parents moved to Atlanta when Ellie was too young to remember, but as she became older, they let her spend a month during summer vacation with Grandma. Ellie had a lot of fun with Luke and Holly, but her favorite times were when it was only Luke and her.

As she grew older, she stopped visiting as often, and soon, not at all. Caught up in her career, she couldn't –no she didn't—find the time. The longer she was away, the easier it became to stay there.

A rustling of an animal brought her attention to the surroundings. Crisp, clean air that just didn't happen in the city and all the colors and types of flora created a breathtaking background.

"Grrrr." Clarence had ventured off to check out the rustling and was currently jumping around a tree and growling. She saw the squirrel nearly up to the top, running around the trunk in circles.

She stood and watched the grand chase until Clarence suddenly turned his back to the tree, lifted his head, and marched over to Ellie. If he weren't worn out from the great chase, maybe he'd have some answers.

"What am I going to do, Clarence?"

Clarence cocked his head as though contemplating his answer.

"I can't keep living like this. I love Gage more than words can say, but he can't even stand to touch me. I guess he put it out of his mind until he had to tell me. But now, all he sees when he looks at me is an unfaithful wife."

"That's not what I see at all." For just an instant, Ellie thought Clarence had answered her, but she recognized the voice. Somehow, she wasn't surprised. He had always been noble.

"It's okay. You don't have to lower yourself to be with me. You can go home." She kept walking.

"You said I see an unfaithful wife when I look at you, but I don't." Gage's words were firm as he put his hands on her shoulders and pulled her to a stop. Just his touch made her want to relax back against him, but she remained rigid.

"You say that now, but you couldn't say it an hour ago."

He gently turned her around to face him. "I'm so sorry, Ellie. I've never been sorrier in my life. I should never have doubted you, and I don't anymore."

"What great epiphany have you had? I still can't tell you why I was with that man, or why my necklace was in that cabin."

Gage's gaze remained steady. "I forgot something, Ellie, but I remember now."

Ellie took a step back, letting his hands slip off her shoulders. "What do you remember?"

"How much we love each other. I forgot you love me, Ellie. You love me enough, even when you didn't remember, your heart did."

She was still unconvinced. "What does that have to do with that man?"

He reached out and gently touched her cheek. "With the love God gave us, you're not going to dishonor our marriage vows any more than I would. I don't know why he was in our SUV, or how your necklace ended up in that cabin, but it wasn't anything illicit. Your father told me from the start, but I didn't get it. I do now." His hand slid around behind her neck. "Just the thought of what hap—supposedly happened destroyed my heart. You own it, you know."

His touch felt so good, she nearly melted against him. Ellie didn't, because she had to know for certain.

"When you look at me, what do you really see?"

His other hand rose to her face. "The woman I love and trust unconditionally. The woman God intends me to spend my life with.

My best friend, my soulmate, my lover, my wife." Ellie saw the truth in his eyes, and for the first time in days, she could breathe.

Without another thought, she took a step toward him, to find herself wrapped tightly in his arms.

"I love you, Ellie. God put me on this earth to love you." Gage spoke with conviction.

"I love you, too." *Thank you, Lord, for helping us remember what is important.*

Chapter 44

You survived your last accident. You may not make it through the next one. You and everyone you care about are in danger.

Fire burned in his chest as   Gage looked at the note again. "Bridgett, did you lift any prints?"

"Only yours and Ellie's."

Gage wanted to hit something. "Is the postmark genuine, Elijah?"

Elijah shook his head. "Doesn't look like it. Somebody went to a lot of trouble to make it appear like this came from Atlanta, though."

"I don't like this." Gage looked around the room, at his team members. "Somebody is threatening my wife, and we're completely in the dark."

Samantha spoke soothingly. "Calm down, Gage. You know she's safe with Kurt there."

"I wish she would have come with me." He and Ellie had "discussed" her decision quite thoroughly. "I don't like the idea of my wife sitting in that insurance office."

Troy stood, his fists closed and shaking, and his chest rapidly expanding with each breath. "That's a threat to Ellie's family, too. I'm going to Atlanta."

"Of course you are," Gage affirmed. "Take the jet, but make sure the pilot brings it back."

"Thanks." Without another word, Troy grabbed the sketch bag always glued to his side and left the building.

"I think this warning is meant for Vivian Wolfe, too. See how he darkened the word, everyone?"

Gage was dialing his phone before Sam was finished speaking. He would arrange protection for all three of them. It only took a minute to get Ross Burnett on the phone. After Gage had explained to his boss what was going on, the man who controlled the center of the country FSA surprised Gage. "I'll get men on all of them. They'll be safe, but in the meantime, you and your wife lay low. That's an order, Donahue."

Too bad Gage was technically still on leave. When he tuned back in to Burnett's words, Gage took a step back. The man who was in charge of the Central United States, with the addition of Georgia and the Carolinas was promising protection through the Atlanta field office. He was also assigning more agents to ensure the safety of Ellie and her family in Shadow. Kurt could only be in one place at a time.

"Thank you, sir." Burnett had never been so quick to assist before.

"I owe your wife." His words surprised Gage. "I heard how she talked you all out of a potential bloodbath. Plus, she ticked off the head of Victory Hills Clinic, who just happens to be my former opponent in college basketball. I was overjoyed when Tom Rogers called and threw a hissy fit about my agent interfering with a prisoner pick-up. What did Ellie do, anyway?"

"The men who came in to get her patient had an attitude she didn't like. She changed it for them."

Burnett chuckled. "I would have liked to see that."

Gage smiled at the memory. "It was a sight when she stood up and informed them they could wait until she and the prisoner finished their hand of Go Fish."

This time, hearty laughter was audible over the phone. "We need more people like your wife in the agency." He sobered. "Let me know if there's any progress in the Proctor case. I'm interested in the Cosart angle."

"Thank you for pulling strings for a warrant." It helped to know the right people. "Elijah will be setting things up later today, and then we'll have ears on Cosart."

"No thanks are necessary, Donahue. Just catch Proctor."

"I plan to."

He switched the cell phone to vibrate and looked up to see Bridgett standing, with the letter in her hand. "I'll check, but I'm sure it's on paper you can buy at any discount store. And I'm positive that it was printed on a modestly priced laser jet printer."

"Then, you can't prove where it came from?" Gage was disappointed.

"I didn't say that," Bridgett protested. "If you find me the printer, I can match it."

"Okay. We'll just start confiscating printers." Gage raised his brows. "Oh, wait. We don't even know which state to start in."

"Hey." A peace-keeping Samantha stood across from the desk as Gage rose. "We realize you're worried about Ellie, but there's no need to take it out on Bridge."

Gage knew that. He was so frustrated--this case would be his last. Although they hadn't discussed it very far, he was sure Ellie would be on board.

"Wait a minute." Jess stood and raised her hands. "We're looking at this all wrong. We need to step back and come at it from a different angle."

Eric leaned against the back of his chair, arms folded. "And what angle would that be?"

Jess ignored him. "What cases was Ellie working on at the time of the accident?"

"Hang on." Elijah began typing on the keyboard. He read from the monitor. "The week before the crash, Ellie was working the Durmont case. She met with Kitty Smith, Opal Lange, Doug Scott, and Perry Hill. And, of course, the Proctor case."

"I know this sounds crazy, but the way this note threatens Ellie with another accident means something. What if the first one wasn't an accident at all?" Jessica spoke to Gage.

"That is crazy," Eric huffed as he stood. "There were no signs of any other vehicle, or anything suspicious. As usual, you're letting your imagination take the lead. It was an accident, Jessica. An accident."

"Engines can be tampered with." Elijah picked up Jess's idea. "The vehicle was too damaged for examining as carefully as we should."

"At least I have an imagination," Jess's glare was focused on Eric.

"A tampered-with engine." Sarcasm eked from Eric's voice. "I suppose a vandal sneaked all the way out to the middle of nowhere and tinkered with Ellie's engine while she and that man were inside getting—"

Gage had to shout to be heard over the instant chorus of angry, raised voices. "That's enough, Eric."

The others quieted as he walked over and stood in front of the older man. "You will not speak of my wife again unless it's with respect." He swallowed, doing his best not to pound the older man into the floor. "I think Jess is right. Somebody not only tampered with the vehicle, they went to a lot of trouble to make it look like my wife was unfaithful." This was the first theory that made sense in the entire mess. "And now the same person has threatened her."

Eric stood, his face inches from Gage's. "And exactly who would want to do that?"

"Proctor." Jess's voice came from across the room.

"Proctor?" Eric threw his hands in the air. "Have you all lost your minds?"

"Enough, Eric," Gage growled.

Bridgett asked. "Why not Proctor? Ellie was working on the case then, and she's involved with it now."

"Proctor's the common denominator." Jessica was excited. "And if Proctor is after her, somehow, Ellie got too close."

"You really think Proctor is threatening her? And her family now, as well?" Eric turned back to Gage and spoke in a more controlled voice. "I think we need to be careful not to develop tunnel vision here, Gage. We all want to solve the Proctor case, but we have to make sure we don't start blaming every crime we see on them."

"It makes sense." Gage was about to say it at least warranted a close examination when Eric reacted.

"If you're not even going to listen to me, I don't know why I'm here anymore." He turned and stomped out of the room before Gage could think of what to say.

"Let him go," Samantha advised Gage. "You both need to cool off."

She was right. Eric's attitude could still be discussed later.

"Are you going to tell Ellie what's going on?" Jessica asked.

215

Gage thought about it. "Not yet. This is still just an idea. But, will you call and give Kurt a heads-up?"

Jess was already dialing the phone.

"I'm going to have to get out in the equipment van if we're going to have ears on Bryan Cosart." Elijah seemed reluctant to change the subject.

"That's okay." Gage would think of— "Wait, Elijah. Run the list of known Proctor abduction sites against locations of the businesses Cosart owned."

"Give me a minute." Elijah began furiously typing.

"You might be onto something." Sam pushed against the much smaller Jessica, evidently determined to see what Elijah found.

"Jess, I need you to help Elijah." Gage usually managed to stay out of his team's arguments, but his partner was blatantly rude. "Come on over here to see what he's doing." He was unsurprised to see Jessica step forward without even a glance at Samantha.

The others stood and gathered behind Elijah as he worked his magic on the computer.

There was excitement in his voice when he spoke. "I've overlaid the maps. The red points are abduction sites, and the blue ones are Cosarts."

Gage's heart pounded so loudly, he had trouble hearing "There are many red points in isolation, but each of the blue ones is within five miles of a red one."

"You know what this means." Bridgett's voice rose. "Cosart could be Proctor."

Gage shook his head as his eyes met his partner's. "I'm certain he's not Proctor. What do you think, Sam?"

"The man is as crooked as the Mississippi river, but I doubt he's capable of masterminding an entire organization. He rattles too quickly."

Gage looked at his partner. "Well, it's time to rattle him some more."

Chapter 45

"Ellie, call the police." Clay Richmond crouched beside Ellie and whispered, even though they were the only people in the office.

"Why?" And why did he appear to be hiding from the window? Hiding behind her?

"There's a man out there—a big, African-American. I've seen him around here all morning, and he walked right up to the door a minute ago. He's probably going to rob us at any moment."

Ellie looked at the man cowering next to her in disbelief. "First, that man is one of my partners in the agency. His name is Kurtis Wright. And secondly, he's not here to rob you; he's here to protect me. You know. Like you're doing right now." She didn't usually condone sarcasm, but he was acting ridiculously.

Clay was just straightening up when the front door opened, and Kurt walked in, poised for danger.

"You okay, Ellie?" His gaze traveled from the now flushed Clay's face to Ellie.

"I'm fine. Mr. Richmond was just a little spooked." She knew Kurt would know why.

He leveled his gaze at Clay. "I see why Gage wouldn't let you work here without some security."

Ellie almost felt sorry for the humiliated man beside her, but the big baby had used her as a shield.

"You can't blame me." Clay managed to muster some indignation as he addressed Kurt. "You were in plain sight. Shouldn't you be hiding or something? So you can catch the perp?"

Kurt's gaze met Ellie's, and she could hear his deep voice, "He's a real piece of work," as clearly as if he'd spoken aloud. Instead, he returned his attention to Clay. "I'm here to keep Ellie safe, not use her as bait. People are supposed to notice me." And with his skills, if Kurt wanted to be invisible, nobody would see him at all.

"I told you, if you insist I stay and train your new assistant, you'll have to accept the situation I'm in," she reminded Clay.

Clay drew himself to his full height. "I would train Dana Gray myself, but I have an important meeting this afternoon."

Ellie steadily met Clay's gaze. "Then you'll have to get used to having Kurt around."

Her boss looked at Kurt and seemed to consider the situation. "I guess it will be okay, as long as he doesn't frighten my customers away."

Did he mean these people continuingly flocking to his door? She bit her tongue.

"If everything is okay here, I'll get back on patrol." Kurt waited for Ellie's response.

She looked at her cowardly boss. "Everything is fine."

Clay waited until Kurt was gone. "I'm sorry for my reaction. My office has been broken into before, and I panicked."

Ellie sighed. "It's okay."

He was obviously uncomfortable. "There's no need for anybody else to learn of this incident then, is there?"

"Of course not."

Clay produced a stiff smile before he returned to his office. Ellie went back to the tedious chore of entering data on the computer.

She was still working on a spreadsheet at one o'clock when Dana Gray walked in. The first thing Ellie noticed was how ordinary the new assistant appeared. With those features, Ellie wondered why Dana tried so hard to downplay them. To avoid attention? There were a myriad of possible reasons, and if Dana chose not to share, Ellie wasn't going to push. With her chin-length, straw-colored hair and nondescript features, she would most likely go unnoticed.

"I'm sorry if I'm late." Dana had a lovely smile. "This is only the second time I've been to the office, and I'm afraid I got lost."

"Oh, that's right. You're new to Shadow." Ellie had forgotten. "What brings you to town?"

"I recently lost my sister, and now I'm all alone. I needed a fresh start, so I closed my eyes and picked a spot on the map."

Ellie smiled. "It must have been a pretty detailed map if Shadow was on it."

"It's such a neat town. I've already heard the legend about the founder of the city and his wife." Dana's demeanor became cheerful. "It's amusing to think that she pushed him under a tree so he wouldn't see his shadow, and he had to keep his promise and settle here."

"Do you realize you're now working for a direct descendant of Virgil Richmond, the man who founded Shadow?"

Dana's smile widened. "Really?"

Within the first hour of working with Dana, Ellie realized two things. The woman, who was a few years younger than Ellie, was sincerely enthusiastic about the job. And the second, more important factor was Dana already knew far more about running an office than Ellie did. The only things Ellie had to show her were the details unique to Clay's business, which took less than thirty minutes.

Dana was busily working on the computer when Clay walked in.

Ellie watched as he greeted his new employee with a casual indifference bordering on rudeness. She felt embarrassed on behalf of the humiliated woman.

"Can I speak with you in your office, please?" She kept her voice as level as she could.

Clay looked surprised. "Of course."

Ellie smiled encouragingly at Dana and followed Clay through the door. She shut it and turned to face him as he took a seat behind the desk.

"I have a couple of things to tell you, so you just sit there and be quiet."

She raised her finger when he started to protest. "You'd better let me speak and get back out front before Kurt shows up again."

Red crept over his face. "Very well."

"After a little more than two hours, that woman already knows more about Richmond Insurance Agency than I do after a year. There is nothing more for me to teach her. Therefore, this is my final day."

"But you—"

"Kurt." He immediately closed his mouth.

"I don't know why the kind man you were becoming vamoosed, but he's evidently moved to Conceit Island. First, you're willing, if not eager, to use me as a human shield. Now, you're behaving horribly toward Dana. Do you realize how rude you just were? You should be bringing her flowers and welcoming her to the office. Instead, you just stuck your nose in the air. Do you think you're Mr. Universe? Because let me tell you—"

"Ellie" Gage's calm voice interrupted her tirade.

She turned from a very red-faced Clay to see her husband standing there, his eyes alight with amusement.

"Just a minute." She wasn't finished. "This is my last day of working here, and I have some things to get off my chest."

Clay cleared his throat. "You're free to leave, Mrs. Donahue."

Gage's mouth twitched with the hint of a smile. "Did you hear him, Ellie? Why don't we go?"

"Because." She whirled back around to face Clay. "You seem to think you're superior to every single person in the county—probably the state. Maybe the world! But listen, Mister, God made every single human, and he loves all of us equally. Every. Single. One. Whether they have money or not. No matter how they look. Do you hear me?"

Gage's hand captured hers. "Ellie, I'm pretty sure the entire downtown just heard you." He tugged her toward the door. "Come on. I came to get you, anyway."

Ellie took a deep breath. "Goodbye." She turned and followed Gage, leaving an open-mouthed Clay Richmond at his desk.

A wide-eyed Dana was sitting at her desk.

Ellie smiled at her. "I guess you heard. I quit."

"Are you sure you want to do that?" Dana's eyes went to Gage for a moment. "This is a good job."

Ellie looked at her husband, who was smiling at her. "I'm sure. I already have a much better offer."

Chapter 46

"Have you heard anything from Atlanta?" Ellie pulled her feet onto the couch and curled against Gage.

He slid his arm around her. "Under instructions from Burnett, Binkley has people on your family around the clock. If anybody so much as sneezes in their direction, I'll hear about it."

It felt good to sit with her like this. Burnett had arranged for Ellie to be reinstated and given her six months to pass her qualifications—with the stipulation she would not carry a gun. Even the big boss could only do so much. She had reclaimed her spot on the AMAR team and spent the week catching up on the past sixteen months. Since Gage was out until all hours combing through the Campbell properties, this was the first evening they'd spent together in days.

"It's weird."

Gage laced his fingers through silk strands. "What is?" She was letting her hair grow.

Ellie looked up at him. "Being an agent again."

He smiled at her. "You've only been back on the job for a week. It won't be long before it comes naturally."

"I guess. Have the bugs turned up anything on Cosart yet?"

"Just the man talks to himself all the time." Gage had listened to an uncharacteristically irate Elijah for nearly an hour this morning. "It's too bad he doesn't have an incriminating soliloquy."

A soft smile lit her eyes. "When I listened to him yesterday, I'm pretty sure he was chewing out one of his employees about Sam."

Gage chuckled. "Sam is making her presence known, isn't she?"

"What's she going to do with all the camping equipment?"

His partner had made it her mission to be an extremely regular customer. "She says as soon as we get the Proctor case wrapped up, she's taking off into the wild blue yonder and living like a hermit for a year."

Ellie wrapped her arms around his neck as she slid onto his lap. "That sounds like a good idea if you'll be a hermit with me."

"Where's the nearest deserted island?" As his lips met hers, he realized they hadn't been able to do this often enough lately. He pushed everything except love for his wife aside and focused on her.

The annoying ring of the cell phone pulled Gage from a deep sleep. Ellie was sleeping peacefully beside him, so he carefully slid out of bed and took the phone into the hall.

"Gage." A very excited Elijah spoke.

The computer expert needed to calm down. "Elijah."

Gage's sarcasm hadn't even phased the jabber box. "I don't know where the call originated, but Mr. Cosart participated in a stimulating conversation. With somebody other than himself."

That sounded promising. "Who did Cosart speak to?"

"No names were used, but it was definitely a man."

"And you couldn't trace it?" Elijah had made certain every piece of gear he needed was set up in the surveillance van.

"Somebody knows what he's doing. I got as far as Waikiki before I lost the call. The lousy thing bounced all over the globe."

"What was said?"

"I think it would be best if you come to the trailer and listen to the recording yourself."

Gage looked through the open bedroom door at the bed, where the spot next to his beautiful wife awaited him. Work. Would there ever come a day when he would be able to forget his job? He resolutely focused on the call. "I'll be there in twenty minutes."

Elijah's response was immediate. "Can you stop and pick up coffee? I should have bullied Jess into covering this shift."

"Anything else? How about a donut or two?" Gage realized he sounded snide.

"Oh." Elijah had evidently heard his boss's grumpiness and drawn a conclusion. "I'm interrupting you, aren't I? I am truly sorry."

"Be quiet." Gage smiled despite himself. "I'll see you soon."

Deciding his customary suit was unnecessary in a surveillance van, Gage quietly walked back into the bedroom and picked up his discarded clothes. He was just pulling his jeans on when Ellie stirred.

She sleepily opened her eyes. "Where do you think you're going? I'm not through with you yet."

He leaned over and kissed her. "I'm sorrier than you can imagine, but Elijah just called. Cosart had a phone call I need to hear."

Ellie sat up. "I want to go. Just give me a minute to get dressed."

Gage started to argue; she'd been so tired. But, then he realized it would be pleasant to have her with him, as well as safer. "Hurry up. We have to stop for coffee."

Elijah made quite a spectacle enjoying it thirty minutes later. "I could drink straight caffeine at this point and still be sleepy."

Gage sat on the chair in front of the recording system and scooted as close to it as possible so Ellie could get past. The vehicle was a little too cozy at the moment.

He turned to Elijah. "Any more calls?"

"No, but listen." Elijah turned a dial.

Bryan Cosart's voice grew and faded as he talked.

"I think he's pacing the floor," Elijah observed.

"This will work. Nobody is going to show up. I've shown what I'll do. I'm safe. I don't have to give up." Cosart's voice faded to unintelligible mumbling.

"He's been giving himself some sort of pep talk ever since the call." And it was evident Elijah had heard more than enough of it.

Gage wondered what had stirred Cosart up. "Let's hear it."

Elijah reached in front of Gage and pressed a button.

Cosart's voice could be heard answering, fear of a call in the middle of the night evident.

"We received your pitiful attempt at a threat," an unfamiliar male voice calmly stated. "You need to remember exactly who you're dealing with, Mr. Cosart."

223

False bravado filled Cosart's voice. "I know exactly who I'm dealing with, and unless you want the FSA to know, you'll help me fix this."

The caller's inflection didn't change as he spoke. "Fix it yourself. You have the means."

Cosart's tone changed. "What do you mean?"

"We know about your private bank accounts, Mr. Cosart. We've always known."

"I can explain that money." Cosart was rattled. "It was left from—"

"It's from the deals you brokered and conducted on the side. Do you really think, after the mess you made, we aren't aware of your every move?"

All courage was gone when Cosart spoke. "What do you want?"

"Take your pilfered money and disappear, or you'll answer for the cash and that other mistake we cleaned up. You know what happens to a person when they cross the boss?"

"I still have proof." It seemed Cosart had mustered one last hoorah. "If anything happens to me, the whole business is over."

Soft laughter came from the speaker. "That is an idle threat. Go ahead and send your supposed proof, and see where it ends up. I guarantee it won't save you."

The line went dead.

Gage was positive of one thing. "This is enough to prove Cosart is working for Proctor."

Elijah frowned. "But what did he mean about where the proof would end up? I don't understand."

Gage turned to ask Ellie. "What do you—?" She was sitting completely still, unblinking, and as white as a sheet. "Ellie?"

He swiveled around and placed his face directly in front of hers. "Ellie?" He fought not to panic when she didn't respond. "Elijah, help me get her out of here. Get her into fresh air."

Somehow, the two men managed to maneuver Ellie to the door. Gage stepped outside, and Elijah handed Ellie to him.

His heart went into double-time when he saw her unmoved expression. "Call nine-one-one." He checked her pulse to find it a little slow, but steady.

"Done, boss." Elijah produced a blanket. "Maybe you need to lay her down."

Gage didn't want her out of his arms, but he knew Elijah was probably right. He gently lowered Ellie to the spread blanket and knelt beside her.

"What else can we do?" The younger man's voice was full of concern.

Gage forced himself to think. She was close to her cousin. If the unthinkable happened, and she didn't remember- "Call Luke Walker and tell him to meet us at the hospital. Ellie needs him."

He could barely hear Elijah on the phone over the sound of his own heart pounding.

The siren's blare beat the ambulance's arrival by seconds. Two EMTs appeared beside Gage.

"Sir, we need you to move, so we can get to her."

Gage looked blindly at the woman speaking to him. "I can't leave my wife."

"Mr. Donahue, you don't remember me, but I'm Barney Nettles." The other EMT was kneeling next to him. "Luke Walker is one of my best friends. I'll take excellent care of his cousin."

"My wife—take care of my wife."

"I will." Barney's voice was nearer. "But you need to move."

Gage felt hands on his shoulders and someone pulling him to his feet. He didn't resist as whoever it was pulled him a few yards back.

He watched as Barney shone a light in Ellie's eyes and said her name, with no response.

Barney looked back over his shoulder at Gage. "She's suffered from head trauma before, hasn't she?"

Gage couldn't seem to speak. Then, from behind him, came Kurt's voice.

"She was injured in an automobile accident sixteen months ago."

225

"We need to get her to the hospital to be checked out." Barney looked at Gage again. "You can ride in the front seat of the ambulance."

"I'll bring him." Kurt's calm voice was right beside Gage now. "We'll be right behind you."

Gage managed to stand and watched helplessly as they loaded Ellie onto a gurney. As they slid her into the ambulance, an image from the past replaced what he was seeing. He started trembling.

"Don't do that to yourself," Kurt ordered. "This isn't the crash. She'll be fine." He put his hand on Gage's shoulder. "Come on."

Gage vaguely wondered where Kurt had come from as they followed the speeding ambulance across town. His thoughts were consumed with his wife, though. He sent a prayer out, asking that she be okay. That he wouldn't lose Ellie.

Chapter 47

"You and Romeo can lie there and watch me."

A cruel voice. Ellie turned her head. Wheat-colored hair was hanging over the eyes of the man lying next to her. His features were rough and unshaven.

"Ellie, sweetheart, please wake up." A new voice, one she loved, was there. "Please, Ellie. Open your eyes."

"I think she's trying to, Gage." She knew that voice, too.

"Luke?" Was that wispy sound her voice?

"Hey, Peanut." Luke's voice was closer.

"Don't--" She tried again. "Don't call me that."

"Well, then, open your eyes," his deep voice instructed her.

Ellie fought the darkness and forced her eyes open. Luke's familiar smile greeted her.

"Hey there, Peanut."

"Hey, Motor Mouth." They hadn't used those nicknames in years.

She looked past her cousin and realized where she was. This was a hospital room. Feeling a tight grip on her hand, she swung her gaze to the man sitting there.

"Gage." He lifted his eyes and looked at her, heartbreak rapidly disappearing from his features.

"You remember me." He leaned over and kissed her hand.

Of course, she remembered him. Why wouldn't--Oh, no. "I remember everything, Gage. You're my husband, and I love you very much. This isn't like the last time."

"I've been praying it wouldn't be." He reached up and pushed the hair off her forehead. "You gave me quite a scare, Ellie."

That, she didn't remember. "What happened?"

She saw him exchange a glance with her cousin before he answered. "You and I were in the surveillance van with Elijah. Do you remember?"

For a moment, she struggled through the fog in her brain. Then she remembered. "The man on the tape—I recognized his voice."

Gage's hand stopped in mid-caress, and he sat straight. "Who is he?"

Ellie once more fought to remember. "All I know is he spoke to me."

"Okay." Gage stood. "Just tell me what you remember."

The man's voice. Those words. The man lying next to her. She started to tell Gage all of it, and then she realized what it seemed like. Tears started pouring before she could stop them.

"What is it, Ellie?" Luke was back beside her. "Maybe we need to let her rest, Gage."

"Tell me what's wrong, Ellie." Gage was pleading. "Please don't shut me out."

"You'll think—I don't know—It seems—."

Her husband's eyes searched hers and obviously knew something was wrong.

"I'm getting ready to head for home." Luke stepped closer to Ellie's bed. "Do you want a ride to your car?

Gage seemed about to say no, but then he placed his hand over hers, "Maybe Luke's right." His lips were warm against her forehead as he kissed her. "We can talk later."

Ellie knew she was a coward, but she closed her eyes and nodded. She had a respite but didn't even think of not telling him everything—eventually. Ice scattered around her backbone. And, once again she dug deep into her retrieved memories, trying to find the truth.

She knew one thing for sure. Even though it didn't make sense, when Gage heard it, he would once more think she cheated. And no matter what she remembered or forgot, she knew deep in her heart she had never been unfaithful to him. It was her last thought as darkness claimed her.

When she next opened her eyes, Jess was sitting in a chair, rapidly writing in a puzzle book.

"Jess?"

Jessica looked up from the book and smiled. "I was beginning to wonder if you were going to sleep the day away."

"What time is it?"

"A little past four o'clock in the afternoon."

Ellie was surprised. "I slept that long?"

Jess grinned. "Well, the doctor might have helped you. He said you needed the rest."

Ellie looked around the room. "Where's Gage?"

"I chased him out of here." She wrinkled her nose. "He needed to shave, and Ellie, the man stunk. I told him to stay home and get some sleep, but I figure he'll be gone two hours, tops.

The horrible memory returned to Ellie. "Jess, you believe I'd never be unfaithful to Gage, don't you?"

Her friend's steady gaze met Ellie's. "I'd stake my life on it."

Ellie felt tears building. "I remembered--what am I going to do?"

Her friend stood and walked to the bed. "Maybe you should start at the beginning."

"I remembered something." Ellie took a deep breath. "I remember a man speaking to me—the very same one who called Cosart. He told me Romeo and I could lie there and watch him." She closed her eyes in misery. "I don't know what he was telling us to watch, but there was a strange man in bed beside me, Jessica. I remember it."

"Oh."

A tear escaped. "See? It sounds like I was unfaithful to Gage, and I know there must be another explanation for what I'm remembering. I could never be with any man except my husband."

"Well, of course, you couldn't." A multiple-colored female version of a Mohawk bounced as Jess jumped up from the chair.

Hope filled Ellie's heart. "What do you mean?"

"There are a couple of reasons." Jessica held up a finger. "First, you have your memory back except for that exact time, don't you?"

Ellie nodded.

"And you called the man beside you a stranger?"

She pictured the man she remembered. It was hard to visualize his features under the whiskers, but Ellie was certain she didn't know who he was. "Yes."

229

"Well, unless you took one look at him and decided his manly figure was worth throwing away four years of marriage, the idea you ran off for a liaison is ridiculous." Jessica held two fingers up. "And from what you remember, it's obvious the man telling you to watch him wasn't the one lying beside you."

Ellie's mind raced. "That's right."

"So, since when do secret lovers sneaking off for the afternoon bring an audience?"

Ellie breathed a deep sigh of relief. "You're right."

"Of course she is." Gage's voice came from the doorway.

Both women turned to look at him. Ellie had to ask. "You heard?"

"Enough to know why you didn't want to tell me." He walked over and leaned down so his face was inches from hers. "I told you, I know you'd never be unfaithful." His lips caught hers and held for a moment.

"Well, since Peppy LePew is back, I'll be on my way." Jessica leaned down to pick up her purse, a saddlebag according to Kurt.

"Wait," Ellie requested. "We need to find out what my memory means."

"Tell me one more time, exactly what you remember." Jessica didn't seem the least bit upset to stay longer.

Ellie described her memory in as precise of detail as she could. "What are you thinking, Jess?"

The other woman held up a hand. "I don't know. Give me a minute, here."

Gage spoke from Ellie's other side. "While she's thinking, I've got some news for you."

Ellie swung her gaze to him. "I hope it's good."

Gage grinned. "Bryan Cosart finally lost his temper."

"What do you mean?"

"Sam was making her daily trip to the store. Cosart saw her looking at sleeping bags, and went off on her. He knew what she was doing, and he was going to sue her for harassment and entrapment. He finally picked up a basketball and threw it at her."

Ellie tried to picture Samantha dodging a ball. "What did Sam do?"

"Single-handedly took the man down and handcuffed him in front of employees and several shoppers." His smile deepened. "Sam hauled him in for assault."

"So, he's in jail right now?"

Gage glanced at Jess before he answered. "Eric and Sam are tag-teaming him. If he doesn't lawyer up, they may get him to crack."

Guilt filled her. "Wouldn't you rather be the one to do the questioning?"

The light in his eyes made her heart stutter. "Nothing is more important than you."

"Okay. I have a theory." Jess was back in action.

Gage and Ellie looked at her expectantly.

"First, we've determined somebody tried to kill Ellie and set it up to look like she was getting her groove on." Jess's gaze went to Ellie. "I don't know why you were there, or who you were with, but for some reason, the second man was there, and he tried to kill both of you."

"But we thought Proctor was involved." Ellie was confused again.

"I'm not saying he isn't." Jessica's eyes lit as she bounced on her toes. "Wait a minute. Just listen."

She appeared to mentally organize her thoughts. "Let's say you're involved in something illegal. You hit your head on the bathroom door one morning and realize you're no smarter than the peacock in that terrible car dealership commercial. This revelation gives you a change of heart. You want out, and you want to shut down the organization. You know it's already under suspicion. Who do you go to for help?" She answered herself. "You'd go to somebody familiar with the crime. You'd go to somebody already trying to stop it."

Ellie saw understanding light Gage's face and envied him. "I'm not following."

"The man you were with was some kind of informant. Something about you made him determined to work with you. The other guy somehow found him and thought he took care of both of you." Jess's eyes widened. "It's still Proctor. I don't know who, but somebody sent the note to warn you. You're still in danger because Proctor thinks you know something incriminating. "

"But I don't remember..."

"Maybe not yet," Jess agreed. "You'll get it back the same way you learned that you're married."

Gage winked at Ellie, who was trying not to blush at the very personal actions after her memory returned.

"Uh--sure." Ellie didn't miss the grin on her husband's face. He was enjoying himself.

"All right, let's get back to the crime and criminals." Jess's smirk announced her knowledge of what Ellie and Gage had shared.

"So, the person warning her is one of Proctor's people." Gage picked up Jess's idea.

Jessica nodded. "Or he may be threatening Proctor. If Proctor somehow finds out this new person is in contact with Ellie, it might give our new friend some leverage to use against his boss."

"But, I don't know anything." There were too many people. A dead informant, if Jess was right, the man who tried to kill Ellie, and now somebody threatening or warning her. And it all came down to something she supposedly knew?

Gage's hand caught hers. "You know what one of the men looks like."

All the good it would do. For some unknown reason, Troy was on guard duty in Atlanta. "I guess I can look at mug shots or try to work on a sketch with somebody besides Troy."

Gage looked at his watch and smiled. "We'll see."

Jessica smiled happily. "I'll take that as my cue to leave. Besides, a big hunk of a man named Kurt promised me Italian cuisine."

As the door closed behind Jess, Ellie could hear what sounded like a bunch of happy people.

She turned to her husband. "Do you think something is wrong?"

"Nope." He barely finished speaking when the door opened.

"Annie!" Her carbon copy, younger sister walked in, with Troy right behind her. But that wasn't all. Aunt Viv and Ellie's dad were there, too.

"What are you all doing here?"

"Troy has been like a lost, little puppy without the team." Annie crossed her arms. "I'm tired of his pity party. We can't have fun with him like this."

Ellie was confused. "Why would you expect to have fun with Troy? He's there to keep you safe, not entertain you."

Troy looked nervously at Gage. "You haven't told her?"

Gage grinned. "I've had to tell her everything else. This is on you."

"Tell me what?"

"Patience, Ellie." Her father stepped forward. "Give them a chance to answer you."

For the first time since Ellie met him, Troy appeared flustered. "I meant to tell you sooner. I really did."

"I should have been the one to tell her. She's my sister." Annie put her hand on his shoulder.

There went Ellie's temper. "If somebody doesn't tell me what you're talking about, I'm going to get Kurt's gun and shoot you all."

Troy winked at Annie. "We're safe, then."

"Troy Alexander Wright." Ellie would have punched him if he were two inches closer.

"We're engaged."

Ellie was stunned. "To each other?"

"Yes." Troy took Annie's hand in his, and sure enough, a diamond sparkled on her finger.

Once more, Ellie felt like she had stepped into another dimension. "When did this happen? Is this another engagement I've forgotten?"

"No." Troy slid his arm around Annie. "It started while you were in the hospital."

Annie smiled lovingly at him. "I was upset about you, and so was he. We discovered our feelings as we comforted each other and—"

"I love your sister."

Annie threw an entreating glance her way. "Please say you're happy for us."

Troy and Annie. "I'm happy. Surprised, but happy."

"If I can get a word in, perhaps Ryan and I can greet our girl?" Vivian gently pushed past Annie.

"Hi, Aunt Viv." Ellie looked past her, at a broad-shouldered, gray-haired man. "Hi, Dad."

Ryan playfully shoved Troy out of his way. "I'm going to have to get surgical privileges in this hospital if you're going to start hanging out in it."

Vivian took Ellie's hand. "Don't let his teasing fool you, honey. We arranged to use the network jet the minute Gage called."

Ellie couldn't have heard her godmother correctly. "You flew?"

A becoming blush appeared on the older woman's face. "Adam piloted, and I was with your father. I knew I'd be safe. Besides, getting to you was more important than a little phobia."

"It wasn't that big of a deal." Ellie felt bad because her family had reacted so strongly. "I just had a reaction to memory."

"Viv's and my engagement?" her father quietly asked her. "Gage told us you remember."

"I'm sorry for acting like a spoiled brat when it came to your marriage announcement." Ellie couldn't have them thinking their news affected her health. "I mean, I remember your engagement now, and it doesn't upset me at all." She smiled at them. "I'm happy for you."

Ellie knew she'd found the right words when a tender look passed between them.

"What did you remember?" Annie was the curious relative now.

Ellie exchanged a look with her husband and remembered her training. "It's an active case, sis. I can't give you any details."

"Well, I hope it helps you catch this person you call Proctor." Vivian stood straighter. "Thanks to him, those FSA agents are trailing my every waking moment. Why, at the courthouse yesterday, I feared one was going to follow me into the ladies' room, and then I almost ran into him when I came out. People probably thought he was peculiar standing outside the ladies' room."

"I'm sorry, Aunt Viv." Ellie didn't like thinking of her godmother being uncomfortable, but her safety was more important.

Viv waved Ellie's apology away. "I guess it's not exactly awful. Only, I didn't know what to say when I met with Crawford, and he questioned me about the strange man hovering around our table. I made something up about trying out a bodyguard, but I doubt believed me."

Ellie was about to respond when a knock on the door announced the arrival of Dr. Tindell.

His eyes swept the room. "It looks like my patient is having a party."

Ellie felt her face heat. "More like a family reunion."

The doctor looked at the others. His voice was pleasant when he spoke. "I need to have a word with Mr. and Mrs. Donahue. The rest of you will find a waiting room at the end of the hall. I'll come fetch you in a few minutes."

Ryan stepped closer to the doctor. "I'm her father, and a heart surgeon out of Atlanta. I'd like to stay and hear what you have to say."

Dr. Tindell smiled politely. "I'm sorry, but I must insist. I assure you, it shouldn't take long."

"Go ahead, Dad." Ellie felt Gage grasp her hand tightly. What had the doctor found?

The door had barely closed behind her family when her husband spoke. "What is it? Did the CT scan show something?"

The physician smiled brightly. "Not at all. It came back clean."

Gage's hand tightened. "Then, what is it?"

Dr. Tindell's eyes met Ellie's. "It's your blood work."

Her blood work? Did she have some sort of disease?

"What's wrong with her blood?"

The doctor turned to Gage. "Nothing. It just indicates your wife is pregnant."

At that moment, Gage looked like a goldfish with his mouth opening and closing. "You mean, she's going to have a baby?"

An amused expression appeared on Dr. Tindell's face. "That is the natural conclusion to a pregnancy."

Ellie was speechless. She couldn't take her eyes off Gage, who was now staring at her.

"You're having a baby. We're having a baby."

"But how?" She finally found her voice. "After the accident, the doctor had to remove—"

"I can assure you that you have enough of the organs necessary for a normal, healthy pregnancy. It's rare, but I've seen other women in your condition conceive."

It was finally sinking it. "Gage, are you happy? Is this okay?"

Her husband's smile would have put the sun to shame. "This is better than okay. You're having my baby."

Before she quite knew what was happening, Ellie found herself cradled in her husband's arms as he turned them in circles.

"It's a miracle, Ellie."

Ellie spoke through her laughter. "I know." It would also be a miracle if she didn't toss her cookies while he was spinning her around. "This is kind of drafty, Gage. My gown has an open back door."

Gage stopped immediately, but he cradled her against his chest more tightly. "Thank you, Dr. Tindell."

"You are most welcome, but this gift isn't from me. It's from our Maker."

And Ellie would thank him for the rest of her life.

"If you'd like, I can give you some time alone before I send your family back." The doctor's understanding eyes sparkled.

Gage's eyes hungrily searched Ellie's face. "Just give us a minute. I don't want my in-laws to worry." The doctor was barely out the door when Ellie was being kissed like she'd never been kissed before. She'd always thought Gage's kisses were full of love, but this—this was off the charts.

She pushed aside all thoughts of criminals and cases. They were going to have a baby.

Chapter 48

Proctor's right-hand man had been in Shadow—still might be there for all Bryan knew. He heard the FSA agent mention him. Of course, she hadn't known who she was speaking of.

How ironic it was, that he was safe in jail. He'd been set to pay bail when it struck him, at least for the time being, he was in a place his boss couldn't touch him.

Proctor. He'd never had the guts to call his boss the name before, unsure of its reception. He still didn't know what the response would be, and if everything worked out, he'd never find out.

Sitting in a jail cell had proved beneficial. With no distractions, Bryan came up with a good plan. He would stay right where he was and play the wrongly suspected businessman. When Proctor's employee left Shadow, he'd pay his bail and disappear. He had access to enough money to start over somewhere else—say, a country with no extradition.

But, before he left, he thought he'd leave a gift for the FSA. Something they'd nearly had once before. He'd leave, knowing he had ended Proctor.

Chapter 49

Keeping his mind on work had never been more challenging. Gage looked at the photocopy in front of him and tried to focus on the adoption certificate. While Elijah and Jess were in his office examining each of the shipping companies on Cosart's list, Gage and Sam were poring over the illegal adoption cases they'd solved, in the hope that something new would appear.

Gage couldn't concentrate now, though. All he could think about was the fact he was going to be a father. When the doctor said the chances were low, Gage shoved the idea of having a child right out the door and locked it. He was thankful she was alive, and it was enough. But now...

It might have been his imagination, but Gage thought there was a special glow about Ellie this morning. She was so happy she hadn't even argued when the doctor instructed her to take a couple of days off to rest. It gave her more time to spend with her family, anyway.

They had no sooner been told about the baby when Ryan and Viv promptly announced they were rescheduling their calendars and extending their stay. They would be there all week. Annie had already planned a two-week visit so the sisters would have some much-needed quality time.

He hated leaving Ellie this morning, but she was happily ensconced on the sofa between her sister and Vivian. They were looking through catalogs full of baby clothes and what Viv called "the good stuff."

He wasn't so sure about it all being good. The contraption Annie was excited about looked like a miniature torture device to him. He wouldn't want to be strapped in a hammock and continuously bounced, even if it did play music.

"You sure look awfully happy." Samantha's voice coming from beside him at the conference table interrupted his thoughts. "Did you discover Proctor's name and address on one of those?"

Since it was so early in the pregnancy, he and Ellie had decided not to share their news with anybody outside the family yet.

He had to think of something fast. "I was just thinking of something Ellie said. Something private."

An audible sigh was her response.

"Samantha, go home by three at the latest, and get some rest."

"But—"

"That's an order."

The middle of her forehead wrinkled. "Fine." Samantha sat up straighter and changed the subject.

"Ellie and Troy are doing their sketch today, right?"

"Yes." But it was against his advice.

"Is she up to that?"

Gage was unhappy Ellie had to give even one moment of her day to the case. "I guess she has to be."

"You surprise me. Shouldn't you be more excited about this? Ellie may very well identify someone very close to Proctor, and I'm sure the baby will keep her happy while we're on the road."

"Wha—do you think I'd ever leave my wife and child to travel for work? Her cheeks were ruddy. "I won't need to worry because—" He looked at the document he'd just turned over. "How closely did we look at the attorneys on these records?"

"What do you mean?" Samantha's brows were lowered. "We dug pretty deep, and there was no evidence of involvement from any of the ones who supposedly signed the papers."

"Not those attorneys." He leafed through a few more pages. "The attorneys who represented the adoptive parents after we recovered a child."

Sam shrugged. "I'm sorry, Gage, but I don't understand where you're going with this."

"We've looked for patterns and connections everywhere else. If those parents all bought their children from Proctor, doesn't it stand to reason Proctor might be linked to their attorneys? He'd want to make sure they got off—that they didn't give him up."

Her confused expression slowly became one of comprehension. "Proctor may have even arranged for their representation."

239

"They'd all be linked to Proctor, and if we find the link—"

"We'll find Proctor." Sam's eyes lit with enthusiasm. "Where do you think we should start?"

Before Gage could answer, his phone rang. Kurt was on the line. "Boss, somebody bailed Cosart out of jail."

"Who?" Maybe it was what had the usually calm man excited.

"Nobody knows. The money just showed up in an envelope with instructions to pay his bail."

"So, he's back on the streets." Samantha would probably be at the sporting goods store within the hour.

"Not because the man wants to be." Kurt gave a rare on-the-job chuckle. "He threw a fit. Claimed he knew his rights. He didn't pay his bail or give anybody else permission to. Sheriff cut him loose anyway."

Something was going on here. "Kurt, do you know where he is now?"

"I followed him straight to his house from the jail. The curtains are closed, and it appears to be locked up tight. It looks like he's hiding, Boss."

"It's exactly what he's doing." Gage had an idea. "If he's hiding from the person who bailed him out of jail, he's probably feeling vulnerable right now. Why don't you have a talk with him?"

Comprehension was in his agent's voice. "You mean offer him safety for information."

"Exactly."

"Will do, Boss."

Gage disconnected the call and summarized the situation to Samantha.

"I hope Kurt lets me know if he goes back to his store." She grinned. "Maybe I can get him to toss a hockey stick my way." Suddenly, she sobered. "But, while we wait to see if Cosart cracks, shouldn't we explore your theory?"

Gage considered their options. "We need to look closely at the lawyers. Maybe they're pen pals or something." The thought was irrational, perhaps even silly, but he believed there was something to find.

Sam frowned. "The Proctor files haven't all been entered into the computer system. Other than the documents the team brought, we don't have anything. That information is in Atlanta."

Was he taking a hunch too far? Gage couldn't explain it, but he felt like they were on to something. "I guess I'm flying to Atlanta."

Chapter 50

"Troy, you shouldn't have." But, as she looked at the tiny, white booties in her hand, Ellie was glad he had.

"I know it's too soon to be buying a bunch of baby gifts, but now you can tell the newest Donahue his very first present came from Uncle Troy."

"Uncle Troy." Ellie laughed. "I'm still getting used to you and Annie being a couple."

Troy's smile disappeared. "Are you okay with it?"

Her answer was sincere. "I couldn't have chosen a better man for my sister."

Relief covered his face. "I really love Annie, you know."

"I believe you." Ellie looked at the clock. "Maybe we'd better get this sketch taken care of while she's napping. I don't need any distractions."

Troy situated his sketch pad and pencil. "I'm ready whenever you are."

Ellie tried to think of the questions she'd ask if she were interviewing a witness. "His face isn't wide or narrow, it's average—with a slightly rounded chin." She pushed aside the unsettling fact his head rested on a pillow next to her as she visualized the man. "I couldn't see it, but I have the impression of a long forehead. And his eyes were completely covered by hair.

She once more pictured the man. "He had a long, narrow nose, and it looked like it had been broken before." Ellie waited while Troy drew. "His mouth was an average width, but his lips were full." And the most prominent feature. "His hair was like straight straw, and it was really long." She tried to think of how to describe it. "Not like he chose to wear it long; it was more as though he hadn't been able to get it cut in a long time. It was the same with his facial hair." She visualized the ragged edges of stubble on his cheeks. "He may have shaved, but I'd guess not for at least a week."

"Beard, mustache, or both?"

"Both, but neither were growing too well."

With Troy gently prompting, and Ellie doing her best, they finally produced a sketch. Troy turned it around. "Is this him?"

"Can you bring the hair farther below his left ear?"

"This?" Troy held the sketch out.

Right down to the hair hanging over his face, the sketch was identical to the man Ellie remembered lying next to. "That's him."

"That's who?" Annie's sleepy voice came from the doorway.

Troy smiled at his fiancée. "Just a man we'd like to identify."

Annie walked over, leaned down and put her arms around his neck. She glanced at the sketch, and then she frowned.

For some reason, Ellie's heart suddenly took off like an oil pump. "What's the matter, Annie?"

Her sister looked up. "I've seen this guy before, Ellie. He was at your house the morning of the accident. With everything happening, I completely forgot."

"Tell me what you remember." Ellie had never been so happy for her sister's gift of a nearly photographic memory.

"I stopped by to return the necklace you loaned me." Annie seemed entirely focused on the recollection "You and Gage had both already left for work, so I let myself in with the key you gave me. When I opened the door to leave, this guy was just standing there." She raised worried eyes to her sister. "He scared the laces out of my shoes."

"What did he do? Did he say anything?" Ellie prayed her sister's memory didn't fail. It rarely had before, but the way this entire case was going, nothing would surprise Ellie.

"He said he needed to talk to me." Annie frowned at the memory. "I was just about to shut the door in the creep's face and lock myself in until he went away when he looked at me in a strange way. He said something like, 'it's not you' and turned around and left."

Troy spoke up. "Was a storm door between you and him?"

"Yes, thank goodness."

"Then, he thought you were your sister." He turned his eyes toward Ellie. "When he got a close enough look to see she wasn't, he left."

It made sense, but Ellie needed to know more. "Did he give you his name?"

Annie closed her eyes as she thought. They were lit when she looked at her sister. "He didn't, but he was wearing an old uniform shirt. I could see the stitching from where a name patch had been."

Please remember, she silently begged her sister. "What did it say?"

"It had a truck on it, and you know how I automatically use word association to help me remember names—the word cake comes to mind."

Troy looked puzzled. "So, a guy named Cake wanted to see Ellie?"

Despite the seriousness of the situation, the sisters shared a smile before Annie explained. "No. I associate other words with names so I can remember them. It's not very professional for a teacher to forget what to call parents."

"Cake," Ellie prompted her sister.

Annie frowned in concentration. "Crocker doesn't seem right. She scrunched her nose. "And I'm positive it wasn't LuLu." Suddenly, a triumphant smile appeared on her face. "Duncan. His last name was Duncan."

Unless the guy was her thirteen-year-old paper boy, Ellie couldn't picture anybody named Duncan. Still, "What about his first name?"

"I'm trying to visualize." Annie finally shook her head. "It was just an initial, and I'm not sure, but I think it might have been a T or J."

It wasn't much, but it was something. "Thank you, Annie."

"Is he a criminal? Was I close to a murderer or something?" Ellie saw the strength of her seemingly unphased sister.

Troy answered his fiancee. "It's FSA business, but let's go for a walk, and I'll tell you what I can."

A subtle tip of his head and Ellie knew he was giving her privacy. She needed to process what Annie had just told them and figure out her next move.

Within two breaths, she realized she would need help. Usually, she would call Gage, and he would take care of it, but he and Sam should be in Atlanta about now. They had found something in the Proctor case needing closer investigation, and taken the jet. It would be late before Gage returned, so Ellie needed to decide.

She finally dialed Elijah. He immediately agreed to prepare a list of every T and J Duncan licensed to drive semis, no questions asked. He'd have the information ready for her by eight in the morning.

After she had hung up, doubts assailed her. Was she about to discover the identity of the man who died in her accident? What else might she learn about him? And did she want to know?

Chapter 51

"Lincoln Ames." Gage waited while Sam typed the attorney's name into the computer. "He's the last one."

Samantha began pulling up basic information on each of twelve attorneys. The musty air swirled around Gage as he moved his chair nearer the monitor.

"Wilma Majors and Edward Black graduated from law school together," Sam observed. She scrolled farther. "But I don't see anybody else who went to that school."

"Wouldn't it be nice if Proctor was a law professor with all these attorneys his students?" Gage was trying to maintain a positive outlook.

They silently read details on each attorney but could find no link.

It appeared the people didn't have anything in common. "What about locations? Some of them aren't in the same city as the adoptive parents. Black handled a case in a town over fifty miles from his practice."

Sam appeared skeptical. "Most of these are pretty large cities. It'll be difficult to find even one thing tying them together." She pulled up a split screen on the monitor and began typing the locations anyway. "They're not alphabetical," she observed. "And the first letters of their names don't spell anything."

Now, that would have been wonderful. The cities could provide Proctor's name. "Let's see what the addresses look like on a map." They had never determined a pattern to the Proctor kidnapping sites, but maybe the representing attorneys were in some sort of order.

After a few minutes of Samantha typing, a map of the country appeared on the monitor. Twelve spots were indicated with bright red dots—each in a separate state. Something niggled at Gage's mind. "Can you highlight the states?"

"Why?" Her expression made it clear that she looked at this as wasting time.

He didn't know. "Something about it seems familiar, but I don't know why. Please highlight the states."

Samantha silently entered another command.

Gage looked at the map now displayed on the screen, with twelve red states against the blue country. Why did it seem like he should recognize it? "Just the highlighted states."

This time, she didn't question him. In moments, a red figure filled the screen. It looked familiar, but not quite right. Where had he seen— "Find the logo for the United Legal Assistance Network."

"I don't underst—" Sam stopped in mid-sentence as an image appeared. Other than three additional states, it was identical to the one they'd just been looking at. The logo displayed the fifteen states represented in the network.

"It's on the wall in Viv's office." The implications were stunning. "Go to their website and pull up the list of participating attorneys."

Wordlessly, Samantha followed his instructions.

Gage picked up the printed list of attorneys they'd been working on and compared it to the one on the screen. His heart picked up speed as he found what he was looking for. "How did we miss this?"

Sam turned and looked at him. "They're all part of the network, aren't they?"

"How did we miss this?" he repeated.

"Once we return the child, and all the suspects are in custody, our job is finished," Samantha did not like making mistakes. "We had no reason to pay attention to who represented them in court."

As the realization of what he was looking at sank in, a piece of sizzling stone sat in his stomach. Proctor had gotten to these lawyers and was using what was intended to be a benevolent organization to kidnap and sell children. "Proctor is using Vivian Wolfe's good intentions for evil purposes."

Samantha's eyes were perfect circles. "Listen to yourself, Gage. You're not thinking logically."

What was she saying? Vivian had set up the network to— "No. It's impossible." He refused to even entertain the notion.

"You said it yourself, Gage." Sam's face was fiery red. "She set it up. She supervises it."

"No, Sam. I just don't believe it."

Samantha softened her tone of voice. "Vivian Wolfe is known for representing the underdog. Who could be more of an underdog than parents who want a child and can't have one? I don't think money is her motivation. I think, in her mind, she's removing children from less than ideal situations and giving them to people who would make better parents."

Everything in Gage wanted to deny the possibility Sam was right, but he couldn't. "If Viv is working for Proctor, it's going to kill Ellie."

"I don't think she works for Proctor." Sam's gaze was steady. "Gage, she is Proctor."

Chapter 52

Bryan was determined to ignore the FSA agent pounding on his front door. The man had knocked and rang the doorbell every half-hour on the dot for the past three-and-a-half hours. Something told Bryan it would continue all night if he didn't answer.

The persistent agent was putting a kink in Bryan's plans. With packed suitcases in the trunk of his car, he was ready to leave. He gave a moment's thought to driving out of the garage and continuing. It would be senseless, though. The agent would simply follow him.

The police told him his bail came from an anonymous source, but he knew exactly where it came from. Proctor couldn't get to him while he was behind bars—at least not without people knowing—so he had been freed.

Now, he needed to somehow elude the FSA and get past any of Proctor's people who were most likely in town. And he needed to do it soon.

The sound of an engine drew his attention to the window. He held the blinds just far enough apart to see the dark truck pull away from the curb.

His heart sped. This was his chance for escape. He hurriedly grabbed his keys and rushed through the kitchen door, into the garage. Glad he'd thought to back in, he slid into his car and started it. Relief spread throughout him as he realized his plan would work.

The automatic door had never taken this long to open. Bryan looked in the passenger seat to make sure his new identification papers were there. When he looked up, his breath caught in his throat.

There, in the beams of his headlights, stood one of the FSA agents, waving and smiling brightly.

Different scenarios flashed through Bryan's mind. Put the car in drive and gun the engine; the intruder would jump out of the way. Hit the remote and close the door, as though he'd seen nobody. Or slam his own head against the steering wheel until he knocked himself out.

He finally exhaled deeply and turned off the ignition. The pleasant expression on the agent's face didn't change as Bryan got out of the car and walked around to stand in front of it.

"Hey, Mr. Cosart. I hope I'm not catching you at a bad time." The agent's demeanor didn't change.

Bryan's voice was flat. "What do you want?"

"Just to talk for a few minutes. That's all."

This was just great. "What about?"

His visitor smiled sympathetically. "You seem to have gotten yourself into a pickle. I may be able to help."

Right. "Like you helped me before?"

"Oh." The agent's smile would melt butter. "Things are different now."

Bryan looked through the open garage door. "Where'd your partner go? The big guy who kept knocking on my door?"

"Agent Wright was called away on an urgent matter." The agent took a few steps toward Bryan. "Wouldn't it be better for us to talk inside?"

Was there even a choice? He watched the agent hit the button that closed the door as he walked into the garage.

Bryan led the way past his car, hoping the manila envelope lying in plain sight wouldn't attract the agent's attention. That's all he'd need—a member of the AMAR team finding his new identification papers.

It wasn't until they were in the kitchen Bryan wondered something. "Where is your vehicle? I didn't see you when your partner arrived."

His answer was the sound of a deadbolt latching. The agent turned deliberately to face Bryan.

It took a moment for Bryan to process what he was seeing.

"Hey, I'm not armed." He held his hands in the air. "There's no need to aim a gun at me."

The agent smiled again, and for the first time, Bryan got a good look at the other person's eyes. They were empty, entirely void of emotion. "What is this about?"

A gesture of the pistol accompanied the response. "You would know better than I."

"Listen, why don't we go down to the police station and talk this over?" Suddenly, the police—even prison seemed preferable to facing the emotionless person in front of him.

A brow curiously rose on the agent's face. "Why would I take you there, when I paid money to get you out?"

"You—" Bryan finally realized this was a battle he wouldn't win. "You're not with the FSA."

A droll smile was the response. "Oh, but I am. The agency doesn't appreciate good agents, nor do they pay us enough." The gun swung toward the living room. "Let's take a little tour of your house. I'm a bit of an architecture addict."

No. This couldn't be the way he—no. Newly resolved, he stood taller. "I know Proctor is paying you to do this. I have money. I'll give it to you. I'll give it all to you just to walk away."

The agent finally showed emotion—sadness. "It's too late to walk away. It's been too late for years." The strange looking pistol was tilted toward the floor.

Bryan felt ice-cold terror throughout his body. What had his mother always said? God, if you're real, can you—. What was he doing? He'd never be forgiven for all the lives he helped ruin. God wouldn't listen to a man with such an evil past. It was too late, but he still felt like he needed to say something. I'm sorry. He wasn't even sure there was anybody to hear his words.

Chapter 53

"Does the network handle many adoptions, Viv?"

Ellie wondered why her husband had brought up something not exactly dinner table conversation.

Vivian didn't seem to mind, as she swallowed a bite of cake. "I suppose we handle a fair number. Why?" She smiled warmly at Ellie. "You two don't need to consider adoption anymore, do you?"

Gage shrugged. "We may decide to later."

They may? This was the first Ellie had heard of it. They'd never actually discussed children at all, let alone adoption.

"So, if we were to adopt, how would we go about it?" Gage appeared to be on a quest.

Ryan chuckled. "Ah, getting free legal advice, are we, Gage?"

Gage's smile didn't reach his eyes. Something was going on here.

"I'm just curious." He directed his attention back to Viv. "Could you just walk us through the process?"

"Gage, she's eating." And, Ellie was two seconds away from pouring her glass of water over his head.

"I don't mind," Vivian shared a warm smile with Ryan before turning back to Gage. "It depends on the kind of adoption you want."

"It seems to me, the important part of the process would be making certain the child was in a good home. What do you think, Viv?"

"This is your relative speaking and not as a legal expert." She didn't seem to even notice his barrage of questions.

"So, an adoption agency? Private adoption?"

Viv didn't like the idea of adoptions costing money. Gage knew that as well as Ellie did. What was going on with him?

"No. I would recommend adopting a child from the foster care program. Our organization mainly promotes adoption of those placed through the Children Services program."

Gage hadn't taken his eyes off her. "Why's that?"

Sadness tinged Viv's eyes. "Many of them have come from unbelievably nightmarish living situations. They deserve to know the stable environment and happiness good parents can give them."

"Tell them about your Benefit," Ryan placed his hand over hers.

Viv looked up through incredibly long lashes. "It's not a big deal."

"Nonsense." If she weren't going to tell them, apparently her fiancé would. "Vivian is hosting a networking banquet in a few weeks, with all the proceeds going to child services."

"It was Adam's idea," Viv protested.

"Adam Spencer?" Ellie tried to steer the conversation away from her husband's obsession. "He's the attorney you hired, isn't he?"

"I hired him nearly a year ago, but I've known his family for years." And it was apparent she liked them. "Adam is a bright, young man, and mark my words—someday I'll be saying I knew him when." Her smile dimmed. "It's a shame he was only able to stay overnight. I would have liked you to meet."

Determined to keep the conversation from returning to adoption, Ellie sat straighter. "That's right. You said he flew you here." Ellie had forgotten. "So, he has a pilot's license."

"I'm sure we'll meet him later," Gage interjected. "But back to adoption—since we'll reside in Illinois, you'd have to refer us to an associate, wouldn't you?"

If Viv was bothered by Gage's fixation on her work, it didn't show. " Charles Crawford, the first to come on board for the network, put so much money into the project, I was happy to sign him as a co-manager. He'd take good care of you." For the first time, she seemed concerned by his questions. "Are you determined to do this? Because adoption is a significant step, and frankly, I'm worried about the stress it would put on Ellie while she's pregnant."

Ellie noticed Gage was working hard to avoid direct eye contact with her. "No. Not right now. I'm just thinking ahead."

Gage's strange curiosity puzzled Ellie, and she didn't protest when the conversation returned to Viv's Benefit.

253

She waited until they were behind their closed bedroom door before she questioned her husband.

"Why haven't you told me you want to adopt? Hearing the news with my father and Aunt Viv was awkward."

A ruddy color swept up his cheeks. "I don't want to adopt. At least, not now."

"Then, why all the questions?"

Gage led her to the bed. "Sit down. I have to tell you something."

She sat on the edge of the bed. "I'll listen to you, but first, can I share my findings from the sketch?"

He frowned. "At dinner, you said it was unrecognizable—it was useless for identification."

"I lied."

"Why would you do that?"

"I didn't want to be peppered with questions I couldn't answer." Her news would surely cheer him up. "Annie recognized him as a man who came to the house, looking for me the morning of the crash. She remembers a name on his shirt—T or J Duncan, and there was a truck on the patch, so he was probably a truck driver. If we find out who he is, we might find out who tried to kill me. We might find Proctor."

Gage sat silently, seeming to contemplate her words. "Do you recognize the name?"

She had tried very hard to. "No. But since you were in Atlanta, I asked Elijah to prepare a list of licensed truck drivers with it." Had she acted rashly? "I hope that's okay."

"Of course it is." A worried expression came to his face. "But I don't think you should set too much stock in it. Annie may not be remembering correctly, or he may have been wearing somebody else's shirt. We don't even know for certain the guy is linked to Proctor. There are a lot of variables to consider."

Her husband had a point, but his lack of enthusiasm disappointed her. "Okay."

His frown deepened.

"What's wrong, Gage?" Surely, he wasn't having doubts about her and this stranger again, was he?

"Ellie." Gage knelt in front of her. "I have to tell you something, and I need you to listen."

She was filled with trepidation. "Okay."

"Sam and I noticed something about the attorneys who represented the adoptive parents after we recovered children from the Proctor network."

The breath caught in Ellie's throat.

"You have to know—each one of the lawyers is a member of the United Legal—

Suddenly, Ellie knew what he was going to say. "No, Gage. I don't care what you and Sam think you've found. Vivian is not involved with Proctor. We need to look for this Duncan man."

Gage leaned closer to her. "You're looking at too many maybes with the Duncan theory when we need to look at facts, Ellie. Not only might Viv work for Proctor; she might be Proctor."

All rational thought flew out the window. "You and your partner may have decided that, but neither of you knows Aunt Viv like I do. Vivian Wolfe helps people. She would never hurt them."

Gage spoke calmly, but firmly. "She may not see it as hurting people. She's removing a child from a lower-class home and placing him into a stable environment."

"Don't!" Ellie stood so abruptly she nearly knocked him over, and brushed past. Fury emanated from her as she whirled on him. "Don't you dare take her words and use them against her like that."

She took a step back as he stepped toward her.

"Ellie, think about the facts."

"No." She put her hands up to keep him away. "You can just go confer with Samantha again if you want someone to agree with you."

She stepped out of reach as he tried once more to touch her. "Ellie, I'm sorry. I didn't want to have to tell you. The last thing we need is for you to be upset. It can't be good for the baby."

"The baby?" Ellie fought to keep her voice down. "Why, Aunt Viv is probably upstairs in the guest room plotting how to steal our baby and sell him." She was hanging on to her temper by a hair on her head. "If you think she's Proctor, you're saying she tried to kill me." At the thought of that accusation, rage filled her. "Vivian Wolfe, the woman who has been like a mother to me, loves me and would never harm a hair on my head."

Gage spoke soothingly. "Okay. Calm down." She backed out of his reach again. "We'll talk more in the morning after we've both had a good night's sleep."

The tears in her eyes aggravated Ellie even more. "I'll have a good night's sleep in the bed. You can try for one on the couch."

Gage's voice was firmer. "This is childish. You're not thinking rationally."

"I don't care. Get out of here, or I will. I have a meeting with Elijah in the morning—to see what he found out about the man Annie remembers. Of course, you'll probably call and order Elijah to ignore my foolish theory, since you and your partner have already figured everything out."

"Ellie, listen to yourself." He stood firmly in front of her. "I don't understand these innuendos about my partner. You know that's not possible. Never would Samantha and I have any kind of relationship other than working together. You have to realize how unreasonable you're being."

"Fine." She swiveled around and stomped to the linen closet, where she grabbed the first sheet she saw.

"Wait, Ellie." One long step put him between her and the door. "I'm sorry. You're right. We need to check the name Annie gave you before we jump to any conclusions."

Ellie snorted. "Don't you patronize me. It's apparent you've already jumped." She reached over and grabbed her pillow off the bed before rushing out of the room.

An hour later, she was lying on the couch, still unable to stop crying. Had she acted childishly? Probably. But just because Gage and Samantha reached a conclusion didn't make it the right one.

She rolled over and plumped her pillow, nearly knocking Fat Ollie from his perch on the armrest.

Ellie wasn't going to blindly accuse her mother's best friend—her father's fiancée. She was going to find out more about T or J Duncan. He was a good lead. A strange man—probably Proctor's man—had killed him and tried to kill her. It was hard telling what information they would discover when they investigated further.

Ellie closed her eyes, determined to go to sleep.

Chapter 54

Gage walked sock-footed across the living room, hesitating behind the couch. He should have slept there. A husband should always be able to tell when his wife wasn't going to calm down and come back to bed. Should he wake her now? She would be furious if he didn't.

He just couldn't bring himself to rouse her from sleep to tell her a neighbor had just found Bryan Cosart's body.

A few minutes earlier, Gage answered the phone to hear Mitch Landon inform him the body was Cosart. Since the dead man was part of an ongoing agency investigation, AMAR would take the lead on the case. Calling Samantha might not be the best idea, but she seemed more rested than the others.

He glanced at his watch; four-fifty-five. Ellie wouldn't be planning to meet Elijah for at least three hours. He'd let her sleep.

He detoured to the kitchen and left a note for her to find. He was undoubtedly making a huge mistake in leaving her behind, but it certainly wouldn't be the first.

It took a few minutes to swing through a drive-through to pick up a cup of coffee—strong and black. Caffeine roused him, and during the drive, thoughts of the woman who owned his heart took over. Even though Ellie had been unreasonable the night before, his wife was partially right. He had been too quick to agree with Sam and not given Ellie's theory equal credence.

His having a female partner had never caused any friction in his marriage, but this was the first time his wife and partner totally disagreed. Seeing marriages fall apart because of opposite gender partners, he had always been careful. He never wanted to place Ellie into a situation in which it seemed he was choosing Samantha over her. Dear Lord, is that what I've done?

He heard his wife's pain-filled voice referring to Samantha in such a critical manner...that's exactly how she perceived this. It made sense.

A groan began in his gut and crept up to his lungs before he set it free. He had just compounded the problem by leaving Ellie at home and meeting Sam at Cosart's house. It was too late now, though. He couldn't take the time to go back for his wife. He could only pray he'd be able to fix it later.

Several squad cars were in front of the house and in the driveway when he pulled up and parked. Kurt must have given up and called it a night.

He shut his door and walked up the drive, where Samantha stood. "You look like Ellie made you sleep on the floor."

Gage wasn't in the mood for teasing. "Not today, Sam," He shouldn't have snapped at her. "I'm sorry. You're right about a rough night."

Samantha placed her hands on her chest. "Is everything okay? Is it Ellie?"

He was not sharing his marital issues with Samantha.

"I've been thinking, and we need to step back from Vivian Wolfe a little—to get the big picture."

"We are looking at the big picture." A look of comprehension filled her eyes and was quickly replaced by antagonism. "Let me guess. Ellie is mad at you because we suspect her godmother. So, you're going to tiptoe around and blow the best chance we've had to crack this case, just to keep your wife happy."

Gage stopped in his tracks. "I let you act as my partner, but that can change anytime."

"Nobody else—"

"Any one of the team members can step into your position." Dark pink crept up Samantha's face.

"I'm sorry." She blinked several times, but one tear escaped. "I know everyone is exhausted, but..." She drew a deep breath. "My step-mother called a couple of hours ago. My grandfather passed away.

"I'm sorry, Samantha." Not for his attitude, but her loss. "Do you need some time off?"

Her red hair was a cloud around her head. "Thank you, but my family—I'm not going."

He knew about family issues. "Okay, but if you change your mind, let me know."

A nervous smile appeared on her face. "Thank you." Her gaze hit the ground before rising and meeting his. "I didn't mean to say anything against Ellie. We may not be best friends, but you must know I care about her."

He had to give her that. Gage had no memory of it; he'd been focused on his wife, but soon after, an unhappy Jess had mentioned there was something "squirrelly" about the way Samantha sat in the mud and, loudly sobbing, stared at the wrecked vehicle below her. No time for memories; he still had something to tell Samantha.

"I know, but you need to understand something." He should have done this a long time ago. "My wife is a gift from God, and other than the Lord, nobody or nothing will ever come before her with me. Not this crew, not this job...nothing, Samantha."

"I don't know what else to say other than giving her a heartfelt apology." Wiping the tears, she stood taller "I'm so tired."

Gage shook his head to clear it. "As you said, we are all tired. I'm finished talking about this."

Mitch emerged from the front door of the house and headed for Gage.

"Sorry to get you out of bed for something this unpleasant."

Gage appreciated the sentiment. "What's the story?"

"I'll let you see for yourself." Mitch gestured toward the door. "Nothing has been moved."

Gage saw a huge yawn on one of Mitch's deputies and almost pointed it out to Sam. He turned back to face his partner. "Unless the sheriff has a problem, Jeff can walk with you to any neighbors who haven't been spoken to."

"They're probably all in bed," Jeff ended his statement with his mouth hanging so widely open, his neck appeared to disappear.

"Especially in a small town, a gunshot and police activity will rouse neighbors," Gage said.

Mitch put his hands on his waistline. "Jeff, take this agent around, and seein' as how enthused you are, stay back and let her talk."

A small breeze rearranged Sam's bird nest of a hairdo. What was with that, anyway? She was very self-conscious and would normally have it under a bandanna rather than let people see her like this. He started to ask but quickly realized his question wasn't work-related.

Sam walked over to the deputy. "I think that's a good idea. Yawning every two seconds won't induce them to speak."

"Like that mess of red hair is going to look professional? I am at least wearing my uniform."

As soon as Gage saw the faint flush creeping up Samantha's neck, he spoke sternly. "You are both professionals, and you will act like it, Samantha, or enjoy some unpaid leave."

Mitch nodded at his deputy. "I'd threaten you with the same thing, but since you don't seem able to control those yawns, you'd probably be happy about it."

"I'm sorry, Agent Hughes." Jeff seemed sincere.

"I understand." Samantha held her hand out to shake Jeff's.

"Come on in, Gage."

Seeing the new friends head to the front door of a house, Gage followed the sheriff. The moment he stepped into the foyer, he was struck by how clean the small room was. "Is the entire house this organized?"

"Yep." Mitch gestured, and Gage followed him into a dining room. Mitch pointed to a cabinet full of dishes. "You'd never have guessed it from seeing his mess of a store, but the house looks like it belongs to a person with some kind of obsessive personality."

Cups in the glass case had their handles lined up at precisely the same angle. Gage paused at the bookshelf long enough to observe the books were in alphabetical order, by the author.

Mitch turned to Gage. "His clothes are hung in his closet neater than you'd see them in a store. He has all the pants on hangers in one closet, none exactly alike, and then they're organized by color."

Hardy entered the living room from another door, apparently having heard his boss. "The shirts are crazy organized. It took me a minute to figure it out, but Cosart has the colors together in Roy G Biv."

Mitch looked at his deputy like he'd jumped out of a tree,

yodeling. "Who?"

Hardy grinned. "Roy G Biv. They're colors. Haley had her Sunday school class use it on a rainbow picture. She told me what it means. Red, orange, yellow, green, blue, indigo, and violet. It has something to do with the spectrum."

Mitch's brows went up as he looked at Gage. "And this is the man who piled baseball cleats on top of tackle boxes."

Gage looked around. "Where is he?"

Mitch gestured toward a door. "In the study."

Gage had taken a couple of steps before he realized the sheriff and deputy were standing and watching. "You guys coming?"

"We'll just let you go in and look. We'll see what you think." Mitch turned and led Hardy across the room. Well, okay, then.

Gage walked through the door. Taking center stage was Bryan Cosart, slumped to the side in a chair behind the desk. A quick scan showed Gage this room was different from the rest of the house. It was a mess.

He walked over to the body and looked closer. A bullet's exit wound had virtually destroyed the cap of his skull.

A pistol lay on the floor under Cosart's right arm as it hung lifelessly. Gage knelt to see what appeared to be a forty or forty-five caliber, a powerful gun.

As he began standing, the computer screen caught his eye. He was shocked to see a note to himself.

Agent Donahue, I cannot go to prison. I know what happens to men like me there. I know it's too late to atone for all I've done, but at least, I can tell you where the Jones girl is. She's in Flexton, Tennessee. Her name is Betsy Stewart now. - B.C.

Gage looked around the room more carefully. It had been organized, just like the rest of the house but was now trashed.

Why would Cosart have thrown books off shelves and left papers strewn across the floor? Each drawer of a large filing cabinet was open, and it was apparent its contents were a mess.

"You were looking for something." But it didn't make sense. A man who kept his home obsessively organized would have no reason to hunt for anything. "Somebody was looking for something." He amended his statement.

He raised his voice. "Sheriff?"

Heavy footsteps tapped on the hardwood floor as the big man walked into the room.

Gage turned to him. "When Cosart's hand is checked for gunshot residue, have the coroner look for signs of another object overlapping it."

"Think he shot himself?"

Gage looked at the computer screen again. "Maybe, but I have a feeling he had help."

"What about Destiny Jones? You believe that?"

That part of the note gave him hope "I'll call headquarters and ask Jessica to contact the nearest field office and locate Betsy Stewart. Hopefully, we'll have Destiny Jones back to her parents soon."

"So, if it turns out she is Destiny, Cosart was Proctor?"

"No."

Mitch's surprise showed. "What do you mean?"

"I mean, the person who shot Cosart is most likely Proctor or one of his people." Gage tried to imagine Viv hiring someone to set something like this up. Ellie was right. The idea was absurd.

A familiar, white-haired man bustled in.

Gage couldn't stop a smile. "I think you're too late, Dr. Tindell."

The physician grimaced at the body. "This is what I get for being a small-town doctor. We really need to find a new candidate for county coroner before our next election."

Mitch sounded amused. "Ah, you love it, and you know it."

Dr. Tindell looked at the sheriff incredulously. "I assure you, I could live my entire life quite contentedly without seeing a brain splattered on the wall."

Gage silently agreed with the doctor. "I need to make that call." He considered what else needed to be done. "The computer's CPU will need to be sent to Elijah, and I would like to speak to the neighbor who found him."

"Sure." Mitch didn't look heartbroken to have someone else

in charge. "Anything else?"

"I'd like to send Jessica and Bridgett over, just to look around."

The doctor looked up from the body. "Perhaps Miss Monroe would care to assist with the autopsy."

Gage could already hear his agent. "I'm sure she would." After she was finished gagging, Bridgett would throttle Gage.

He left the sheriff talking to the doctor and headed out of the house. Two men in dark blue uniforms met him at the front door.

"Hello, Agent Donahue. How is your wife?"

Gage looked at the man and recognized the EMT who helped Ellie. "Barney Nettles, right?"

Barney smiled. "Luke told me they kept Mrs. Donahue in the hospital overnight, but I haven't seen him lately to ask. Is she doing okay?"

Other than wanting to skin him alive? "She's fine. I appreciate what you did."

The stocky man blushed. "I was just doing my job."

"I appreciate it, just the same."

Gage walked on out to see Sam talking to a woman who went to the same church as he and Ellie. What was her name? Her husband did something for the school district. Dennis something. Bryan drew a blank.

Sam's face was as red as he'd ever seen it as she watched him approach. Something had made her angry.

"Gage, this is Jennifer Ewing. She's the person who found Mr. Cosart."

"Pleased to meet you, Mrs. Ewing." He almost dropped her hand; it reminded him of fish he'd had to flush away. As she pulled her hand away, Gage spoke. "I need to have a word with my agent for just a moment." He turned to Samantha and lowered his voice. "Where is Jeff?" There was no way they did an adequate job if they were already finished.

"Mrs. Ewing was frightened to walk down here by herself. I left Jeff listening to a lady named Liddie Sparks tell him for the fifth or sixth time he looked like their son." She seemed more herself. "I need to head back before she talks Jeff into believing he's her long lost son."

Gage managed a smile. Hopefully, she was back to being herself.

He waited until she headed down the sidewalk and then turned to the neighbor."What led you to enter Mr. Cosart's house, Mrs. Ewing?"

"Why, the music, of course."

"Music?" Nobody had said anything about music.

"Yes. It was so loud, it woke me." Jennifer pursed her lips. "Dennis didn't move, but he could sleep through a train wreck."

Gage suddenly remembered this woman's reputation. She liked to talk. "How did you get into the house?"

"Well, I put on my housecoat and came over here." She frowned. "I just got dressed. I shouldn't have done that, should I? My housecoat is probably evidence."

Not unless she had taken it off and used it as a dust cloth. "Ma'am, how did you get into the house?"

"The door was open." She acted as though Gage should already know that. "I knocked and rang the doorbell, but he couldn't have heard me over the music. The thing has one of those annoying sound systems with speakers in every room, and the music was blasting."

Gage silently counted to ten. "So, you walked in. Then what did you do?"

"I yelled his name as loudly as I could. When he didn't answer, I went looking for the machine." Jennifer smiled proudly. "I found it, too, in his bedroom. He must have planned on sleeping soundly because he set it to go off like that at four-thirty. Why on earth would anybody want to wake up to that cacophony, I ask you."

"And, after you found it?"

"I shut it off." Her hands flew to her face. "It was heaven. My ears were still ringing, but it was finally quiet."

There were most likely prints on the items she touched– lights, the stereo, and doorknobs. Gage felt bad for her, though, so he wasn't telling her she actually did mess up the scene. "Then, what did you do? How did you discover the body?"

The woman's face turned a bright pink. "I always wondered what the inside of the house looked like, but Bryan Cosart lived like a hermit. I'm pretty sure Crystal Stanley never even went inside, and he dated her."

"You went exploring."

For the first time, Jennifer's composure slipped. "Mr. Cosart...I've never seen anything like it before. Except on TV. Should I have tried CPR?"

Gage highly doubted she would have been capable of touching Cosart. "No. I'm sure it was too late when you found him. Did you hear anything else? Maybe loud noises during the night?"

She crossed her arms. "The Richey boy was shooting off firecrackers again. One of these days he'll get those things too close to a car and blow the whole block up."

Firecrackers the night a man was shot? Right.

"Do you know what time you heard the firecrackers?"

Jennifer had regained her composure. "It was when David Letterman was giving his top ten. I missed number one. It was ten ways--do you ever watch that show? Dav--"

"Mrs. Ewing, a life has been taken. Other than to ascertain the time, the show you're describing is inessential."

The nosy woman tilted her head. "You're married to Luke Walker's cousin, aren't you? And she forgot you were her husband for so long." She clasped her hands over her chest. "It must have been hard to date her when she was already your wife. How did that work? Do you have to learn to live together all over again?"

"We're happily married. Can you tell me what time you heard the firecrackers?" Dennis Ewing had Gage's sincere sympathy. The man must have limitless patience.

"I suppose it was about a quarter after. Why does that--" Jennifer's mouth dropped open. "It wasn't firecrackers going off, was it? I heard Bryan Cosart shoot himself."

"I don't know that. You'll need to go to the police station and give them your statement, though." And the deputy who took it would need a bottle of aspirin on hand.

After more reassurances that she couldn't have saved Cosart's life, it was with no small pleasure Gage watched Jennifer Ewing walk away.

Around a dozen neighbors were inching their way closer, three with cameras and even more with their phones held up. Typically, he would have found Mitch and ask for deputies, but today...He was not in the mood to walk away. Instead, he walked over and stopped a few feet from them.

After he flipped out his badge, he made eye contact with every one of them.

"One of your neighbors has passed away, and this is the way you show respect?".

"But people do it all the time," one woman yelled.

"That doesn't make it legal. This is a federal case, ma'am." He always wondered why people would want to be present at a tragedy. "I will give you all one chance. Put your cameras and phones away. After I walk away, agents will be here shortly to confiscate every imaging device within sight."

"How would you feel if this was your mom, dad, someone you love, and strangers were outside taking every picture they can?" Samantha now stood beside Gage. "My grandfather just passed away, and I love and respect him enough to stop him from becoming a news article."

Muttering, the small crowd turned and began their walks home, Gage hoped. He'd seen the lengths to which some reporters and photographers would go.

Chapter 55

"And Kurt wore one of Jess's skirts to the bowling alley last night." Elijah's voice penetrated Ellie's consciousness.

"I'm sorry. I wasn't listening."

"You don't say." He leaned forward in his chair. "What's going on?"

"I just feel like this Duncan name needs to be thoroughly investigated, and nobody will help me." They were too busy trying to prove Aunt Viv was Proctor. Gage had even come right out and said her theory possessed "too many maybes."

"What am I? A useless nano byte?"

"You know what I mean." Ellie sighed. "Besides, the computer Gage called about will be here any moment. You won't be able to help me."

Elijah's consoling smile nearly brought her back to tears. "I'm sorry, Ellie. Maybe the girls will help you when they get back."

It wasn't enough Gage refused to look past Viv as a suspect. He seemed determined to make it virtually impossible for her, too. Not only had he appropriated Elijah for some new case, but he also shanghaied Jess and Bridgett.

"I'll just do it myself." She picked up the folders he'd given her. "Thank you, Elijah."

"I don't know what's going on between you and Gage, but don't let this job come between you." The pain in his eyes caused Ellie to wonder about the past Elijah very rarely spoke of. He reached up and patted her arm. "Your marriage should come first."

Yes, it should. "Tell Gage that." Ellie walked down the hall to the office she shared with Jessica. As she sat at the desk, there was no way to stop her smile. Jess kept a line of bobble-head animals in a semi-circle facing her. Ellie knew from experience when Jess became frustrated, she would whack them and set them all to nodding. She claimed at least that way, somebody agreed with her.

Ellie decided to try it out. She patted the animals, and once they were all merrily bouncing away, she couldn't resist nodding back at them. It was a good thing nobody had seen her. They'd think her brain injury had recurred with a vengeance.

She sighed and opened the first folder. The driver's license photo, Thomas Duncan, of Malton, Utah was at least ten years older than the man she remembered. And his face was too full, too round. She closed the folder and went on to the next one.

After examining over thirty files, Ellie had a stack of "maybes" set aside. None of them seemed quite right, though. The problem was she hadn't seen his unshaven face. Since she hadn't seen his eyes, it was impossible to know their shape, color, or if they were dark or light. And his haggard hair hid his bone structure and shape of his face.

Maybe, with his artist's eyes, Troy could pull features out from under the whiskers. If he could produce a sketch with no facial hair, Ellie might be able to find the right man. Troy had been given the day off, so he and Annie planned a quiet day at home. Since Ellie's dad was spending the day with Uncle Richard, and Aunt Viv was in Pattinton, having yet another meeting with Charles Crawford, the young couple had the place to themselves. As much as Ellie regretted intruding, it was necessary.

Annie answered on the second ring.

Her greeting was immediately followed by a garbled noise, then "Ouch, Fat Ollie!" More sounds of yelling were followed by her sister's slightly calmer voice. "Your silly cat just attacked me. That walking hairball thinks he's a tiger stalking prey in the jungle."

"He hasn't gotten used to a big house yet." Ollie roamed about the place and had become much more aggressive, often pouncing on bare feet or furry house slippers.

Annie sighed. "What do you need, sis?"

"I'm sorry to do this, but I really need to speak to Troy."

"Me, too." Her sister's voice was full of disappointment. "He and Dr. Grant went to Pattinton. They're doing some kind of sketch for the police chief."

Ellie was surprised. "Why didn't Troy call me?"

"I asked him that, too." Annie was unhappy. "He said Gage told him you were busy, and Dr. Grant could handle it."

"Oh." She wasn't sure how she felt about that. "I guess I'll see you when I get home."

"We're all going over to Uncle Richard and Aunt Anita's for dinner, remember?"

She'd forgotten they were barbecuing steaks for her dad and Aunt Viv's final evening in Shadow. "Will Luke and Holly be there?"

"Yep." There was a smile in Annie's voice. "And Luke promised they'd bring Clarence."

Ellie laughed for the first time all day. Uncle Richard's pups, Maxine and Minerva, hopped and cavorted around Clarence like the mutt was a movie star, and Clarence looked at them with disdain. Ellie could sit and watch them for hours.

"It's good to hear you laugh." Annie was quiet for a moment. "I saw the blankets. One of you spent the night on the couch, didn't you?"

Ellie's laughter dried up immediately. "I don't want to talk about it. I really have to go."

She disconnected the phone and picked up the first possible matching Duncan folder again, determined to focus.

Loud voices from the front of the building stopped her.

Elijah and Kurt stood facing each other when Ellie walked into the room. Kurt's fists were clenched at his sides.

"I did not play a practical joke on you," Elijah said calmly.

Kurt stepped forward. "You sent me on a wild goose chase, so don't stand there and try to tell me you didn't."

Elijah raised his hands. "I really have no idea what you're talking about, but if you calm down and tell me, maybe I can help you figure it out."

Ellie stepped forward. "Kurt?" She waited until he looked at her. "You know Elijah. If he played a practical joke on you, he'd be bragging. Why don't you tell us what happened?"

Kurt's gaze held hers for a minute before he drew a deep breath and relaxed his hands. "I was at Bryan Cosart's, waiting him out. The guy was home, but he wouldn't answer the door, and I wasn't going to leave until he talked to me."

"I knew you were at Cosart's house," Elijah admitted. "But when I didn't hear anything, I figured it had gone south. What happened?"

"I got a call from somebody saying he was you. He sounded like you."

"He wasn't." Elijah's demeanor didn't change.

"I believe him, Kurt." Ellie was thankful that, for such a physically fit and well-trained man, Kurt was slow to lose his temper.

"Okay." There was still doubt in Kurt's eyes. "So, you—he told me a girl's body had been discovered about fifty miles outside Chicago, and tentatively identified as Destiny Jones. Gage wanted the whole team to meet at the police station in a town called Tippen ASAP. I drove for hours to get there." His dark eyes were twin lasers. "Tippen police thought I was nuts. There was no meeting, and they knew nothing about a body."

"I've never even heard of the town," Elijah assured him. "I'm as much in the dark about this as you are." He looked at Ellie. "Okay, shrink. Who and why?"

Ellie didn't have to think. "As for the who, I have no idea, but the why? The caller wanted to get Kurt away from Bryan Cosart."

Elijah seemed unconvinced. "Who would want to do that?"

"The person who murdered Bryan Cosart." Gage's voice came from behind Kurt. Ellie looked to see her husband, with Samantha beside him, of course.

Gage included the others when he next spoke. "Cosart's body was discovered early this morning. The scene isn't completely processed yet, but I know as sure as I'm standing here, we're looking at a murder staged as a suicide."

"You mean after I left?" Kurt's anger had changed to curiosity.

"What time did you leave?" Gage asked calmly.

"About ten-thirty."

Gage nodded. "The neighbor heard what she thought were firecrackers around thirty to forty-five minutes later."

Ellie had to bite her tongue to keep from speaking. She supposed Aunt Viv had sneaked past her sleeping on the couch, and tiptoed out of their house, to do all this. Fat Ollie was probably her accomplice. "I'm sorry about all this, but I have work to do." She

271

turned to leave.

Her husband's quiet voice halted her. "There was a note on the computer screen. It alludes to Cosart being Proctor. He left the new name and location of Destiny Jones."

Ellie spun around, eager for good news. "She's been found?"

Samantha answered. "Not yet. I just notified the Knoxville office not too long ago. It will take some time for them to locate her and confirm she is Destiny."

"Well, it sounds like good news." Without another word, Ellie turned and walked back to her desk. So, as she'd suspected when she read Gage's note, he hadn't gone to meet with the sheriff; he went to a crime scene with Samantha, and without Ellie. So, now he and Sam could put their heads together and come up with a way to connect Aunt Viv to Cosart's murder.

"Cosart wasn't Proctor." Gage's voice startled her.

She looked at him. "Of course not, because we all know who is."

He stepped closer to the desk. "Listen. I'm sorry. You were right. I jumped the gun. I want to look at what you've found on Duncan."

"Well, isn't that big of you?" Ellie couldn't keep the sarcasm from her voice. "How dare you leave me this morning? Team rules, Agent Donahue! Your rules. We're all equally important. Or so you said."

"We are."

Ellie was good and mad. "Well, apparently that applies to everyone but me. You left me, a trained agent on your team because I refuse to jump on the 'convict Vivian' bandwagon, and you didn't want to deal with my crazy theories. No, you chose to meet someone who agrees with you. If any of the rest of us had done that, you'd rake us over the coals."

Gage's voice was steady. "That's not why I left you, but you're right about the rest. I'm sorry."

"Well, so am I." She'd show him sorry. "I quit." She brushed past him and walked out of the office, barely noticing the shocked expressions on Kurt's and Elijah's faces as they looked at her. Sam stepped over and stood squarely in front of the door.

Ellie spoke with barely controlled rage. "I'm giving you ten seconds to get out of my way. Or I'll forget I'm pregnant and show you how well I remember Kurt's teaching." She wasn't a shooter, but Kurt didn't stop training her until she was an excellent fighter.

"You're pregnant?"

Aggravation she'd let it slip worsened the situation. "Go ask your partner." She shoved her way past a now unresisting Samantha. Ellie was finished.

Chapter 56

Gage had never in his thirty-seven years been responsible for a mess of this proportion. He'd started out the door right behind Ellie, but Kurt persuaded him to wait and let her cool off.

He did what he could to make things up to her, spending the day immersed in the lives of four different T. and J. Duncans. Since their files were separated from the others, and they shared similarities, Gage assumed Ellie considered them possible matches. One of them turned out to be an intriguing candidate. He almost called her, but then decided it would be a better olive branch if given to her face-to-face.

He would also be able to give her some good news. Betsy Stewart had been located, and through fingerprints, was conclusively identified as Destiny Dawn Jones. Henry Baker, the agent he'd spoken to, was quite impressed with the school district and Shadow County Sheriff's joint fingerprint collection of area children. It made his job much easier. The people who had her, Dean and Rhonda Stewart, swore they legally adopted her and lawyered up. So far, they weren't talking. The agency had the forged adoption papers, though.

The drive home had never seemed this long before. Maybe he should have ignored the others' advice and gone after his wife. Sam must have told the others what happened because there had been various reactions. Troy was unhappy with Gage, not only because of Ellie but also because he'd been forced to work with Eric.

Thinking of his team revived doubts he couldn't quite tamp down. Somebody wanted Kurt out of the way to get to Cozart. That person would have to know several things. Namely, Kurt's phone number, what he was doing, and what to say that would induce Kurt to leave without further questioning his caller.

No matter how Gage dressed it up, he couldn't ignore the probability one of his team had turned. However, he couldn't, for the life of him, figure out which one.

One thing Gage was confident of was that Kurt would have never turned to Proctor. He was honest and shared his opinions. Plus, the weapons expert treated Ellie like a sister. Gage trusted his agent to the end, but Kurt would probably have to prove himself to his peers.

As for the others, he tried to think about each one objectively.

Elijah was the member who could most easily pull it off. Gage thought of all the technological marvels his computer expert had demonstrated. He would have to be examined.

As ludicrous as it seemed, Jess had to be considered. She most definitely could alter her voice. And size didn't matter when a gun was involved. Although she was almost always a fun-loving, cheerful woman, he knew better. Her past had nearly destroyed her. The fact was, she was almost always at an AMAR office or investigating. He didn't believe Jessica was the traitor, but again, she would have to prove herself.

Eric was probably the least tech-savvy member, but even he knew how to use voice-altering devices. The psychiatrist had become quite a grump, but Gage highly doubted it would bring him to endanger the team. No, Gage thought it was because the agent wanted to retire and wasn't sure what he'd do without his job. Unfortunately, Gage couldn't get a reading on the man Eric had become. It concerned Gage that the older man had been routinely disappearing with a generic excuse when he showed back up. Gage had written him up, but hadn't yet turned it in. Just as his peers, Eric just didn't seem like a traitor.

Bridgett concerned him. Yes, the chief of the entire USA's Federal Safety Administration branch recommended and endorsed her. Even with her queasy stomach, Bridgett did her job. But, even Jessica, who he frequently assigned with Bridgett, expressed concern about her. The open, share anything Jessica couldn't get a single reply to a personal question. Since Bridgett's files were redacted, Gage could only tell Jess to do her job and learn to live with her curiosity. Pretty much how Burnett answered Gage.

At the thought of Troy being a spy, Gage felt a smile tug at his lips. If he ever did something illegal, Annie would beat him, and her sister would finish him off. Plus, Troy was a sketch artist and not bad with a camera. He could hear Eric now. "He exercises five days a week and is nearly as muscular as Kurt. He has the training. How can

275

you not consider him a suspect?"

"Get out of my head," Gage growled.

Which left Samantha. Before this morning, he would have dismissed the possibility of her involvement with no hesitation. Yet, she was keeping a secret, a big one if Gage's hunch was right. Her personal life wasn't the agency's business unless it conflicted with legalities. A few of the things he heard her say gave him concern for her soul as much as her possible involvement with Proctor.

Gage pulled into his driveway and parked. Before he went in to face his wife, he needed to do one more thing. He picked up his phone and resolutely dialed a number.

Ross Burnett was unhappy, to say the least. "You'd better be calling to tell me Proctor is safely behind bars. I just sat down to a perfectly grilled porterhouse."

"I'm sorry, sir. I wouldn't bother you if it weren't important."

The director must have heard the gravity in Gage's voice. "What's going on, Donahue?"

Gage decided to spit it out. "I have reason to believe one of my team has turned. I need a Code eight investigation. I'm certain that two of my agents are innocent, but we'll need the poly and questioning for them, too."

A long silence met him. "You know what this will do to your team."

Yes, he did. "It's not much of a team if one of them is working for Proctor."

Burnett cautioned him. "Just know, once you open this door, it can't be closed."

"I know."

A deep sigh came from the phone. "I'll have Lorrie DeWitt fly down tonight."

She was the agency's top polygrapher and proof of how seriously the boss was taking this.

"Simon Fisher and his team will be there first thing tomorrow. To keep this on the up and up, you need to back completely out and let Fisher take care of it."

He would gladly step aside. "Thank you, sir."

"I hope you're wrong about a traitor."

"So do I." Gage heard his boss disconnect the call. After tomorrow, his team would no longer be the same cohesive unit. They would look first at him with anger, and eventually at each other with suspicion.

He picked up the Duncan file and got out of the car. He was halfway to the house when he realized Ellie's car wasn't there. His heart leaped to his throat. Hadn't she made it home?

Gage rushed into the house and nearly steamrolled his sister-in-law as she was coming out the doorway. "Where's Ellie?"

"Wouldn't a good husband always know where his wife and unborn child are?

"I thought she was here." He swallowed hard at the thought of losing Ellie again.

Annie reached up and twirled her pointer finger in the air. "Whoopity whoop whoop!"

"Listen, you can be angry—even furious--with me. I just want to fix things with my wife."

Annie looked like she was ready to lock him in the nearest closet. "She's already at Uncle Richard's. She wanted to go for a walk."

He'd forgotten the barbecue. "If you wait a minute, I'll catch a ride with you. There's no sense in having both Ellie's and my vehicles there."

"There's lunch meat in the refrigerator. There's no need for you to come." Annie had a milder temper than his wife unless somebody was hurting those she loved. When Annie lost it and chewed out the guilty party, Ellie seemed like Mary Poppins.

"Listen, Annie. Ellie is my wife, and I'm going to spend the evening with her. If you don't want me to ride with you, I'll drive myself."

"Fine." She brushed past him as she walked back into the house. "But if you end up walking home, it's your own fault."

"I'll take my chances."

She turned and huffed at him. "Are you going to change clothes or are you planning to wear something that looks like you slept in it?"

Gage was surprised. "You'll wait for me?"

"You've got five minutes. Hop to it."

She didn't have to tell him twice. He wasn't going to waste any time getting to his wife.

Chapter 57

Ellie watched a dragonfly zoom around her bare feet as they dangled over the pond. She had been a teenager the last time she sat on the dock. It surprised her that it was still there. And, sturdy, too, since Clarence had flopped down beside her.

She smiled at her memory of the "Lake Walker" dock. Never mind Uncle Richard's pond was four-feet-deep on a good day, and the only boat they had was her Barbie Doll's. After watching a fishing program on TV, Luke claimed every lake had a dock. At ten, Ellie believed every word from her much wiser twelve-year-old cousin. After five days of wading in mud and water with boards and nails and four large fence posts, the two of them managed to construct what might pass for a dock. Of course, it stood at one level all the time, which on average was two foot above the water.

The sound of rustling grass announced the arrival of Uncle Richard's dogs. The puppies had shown up at the farm, presumably dumped, a few months ago. Much to Aunt Anita's horror, her husband bonded with the canines, and after a fruitless effort to find their owner, claimed them as his. They seemed to be some sort of bird dog mix and were already nearly as tall as Clarence. Ellie's distressed aunt practically went into shock when the vet told them the pups were only about six months old and still had some growing to do.

Maxine and Minerva charged into the pond, falling all over themselves. Clarence, from his prone position next to Ellie, raised his head and seemed to roll his eyes. If he could talk, she was sure he would deny they were the same species.

What was she going to do? She had quit her job and walked out. Had an FSA agent ever done that before? Somehow, she had trouble visualizing Kurt stomping his foot and leaving in a snit.

"Penny for your thoughts."

Ellie wasn't surprised that Gage stood behind her. Staring straight ahead, she decided to speak her piece.

"If you hadn't been so determined you and Samantha already identified Proctor, you would have given serious consideration to my

279

lead. But because I'm your wife, you think I'm focused on a crazy theory and won't back down because I can't bear to suspect my godmother."

"I'm sorry." Gage sounded sincere.

She tilted her head and looked up at him. "Yeah, well, I'm feeling like a toad's navel lint right now."

Gage pushed Clarence over and sat beside her. "I know I made a mess of things. All I can say is I'm sorry. And you were right. I focused on Viv too quickly."

"What changed your mind?"

"When faced with everything...you're right, Ellie. This isn't Vivian's work."

If he was waiting for her to jump up and do a happy dance, he was out of luck. "You should have known that right away. She's been close to you since we were married."

"I know." His eyes met hers. "I tried to make up for this mess. I spent the day going over your Duncan files. I found one I think is promising." He reached over and took her hand, lacing their fingers together.

Ellie still wasn't ready to kiss and make up. "Why is it promising?"

"Timothy Duncan is an independent trucker who promotes himself as available for nationwide shipping, but that's not the most significant detail." His hand tightened on hers. "He dropped off the map. There is no record of him driving a route since a couple of months before the crash. The landlord of his apartment building said he stopped paying rent and disappeared about then, too. And his cell phone number is no longer in service."

"So, even if he's our guy, we're back to square one." She was beyond disappointed.

"According to the records, he leases a bay for his truck at Brown Shipping in a little town in South Carolina. They may have something on him." Before she could say anything, he continued. "I called their office this afternoon, but it was already closed. I'll try again tomorrow."

That satisfied her. "What happened with the girl Cosart identified?"

Gage looked at his watch. "Destiny Jones should be safely returned to her parents within the hour."

She felt tears tingling behind her eyes. "Th—that's miraculous." Pregnancy hormones already? She shifted her focus. "What have you found out about Proctor? Have the people who had Destiny talked?"

"Not the last time I checked." He didn't seem surprised. "They were claiming they thought the adoption was legal and lawyered up."

Ellie was afraid to ask. "Do you know what lawyer is representing them.?"

Gage was hesitant to answer. "It's a member of the network, Helen Boynton, but it doesn't mean Viv's involved. You're right. I was just caught up in the excitement of putting Proctor out of business."

Her voice was quiet as she spoke. "You were caught up in enthusiasm with Samantha, you mean. It's a shame you couldn't have given me the same consideration."

"Please, tell me you don't think I'm—"

"Of course, I know you're faithful." She decided to get something off her chest. "I'm worried about her, Gage. There are times she acts like the Samantha I remember, but then...it's almost like she has her mind on something else."

"I noticed that, but I just haven't had time to sit down and talk to her. She nelt's most likely her still adjusting to her grand Gage seemed fascinated with

Ellie's wedding rings. "I have another agent I'd like to give my job to.

She'll get a recommendation from me when Clarence there flies a jet."

Although this was a serious conversation, Ellie couldn't stop a smile. "You never know with that dog."

His smile morphed into a straight line, and with his hand on her cheek gently tilted her head to face him. "I'm sorry. I should have thought of you as an agent, not just my wife."

"That's it, though." She looked into his love-filled eyes. "I am your wife. I'm not sure you can see me as an agent, too."

"I promise I'll never brush you aside again. I'll give your ideas and participation the same consideration the rest of the team receives." His gaze dropped. "At least while AMAR exists."

"What do you mean?"

"You may as well know." Gage's hand tightened on hers. "I think one of my agents has turned. And he or she got rid of Kurt and killed Cosart."

Ellie's thoughts spun through her mind like a cyclone. "It's not possible. What would ever induce one of them to work for Proctor?"

Gage shrugged. "I don't know. I've already gone over Binkley's head and called Burnett again, though." ." Her heart broke when she saw the pain on his face. "A Code eight investigation will begin tomorrow."

"A Code eight...they use a polygraph test." The enormity of Gage's dilemma was sinking in. "They're all going to—"

"They'll be enraged with me at first. Then, they'll start looking at each other differently. Could she be the one? The trust will be gone."

"So, you're going to destroy the team."

Gage sadly shook his head. "No, Ellie. The agent who turned already has."

Six years together. What this had to be doing to Gage. "I'm sorry."

"I'll deal with it." An intensity appeared in his eyes. "Right now, I need to make everything right between us. I plan to never sleep apart from you again."

Ellie was ashamed. "I overreacted. I was hurt, and I struck out. Would I respond so dramatically if your partner were a man? I honestly don't know." She met his gaze head on. "But, I'm your wife, and I love you."

"I love you, too, more than words can say." He slid his hand behind her neck and leaned over to kiss her.

Laughter bubbled and escaped when Ellie felt Clarence's rough tongue slather across their cheeks.

Gage pulled his mouth away and turned to the dog. "You can go kiss Maxine or Minerva if you want some lovin'. This woman is taken." His lips returned to hers.

Chapter 58

"What do you mean, you need to speak to me?" Jess's bright green pigtails shook as she demanded an answer from Simon Fisher. "I know you don't think I need to take a lie detector test."

Gage spoke firmly. "Jess, he or one of his team is going to be speaking to everyone—not just you." He was most likely a coward, but he'd let Lorrie Dewitt and her team be a surprise. The first one back out would tell the rest of them.

Jess whirled on Gage. "What about? This is a bunch of hooey! I have too much work to do on the Proctor case—or have you found somebody better equipped to organize and search the abduction data?"

The team had been relieved because of the information they received from Brown Shipping. The company confirmed that not only had Tim Duncan kept his truck there until approximately eighteen months ago, he often drove for them. And even more incriminating, Cosart's store was a regular customer. Unfortunately, their computer system was being updated and therefore inaccessible for the next twenty-four hours. They were eager to provide detailed information to the FSA, so they promised to call the moment it went back online.

Undaunted, Jess was preparing a list of abductions to compare with the Cosart shipping schedule when they received it. "You'll have time to work on it. Just go with Simon right now."

Elijah walked out of one of the offices with an agent behind him. He glared at Gage.

"This is wrong, Gage, and you know it."

"What is wrong?" Jess turned back to Gage. "What is Elijah talking about?"

With a scowl on his face, Elijah answered. "Gage thinks one of us is working for Proctor, and the DeWitt Doubters are back there to give us polygraph tests."

"What?" Jess looked at Gage incredulously. "Did you scrub your head too hard when you showered? Cause you've lost some brain cells, Gage Donahue."

Simon spoke from behind the angry woman. "Agent Bannon, you can either come with me or be transported to headquarters in Atlanta for a personal meeting with Director Burnett. Those are my orders."

Eric entered the room with a puzzled expression on his face. "What's going on in here? I could hear Jessica from the sidewalk."

Jess's eyes drilled holes through Gage. "Ask Agent Donahue." She turned and stomped into the office, with Fisher behind her.

The agent who had questioned Elijah addressed Eric. "Are you Dr. Eric Grant?"

"Yes." Eric looked at Gage curiously."

Elijah's voice was laced with anger. "Carl Gaviola is going to haul you into the office and question you like a common criminal before he lets the DeWitt crew hook you up to a polygraph machine."

"Why?"

Before Gage could reply, Elijah did. "Our boss suspects one of us is a Proctor goon."

Eric's gaze leveled on Elijah for a moment before shifting to Gage. "Why?" he repeated.

Gage decided the answer was simple. "Cosart."

The older man nodded. "I understand."

"You understand?" Elijah looked at Eric like he thought his co-worker was crazy. "What's going on around here? Is stupidity contagious?"

Eric turned and spoke calmly to Elijah. "Somebody made sure Kurt was out of the picture and then killed Cosart. It makes sense it could be one of us." Leaving an open-mouthed Elijah, he silently turned and followed Gaviola out of the room.

Unfortunately, none of the others took it as well as Eric, and by noon, he and Ellie were the only people speaking to Gage.

Since a team meeting had already been scheduled, Gage had that to look forward to. When he walked into the conference room, it was to see a just arriving Samantha listening to a still irate Elijah.

She shook her head. "I don't care. He won't expect me to be questioned."

Agent Fisher, who had been expecting Sam's arrival, walked in next to Gage. "Agent Hughes?"

Sam smiled at him. "How are you, Simon?"

"Good." Fisher didn't smile. "I need you to come with me, please."

Her smile dimmed. "You don't need to speak to me. I'm Gage's partner."

"I have my orders." The agent spoke firmly. "You need to come with me."

Sam looked at Gage with disbelief in her eyes. "Say something, Gage."

He did. "I'm sorry, Samantha. They're seeing everybody."

Her eyes narrowed. "Of course they are. Has Ellie been in there yet?"

It was Agent Fisher who answered. "Agent Ellie Donahue is not on our list."

Sam scowled at Gage. "Isn't this nice? We've worked together for six years, and you don't trust me, but you think a woman you've known a little more than half that time—"

"You're talking about my wife." Samantha had just stepped way out of line.

It seemed she wasn't finished. "Have you ever wondered about the timing? It's awfully coincidental Proctor went off the grid while Ellie was out of commission. Maybe she didn't have her inside person to cover for her." Her voice had risen as she spoke. "How do you know Ellie wasn't a plant from the start?"

"He doesn't." Ellie's voice came from behind Gage. "Simon can ask me questions. I'll take a polygraph if it helps at all to clear this up."

Gage turned to his wife. "You are not a suspect."

Simon agreed. "Director Burnett gave me strict instructions. You are not on the list."

Ellie hadn't taken her eyes off Samantha. "Put me on it."

Gage stepped closer and murmured, "you don't have to do this."

Her gaze finally shifted to him. "I know. I want to."

Gage was somewhere on the road between frustration and pure anger. Where had this Samantha come from? Had Sam always had this attitude toward Ellie and managed to hide it, or was it new? Whatever the case, he didn't like, nor would he stand for it. "It'll be a waste of time, but I won't stop you." He turned to Samantha. "And you can either go with Simon now or be flown to Atlanta for an unpleasant interview with Burnett. It's your choice."

Fisher held out his arm. "After you, Agent Hughes."

Her eyes sparkling with anger, Samantha brushed past Gage as she followed Simon.

The investigating agent smiled sympathetically.

Gage waited until they left and made sure nobody was within hearing before he turned to Ellie. "You really don't have to do this. I know you don't work for Proctor."

"You have enough to deal with." Her eyes met his. "If this will help in the least, I don't mind. Besides, if I spend one more hour entering data on past abductions, I'm going to cry. It's hard to believe even counting the children who have been found, there are still so many out there."

"Don't let it get you down." His wife was soft-hearted. "We can only handle so much. If we find one child and return him to his parents, that's one reunited family. We have to look at the successes instead of what we haven't accomplished."

The corners of Ellie's lips turned up. "Have I told you lately I love you?"

"Not since this morning." He returned her smile. "But I never get tired of hearing it." And he prayed she'd never stop saying it.

Chapter 59

"You don't look very relaxed," Mavis scolded Ellie.

Ellie looked up from the catalog she'd been blindly staring at and focused on her friend. "I guess I'm more tired than I realized."

Mavis stood up from the chair and walked over to sit on the couch beside Ellie. "Is something wrong?"

Other than her husband's partner had come right out and accused Ellie of being a spy, and now Gage was stuck in something called an information verification meeting until who knew when? "Just a rough day."

"Well, you're here now," Mavis declared. "So, forget your day, and let's look at maternity clothes and baby goodies."

After Ellie had blown up and told pretty much the entire AMAR team, she and Gage decided they could tell their friends. When she told Mavis, her friend literally jumped for joy. Apparently, her enthusiasm hadn't stopped there, either, since the moment they finished their dinner, Mavis dragged catalogs and newspaper inserts out from where she'd stashed them in the closet. For the past fifteen minutes, Ellie had been "looking" at a pair of adjustable pants guaranteed to make it from conception to birthing.

Mavis picked up a stack of newspapers, so Ellie forced her attention back to the catalog.

"Hey, isn't this your godmother?"

Ellie looked over at the paper Mavis held. Sure enough, Viv was standing proudly among a group of people, all smiles. "What is that?"

"It's a pullout from the U.S. Bullet. There's a whole section in here about a big charity banquet." Mavis unfolded the paper and spread it between them.

Ellie reached over and pointed. "I recognize these men." She placed her finger on a gray-haired man. "Stanley Vickley is her associate from Ohio, I think." She pointed to a woman. "She's Madge Heward, from one of the Carolinas." A very familiar face caught her eye. "That older man behind Aunt Viv is her partner, Charles Crawford." Other faces looked familiar, but she couldn't name them or their states.

"So, she has partners in how many states?"

"Fifteen, so far, but Eric is her only partner. The rest are members."

"And, these lawyers do what? "

Ellie tried to find the easiest way to explain a complicated system. "Each attorney in the network agrees to accept so many new clients pro bono. It's somehow based on the count of clients already on their list. In return, according to Aunt Viv, Maxim and Maxim are the best attorneys in the continental country. It helps their image and sure is a blessing for the people who can't afford a lawyer."

Mavis looked at the paper. "Wow! I guess I didn't realize the size of her network."

"Yeah. One person can make a difference, can't she?"

Mavis studied the photo. "Wait. These people are all...older. Who's this guy? Look at those muscles, Ellie. Where can I find one?"

Aunt Viv was posed beside a well-built younger man turned to the side. His profile and expensively cut brown hair were all that was visible.

There was something familiar and unsettling about the man. "I don't know."

Mavis read. "Vivian Wolfe with the up-and-coming attorney, Adam Spencer." She waggled her eyebrows. "Please tell me he's single."

Ellie had forgotten about Aunt Viv's new employee. What had she said about him? "He's single, as far as I know, and he's been practicing law for around ten years. Aunt Viv is very pleased with him." She remembered something else. "Since he's a licensed pilot, he's been acting as a liaison between Aunt Viv and her associates. That way she doesn't have to travel or depend on others making it to Georgia."

Ellie smiled as she remembered her godmother's words: "Teleconferencing is too impersonal, and the camera on my computer adds at least ten pounds."

She glanced at Mavis to see her eyes still on Adam.

Weirder meetings had placed together two people. "He must

be a good guy because Aunt Viv likes him."

Mavis waggled her precisely trimmed eyebrows. "Just promise me if he's ever in town, you'll introduce us."

Ellie laughed despite herself. "I promise."

"Now, have you seen the dress on page twenty-seven? You'll look great in it."

Finally pushing unpleasant thoughts away, Ellie relaxed and let her friend lead her through maternity clothes. Worrying would do no good; the Bible said so. It was all in God's hands, and she trusted him.

Chapter 60

Ellie's terrified scream woke Gage instantly.

He reached next to him, only to find her sitting straight up in bed. "Ellie?" He sat up beside her.

She turned toward him. In the soft light from the hallway, he could see wide-eyed fear.

Gage remembered how she'd frozen up before. "Stay, Ellie." He quickly got up on his knees to face her. "Stay with me, please."

"He was dead." Disbelief and horror warred in her voice. "Tim Duncan was dead."

He didn't understand. "Did you have a nightmare?"

"No." Ellie's lips quivered. "I've remembered, Gage." Her eyes were awash with tears as she looked imploringly at him. "I remember, Gage. I remember everything."

"Shhh." He scooted around and pulled her onto his lap. "You don't have to talk about it right now."

She buried her head against his neck. "It's so awful."

He held her snugly against him. "You're safe. I won't let anything happen to you."

They sat, for what length of time Gage couldn't tell, until finally, she spoke.

"He didn't say who he was, but now...Tim Duncan called me at the office. He said he had proof of who Proctor was. He would only give it to me if I came alone to the old park on the south edge of town." A shudder went through her. "He gave me ten minutes to get there."

"You should have taken back-up, Ellie." Gage kept his voice gentle.

"I know." Ellie blindly turned and buried her head against his chest. Even muffled, he could understand her. "You wanted to take Proctor down so badly, and it was my chance to get them for you. I didn't think."

"Ok, sweetheart." Gage tightened his arms. "I understand." This was not the time for lectures, nor would anger help his wife. "Just tell me what happened."

Ellie's voice was soft as she began to talk. "He knew who I was because the moment I closed the car door behind me, he appeared. He said he had a flash drive naming everybody from top to bottom—the entire Proctor team. He stole it from Bryan Cosart."

The proof of Cosart's crimes didn't mean anything, not compared to his wife.

"At first, he seemed so nice, and I...and I almost felt sorry for him." Gage hugged her tighter against him when he heard her wavering voice. "Then, he...he changed"

"Before we go any further, please answer just one question," Gage gently turned her to face him. "Please, tell me the truth, Ellie. Did he hurt you in any way?" With the accident, who knew how many of those bruises were already there. Or if the Duncan guy...

She shook her head. "No, but when he...I was afraid."

Only because of how deeply he loved his wife was Gage able to contain his own rage.

"When he grabbed my arm, I forgot every self-defense method Kurt taught me. He would be ashamed of me."

"No, he wouldn't, sweetheart. You just wanted to get away from danger. Not one of us knows how we'll handle any situation until we're smack dab in the middle of it.

Her chest shook as she drew a deep breath, and he was reminded of his wife's strength. "He said he hated Cosart because Cosart left Kristin Baker in jail. "

"Wait." Gage had to wrap his head around this information. "Kristin Baker was in one group, and Duncan with another?" The agency and AMAR had been operating on the theory that once formed, teams stayed together. It looked like they were wrong.

He looked down at his wife and wished he could take her place in all this.

"He was crazy about her." Ellie leaned back, and Gage gently used his thumbs to wipe away her tears. "He yelled, practically screamed at me that he hated Cosart. And, he ranted about how it was all Cosart's fault in the first place."

"Did he explain?" Gage hated to interrupt her, but if she didn't clarify her phrase, something important could be missed.

"He claims he was on the phone with her when Cosart told them all the vehicles were gassed up and ready to go. He heard Cosart, and had never stopped blaming him." Ellie shuddered in Gage's arms. "He was going to hold onto the flash drive until Cosart got Kristin out of jail."

"But he didn't blackmail him?"

"He knew he was part of an illegal child-selling ring, but he thought Cosart was the top of the ladder. Then, he looked at exactly what he'd taken."

"But, he didn't give you any names?"

"No. I asked, but Duncan said no information would come my way until he had a deal."

"So, he checked the drive pretty thoroughly." Gage wondered if anyone knew whether Duncan was good on computers.

"Yes, and he said how he wished the flash drive had stayed hidden because it could be the end of his life. If the drive weren't missing when he disappeared, they would have no reason to hunt him."

"He went on the run?"

Ellie nodded. "He'd been hiding nearly two months when he asked himself how much longer it would take them to find him. He had to do something major."

"He found you." A familiar voice spoke in Gage's mind; *I told you that's what happened.* Once more, Jess was right.

"He saw me on a news clip and thought I looked more understanding. First, he found our home address and tried to see me there. He ran into Annie, instead. He was ready to go back on the road when he saw me walking into our building."

Gage kissed her forehead. "I understand why you went with no backup, but, please Ellie, don't ever do that again."

"I learned my lesson."

"And, he asked for what in exchange for the information?"

"He believed if he went to prison, when inmates discovered his crime was child abduction, he would be as good as dead. So, he asked us to not put him in as a child abductor, and at a prison not far from Kristen Baker's."

293

At least she hadn't corrected Duncan with information he'd more than likely be in a federal prison. "That wasn't a bad deal. He wasn't asking for freedom."

Ellie's lips clinched, and a fury unlike anything he'd seen on his wife took over her features. "He told me he hadn't ever hurt a child, not even if they woke up from the drugs. He had a special, soundproof compartment fixed for them." Ellie's fists clenched, and Gage half expected flames to burst from her mouth. Before he could say anything, she returned to her story. "He bragged because he could keep them without being heard. Like he cared about the children. He kept them in a compartment, Gage; A terrified child with no idea of where he or she was, crying and screaming"

"I'm so sorry, Ellie." Gage kissed the top of her head.

She turned and looked at him. "I'd tell you I wish I had my gun with me that day, but I'd be lying."

"Why?" Gage was worried about her anger. Would it send her back into the hospital?

"Because, Gage, I would have shot him. I would have killed a man."

He drew her into his arms again. Not the most comfortable way to sit, but he needed to hold her as much as she needed him to.

Gage saw her anger fade to trepidation. He whispered in her ear, "You're frightened. Don't be, Ellie. I have you."

Her chest rose as she pulled away and looked at his face. "I'm not afraid of anything like that. This next part will make you furious. I know it wouldn't be at me, but—"

"You don't need me angry. You have a supportive husband right now."

"Duncan pulled a pistol on me and ordered me to drive us to his hiding place."

Gage wanted to slug the man for frightening her, and if that gun had...no, she was safely in his arms.

Ellie rested her cheek on his shoulder. "It was so strange. He's holding a gun to make me drive, but he kept saying he was sorry, over and over."

"Don't be angry with me, Ellie, but I don't think Tim Duncan was an entirely bad man."

Bright green eyes were inches from his face. "Explain that, please."

"Duncan was a truck driver, and we don't know why he worked for Proctor—but the man had a conscience. He could have blackmailed Cosart or destroyed the drive. Instead, he was trying to fix things as well as possible, plus taking responsibility for his crimes."

"I believe you," she whispered, "but he would have shot me. I can't get past that right now. I'm praying for a way to deal with this."

"I understand."

"You know he took me to the cabin."

"That's where the flash drive was?"

He felt her nod against his shoulder. "He thought he'd chosen a place where nobody would find him." Gage felt goosebumps rise on her arms.

"He was true to his word and put the gun on a table as soon as we entered the cabin. He was just walking toward the fireplace when another man met him in the doorway."

As badly as Gage wanted to know everything, especially identities, he couldn't let his wife wear herself out. "You're safe, Ellie, and you don't have to do this all at once."

She either hadn't heard his words or more likely, was ignoring him.

He pulled her down with him and held her tightly against his side. Then, he continued to listen.

"This man had his pistol aimed at Duncan and told me if I so much as breathed hard, he'd shoot my boyfriend. Then he demanded to be told where the data was hidden."

Ellie started shaking. "I'm still not sure what happened. There was a struggle, and Tim Duncan collapsed. He was...he was dead."

Gage knew perfectly well this stranger needed the flash drive and would have more trouble with Duncan. So, he permanently rid the world of the truck driver.

"The stranger was furious. I saw him coming for me and tried to run, but he...he was so fast, and--"

"Shhh, Ellie. He won't touch you ever again."

Wiping tears from her cheek, she nodded. "He carried me into the bedroom and tossed me on the bed." Her body trembled so hard he thought she might go into shock.

"Listen to me." Gage made sure she saw his eyes. "You're safe now." He would tell her that every minute of every day if she needed his reassurance.

"He thought I was Tim's girlfriend and said I better tell him where the flash drive was. I was so afraid."

"Anybody would have been."

After a few deep breaths, Ellie continued. "I didn't know what he would do, so I told him the truth." Her eyes were tightly shut. "He laughed and told me how stupid I was to get involved. If I wanted to stay alive, I'd lie there and not move. I was trying to figure a way out when he walked back in. He was carrying Duncan's body."

"He told me he had to hunt the stupid thing, then he said...he said, 'You and Romeo can lie there and watch me. Then...Then.'"

"He placed him beside you."

"It was like I wasn't me anymore." She sounded exhausted. "I couldn't speak or move. All I could do was stare at that dead man."

"Fear is normal," Gage assured her. "You were terrified. Most people would feel the same way. I would feel the same way."

"He didn't have to look very long." He twisted so he could see her face. If keeping her eyes closed helped her, she could keep them closed all day. "He was making noise in the kitchen; I could hear pots and pans being thrown. When he walked back in, he raised the drive. For a moment, I thought it was over. But, he had a f...fireplace poker in his other hand."

"'Concussions and broken necks aren't out of place in a car accident autopsy.' He had the evilest voice; I think if I had looked into his eyes, I might see who he was worshiping." She closed her eyes tight. "He dragged me off the bed and..." Bloodshot eyes seemed to beg Gage to make it go away. "He kicked and hit me. The last thing I remember was the second time he brought the poker down."

Now it was Gage fighting a rage unlike he'd never felt. "I'm so sorry you went through that." No wonder she hadn't remembered. It was a nightmare. One from which if he found the man, Gage might break the law and give the man double what Ellie had. He placed his chin on her head and asked for words that would help. "Satan has a lot of control over those of us not accepting the Savior."

"The way he hit me...The first time I saw the iron coming down and I kicked him in the groin. His expression was pure evil, Gage. He told me to run and see how far I'd get since he even had an extra gun."

"What does your training tell you?" Gage realized what he sounded like. "I'm asking as your husband, not an agent."

"I know." She reached up and kissed his cheek. "FSA says to keep myself safe, but he had a gun, and I...I was terrified. When I felt the iron hit me the second time, all I remember is darkness."

"Maybe we should get up and have a cup of tea—maybe a little toast.

"I need to tell you." Ellie paused as though waiting for him to complain. He would do whatever it took to help her. "I remember opening my eyes to see a bridge's rails growing close way too quickly and then open air...I don't remember anything else.

Gage fought back the rage once more blaze through his body. This stranger traumatized and nearly killed Gage's wife.

"Gage?" Tears were in her eyes as she looked up at him. "Don't let him drag you down to his level. You love the law, and you love Jesus."

Just like that, Gage felt a deep love in his heart and held her tighter. He focused on comforting and reassuring her. "It's okay, now, Ellie."

Ellie pulled back and looked into his face. "No, it isn't." Her eyes were full of pain. "I know who the other man was. I saw his picture in the paper this evening. He had his back to the camera, but I'm positive Adam Spencer is the man who tried to kill me."

Gage didn't know how much more his wife could take. "Who is this Adam Spencer?"

297

Even though he felt her heartbeat taking off like a tap dancer, she was strong, and somehow she managed to keep going. "He's Aunt Viv's assistant. Darkened eyes looked up at Gage. "Samantha was right. Aunt Viv must be Proctor."

"Calm down." He rubbed her back. "Now, you're leaping to conclusions. Let me check this Adam Spencer first. I'll have him arrested. We'll see what he says."

A small glimmer of hope appeared in her eyes. "Okay."

"Stay here." Gage kissed her forehead. "I'll be right back."

As he picked up the phone and dialed Atlanta, he prayed his wife wouldn't be hurt anymore, and that this mess wasn't as it appeared.

Chapter 61

"The car is in Bay twenty-one. Here are your keys." The woman spoke loudly enough to be heard over the sound of a plane taking off.

Ellie managed to thank the attendant as she accepted the keys to a rental car. A taxi wouldn't provide enough mobility, and there was no way she could call the agency for a vehicle. Not when she was going against so many FSA rules.

Her mind drifted as she drove familiar streets. Gage would be furious with her, but she had to confront Aunt Viv herself. Regardless of the evidence, Ellie couldn't believe her godmother would hurt her or any human being. Yet, she needed to hear Viv say she wasn't Proctor with her own two ears.

Just as there had been another explanation for Ellie lying in bed with a strange man, there must be one for Aunt Viv's network being used as part of a child abduction ring. But what about the man who tried to kill Ellie being Viv's assistant? She pushed the question aside. She had to believe that Aunt Viv would answer her, and everything would make sense and be okay.

Lost in her thoughts, it didn't seem like very long before she pulled into the drive of a house she'd always considered her second home. Usually, Ellie would think nothing of showing up unannounced, but this time was different. She was there to accuse the other woman.

Vivian's car was visible through the garage door windows, so she hadn't left for the office yet. Ellie hoped that would be the case.

Her hand shook as she rang the doorbell.

"Ellie." Aunt Viv smiled warmly as she swung the door open. "I'm so happy to see you." She stood back to give Ellie room. "Come in."

Vivian led the way to an elegant living room, where they both sat in their usual places—Vivian on a Victorian chair and Ellie on the sofa.

"What on earth are you doing in Atlanta?" Vivian didn't give

Ellie a chance to answer. "Don't tell me those FSA people are sending you on some kind of assignment. Not in your condition."

"I'm not here for the FSA." Now that she was face-to-face with her godmother, Ellie found it harder than she'd anticipated. "They don't know I'm here." And what's more, she would be in a lot of trouble when they found out.

Vivian appeared confused. "Then, why are you here? You and Gage aren't having difficulties, are you?"

"Gage and I are fine." At least they were before Ellie did this. "I'm here to see you, Aunt Viv. I need to ask you something."

"Why, honey, what could you possibly need to ask me that you'd have to do it in person?"

Ellie took a deep breath. "The FSA has reason to believe lawyers in your organization are part of the Proctor Kidnapping ring. You set the network up, and you coordinate it."

The confusion in Viv's eyes slowly turned to shock. "You're not saying—they can't possibly believe I'm this Proctor person."

"Are you, Aunt Viv?" It was horrible, but Ellie had to know.

Viv's lips trembled. "You can ask me that? You can sit there, and for even one moment believe me capable of such a thing?"

Ellie's heart twisted at the raw pain on her godmother's face, but she couldn't back down. "I remembered who tried to kill me. It was Adam Spencer—your employee."

"Adam?" Vivian came to her feet. "That's impossible. He would never do anything like that." She shook her head. "Something is very wrong here, Ellie."

"It was him." Ellie stood and walked over to stand in front of Viv. "I'm giving you a chance to explain everything. If you've done this, maybe there's a reason. You thought you were providing children with better homes. Please, Aunt Viv. Help me understand."

Vivian drew a deep breath and stood straight. "I can't help you understand because it's not true. I'm telling you, Ellie Lynette Donahue, the FSA—and you—are making a terrible mistake."

"It seems your goddaughter has a habit of making mistakes." Both women turned to see a heavy-set, balding man with a pistol aimed at them.

"Charles." Vivian stepped in front of Ellie. "What are you doing?"

Ellie pushed fear away. Then, she wondered if perhaps the man dancing in a circle was intoxicated. "Let me call a cab to take you home," she offered.

His whirling stopped, and he pinned his evil eyes on her. "I'm not intoxicated, you brat. I'm just beyond joy that you've stuck your nose in, and now you're trapped."

"Oh, me, too." Ellie didn't so much as blink at his stance. "Please, tell me you're buying matching dresses for Aunt Viv and me."

Any trace of humor or his so-called ecstasy disappeared. "Vivian, old dear, because of this pesky young woman's propensity for showing up at inconvenient times, I'm altering my plans. I thought I'd only have to kill you."

Chapter 62

"Why?" Gage asked the sheet he'd just pulled from the fax machine. A ringing phone interrupted his conversation, which was just as well.

"I'm looking at it, Simon," he said with no greeting. The agent identified as having a hefty bank account on Adolfo Island was photographed with someone who had been on the run from the Secret Service for going on three years. Whether it was guilt or some game being played, all the extra training on beating a lie detector test appeared to have been used to confess.

"I'm sorry, man." The other agent cleared his throat. "Did you have time to read DeWitt's report?"

"Don't have one." Gage turned to look at the fax machine, but no reports were there. Then, a sliver of white under the machine caught his eye. When he pulled the paper out, not only was it the report; Lorrie DeWitt had coded it.

"I take it you decoded the report," Gage said as he fed the paper into the scanner. Unless Lorrie hadn't followed protocol, Gage's identification code would be the only way to open the message.

"No," Simon answered without hesitation. "Lorrie sent a note to me, saying if I even tried to read it, she'd bring all ten of her grandchildren to visit Uncle Simon for the weekend."

Normally, both men would have chuckled at the agent's routine threats to gift colleagues with her grandchildren. Today was different. Nothing was amusing enough to get through a haze of disappointment. "I need to do this, Simon. Thank you."

"Call if you need anything."

Gage placed his phone on the desk and looked at the gibberish on the screen. She had double coded it? He typed in his backup code and watched as groups of letters became words.

I have an official file, but this is between the two of us.

Gage wondered if his entire team was on the take. He drew a deep breath and read.

A few of the second subject's answers put the examiner on alert. He reports that he went off script and managed to slide a few extra questions in. Photos are in an attached file, and it'll take both your codes and the date of birth of my first grandchild.

Gage, when you look at the formal information and photos, keep in mind that our subject will answer for this. Legally. Don't let your temper get away, please. You're a good guy, and the entire department is happy you have your wife back.

What was this about? There was only one factor that would tempt him to forget legalities—the photo file opened, and he sat back, unsure if he could breathe. As he flipped through the file, disbelief surrendered to anger, which if he wasn't careful would put him in the trouble Lorrie DeWitt warned against.

Gage picked his phone up and hit a speed dial.

"Fisher here."

"Simon, I need a favor."

"Anything I can do. I meant that."

"I need you to talk to Burnett for me." The boss would have received these reports before they came to Gage. "Tell him...tell him I need to handle this in my own time. He'll understand."

A dry laugh came from Gage's phone. "Already set up for you. When Burnett told Binkley that you have total autonomy, I guess Binkley threw a bonafide temper tantrum, complete with stomping and yelling. One of the ladies on the team said she wouldn't have been surprised had Binkley lay down and kicked his feet. "

Gage couldn't so much as move his mouth, let alone smile. "I need to get off here and figure out how to handle all this. Thank you for taking charge of the polygraphs."

"I hope my team doesn't endure something like this. If you need any more help, give me a call. I'm sorry, man."

After laying the phone down, Gage propped his elbows on the desk and rubbed his temples.

Just as he stood, Eric appeared at Gage's office door.

Gage froze between the desk and chair and looked at the other man.

Eric's eyes met his, and Gage watched as awareness was replaced by a calm acceptance. Eric closed the door as he walked in, and Gage felt disbelief. Then, Eric spoke again. "The polygraph test..."

"Why?"

"I have a daughter."

"What?" As far as Gage knew, the man had never even been married. And what was Eric's point?

"I didn't know she existed until the day after I joined AMAR."

"I'm supposed to care about this because?"

Eric's eyes met Gage's and for the first time Gage saw how drained the man appeared.

"It's the same old story, Gage." Eric drew a deep breath. "Sixteen years old, and the world seems to be yours to own. Our parents agreed with each other and made us get married."

"So, she was already--?"

"No, but she could've been." Shame covered the older man's face. "We only lasted four months before our pastor stepped in and convinced our parents to let us annul the marriage."

"And, she really was pregnant?"

Eric sank into the only other chair besides Gage's. "Turned out to be two months when she went to the doctor after our divorce. Then, I heard she died giving birth to our child." He stared at the front of Gage's desk. "Turned out, my former wife died, but Felicity was healthy." His gaze came back to Gage. "It's all a mess, Gage. Her parents were going to make us have a proper divorce, and I wasn't sure whether they could do that. She was scared, so she ran away to have our daughter. When she died, her parents washed their hands of my daughter." Even through his sorrow, pride shone from Eric's eyes. "She's smart, Gage. I'm proud of her. She is a respected physician at a hospital in St. Louis. She found the paperwork in an old suitcase of her mom's, had a DNA test done, and there we were."

"If you are so proud of her, why didn't you tell us?"

"The call I received was a nightmare. The person running the ring we were after sent me a video clip with his message. If I wanted the beautiful young bride-to-be wearing a white dress instead of a blood-red one, I would answer calls and do what I was told. Indefinitely."

"We would have helped you," Gage forced himself to lower his voice. They could have discovered who was calling Eric. This could have been all over a long time ago.

Eric leaned forward and tented his hands on the desk. "You've been trying to take Proctor down for how many years? And, you've yet to succeed. Why would this have been any different?"

Gage read the agent's face. "Okay. I believe that's how it started, but it became a game to you, didn't it? Do the assignment from Proctor and keep us from catching on?"

A twisted smile graced the older man's face. "If I hadn't made a game out of it, as you say, I would have gone insane. Imagine Ellie always in the sights of a gun, and can you tell me you'd be able to handle it?"

"Well, since my wife suffered a beating and near death in a staged crash going on two years ago, and for most of that time didn't know me, I'm not insane."

"You may as well know what it was like, helping the Proctors. Not only was my granddaughter safe, Proctor gave me more money than I would ever earn as an agent, just for turning my head or laying a false trail."

That wasn't all he'd done. "You killed a man."

Eric's eyebrows went down. "I didn't kill him. I couldn't; I was ordered to and had him set up, ready to be shot, when I looked into Cosart's eyes and saw the same fear I'd seen in so many other faces. Good, bad, it didn't matter. No matter what you think, murder is a line I wouldn't cross. " With eyes that Gage would like very much to punch, Eric looked as angry as Gage felt.

"So, who killed him?"

Unless Eric was an award-winning actor, he was being truthful.

"I don't know." He leaned his head back before bringing it up, and Gage saw only honesty and the desire to fix things. "I knew there was someone...the boss's number one person. I couldn't find anyone who could claim to have ever seen him."

The image of his wife, always loving and trusting popped into his head. His wife had almost died. Gage remembered Ellie's terror, and when the lit candle in his stomach became a forest fire, he yelled, "What about Ellie? Did you know they planned to kill my wife?"

"No." Eric met Gage's gaze steadily. "I only knew about the things I was instructed to do."

"And, who instructed you? The head of Proctor? Tell me his name, Eric."

"The person who contacted me altered their voice, but the only thing I'm sure of is I was listening to a pro."

"So—" Eric's words sank in. "Are you telling me you have no idea who he is?" And if the man in front of him wanted to remain standing, he'd better answer quickly.

"I swear I have no names, contact information, anything. It's too late, but I'm sorry for the way I treated Ellie. Felicity's mother resembled your wife, and with all that's going on, I became frustrated with her."

Gage lowered his voice. "I don't care about your wife and child situation, Eric. Because of your desire to play games, there have been countless victims falling prey to the Proctors. You are every bit as guilty as the people taking those babies and selling them."

"I know." Finally, Eric had regret on his features.

Gage realized what was missing. "The polygraph...we all know you could have tricked it, but you didn't. You wanted to be caught."

The older man's face fell. "It's kind of like a suicide by law enforcement. I'm too big of a coward to confess." The usual suave doctor seemed twenty years older. He drew a deep breath. " Charles Crawford has been running a vast network, with more teams than you realize, for many years. Vivian Wolfe's idea for the United Legal Assistance Network gave him a means to legitimize the one he already had set up. There's a flash drive with proof of everything, somewhere at Cosart's house. Unless the murderer found it, the drive should be there."

Gage didn't take his eyes off Eric as he picked up his desk phone and dialed. "Elijah, please come in here."

Elijah appeared behind Eric within seconds.

Gage spoke. " Charles Crawford is Proctor. Call the Chicago office and have him taken into custody immediately."

Elijah's eyes darted from Gage to Eric in confusion. "How?"

"Please, just do it."

Without another word, Elijah turned and left.

Eric calmly pulled out his gun and badge and placed them on Gage's desk. "I'm sorry, Gage."

"That's not enough." Not bothering with the phone this time, Gage raised his voice. "Kurt!"

Kurt appeared in the doorway, with a half-eaten banana in his hand. "Yeah, Boss?"

"You need to cuff Eric and drive him to the station," Gage said. "Until you can prove you didn't, you're under arrest for the murder of Bryan Cosart, and that's just for starters. Simon Fisher will be there shortly." Eric was facing federal charges.

The banana sank as Kurt's eyes flew from the gun and badge on the desk to Eric. Comprehension dawned on his face and was immediately followed by anger. "You?"

Gage spoke calmly. "Kurt, please just take him in."

As Kurt turned to throw his snack away, Gage saw the pistol in Eric's hands.

"No!" Gage shouted. Kurt turned and reached for the gun, but it was too late.

"Tell my daughter I'm sorry." Eric pulled the trigger.

After the ambulance left with a still breathing Eric, Gage left his office and joined Elijah,who sat at the conference table. He was on the phone and didn't look happy, which was even more evident when he disconnected the call and slammed the phone on the table.

Gage jumped. His mind had still been on Eric.

"What?" Gage asked.

"The Chicago crew can't arrest Crawford. His secretary said he has a meeting with his associate in Atlanta today."

Before Gage could speak, his phone rang. He recognized Annie's number. What now? Fat Ollie was on a crime spree?

"No bad news, please, Annie," he asked.

"I'm sorry, but Ellie told me to wait until now to call you. I tried to talk her out of going."

"Going? Going where?" As far as Gage knew, she would be arriving at work anytime. After the trauma of remembering everything, he'd left her to sleep late.

"She only told me she had to see Aunt Viv. She flew to Atlanta."

Gage's heart went into his throat. Crawford was in Atlanta, and so was Ellie.

Chapter 63

"You're insane." Ellie glared at the man behind the wheel of the car. They'd been driving for nearly an hour, and she was tired of being silent.

He glanced her way and shrugged. "You're the doctor."

"That's right, and I can arrange for you to have a new wardrobe and live in a lovely white room." Keep him off-base. She heard Kurt's voice as clearly as if he were beside her.

Then the lawyer scowled, or maybe it was a rueful grin. "I'm sorry. I don't have much imagination. I'm afraid Adam is much better at this sort of thing."

On this bumpy road, Ellie was worried about Aunt Viv lying unconscious in the trunk. It was hard telling what was in the tiny bottle Crawford forced down Viv's throat. And Ellie was helpless, with her hands tied behind her and her ankles strapped tightly together. Every time they hit an unusually large pothole, her shoulder jammed against the seatbelt, and it felt like something was dislocating.

This nightmare began while they were still in the house. Ellie had to try something. "Nobody will believe the note is real." Truthfully, she wasn't sure if Crawford's plan would work, so she prayed over and over while the crooked lawyer spent over an hour trashing Aunt Viv's house. Then he used her computer to produce a letter, claiming his clues would work together. "They'll think Spencer murdered his boss and then everything will prove Viv is Proctor and implicate Adam Spencer as both women's murderer." He freely shared with Ellie how leaving a message wouldn't be necessary but for her presence. Then, the man had walked around the house, holding quite a discussion with himself before deciding one of the women must be capable of walking. He couldn't very well tuck one under each arm and haul them around, could he?

A sound—a croon brought Ellie's mind back to the vehicle they were in. "They'll have no choice but to believe the evidence I've prepared." Crawford seemed to be admiring his own reflection in the mirror on the sun visor. With any luck, the sunshine would glare off the bald spot on top of his head and blind him. "It's taken months of preparation, but I'm getting out of the business. With Ms. Wolfe taking the fall, there will be no reason for the FSA to continue their quest."

He was a ninny of the highest degree. "Don't you think they'll look at Aunt Viv's partners? All those other attorneys aren't going to let you ride off into the sunset."

"You are naive. Records will show that your godmother, with Adam Spencer's assistance, has been solely responsible for each and every adoption. She took advantage of the attorneys in her network. They'll hold no blame." If he primped anymore, Ellie was going to gag. "I've even arranged for the man who took care of all the dirty work to be your godmother's employee."

Ellie had found a flaw in his plan. "Proctor's been active for years. Adam hasn't worked for Viv that long."

"Not openly," he conceded. "But the records place him on Viv's payroll years sooner."

"You used Aunt Viv."

"We all use each other; didn't you know that?"

"Who's been using you?" Ellie asked. "You're the head of this national crime team, and you're telling me you're being used. By whom? Your second-in-command? The man must be crazy to work for you!"

The corner of his mouth moved up. "And, I've heard you were a genius." He glanced at her, his smirk growing. "Spencer is my second. He enjoys the extra I pay when he has to remove a person from this earth. Given enough time, I would have him taking more lives. If your husband hadn't messed this up, Spencer would answer to me for the rest of his life."

Ellie didn't miss his vehement declaration that Spencer was Crawford's to order. Now, Ellie understood. "He won't answer to you, will he? He's somehow got you in quicksand with no way to pull yourself out, and you're running away. That's the real reason you've chosen to do this now. You wouldn't be shutting it down if it weren't for him, would you?"

"Enough!"

Ellie wondered if she sat down with him—on the other side of iron bars—she could diagnose whatever this man had. Before she could take a breath, he began bragging. "Vivian suited my needs perfectly."

Ellie would like to twist the conceited dolt's nose upside down and send him out in a hard rain. "She wanted to set up goody-two-shoes lawyers across the country to help the poor and down-trodden. It was ridiculously easy to lead her to the associates already working with me. She made a significant portion of my organization legitimate. We would have expanded the network to cover even more of my people if the FSA had stayed out of it."

Apparently, his mouth was in drive. "I even finally managed to be rid of Cosart, the fool. He stole the wrong piece of information from me and then let an angry driver boost it from him. I should have finished Cosart when I found out what he'd done, but I thought he might be useful later. Then, what does he do? He sends a note to you, warning your godmother, to make sure I knew he would turn me in. It was a pleasure ridding the world of Bryan Cosart. I should have had him taken care of long ago."

This man had no conscience. He wouldn't hesitate to kill her. Her baby. "Gage won't believe your lies. He won't stop until he figures everything out and destroys you."

For the first time, the polished lawyer seemed rattled. "Gage Donahue has been quite a pest during the past six years." He tilted his head and looked down his nose at her. Some of his cockiness returned. "You know, it was a lucky coincidence of all the FSA agents, Duncan chose Donahue's wife to confess to. It made my life easier when Adam took care of you. The months Donahue was out of commission, my inside person easily kept my activities off FSA's radar.

He only had one insider, though, didn't he? Had one of the AMAR team overseen this the whole time? An agent shot Cosart. Just as she started to ask who it was, Ellie noticed where they were. Her heart stuttered, and panic began to set in.

"Why did you bring us here?"

The lack of emotion in his voice chilled Ellie to the bone. "Of course, this is where Adam would kill you. It's such a shame Vivian will get here too late and wind up dead herself. And, if only I hadn't missed my flight to Atlanta, I would have been here to save both of you."

Ellie could only do one thing. *Please, God, don't let this man succeed. Don't let him kill my baby. I need a miracle. Somehow, I need Gage.*

Chapter 64

Gage thanked the Lord as he pulled into the driveway. The agency jet had made record time, and miraculously, no law enforcement showed up during his frantic drive from the airport.

Ross Burnett, himself, was standing on the front porch.

Gage ran past the car he assumed Ellie had rented and straight to his boss.

"Ms. Wolfe's garage door was open, and her car was gone when we arrived." Gage vaguely noticed other agents walking the exterior of the house.

"What did you find inside?"

Burnett's expression was grave. "The house has been turned upside down, as though someone was looking for something." He held out a piece of computer paper. "This was on the table. Do you know what to make of it?"

Gage accepted the paper and read with growing dread.

I may not have found the files, but I've got your princess. If you don't want her dead for real this time, bring what you owe me. We're where it started. - A

Gage's mind raced. Viv's princess had to be Ellie. They hadn't located him to arrest, so "A" must be Adam Spencer. He took her where it started. Where what started?

Then he knew. He didn't have time to explain it right then. "I need to check something out." He pulled out his phone and dialed as he jogged back to his car. He could only pray he was right.

Chapter 65

Ellie had never wished for her gun, but this man had no conscience. Even though he had her in an uncomfortable chair, with her shoulder aching, she was more concerned about Aunt Viv.

"Don't drop her!"

But it was too late. With a smirk, Eric released his arms and Aunt Viv landed on the hardwood floor.

Please, don't let this monster win. Tell me what to do. Please show me—

"Are you praying?" The monster threw back his head and laughed. "Nobody is listening to you. God doesn't exist; he's a fairy tale."

"It's never too late to ask forgiveness. I'll pray for you and explain what Jesus has done to set us free from sin."

"Stop trying to convince me!" He picked up a book and threw it so hard it broke a mirror. "There is no God, you stupid woman. No God at all!"

"And you're basing that statement on what?" She had a feeling that at some time during his life, he believed God failed him.

"If he existed, the world wouldn't be full of murderers and liars. If he existed, he would have stopped an intoxicated driver before he slammed his car into a teenager's and killed her."

Ellie knew now why Charles Crawford was angry with God. "We're all sinners, . God gives us free will, and we should use it to get closer to him. He loves us...he loves you. And, he will forgive if you just ask him."

"Shut up." He waved his gun at her again. "I don't want any preaching."

What should I do now? When no answer popped into her mind, she decided to stop talking. Perhaps her words would soak in.

"Hmmm." Eric stood closer to Aunt Viv. "How am I going to set this up? Wait. You're experienced in being kidnapped and nearly killed. So, you tell me how I should stage this."

After an apology to the Lord, Ellie lost her temper. "Why don't you drop the gun on the floor and lie down in front of it and play dead. You'd look like the fool you are; if you really think you'll get away with this."

His smirk was back. "I've heard about your wit. I would have knocked you out and kept Viv with me, but she wouldn't have shut her mouth at all."

"This is foolish and unnecessary." Ellie decided to try again. If she didn't do all she could, she and the precious baby in her womb would die. "Just leave. I don't know where you're going so you could be long gone before anybody finds us. Just leave," she repeated

"I think I should shoot Viv first." Plainly, he wasn't affected by her words. "Because Spencer's a red-blooded male, and if you can stop those annoying speeches, you're quite attractive."

"How do you know what I would do?"

The voice that terrified Ellie and the man to whom it belonged stood in the doorway. He held a pistol loosely by his side. "Come on, Crawford. How can you know me, when we only see each other at one of Viv's horrible fundraisers."

"Good!" How could Eric mastermind the Proctor organization this long? His lying skills were just about worthless. "We'll finish these two off and get out of here."

Seemingly undisturbed by the older man's gun, Adam still hadn't raised his. "You must think I'm stupid."

Eric would never have a star on Hollywood's Walk of Fame. "I don't know what you're talking about."

"I found the files." Hatred and anger molded his handsome face. "I know you were leaving me to take the fall right along with Vivian." He gestured at Ellie. "And her."

"I ... you're wrong. I planned to take you with me."

"Right." Spencer nodded. "Because you're such a soft-hearted man."

Ellie had been thinking in circles, trying to process what the two men were saying. She finally understood. "That's why the note you left at Aunt Viv's –the one in which you threatened to kill me—has Adam's signature. You want him to take the fall."

"No, I wouldn't do that."

"Yeah, you would." Adam looked steadily at the older man. "You would throw your mother off the bus if it got you a cheaper fare."

"But, I—"

Ellie shivered when she recognized Cartwright's pistol as one of Kurt's favorite models. One her friend described as the most powerful gun legally obtainable. "Just be quiet while I figure out what to do with all of you."

All of them? There went Ellie's fervent hope that Adam would be so angry with Crawford, he would just leave her and Aunt Viv alone.

Adam's arm was steady as he raised his gun. Apparently, he was finished with this discussion. "Drop your fancy weapon, old man." Any of the courteous businessman Aunt Viv spoke of was gone. Hatred and evil oozed from his pores.

"Okay." As though placing his weapon on the floor, leaned forward, and then—even if it was only a few moments—everything went into slow motion.

Ellie closed her eyes as the pistols fired. Even though she knew what had happened, she forced herself to open her eyes.

Charles was on the floor with his chest bleeding in two places.

"Viv...sorry." He seemed to be apologizing to the woman, still lying motionlessly.

"I told you." Ellie didn't have time to cover her eyes or turn away before Adam shot again. She didn't have to wonder. Charles was dead.

Her eyes met the emotionless expression in Adam's gaze. Then the voice that haunted last night's dream spoke. "Well, here we are again."

Ellie knew she shouldn't show fear, but the image of Tim Duncan's lifeless body wouldn't go away. A moan brought both their attention to Aunt Viv. When Ellie watched Adam aim the gun at Aunt Viv, she lost all fear. This monster was going to kill the mother she had taken for granted.

"No!" She managed to jerk herself forward enough that, even with her arms and legs bound, she rocked back and then brought the chair forward until it crashed into Adam.

An excruciating pain filled Ellie's skull when she hit the floor. What if she'd hit the same place as before? Her vision blurred, and when it cleared it was to see that he merely stumbled before turning his attention back to her. He smiled at her; she knew this couldn't be good. Ellie was completely vulnerable. She had no way of protecting herself without the use of her limbs.

While he nearly dropped her and used a string of words Ellie hoped to forget, he finally had her sitting back up on the chair.

"Ought to left you down there." Adam smirked. "But then you'd miss the show."

"Adam."

Ellie closed her eyes again, only seeing the gun swerve to aim at Aunt Viv.

"I wish you hadn't woken up." Was that contrition in his voice? "But, it's too late now." The gun swept back and forth between Ellie's helpless form in the chair to Aunt Viv, who wasn't steady by any means but had managed to scoot across the floorand pull herself up to lean against the recliner

Please, Father, give me the words to help this man see he can make the decision to change.

"You have the names of the Proctor group." At least Ellie thought he must. She was surprised at the steadiness in her voice. "That is worth a lot to the FSA. You can make a deal; just let us go."

His lips were a straight line before he smirked. "You can't believe Duncan and Crawford are the only two I've killed. Your wimpy sidekick failed to follow orders when he left big-mouth Cosart alive." A corner of his lip lifted. "I didn't even bill them for offing that brainless man. It was just plain fun."

Keep him talking, but not about the murders. "But, you have more information they need very badly. I will speak to my husband about getting you a deal."

His eyes flashed, and just for a moment, Ellie saw what looked like regret, but it was gone more quickly than it came. "What kind of deal are they going to give a hit man. I'd end up in prison, and that isn't going to happen."

Ellie came within a breath of telling him he'd more than likely end up with federal charges and receive a death sentence. That would surely set him off.

"You'll have an attorney who cares about you." Vivian still sounded too weak as her energy disappeared and she slumped sideways.

"Undo my hands so I can help her get on the sofa." Ellie didn't think he'd let her, but Aunt Viv was in too much pain to lie on this cold hardwood floor.

"I'll take care of Vivian."

Unsure what he planned and helpless to stop him, Ellie sent a smile to her godmother. "I love you."

Vivian produced a small smile. "I love you, my girl."

"Oh, isn't this cozy?" Adam enunciated. "I think I'll get a tissue to dry all the tears you're making me cry."

When he turned his gaze to Ellie, she shuddered. For there was nothing in his eyes—not empathy, not even anger or hatred. Although she knew it wasn't how God worked, she couldn't shake the notion that the eyes were the window to the soul—and if that was true, his had followed the enemy. She once more apologized to her Savior; she should still try to get this man right with God. But, she couldn't this time. Something deep within told her to stop before he lost control and shot her or, worse yet, Aunt Viv.

"So, now I have to figure out how to get rid of you two." His head turned and again, sorrow at hurting Aunt Viv softened his features.

Vivian Wolfe was not a famous lawyer for her looks. She had dealt with people worse than Adam. And, Ellie saw in her eyes that she knew somewhere down deep he was a human being with real feelings.

"Your grandfather will be there for you. He loves you, Adam. Forget your parents. Think of Robert. And, I promise to represent you. You know me, Adam. You know I don't lie."

This time, shutters came down, and his eyes were an empty brown. "I only have 2 people to get rid of, and then nobody will know I was involved." He turned and stepped over to 's crumpled body. "Crawford, over there, is going to shoot both of you."

The breath caught in Ellie's throat. He was going to use Charles's gun and stage this to look like a murder-suicide. It wasn't much different than what he'd done to Tim Duncan and her. She had one last card to play—one chance to make him see reason.

"If you kill me, you're killing my baby." His expression didn't change. "I know you don't hurt children. Proctor—you have transported them to other families, not harmed them. So, please don't hurt my baby."

He nodded. "Maybe I won't kill you." He raised his gun and aimed it at Vivian. She looked at Ellie, and Ellie saw the love flowing from her eyes. And acceptance. When she closed her eyes and clasped her hands against her chest, Ellie knew she was praying. She had finally found her way to God when her life was about to end.

"No." Ellie calmly and firmly told the crazed man. She was a psychologist, so why was she accepting this?

He turned his head and looked at her again. "Okay." The gun swept toward Ellie. "Give me one good reason to let the old woman live."

"Take me with you."

"Ellie!" Vivian was the color of her white blouse.

"Go on," Adam urged. "Let me hear what you'd do to save your aunt."

You can do this. Could that be God, answering her prayer? *I am with you, Child.* A deep calm settled her soul. She had the Ultimate Help "A pregnant FSA agent is the best hostage. You could have a free pass to a country with no extradition."

His head tilted, and he seemed almost amused. "I know the FSA policy on kidnapping. I am quite familiar with the legal repercussions."

"But—" He had to realize this by himself, or he wouldn't believe it.

"The head of AMAR would do anything to get his wife and baby back." And, wasn't he proud of himself for thinking that one up.

"So, let's go." She tried to appear frightened, but help was coming.

"Take me," Vivian begged. "Not her and the baby. She has a life to live." Her words were rushed as she had his attention. "You said yourself I'm old."

That brought a droll laugh from the murderer. "I'm sure the FSA will want this woman back; who cares about you enough to be a bargaining chip?"

"It's okay." Ellie hoped Aunt Viv could see the optimism in her eyes. "No matter what he does, I'm loved by our Lord. He will be with me." She would either go on with her earthly life or be sent to her eternal home.

"Let's—" The sound of a helicopter interrupted Adam. Could that be an FSA chopper?

His satisfied expression stopped her hopes. "Sounds like our ride is here."

With the ease of waving, the gun was pointed at Aunt Viv.

"Nooooooo!" Ellie screamed, trying to maneuver around to help her godmother.

Before she barely took a breath, the gun went off, and Aunt Viv crumpled.

"No." Ellie scooted away, but Adam leaned over and proceeded to untie her ankles.

"Don't be trying anything, or I'll shoot her again."

"She's gone."

He shook his head. "Not yet, unless you don't keep up your end of our little deal." He pulled the last knot apart, and Ellie felt pins jabbing her feet as they woke up. "Look for yourself. Her arms . . . She won't be able to get help."

With that statement, he stood and grabbed her shoulder. She bit back a cry of pain as he yanked her into an upright position. Ellie felt something give in her shoulder and for a moment, thought she would pass out. But, she was supposed to go with Adam. She didn't know why, but she believed God was talking to her. She dug for strength and steadied herself.

Before she could move closer to Aunt Viv, Adam yanked the arm that hurt and jerked it toward him.

"Ohhh..." She groaned with the pain. "P...please untie me. You're hurting me."

The smile he produced was void of any emotion. "I told you I won't kill you. I never said it would be a painless trip."

She summoned every bit of strength in her and stood straight. "It makes you happy to hurt a helpless woman?"

"Helpless?" Adam planted his face so close she could smell the coffee on his breath. "I've seen videos of your helplessness."

He knew she could fight. "In case you didn't get it the first time, I am pregnant. I won't do anything that might hurt my baby."

Adam pursed his lips. "Is that right?" Evil flowed from him like rays of the sun. "Then maybe I'm aiming my gun at the wrong place." He swiveled around and aimed at her. Only this time, it was her stomach.

"Please?" She begged.

"Huh uh." He stepped back and steadied his arm. He was going to shoot her baby.

Please, God. The silent prayer was all she could muster. *Please.*

Chapter 66

Please, God.

The simple prayer had become a mantra for Gage. He leaned down to avoid yet another low-hanging branch. Following the investigation into Ellie's crash, and when they were finished with the cabin, Gage came out to see if he could find anything to help explain why his wife had been in bed with another man. While he didn't find anything to support his quest, he became very familiar with the woods surrounding the house. He was banking on the forest being unfamiliar to Spencer.

It wasn't a long walk, but even in this thick undergrowth, he had to be silent. Fear for his wife made him want to put his head down and charge through the brush, an idea which he was certain would not end happily.

After he called Burnett and explained his plans, his boss promised to gather all the FSA agents he could find. As far as Gage knew, they would be pulled in by the creek. A deserted road was barely visible—a perfect place for hiding.

He was trying to trust God to get him there in time. He wondered if Adam and made this plan together, or if they were enemies. Maybe they'd argue and shoot each other.

He finally made it to the top of what he had disdainfully christened Cactus Hill. Of course, there were no cacti, but the brambles from all the fir trees seemed to attack him. If he could make it down the southeast side without making noise to warn Spencer of his presence, he would have a shot.

It took him forever to get down the hill. He looked at the hill just east of Cactus Hill and wondered if everything was ready.

A flash of light reflected, and he realized it was the helicopter he'd heard. He had to get to that cabin before Ellie was hurt. He didn't know how, but he felt in his bones that his wife and baby were all right.

The sound of a gun firing froze him.

"No, Please, no." He no longer cared about being quiet, but before he took a step, he heard the voice he wanted.

"I need to go see if Aunt Viv is okay." Then a pain-filled sound came from his wife. "Will you let go of my arm?" Even in these circumstances, Gage was proud of his wife's courage. She told him it came from trusting God.

"Shut your mouth or I'll tie you to the chopper's skids."

They were making as much noise as a stampeding moose. If Gage knew his wife, she would make as much ruckus as possible. He changed direction and took off faster. Now, Gage was sure of their destination and needed to be there first. Parallel to his wife and the kidnapper, he took a detour. With steep hillsides and incredibly thick brush, he might wind up with a broken back. Still, it should shave a few precious minutes of time.

Ellie was alive. Now, if he could get her back before Spencer changed that. Just like after the car crash, Ellie was alive.

Chapter 67

Adam practically dragged Ellie from the house and headed toward the forest. When they were a few yards into the woods, Adam laughed. Ellie found no humor in any of this.

"I don't know why you're amused, but in case you didn't notice, the old lady lawyer missed your head by a few inches."

He pulled her uninjured arm to keep her with him. "I didn't know Viv had that in her."

"Well, why don't we go back and let her show us again?"

He stopped, and Ellie nearly lost her balance. She didn't think he realized he was no longer holding her sore arm, so she produced a realistic "ouch" to help. The truth was, there was no way for her to break a fall. And, she didn't know or want to find out if falling on her stomach could hurt the baby.

After staring curiously at her face, Adam smiled—an authentic one. "I may keep you around. You have the wit your aunt always talked about, and you're not ugly. You might be good entertainment."

Wonderful. A murdering madman had given her an exceptionally strange compliment. A gasp left her lips when he yanked her and began walking faster.

"Why are you holding onto me so tight?" Ellie wanted to take that gun and whop him upside the head. "Do you think I'm going to jump up and do a Tarzan thing from tree to tree?" Aunt Viv had scared Adam when she lifted her upper torso and fired Eric's gun. She had used every bit of strength to protect her beloved daughter, and Ellie now realized that's exactly what she and Annie were—Vi's daughters. Their mom had left them in her dear friend's hands, knowing Vivian would love her girls. Ellie had always been blessed with a mother; now if she could share her epiphany with Aunt Viv.

"Your godmother's quite a shot for an old lady."

She had better aim than Ellie because the wood was peeled off the doorway not three inches from his head.

When he'd dragged Ellie between Viv's aim and himself, she came close to asking if he might be related to Clay Richmond. She was once again between a coward and danger, or in Clay's case, ridiculous assumptions.

It took every molecule of Ellie's control to hide her fear. "Untie my hands, and I'll show you entertainment." She wouldn't, though, because of the small life inside her. "Where are we going? I haven't been here before, but I'm fairly sure you won't find an airport or rental cars."

He loosened his hold on her arm. Now, if she could move her other arm, which she couldn't now, she had a good chance of getting away from him. She could use her upper body strength and the adapted kickboxing Kurt worked so hard to teach her.

"Something better."

"Like what?" Just as they struggled through the last patch of brush and topped the hill, she froze. "That's not real." She shook her head. He'd mentioned tying her to skids, but she hadn't processed it until now.

"I saw Eric's files, remember?" Now, he seemed to think they were going for the blue ribbon as he ran up the hill, tugging on her bad arm again. Unbelievably toward a sparkling silver helicopter. Parked, if that's what one did with choppers, in a clearing just big enough for it to have landed.

Ellie wasn't stupid. If he got her into that helicopter, her landing would be a long way down with no parachute. *Okay, Lord, help me out here. Please.* "The pilot seems to have left."

Adam shrugged. "He probably took off when he heard your crazy aunt shoot at me."

"You were going to kill my BABY!!"

"I still might." But something by the helicopter caught his attention. "Looks like the pilot stuck around after all." His hand tightened on her aching arm. "And, don't bother trying to sweet talk him into helping you. Guys that work for Crawford only care about money."

Ellie glanced up, expecting the pilot to be angry. Only, when she saw the man, in faded jeans and a jacket she'd given him for his birthday, even from behind, she recognized her husband. "Maybe our pilot will think I'm pretty and forget money."

Adam ignored her and spoke to the man at the head of the helicopter. "Get this bird started."

When the "pilot" didn't seem to hear Adam, his grip tightened on her arm. "Okay, Bud. You fly, or I shoot you and fly this bird alone. I have a pilot's license."

The man slowly turned, and with a muttered curse, Adam yanked Ellie around, and she once more found herself in what was becoming a horrible habit. "Do you cowards have a how-to book? *Cowards for Dummies*, maybe, or how about *You Can Be a Coward too?*"

"Shut your mouth," Adam put a little more oomph in his yanking--another bad habit. "I will shoot you, woman, and I mean it."

"I don't think you will." Finally, she seemed to have stunned her would-be captor. "That man facing us will be on you like needles on a cactus."

"Let her go." Gage's gaze fell on Ellie, and she recognized the deadly calm expression on his face. She had only seen this once, right before he knocked an abusive husband out cold. "Let her go, and I'll take you in. All peaceful, and we can all walk away."

"How are you gonna stop me?" Adam demanded, squeezing Ellie's shoulder even harder. This time, she couldn't stop a pain-filled gasp. She had no doubt that her shoulder was injured. "You don't have a gun."

Now, that was a disturbing thought. Gage's hands were hooked to the front pockets in his jeans. They weren't skin tight, but there was no way a gun even as small as Jessica's could fit.

"Don't need one," On the surface, Gage was calm and authoritative. Ellie knew if he could get his hands on Adam, the peaceful man in front of them would quickly overtake her kidnapper.

"What are you gonna do? Make faces at me? Use your thumb and finger to make a gun?"

Ellie heard Adam's voice pattern change and knew Gage was knocking her kidnapper off-track. Cartwright had to know an FSA agent wouldn't stand with his hands in his pockets and calmly tell an armed man to let his wife go. It didn't make sense unless...

"This is your last chance." Gage seemed emotionless. "Are you going to let her go?"

"Sure." Adam yanked her even closer as his human shield. "I'll give the location of the safety deposit box, and you can have plenty of proof to destroy the doctors and lawyers."

"Fine." To anyone who didn't know Gage, he would appear almost relaxed and nonchalant. In reality, he was barely able to control his temper. "So, just get in the helicopter and leave. You're not taking my wife with you. Wait until you're somewhere safe from the law and give me the information. You don't need Ellie."

"I'm taking her with me. Then I'll leave her somewhere after I'm safe."

"You aren't taking her," Gage repeated.

"Again, no gun. And if you try to physically attack me, I will kick your wife's stomach."

A twitching muscle in his cheek was the only sign Gage was about to explode.

Well, Ellie was beyond angry. "You stop threatening my baby! And, while you're at it, stop posturing. The only reason you want to take me is to get even with him. Are you a child?."

Adam's voice was coarse sandpaper. "He made my job a nightmare. It was hard enough to keep Vivian Wolfe from the truth, and with Mr. Perfect Agent nosing around, I had to...take care...of more people than I should have, so, yes," he nodded his head. "I want to make him hurt."

Gage's gaze shifted to Ellie for a moment. It was long enough for her to get the message. Trust me. "Is there anything I can say or do to change your mind?"

"No." Adam shoved Ellie a little farther, once more grabbing her throbbing shoulder.

"Do not hurt my wife again." Gage was suddenly a tall and extremely muscular man trained in almost as many fighting methods as Kurt.

Any other day Gage would remain calm, but today his wife and baby were in danger. And, if Gage charged Adam it would get ugly very quickly. She met Gage's gaze and hoped he knew what she

327

was planning. He nodded so subtly that had she not been waiting for a signal, she would most likely have missed it.

"Okay." Gage had a sad expression on his face. Then, in his calm voice, said, "down." Adam's grip was way too tight for her to get completely away, but what she could do was give her husband a clear shot. If he had his gun.

Before she could try to figure that out, a funny whirring noise had her looking toward it. Just as she realized what it was, a red hole appeared in her captor's forehead, and he went down fast and hard, his death grip taking her with him. As much as her husband disliked taking a life, a wound would have given Adam the time to shoot her. She didn't have to look to know he was dead. She knew only one person who could have shot that well, and just before the pain finally took her under, she saw Kurt run into the clearing. Then, her world went   dark.

Chapter 68

"Gage's heart finally started beating again as he ran to his wife.

"'Bout didn't give me enough time to set up." Kurt lifted the man so that Gage could separate the dead man's hand from Ellie's arm. Even in death, this man wanted to hurt her.

The distant sound of sirens, police cars, and ambulances was growing louder.

"FSA won't see us up here. I'll go down and tell them where you are." Kurt dropped Spencer's body to the side and took off at a dead run.

"Send someone to Vivian, please!" Gage called out. While he knew from the pain on his wife's face while being manhandled something was hurting, she was okay for now. Vivian had lost a lot of blood, most of which was after she managed to fire Charles Crawford's gun at Adam Spencer.

Viv always complained about Ryan forcing her to take shooting lessons and had flat-out refused a gun in her vehicle. Gage highly doubted she would argue about it now.

And what she had done—Gage would be forever grateful to Vivian Wolfe. Even though he knew the woods, he would have never found them before they took off in the chopper. Somehow, she had watched and known the direction Spencer dragged his wife in.

"I love you, Ellie." He gently pushed her hair over and off her forehead. "I love you."

While he would be devastated if something happened to their baby, even the slightest thought of his wife being taken away from him was unbearable.

Lord, she's suffered so much, and I know part of it was my fault. You've placed this deep love for her into my heart, and I want time to spend with her until you take us home. She would be all right. He felt it in his very soul.

Chapter 69

"The baby is safe and sound." Dr. Richard's voice came from far away. Ellie wanted to stay where she was and forget all the pain and sadness. She let the darkness swallow her once again.

The next time the tunnel started to light, Ellie began to seek the darkness again, but Gage's voice came from right beside her. "Ellie, you need to wake up. I need you with me." He sounded frightened. "Don't leave me again; I can't...I can't lose you."

Suddenly, a light brighter than any she'd seen was in front of her. She was drawn to the beauty which seemed to be calling. Just as she had the thought, a woman Ellie hadn't seen in too long stood in the light. "Mom," Ellie breathed.

The woman placed a hand over her heart and blew a kiss to Ellie. Though she couldn't hear her mother, she read her lips. "Later, my love."

Another, deeper voice she loved spoke. "I want our baby, but if it ever came down to a choice, I don't think I can live without you." Gage sounded near tears.

Finally, she knew it wasn't her time to go to her eternal home. Whether her mother had appeared or if it was a hallucination, God had given her a precious gift. Peace in her heart.

Just as she managed to open her eyes, Samantha spoke.

"Is she in a coma?" Samantha sounded worried.

"Gage."

He pulled back, and if she ever doubted his feelings for her, she would remember his eyes at this moment. Pools of deep blue ocea with so much love it caused her heart to clinch.

"You know me."

"I know you."

He leaned down and softly kissed her lips.

"Great. She's awake." Was that Samantha? Why was she even there? "Come on, Gage. She's okay, and we have a ton of paperwork."

"I'm not leaving my wife." He answered Samantha, but his eyes didn't leave Ellie's. Something wasn't right, though. Ellie figured he couldn't share AMAR business with all these people around.

"You'd better leave, Samantha." Jessica was there, and she was unhappy with Samantha. Forget Jess's petite size; nobody who knew the real Jessica would risk her ire.

Samantha's voice was nearer. "But, we have work to do, don't we, Gage?"

She felt a firm kiss on her forehead, and then her husband's voice came from right beside her. "Ellie comes first. I'll get to the paperwork later."

"So, leave." Jessica's command to Samantha was even harsher this time. "In fact, let's both leave. Give Gage and his wife some privacy."

Gage still hadn't taken his eyes off her, and now he was caressing the area between her shoulder and neck. His lips were feathers on her skin as he kissed his way from her shoulder to her cheek and finally made it to the sweetest kiss she'd ever known.

"If you don't get your hiney out that door, I will get Kurt's gun and shoot your big toe."

Ellie felt Gage's laughter just as she started giggling. He lifted his head, and that glow filled his eyes. "I love you, Ellie."

Her heart soared, and she lifted her arms to hug him. A soldering iron took up residence on her shoulder. "Ohhh."

"Hold still," Gage gently guided her aching arm back to its place. "Your shoulder was really messed up. Dr. Richards was glad to have it go well and to be done before, and I quote, *that bossy dad of my wife's gets back.*"

"He's just that way with me because he loves me that much. She drew a deep breath and relaxed her arm, praying it stopped hurting. "I heard...did I hear our baby is okay?"

"Yes." Gage placed a hand over her still flat stomach, where blessed evidence of their love was alive.

Suddenly, she tried to sit up, but Gage gently pushed her back onto her pillow.

"Aunt Viv?" She felt panic building. "He shot her, he shot her."

"She's okay. She thinks maybe Spencer didn't have the heart to do away with her. He's known her since he was a toddler."

"Which floor is she on? Get a wheel—"

"She's not here." He couldn't seem to stop touching her face, and she knew he was trying to come to terms with what happened. But then she realized what he'd said.

"Did they take her to a different town? Bigger hospital?"

"Again, nobody knows why, but it was a flesh wound. Your godmother is in Atlanta right now, or she'd be with you."

"Atlanta?"

Gage hesitated for what seemed a ridiculous amount of time. "Gage, please just tell me." She wouldn't let her mind visit the different reasons her godmother was in Atlanta. There was no way Viv would leave Ellie unless...

"They think Aunt Viv was in on it."

"No." He was frustrated again; Ellie could see it. "But they have to investigate just like if she were a stranger. You know how a later lawsuit will turn out, saying Viv was given special treatment because of her relatives being present."

Ellie knew that, but she was so tired, her mind didn't want to work. She had one question left to ask. "And, Adam Spencer..."

"Is at the funeral home."

She wanted to ask about Kurt, but Gage began talking again.

"They found Spencer's stash of incriminating files. He had enough on Crawford and the other lawyers to put them away. For good."

"But?"

"But, Eric laid quite a false trail, and the more Elijah finds on him, it's amazing what he has gotten away with. Vivian is right there, proving each accusation wrong."

"She can't go to jail. We can't let her go to jail."

"Honey, there are so many top-notch attorneys from around the country with offers to help Viv, your dad has lost count."

"Anyone..." She thought of Charles. "Almost anyone who knows her realizes how amazing she is.

Gage brushed a loose strand of hair from Ellie's face. "Besides, your dad hasn't left her side. He's using his clout and pulling favors from past patients." With his kind heart, Ellie's father routinely made bartering deals with patients. When a thirteen-year-old Ellie asked her dad why he let people work to pay their bills, Ryan explained it gave them self-respect and a purpose.

That made perfect sense.

"Where is my sister? Troy?"

"In Atlanta right now. Troy's parents spotted him in the paper and wouldn't believe he was okay until they saw him face-to-face. They left yesterday and should be back this evening."

She looked around the room. "Find Dr. Richards and tell him to discharge me."

"He already said you're coming home tomorrow. There are stitches in a place where if you move, they'll tear open. He just wants you to be steady on your feet, and for that, you need to rest."

"I have so much to do." She didn't even bother trying to sit up this time. We need to go home."

"And, we will...tomorrow when Dr. Richards releases you."

She looked into eyes so beautiful it hurt. "Okay." His lips were soft on her good hand.

"I love you, Gage."

His features softened as he leaned over and kissed her.

"We'll talk about this later, I promise." Your voice saying those words to me—our love is so strong, it makes me want to stand on a mountain and announce to the world that you're mine."

Ellie had to chuckle. "When the jealous mountain goats are grouchy and think I'm stealing their man, will you protect me?"

"Always." His smile faded into somberness. "Since the day we met, I have never done anything, spoke of, or even felt an attraction to another woman. You are a gift from God, and you're my world. When I said I do, I didn't mean when it was convenient."

Chapter 70

"This is ridiculous. I do not need a wheelchair. It's not as if my legs are broken, you know." Gage hid his smile. After waking up and feeling more like herself, Ellie wanted to go home. Now.

He'd left a grouchy wife long enough to shower and change into the jeans and T-shirt Kurt dropped off, only to find her in an even fouler mood. She was still going strong as he pushed her wheelchair toward the exit. At least he was pushing her, and therefore the target of her complaints. The poor nurse would have been in tears by now.

"I'm surprised you don't strap me to a gurney." A man with his very pregnant wife paused in the doorway to give Ellie a strange look. "Or maybe a full body cast would satisfy you."

Gage smiled at the puzzled couple. "Pregnancy hormones," he murmured, to which an understanding expression appeared on the man's face.

"Hey!" Ellie yelled loudly enough to raise the security guard's attention. Then, the guard saw Gage and with a wink, turned to walk away. "Hey!" She was drawing attention from too many people who didn't know the situation. Seeing a woman frown at her was the flame that lit her fuse.

"Why don't you see if you enjoy a wheelchair ride when your legs are in perfect condition?" She demanded of the other woman, who picked up speed. Gage was relieved when nobody else passed them as he finally made it to his brother-in-law's car.

"Has she been harping like that the entire trip?" Luke called through the open window of his vehicle.

"Yep." Gage stepped in front of the chair and opened the back door of Luke and Holly's car.

"What?" Ellie's sarcasm was in full force. "Do you mean you're going to actually let me stand on my own two feet long enough to get into the car?"

Luke's amused voice came from the front seat. "Be quiet, Peanut, or I'll go home and let your dad come back for you. If you think Gage is overprotective—"

Gage was glad he couldn't decipher his wife's mutterings as she maneuvered herself into the car. He couldn't help but notice, though, she was very careful not to bump her bandaged arm and shoulder.

As he strapped himself in, Gage decided he'd wait and let her dad and Viv explain their good news. If everything went as planned, he'd have a happy wife again.

"You told her yet?" Luke's eyes met Gage's in the mirror.

"Told me what?" And, she was back. "You two go ahead and gang up on me. I'm a pregnant and defenseless—"

Gage felt real happiness as his and Luke's laughter filled the car's interior.

When she drew a breath and got ready to resume her tirade, Gage decided he knew a good way to stop her. His mouth covered hers just as she began to speak.Her muffled protests became soft sounds as his kiss became a pleasant way to settle her down.

"Ookay." Luke's amused voice came from the front.

"What do you need to tell me?" Although Ellie tried to sound ferocious, the tiredness on her face took away any power it might have had.

"I'll show you in a little while." Forget all this; it seemed like ages since he'd been able to kiss his wife. She must feel the same way since she was giving as good as she got.

All too soon, Luke's voice interrupted them. "Hey, smoochers! Everyone is here."

Gage prayed this would please his wife. Maybe he should have done what Jess suggested and told Ellie before leaving the hospital.

"What's going on?" Ellie stared out the window at the vehicles in their driveway.

"They realize you're just beginning to recover, and won't stay late, but the team is flying back to Atlanta in a few hours." Jessica and an unusually cheerful Bridgett had requested the barbecue. "Holly and her mom said they snuck out of the kitchen to keep themselves from sampling Bridgett's baking."

Luke looked over his shoulder at his cousin. "That Bridgett is a gourmet cook, Ellie. She was baking some kind of pie that smelled so good, I tried to get a bite. She caught me, though, and whacked my hand with a spatula."

When Ellie didn't so much as chuckle, Gage realized his wife was fighting tears. Maybe this was too much.

"If you're not up to it, they'll understand."

"Nonsense. They better not have left without telling us good-bye."

"Dad?" Ellie leaned across Gage and peered at the man rapidly approaching the car. "Aunt Viv!" Relief filled her voice.

Meanwhile, Gage chuckled at the sight in his back yard. Since he had no lawn furniture to speak of, it appeared his friends and in-laws had dragged out every piece of furniture not nailed down. There had to be a redneck joke in there.

Ryan reached for his daughter before they were barely out of the car. He looked like her dad, but at the moment, he sounded like a doctor. "You're awfully pale. Three days isn't very long to recover from shoulder surgery as extensive as yours, not with the severe trauma you've gone through. If I'd have been here, I'd have talked your doctor into keeping you hospitalized longer. Perhaps we should all leave and let you go to bed."

Gage wondered how Ryan would treat his grandchild.

"Dad, I'm okay." Ellie's eyes went past her father. She walked around him and only took a few steps before she and Viv were locked in a gentle, yet tight embrace. Because Viv had been in Atlanta, being extensively questioned the past three days, they hadn't seen each other since the incident.

"I love you so much, Ellie." Viv's tears flowed as she spoke. "I'm so sorry I brought those people into your life."

"You didn't. My job did." Ellie looked over her shoulder at Gage. "It's why I've decided to leave the FSA."

A concrete block broke out of his chest and flew away. They had made decisions and plans during the past few days, but he could finally see she was at peace with them.

"I prayed, you know." Vivian seemed shy as she spoke. "When Adam took you with him, I prayed. And God answered me because Gage showed up, and you're okay."

Gage figured there would be plenty of time later to share how God's answers didn't always come that quickly or turn out to be the answer people wanted.

Ellie gave her godmother another one-armed hug. "I'm so glad, Aunt Viv." The women pulled apart and shared a loving look. "When do you have to go back to Atlanta?"

Viv's eyes shot to Gage.

Oh, no. He bit back a smile and calmly announced, "It's your news."

Ryan slid his arm around Viv. "After all this," he gestured toward Ellie, "Viv and I don't want to waste even one moment."

Gage felt her hand squeeze his. "And?"

Vivian answered her. "After we go back to Atlanta and get both of our jobs in order, we are retiring and moving to the old home site on Luke's land."

"Luke was kind enough to sell us the old homeplace and twenty acres. Construction of our new home is already underway." The smile his daughters had inherited made an appearance. "It should be done within the next three months."

"But you're moving here? In three months?" Part of the joy she had just expressed seemed to disappear.

"Sooner, since we're renting Holly's house until ours is ready, we'll be able to move here within a month, at most," Vivian explained.

"After our honeymoon, of course," Ryan added.

"Our wedding will be small and private." Viv smiled up at her fiancé. "Next Saturday."

"Next Saturday?"

Annie appeared beside Viv. "Ellie, you have to come see the wedding dress I found for Aunt Viv." Gage watched as Annie swept Ellie away, and the others made their way back to the group. His gaze swept over Elijah, surrounded by women. For once, he didn't' seem embarrassed. Of course, the youngest one of his admirers was in her forties, so that might be contributing to it.

Georgia Florey-Evans

Samantha approached him. "So, I hear you're heading up the Pattinton office after the rest of your leave is over."

"Yes." Simon Fisher was bored with a small town and glad to be transferred to Chicago.

She smiled timidly. "I guess you heard I'm in charge of the AMAR team now. Scoggins will be my second-in-command."

Gage nodded. "Congratulations. You'll be good at it."

"It'll be strange, not having to go after Proctor anymore." The flash drive Adam Spencer gave up had provided them with everything. And, already the arrested attorneys were giving up names of the others involved, trying to cut deals. It would take a while, but the Proctor organization was crumbling.

"You'll keep busy."

Sam seemed to search for words. "I'm really sorry. I should have never put you in a position in which you had to choose between Ellie and me."

He decided this woman just didn't get it. "Apparently, you are under the mistaken impression there was ever a choice to make. Ellie is my wife—my life. You should have never spoken of or accused her like you did. I won't tolerate it from anybody."

Her surprise was replaced by forced indifference before she turned and silently walked away.

Something had changed in their relationship the day she disrespected his wife. Sam had crossed a line from which there was no going back. He would remember, but he wouldn't miss her.

"Penny for your thoughts." Jess's voice was unusually subdued.

"They're not even worth one cent." Then he took a good look at her face. "You talked to Burnett, didn't you?"

"I had to come clean about Eric." It was unusual to see the normally vivacious woman so sober. "I'd known something wasn't right for a few weeks, but I refused to let myself believe it. I could have shared my suspicions with Simon when he questioned me, but I really should have come forward after we interviewed Dixie Campbell, when he claimed she didn't know she worked for anybody. Dixie mentioned her boss a couple of times, and Alex steered her away from it. If we'd have gotten a name out of her, those men may not have had to die."

"What did Burnett say?"

Her smile was forced. "He lectured me about having too big a heart for such a little body. Then, he gave me three months suspension. To get my head on straight."

"I'm sorry."

Jess shrugged. "I deserve it."

"But I don't," Kurt spoke from behind her. "Just who am I going to harass for the next three months?"

"Not me, I hope." Bridgett had stepped up.

"I never got the chance to thank you," Gage told Kurt after the women wandered off a few moments later.

Kurt met his eyes. "No need to, Boss. I just shot the bad guy."

"That's not all you've done." Gage had finally figured a few things out.

"What do you mean?"

Gage might have bought the other man's nonchalant stance if he hadn't heard the crack in Kurt's voice.

"The night at the surveillance van, when you showed up, I should have known it then." Gage kept direct eye contact with the other man. "You were never on any special mission. I asked Burnett. You were on your own time. You've been here in Shadow, living under the radar and guarding Ellie since she arrived. You never thought it was an accident, did you?"

Kurt shrugged. "I'm just the muscle and trigger man, not the brains. I didn't have any proof Ellie's crash wasn't an accident, but something just didn't feel right. I figured I was probably wrong."

"But you came anyway."

"I couldn't take the chance I was right." Kurt's eyes went past Gage for a moment. "I tried to keep my eyes on her as much as possible, but I'm sorry I couldn't be with her twenty-four-seven. I should have been with her in Atlanta—to keep Crawford from taking her in the first place."

"Everything happened at once. It wasn't your fault."

"I still feel bad," Kurt insisted. "If anything happened to Ellie, I wouldn't have been able to live with myself."

Gage was truly grateful and deeply touched. "I won't ever forget what you've done for my wife, Kurt."

His eyes darkened with sincerity. "I would have done it for any of the team. You guys have been my family."

"I thank you, just the same."

Kurt hesitated. "Ellie doesn't need to know she was being watched, does she? I disappeared when she was with you, and I never invaded her privacy."

"My lips are sealed." This was one thing Gage could live without his wife knowing.

After Kurt had walked away, Gage looked around and finally found Ellie, safely ensconced between Vivian and her aunt Anita, with her father hovering over her.

"Hey, Gage, can I have a word with you?" Troy's voice caught his attention.

"What's up?"

"I have an idea, but I want to run it by you before I take it any further." Troy seemed awfully anxious.

"Okay."

"Lucy isn't too happy about staying in Atlanta since the rest of her family will be in Shadow."

"Yeah."

"The AMAR team isn't going to be the same. Eric is gone. Now, you and Ellie are leaving. I've heard some of the others mention asking for reassignments, too."

Gage thought he knew where Troy was going. "You want to transfer to Pattinton."

Troy grimaced. "Not exactly." He drew a deep breath and spoke his piece. "Ellie and I work well together. We could freelance for departments and agencies all over the state. We'd be able to set our own hours, choose our own cases—it would be our own show. What do you think?"

The one thing Ellie expressed regret about when she decided to leave her job was no longer working with Troy. Gage was certain how she would react. "You'll have to talk to my wife. Whatever she decides is fine with me."

"How soon do you think Ellie will be up to a talk?"

Gage looked at his wife and considered her response if she discovered the offer had been made and she wasn't told about it right away. "Why don't you hang around after everyone else leaves? You can catch a flight first thing tomorrow."

A big grin appeared on the agent's face. "That's fine with me. I won't have to listen to Jess and Elijah play trivia games on the jet."

"Hey, handsome." Lucy leaned against Troy. "Want to help carry hamburgers out? Elijah and Bridgett are arguing about the charcoal, but Luke and Uncle Richard are ignoring them and say they're set to barbecue."

Gage watched the couple head to the house. He turned and headed toward the cluster of people gathered in his yard. He'd been away from his wife long enough.

Epilogue

"Get out of there, Fat Ollie."

Ellie giggled at her reflection as she heard Gage scolding the cat. Since they moved into the new house last month, Ollie had claimed a new nesting site—in the closet on top of Gage's shoes. No matter how careful they were to close the doors, somehow Ollie managed to find his way in. Gage said his shoes were going to be so full of cat hair his feet wouldn't fit in them.

"You'd better not be laughing at that cat." Her husband came up from behind and wrapped his arms around her.

She leaned back and felt him nuzzle her neck. "So what if I am?"

Gage chuckled. "I'd show you, but then we'd both end up late for work."

Ellie turned in his arms, conscious of the seventh-month baby bump between them. She searched his eyes. "Are you happy, Gage? Is your job enough?"

The intensity of his gaze weakened her knees. "God has blessed me with everything and more than I've ever wanted. The cases I have now are as important as those in AMAR, and I'll tell you the truth—I was tired of traveling around, chasing crooks. The best part is, though, that I'm able to come home to my beautiful wife every evening." He winked. "It's an added perk when this sketch artist and gorgeous psychologist come in and work with a witness. I hear she'll be there today."

She felt her cheeks heat at his compliment. "Oh, you."

"Yeah, me." Gage pulled her closer for a deep kiss. It was a good thing Gage was the boss. They might just be late for work after all.

Ending a series is difficult. I find myself wondering what the characters are doing now.

After writing about twins in Myrtle Beach (contemporary romantic *Extended Family* series) my daughter and I kept expecting to see them when we vacationed there.

So, here comes my big confession. Considering every character in this trilogy, one is the most difficult to leave behind. Clarence—I wasn't sure that Luke needed a dog, but once Clarence showed up, he was partially the hero. While not a giant mutt, my Lhasa Apso was the inspiration, and Gizmo thinks he's a person, or at minimum a giant German Shepherd. He hops on his back legs for sometimes so long he wears himself out. And he likes to get in my lap to "rock." Yes, folks, when it storms and my twenty-one-month-old puppy is afraid, I haul him up onto my lap where he buries his head on my shoulder and we rock. He's even fallen asleep like that more than once.

Blessings,
Georgia

Please contact the police and other proper authorities when a child goes missing OR you see something suspicious, err on the side of a frightened child and call it in.

1.800.843.5678

TTY – 1.800.8267653

Catch up on the In Shadow trilogy!
Books 1 and 2 are available at Amazon.com or Georgia's website– www.georgiaevansauthor.com

Her college stalker is back. A furious man wants her dead. And one will do or give whatever is necessary to keep her alive. Who will be the victor?
Set in the fictional town of Shadow, IL, *Hidden* is the story of Luke and Holly. They've been friends their whole lives, and now will the danger bring them closer or tear them apart?

Beau Harding isn't his real name; nor were the ones he'd used during the past couple of years. He's staying out of the public eye, because when he testified and took down the golden boy of a syndicate, he put a death warrant on his head.
Haley Johnson has no family, but the folks in the town of Shadow have taken her in. She's happy and can't imagine moving.
But, then they really see each other, and both feel the same way. God wants them together, but how?
As vandalism turns into murder, Beau knows it's someone after him. He can't leave the people he's grown fond of nor will he leave the woman he loves. When he makes the dangerous decision to take a stand, who will win?

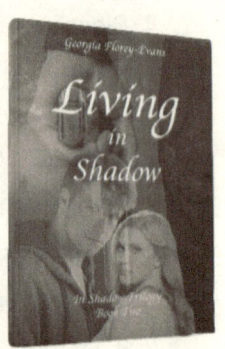